Magda's lithe auburn beauty paid the
way for her survival as a girl.
Her reckless passion for life destroyed
the husband who made her a lady.
But it was a woman's courage that led
her to an atonement of self-sacrifice to
save the life of their daughter . . .

THE DAYS OF WINTER

The new novel by the author of
A WORLD FULL OF STRANGERS
and FAIRYTALES
Cynthia Freeman

The Days of Winter

by Cynthia Freeman

BANTAM BOOKS
TORONTO · NEW YORK · LONDON · SYDNEY

*This low-priced Bantam Book
has been completely reset in a type face
designed for easy reading, and was printed
from new plates. It contains the complete
text of the original hard-cover edition.*
NOT ONE WORD HAS BEEN OMITTED.

THE DAYS OF WINTER

*A Bantam Book / published by arrangement with
Arbor House Publishing Co., Inc.*

PRINTING HISTORY

*Arbor House edition published February 1978
2nd printing . . . April 1978*
Bantam edition / April 1979

2nd printing . . . . . April 1979	5th printing . . . . March 1981
3rd printing . . . . . June 1980	6th printing . . . . . April 1981
4th printing . September 1980	7th printing . . . . August 1981

ISBN 0-553-20523-4

Published simultaneously in the United States and Canada

Bantam Books are published by Bantam Books, Inc. Its trademark, consisting of the words "Bantam Books" and the por-
trayal of a rooster, is Registered in U.S. Patent and Trademark
Office and in other countries. Marca Registrada. Bantam
Books, Inc., 666 Fifth Avenue, New York, New York 10103.

PRINTED IN THE UNITED STATES OF AMERICA

16 15 14 13 12 11 10

For my mother and father with love. Without them, there would never have been Chapter One.

Магда

Spring

The year was 1914. . . . The time was spring . . . the
place was Paris . . . and all the poetry that belonged
uniquely to that magnificent goddess was on display. The
chestnut trees were in bloom . . . the boulevards were
alive with people. Like a Monet painting they sat at the
sidewalk cafés. The boats floated languidly along the
Seine. Montmartre sang with a voice of inspired imagination which was translated onto the canvases, conjured up
from the soul of the artist as he painted under the trees,
hoping for a buyer.

Rubin mused. . . . If life allowed one the freedom to
choose a secret desire, his first love would be painting.
But he felt no bitterness in the fleeting thought. One must
not be tempted by dreams that deny reality. . . . No need
to dwell upon it since his life had been predestined from
the cradle, as it had been for all four of the Hack sons. . . .

The Hacks had been barristers for two hundred years,
starting with Rubin's great-great-grandfather, Isaac, and
perpetuating up to the time of Nathan, Rubin's father. Nathan was also a member of the House of Commons. The
firm of Hack was indeed prestigious; on the door were
five names. There was much reason for Nathan to be
grateful, Rubin knew, especially when he looked back and

considered his blessings. Every two years a son had lain in his arms. When he had looked down at each newborn, just separated from the body of his beloved wife Sara, Nathan had reveled in the knowledge that this child would continue the legacy established by the house of Hack. There had been a Hack in the House of Commons at the time of Disraeli. Yes, Nathan was a proud and happy man. Life had endowed him generously.

Three of his sons had married into families of distinction. Maurice, the eldest, had married Sylvia Rothchild, Phillip chose Matilda Lilienthal as his bride, Leon's great love was the exquisite Deborah Mayer, and now there was cause for further pride. Rubin, the youngest, was betrothed to Jocelyn Sassoon, a name so illustrious that even Nathan stood in awe.

Rubin's thoughts on that spring day, however, were not centered on Nathan's joys, but on his own pleasures as he walked the crooked, cobblestoned streets of Montmartre. His life had been filled with the grandeur of tradition and culture. Sometimes it was overpowering.

When Rubin had left London to visit Paris, he took a room on the Left Bank, which his family was unaware of. He should have been staying at the home of his dear friend Emile Jonet, where he still picked up his mail, but that address would not have given him the thing he was seeking. The Paris he wanted was filled with intoxication, excitement, the feeling of being free that he was not privileged to enjoy at home. He felt stifled at home, but here he felt as though he could soar like a bird.

That evening Rubin walked along the Rue de l'Odeon, turned right until he stood in front of Sylvia Beach's book shop. He allowed his mind to dwell on the past and the present. Ezra Pound . . . James Joyce . . . Rubin tried to imagine the great men and women who had stepped over the threshold of that outwardly unimpressive little book shop. Exhilarated, he felt a compulsion to walk further until he came to 27 Rue de Fleurus, where Gertrude Stein lived. From across the street he looked up, trying to imagine her sitting inside, surrounded by the greatest treasures of modern art like some giant enchantress toward whom everyone felt subservient. For one moment he allowed himself to feel that he would never be privileged to open that door. Then just as quickly he dismissed the thought and replaced it with a joyous feeling that at least he had been privileged to stand on this street so close to greatness. Lighting a cigarette, he smoked it contentedly as he leaned against a lamp post.

Suddenly he laughed out loud, looking down at his dirty canvas shoes and his baggy corduroy trousers above which he wore a brown V-necked sweater. If Father could see me now, he thought, he would glare at me with fierce disapproval. Nathan was a meticulous man who believed that the proof of his status as a gentleman lay in his tailor. Rubin could see his beloved father now in the great London synagogue on Yom Kippur eve sitting in his black cut-away jacket and silk top hat, the *tallis* folded neatly around his neck, communing with God. Not that Rubin was irreverent . . . but Nathan loved God as Rubin loved Paris. The difference, however, was that Nathan must stand before his God dressed as a gentleman, whereas Rubin could stand before his goddess dressed in the garb of Bohemia.

With these thoughts Rubin wandered through the Paris night, along the quay and up the steep stone steps past Nôtre Dame. He realized two things: He had been in Paris for three days and had not written Jocelyn; also, he had not eaten since early that morning. He would accomplish both things at once. He found a shop and bought a postcard and a stamp. Leaving the shop in search of a café, mentally he wrote . . . "My dearest Jocelyn . . . Please forgive me . . . for my neglect in not writing sooner . . . but . . . since I arrived in Paris there has been so much to see . . . Cézanne, Picasso, et cetera, et cetera, have taken a good part of my time. . . . The Museum of Modern Art has haunted my dreams." Stupid, simply stupid, Rubin admonished himself. It was not a travelogue he was writing but a love letter to his betrothed. Begin again, now. . . . "My dearest Jocelyn, since arriving my every thought has been of you. I beg your indulgence for not having written sooner, but getting settled in Paris this year has somehow been difficult. My fervent prayer is that when I return it will be with my Jocelyn so that we may share the beauty that is only to be compared with you. Until then I wait for the moment when my holiday is complete to hold you in my arms. With love, Rubin."

Entering a café, he groped through the darkened room, found a table and seated himself. The café was filled with an assortment of painters, writers and expatriates all assembled for the same reasons, not only to escape the ugly realities of life in a bottle of wine and a cheap meal, but also to reach out in the need to touch one another's lives. To talk . . . to laugh . . . to listen . . . yet not always to hear. It made life bearable to know one had friends in adversity. Rubin sat by himself enjoying the sounds, catching fragments of conversation. The smoke-filled room gave it an atmosphere of such intimacy that Rubin felt himself a part of the camaraderie. He was so carried away he forgot his promise to write Jocelyn.

The shirt-sleeved waiter asked. *"Que desirez-vous?"*

Rubin looked at the large blackboard attached to the wall. The bill of fare was the same each day . . . *escargots* . . . salad . . . onion soup . . . bread . . . *fromage*, and, of course, *vin ordinaire*, table wine, either red or white.

Rubin ordered onion soup, bread, and red wine. Later the waiter could bring Camembert. Suddenly Rubin remembered the postcard with the picture of the Eiffel Tower. Taking it out of his pocket, he began his soliloquy. He got as far as "My dearest Jocelyn" when a hush fell over the room. The strains of a gypsy violin began, and a voice so soft, so sensuous, beseeched . . . no, demanded . . . silence. Rubin looked up from the card, the pen poised in his hand, and sat, unable to move. It was not only the music that aroused him, it was also the girl. He had never seen anyone so magnificent. Her deep amber liquid eyes looked at each man as though she were his and only his. Her hair, which gave the illusion that it had not been coiffed, was parted in the center and hung loosely to below her shoulders. Her skin was silken smooth. The sheer white peasant blouse was cut deeply, revealing the top of her perfectly rounded breasts, which rose enticingly as she sang. Her waist was slim, encircled by an eighteen-inch belt above a black satin skirt which revealed her slightly full hips. The slit on the right side exposed her exquisitely shaped legs. The movement of her body became feline. When she finished the applause was tumultuous. She threw back her mane of tousled hair and laughed, parting the extraordinary red sculptured lips.

There were shouts for her to sing songs Rubin had never heard of. When she sang in Italian she was bawdy and naughty. . . . No one need understand the language, the gestures spoke for themselves. And when she sang in Rumanian she was sad, poignant and lovely, ending in tears. And the song she sang in French brought tears to Rubin's eyes.

Finally, after a long sip of wine, she began a wild gypsy song. As the rhythm gathered momentum, the crowd clapped along with her until the song reached a crescendo. Completely spent, she took another sip of wine, then half whispering, half talking, she said, "*C'est tout. Je vous adore, mes amis, bon nuit, mon ami.*"

Wiping her forehead she left the small stage and joined her friends. Rubin could not take his eyes away from her. He sat in the shadows, watching. He would wait all night, if need be, until she was alone.

Closing time was three in the morning. That was always the happiest moment for Pierre, the waiter, when he could lock the front door and begin putting the chairs upside down on the round tables with the red and white checkered cloths. Then the lights were turned off except for one which cast eerie shadows on the walls.

Rubin had sat so unobtrusively in the corner all evening that Pierre was surprised to find him still sitting there, with just a small amount of wine left in the bottle. He said, "Monsieur, we are closed."

Rubin looked somewhat startled. "Oh! I am sorry, but I've been sitting here daydreaming . . . enjoying the wine and silence."

Pierre narrowed his eyes suspiciously on the stranger. "You have nowhere to sleep?"

Rubin was feeling lightheaded and courageous. He scarcely heard the waiter as he looked at the young woman who sat a few tables away from him.

"Monsieur?"

Rubin looked up. "*Oui?*"

"I asked, do you have a place to stay?"

"Oh . . . oh, *oui, merci.* What do I owe?"

"Four francs."

Rubin paid, rose unsteadily and walked to the table where he stopped, looking down at the magnificent bowed head of soft amber-brown hair. Suddenly the head lifted and a pair of wide eyes flecked with green and gold met his. Close, she was more beautiful than he had imagined. She did not speak, but merely took the wine glass in her hand and sipped, peering over the rim. Her eyes inspected him openly, observing each feature of the handsome young face. Rubin was, frankly, overcome. Jocelyn crossed his mind as he saw himself lying beside this girl. . . . Then he felt awkward, doltish, for staring at her as though he were mute. He found his intermingled feelings both exciting and frightening at the same time. He *wanted* her so—

"Why do you stare at me like that? You think I am so grotesque?" She narrowed her eyes and threw back the heavy mane of hair.

He tried to find his voice as she draped her left arm behind the chair, crossed her legs, then slouched down slightly so that his eyes fell on the low-cut blouse. Finally he answered, "I think you're magnificent."

She laughed, with a sensuous huskiness. She'd heard that too many times to believe it. Shaking her head she answered, "Magnificent . . . only magnificent? That, monsieur, is the best you can say?"

In spite of the bitterness in her voice he repeated, "Yes . . . you are the most magnificent looking woman I have ever seen."

She pursed her lips. "You've already imagined how magnificent I would be in bed . . . yes?"

Rubin ran his tongue around dry lips. "I've imagined all sorts of things this evening since I saw you for the first time."

"You've been here all evening?"

"Yes . . ."

She laughed. "You found the vintage wine and the singing so exciting, so fascinating that you could not find the power within yourself to leave without paying me the homage all great artists deserve, yes?"

"Yes."

"Yes," she goaded him, "but you also have nowhere to go, you are lonely. Let me guess . . . you are a painter or a writer who has not been able to sell your work. You feel that I could help you through the night, am I right?"

"You are wrong. I am none of those things. My name is

Rubin Hack, and my home is in London. I'm on holiday, and I have a room—"

"Ah," she said, shrugging her shoulders, "you have a room, you are English and speak French better than me. So I guessed wrong, it won't be the first time. Life is full of little surprises."

"You're quite right, mademoiselle. If I had not wandered in here this evening, merely by accident, I might never have had the joy of seeing you perform—"

"However, you didn't stay just to pay me compliments, you stayed because you thought it would be easy to share my bed. . . . Don't lie to me, I've known too many men since I was twelve. I pick and choose with whom I sleep. I'm not a whore, you know."

Rubin bit his lip and looked away from the anger in her eyes. "I've obviously offended you, and I haven't meant to. Forgive me. Please."

She searched his face. When had anyone last begged *her* forgiveness? "Sit down, Rubin Hack."

She looked at him as he sat across from her. There was something very different about this one, in spite of the studied Bohemian pose. He was not like the pigs she had met in her travels. She took a sip of wine. "I'm like a million other girls in Paris who have more than their voices to give . . . or sell. Tell me, Rubin Hack, honestly, why me?"

"If I did, would you believe me?"

She shrugged. "Perhaps . . . maybe your lies will sound more sincere than most—"

"I simply couldn't leave without meeting you . . . speaking to you . . . hearing your voice for my ears alone—"

"Ah!" She laughed. "You are a poet."

"No, I'm a barrister, and I have never been so affected by any woman in my life."

She pursed her lips. "And what does that mean?"

"It means I was to be in Paris for a fortnight, but I am going home as soon as I can book passage."

"Really? And why would you do that?"

"Because I can't risk seeing you again."

This time their eyes met. She had known men too long not to believe him. . . . He was more than fascinated with her. But then her eyes grew soft and for the first time she let down her defenses. . . . Rubin had evoked a feeling foreign and unknown to her.

More gently she said, "Out of simple curiosity, why, may I ask?"

"For the very unsimple reason that if I see you again I may not find the power inside myself to leave."

"And what would prevent that? Are you married with ten children?"

"No, but I'm to be married," he answered seriously.

"And your moral principles would not permit an *amour de coeur*."

"Yes, I'm afraid that's it."

"And with your English upbringing you have never had an affair with a woman?"

"Not since my engagement, no. But at this moment, the decision not to see you goes beyond any principles."

"Really?"

"Yes . . . in my fantasies you've already been in my arms, I've made love to you. But even when the fantasy passed I realized that what I wanted was to have you with me, I was jealous of the men who . . . It's crazy, I don't even know your name . . ."

She appraised him carefully. "My name is Magda. . . . Magda Charascu. I am Rumanian, a Jewess from Bucharest, and I wish to apologize for being so rude and sarcastic."

"Please . . . please do not apologize. It is I who should do that, but in my desire to speak to you and my . . . well, I have been presumptuous." The words tumbled out painfully.

Was it possible he did respect her? He certainly seemed to. But how little he knew about her. Magda laughed bitterly to herself.

She was playing the same game she had played a thousand times. The verbal fencing to keep a man from thinking that she could be taken easily . . . or cheaply. But Rubin had affected her physically. She *wanted* to sleep with him. She had from the first moment she had seen him. But *love* . . . hardly . . . Behind her façade she loved no man, no man was worth loving. But love had nothing to do with lust, of course not, so she took only from those she chose, and threw back the others—

Pierre coughed and cleared his throat. "It's three o'clock, Magda."

Magda got up, took one last sip of wine and said, "Come along, Rubin Hack, you may walk me home. *Bon soir*, Pierre, and turn off the light when you leave."

"You tell me that every night."

"And if I didn't you'd forget." Laughing as she left, with Rubin following, she first unlocked the front door, then shut and secured it behind them.

They walked six blocks in silence, then turned onto a narrow cobblestoned alley. After another few steps Rubin found himself walking up four rickety flights to Magda's room. The door was unlocked. Opening it, she turned on the bedside lamp. A clothesline was stretched from one corner of her small disheveled garret to the next. She yanked down the line hung with stockings, a camisole, sheer panties, chemises, and threw them into a corner. Without apologizing for the unmade bed, the dressing table layered with dust, the cheap perfume and cosmetics, she motioned Rubin to sit in the battered, torn red velour chair.

Out of habit rather than modesty Magda stood behind the cheap silk printed screen and undressed, throwing her stockings, skirt and blouse over the top. Seconds later she emerged, dressed in a sheer wrapper through which Rubin could see the silhouette of her exquisitely slim body. Her breasts were firm and provocatively ample, with delicately distended nipples. It was impossible for Rubin not to look. She seemed so casually unaware, almost like a naive child. She had the ability to make her body a natural thing, as unself-conscious as the statue of a Greek nude he had been so affected by at the Louvre. However, she was not a statue. . . . She was flesh and soft, and he wanted more than anything in his life to feel her suppleness yield underneath his body. To touch her, to explore the inner depths of her passion. Out of fear that he would be premature, he sat rigidly, holding himself back with all the discipline of which he was capable.

He watched as Magda went to the small cupboard and took out two glasses. "What will you have, absinthe or wine?"

"Wine."

She handed the glass to Rubin, then lay down on the brass bed, propping the pillows as she sipped. There was an awkward silence between them. Finally Rubin asked, "How long have you lived in Paris?"

"For five years now, since I was fourteen."

How incredible, Rubin thought, a child, a mere girl alone in a place like Paris. Of course, he had guessed how she had survived but it seemed that life had never touched her. Life is an illusion anyway, Rubin thought. We see what we want to see. . . . What's real and what's not lies in the eyes of the beholder, like beauty.

As though she were reading his thoughts, she said, "Don't be curious about my life. It is no different from a million others. If you become hard enough you become strong enough not to let life beat you. Tomorrow or the next day you will be gone. What contribution could I make to your memories?"

"But you've already done that. I will never forget that I have met you."

"Yes, *of course.*" She pursed her lips. "You will remember me as you remember what you had for dinner last Tuesday. I don't feel like playing games this early in the morning. Do you have a cigarette?"

Rubin walked to the bed, sat on the edge and flipped the package. Magda took out a cigarette and put it in her mouth. She waited for Rubin to light it. He struck the match. His hand trembled. Magda watched the performance, then took his hand and guided it. She inhaled deeply, blew out smoke, clouding her face like a veil. "Do you want me so badly that you must act like a schoolboy visiting a bordello for the first time?"

"I want you as I have never wanted anything . . . or anyone in my life," he told her, and meant it.

She reached for the ashtray and snuffed out the cigarette. Unhurriedly, she opened the front of her sheer wrapper and slipped out of it. Then she pulled the sweater over Rubin's head, unbuttoned his trousers and slowly undressed him until he lay alongside her. Passionately, hungrily, he kissed her . . . explored her. And for Rubin it was as though he was entering a bottomless ocean of pleasure. The waves covered him with love, dissolving his want and need, and then . . . the sea became calm and serene, and the whole world was a nineteen-year-old woman named Magda.

She lay still beneath him now, her body damp and

clinging, her face and hair moist with perspiration. She had given him all she had. It was enough. It had taken him beyond the stars.

She held his face in her hands, then ran them smoothly through his thick black hair and looked into his eyes. "Now you will have at least one momento to take home. I hope your bride will appreciate the fact that she is marrying a very extraordinary lover. Now go home, Rubin Hack. I'm tired and quite content—"

"I *love* you, Magda, please understand!"

Closing her eyes and moving away from him she said, yawning, "It's like the measles. You'll recover."

"Magda, I know it's too quick, but it's time, I—"

Half opening her eyes, she looked at him, then smiled. "Go home, Rubin Hack. Not even God is worthy of instant love." Rolling over onto her stomach, she fell into a deep sleep.

Rubin watched her for a long time. Then, unhurriedly, he quietly slipped out of bed. He glanced around the shabby room, overcome that this beautiful girl he had fallen so incredibly—yes, incredibly, but nonetheless true—in love with must live out her life in such a place. With sudden anger he opened the door, hating the injustices of the accident of her birth, and of his. That was all it was. Even God was partial . . . preferential. He gave so much to some, so damned little to others. What had Jocelyn, for example, done to deserve *her* abundance? Or Magda, to be thrown like so much garbage onto the heap of discarded humanity. . . .

Rubin walked in the gray-mauve dawn past the now deserted café, past Nôtre Dame cathedral, down the steep stone steps. Turning right, he followed the Seine, looking below at the derelicts sleeping along its bank.

It was a bitter, frustrated Rubin who unlocked his door. Once inside, he stood against the door and stared up at the ceiling. Turning, he pounded on the door until his knuckles were raw. Finally he went to the washbasin in the corner and stuck his head under the water tap.

When he felt the anger subsiding, he wiped his face and dried his hair. Lying down, he put his arm across his eyes, but the face of Magda was still there. Remembering, recalling the feel of her body next to his, was almost equal to the reality. Now that he had known her, how could he possibly leave? Where could he find the reservoir of strength never to see or touch her again? He buried his head in the pillow. Spent, exhausted, he fell into a restless sleep.

Later, opening his eyes, Rubin was startled to find that it was dusk. Though he had slept for many hours, he awoke with the same heavy fatigue. His first conscious thoughts were sequels to the other ones—all of Magda. Still, he knew there was no out for him, no other course for him but to go home . . . it was his only salvation before he became too self-involved . . . if he stayed in Paris, there would be absolutely no turning back. . . . He was not a man of middle ground. With all the will, tenacity, he was still able to command he quickly got up, washed, changed clothes and packed, simply throwing his belongings into the valise. His hand poised on the door knob, he took one long look around the room and thought of the last few days. . . .

He had arrived in Paris with the love of one woman. A woman he thought he loved, or at least had sufficient affection for to take as his wife, to be the mother of his children. But now he was leaving with a deep, crazily obsessive love for another woman.

He had never, of course, thought of Jocelyn in terms of great passion. She was simply a lovely young woman, altogether worthy of bearing the Hack name, perhaps adding to it. She fit so well into the pattern of his preordained life. The prospect of taking her as his bride had never been questioned in the past. But time had nothing to do with falling in love. He knew one thing: in his life he would never forget Magda nor love anyone else that way. . . . He picked up his valise and hurried out, taking two stair steps at a time, until he reached the street.

After paying the driver, Rubin got out of the taxi in front of the Gare du Nord. He walked into the station and bought a ticket. Sitting down on a wooden bench, he waited for the train that would take him to Calais, where he would board a ship to cross the channel to Dover, then take a train to London where his journey would end at Victoria Station. And Magda would be lost.

Rubin sat, his body wrapped in numbness, watching but not seeing the travelers coming and going. A sudden thought nudged him back to reality. He had not only neglected to write Jocelyn, but his family as well, so they would not be expecting him to arrive home until Thursday of next week. Looking at his watch, he found there was time to send a cable. Getting a form from the clerk inside the small enclosure, he began to write an inane, contrived message to explain why he was leaving so soon. He knew they would be surprised at his rapid departure, since Paris had always been his joy and a holiday he looked forward to each year. Reading the cable to himself, he knew it was impossible, tore up the message, and walked hurriedly out of the station, forgetting about the ticket he had just purchased. He hailed a taxi, which led him back to Magda. . . .

Nervously, he tried not to think about the consequences of his impulsiveness. He could no longer be philosophical. He had no choice. If what he was doing would make him suffer later, after his marriage to Jocelyn—that, of course, would still take place—then that was an atonement he would have to live with, alone. But all he knew or cared about at *this* moment was Magda.

He hesitated before her door, staring at it for a moment, then knocked. When it opened, Magda stood in front of him dressed in the same sheer wrapper, the expression on her face neither joyful nor sad. She merely opened the door wider so that he could come in. Inside, he put the suitcase down. He said, "I couldn't leave."

She lay down against the pillows and looked at him. "You look rather stupid standing there. Why don't you sit down?" He did, on the battered velour chair.

A sardonic smile showed around her eyes. "So, you had to come back? Didn't I give you enough of a souvenir to carry away?"

"I love you, Magda, can't you understand—"

"And can't you understand how many times I've heard that in my life? I don't *believe* in love."

"That's because you've never truly been loved—"

"And *you* truly love me. You adore me. You only met me yesterday! If it wasn't so unbelievable, I would laugh."

"Please don't, Magda. I bought a ticket for Calais, and at the last moment I had to come back—"

"How touching. Why did you come back—to take me out of this place? To rescue me from a fate worse than death? Wait, I know! You came back to take me home to introduce me to your family." She said this with unmistakable bitterness. "Get out of my life, Mr. Proper Englishman. You disturb me. . . . You have nothing to give me. Enough has been taken from me already." Breathing hard she said, "Do you know how my parents lived and ate? . . . Why they survived? Well, I'll tell you. Because they were blessed with a daughter who had a commodity to sell. Do you know what it feels like to starve? When the pains of hunger become so excruciating, so fierce, you thank God you have a body to sell. Who cares if it's right or wrong, moral or immoral? When your belly's empty, you beg someone to take you and get it over with so you can run to the bread line before it's all gone. I died more than once that my parents should never know how the food was brought to their table. And you talk to me about *love*."

Rubin went to the bed, took her in his arms and stroked her hair. "You and I are not really so different, Magda. Life has taken us both in . . . I've got my love for you and my . . . obligations to the life that was, frankly, planned for me. Until now it didn't matter."

Magda shook her head. "You will choose your obligations. Now, please, get out of my life. Go away and leave me in peace. I don't want to be loved by you, it will only destroy both of us. Take your ticket, go back to where you belong and leave me alone."

"Just listen to me," Rubin pleaded.

"No. I don't want to hear any more. I no longer have to sell myself to feed my stomach. Here I finally have some sanity in my life . . . even living in a place like this. My voice and talent, such as it is, pay for these lodgings. And I choose who I sleep with."

"I want more for you than this, Magda. You deserve more—"

She threw back her hair, then laughed without humor. "How stupid you are, living in your little sheltered, narrow world. I 'deserve more'? Since when do we get what we *deserve*? Did my father *deserve* to work since he was six and die at thirty, penniless? Did my mother *deserve* to go on living, wishing she could throw herself into his grave because her life had stopped? Did my brother, my beautiful, handsome Niko, *deserve* to be killed in the war at eighteen? You talk to me of deserve. What do you know about it . . . a barrister!"

With tears in his eyes, Rubin turned his face away so she wouldn't see the hurt in them. Magda took his face in her hands. Taking the handkerchief out of his breast pocket she wiped his eyes. Almost too softly for Magda, she said, "Perhaps you are not so smart about life, but at least, Rubin Hack, you can cry. Under different circumstances I might get to like you. There's more to you than I would have thought."

"Can't you believe that a person doesn't have to be born into poverty to have feelings—"

"It's guilt you feel. You are very rich. I know without your telling me. That is what makes you feel so guilty."

He took her hand and held it tightly. "Yes, of course I feel guilty. Life has given me so damn much and you so little, but I'm going to change that, I'm at least going to take care of you—"

She laughed again, but this time loudly. "I'll become your mistress, yes? What makes you think I want you? Men! What microbes you are. You think all you need to say is 'I'll take care of you,' and I'll come running. I said you were not too smart, and I was right. You don't know Magda, Magda Charascu from Bucharest. . . . You want a mistress, so get yourself one. You'll have no problem, you're very rich. I'll concede that you are . . . quite handsome, not that it would matter to some mistresses. Don't let it turn your head, but you are. It wouldn't matter to most, but you happen to be a very good lover. With all of that you'll have no problem."

"Magda, I love you. Can't you understand? God only knows how much I want you—and *not* as a mistress."

She released her hand from his grasp, lying back against the pillows, bit her lower lip and looked at him. "Light me a cigarette," she said, not taking her eyes from him. "What do you really want from me?"

"Let me make you . . . happy—"

"*Happy?* And how would you accomplish such a thing? You're going back to your world, where you belong, and I'll stay in mine. Now, tell me about happy. What kind of nonsense is that?"

"Magda, I'm going to take care of you so you won't ever—"

Getting out of bed quickly, she shouted, "*Ever?* I think you're crazy."

He took her in his arms. "I don't want you ever to have to do what you're doing, at least I want to make it possible for you to live with dignity—"

She broke away from him, looking at him in honest bewilderment. After a long, tense silence, she said, shaking her head, "Why? What will you get out of this? Nobody does anything for nothing."

"It will make me happy, knowing that when I leave . . . you'll have a . . . well, a decent chance—"

Narrowing her eyes in disbelief, she said, "You would really do that for me, that's all you want?"

"Yes, that's all I want."

Still not believing, she said, "I don't understand you, Rubin Hack. Who does such a thing? You're a fool."

"No, I'm not a fool. I would marry you if I could, but since I can't, at least it will help to know you'll never be in need or—"

"And what about my not loving you? Doesn't that bother you? Because I don't. I don't know how to love anyone. Now, do you still want to support me . . . forever?"

"Yes . . . *yes,* damn it."

Shaking her head, she said, "I thought I knew everything about men. But what I don't understand about you is almost frightening."

He took her up in his arms, placed her on the bed, lay down alongside her. "Don't be frightened. Don't try to understand. We all think we know all the answers and suddenly they blow away like feathers. Please . . . accept what I have to give you. Knowing *I* love *you* will be enough . . . please believe me . . ."

She looked at him, tears in her eyes this time. "I still don't understand . . ."

"I find something . . . magical in you, Magda, that goes beyond my ability to describe it, beyond any logic—which is meaningless anyway. All I know is that you are part of me, and that won't change. Not ever. And don't mock it, please, not now. . . ."

Mocking him was the last thing she wanted to do as he took her gently, then almost violently, speaking his feeling for her the best way he knew how.

* * *

At dawn Rubin woke up to the sound of Magda's soft breathing. He looked at her face in such gentle repose. She slept like a child . . . a lovely child. There were no traces of bitterness, or fear. Nothing in her lovely face revealed whatever inner torment she might be feeling.

Going to his suitcase he took out his dressing robe and put it on, then found the writing case under his shirts. He began to compose a letter to Jocelyn. He looked down at the blank piece of paper for a very long time. He felt chilled, yet beads of perspiration broke out on his forehead. His hand sweating, he began writing the letter, only to tear it up and start another. Five times he got no further than "My dear." Then he forced himself to write: "Dear Jocelyn, please forgive my neglect in not writing sooner. The delay has been unforgivable, but Paris becomes so intoxicating that each day melts into the next and one forgets about time and obligations. I offer my apologies and trust you will understand. Upon my return I will try to redeem myself. May this letter find you happy and radiant as always. My very best regards to your family. With affection, Rubin." Sighing, he moistened his dry lips. With contempt for his own weakness, he quickly sealed the envelope, put a stamp in the corner, and proceeded to dress hurriedly.

Looking like the London barrister he was, he scribbled a note to Magda that he would return by noon. He propped the note against the mirror, took one more look at her sleeping body, and left.

When he returned and saw Magda sitting up in bed against the pillows, his feelings took over again. The guilt he had fought was again pushed aside. Magda regarded him over the rim of her coffee cup.

"Darling, get dressed," he said.

"Why?" she asked.

"I have something to show you."

"You're going to take me on a sight-seeing tour of Paris? Lunch at Maxim's in my black satin skirt? Or the Louvre, to soak up a little culture . . . yes?"

"Something more important than that."

"More important than the Louvre! My, my, my! What

could be more important than that? Just one thing, a Paris bordello. Am I right, Rubin Hack?"

"Don't be so bitter, Magda, please, not today."

"What's different about today? Is it a holiday? A day of great hope and expectations?"

"Yes, it's a very great day," he answered, kissing her gently.

She did not respond to his kiss. Her mouth remained rigid. "Do you know how ridiculous you look," she said, "dressed in your tailored London suit, as though you were ready to walk into Parliament? Look around you, Rubin Hack, and tell me how these surroundings suit you. What a handsome pair we would make promenading the boulevards of Paris together. It's so funny I could laugh." There were tears in her eyes.

"Magda, there's no need to torture yourself like this. I can't bear it . . ." Stroking her hair, he went on, "Get dressed, darling. Please."

She hesitated, then slipped out of bed and went to the wardrobe closet. She opened the doors wide, took out a black wool skirt and sweater and threw them on the bed. She quickly applied a thick layer of lip rouge, penciled her eyes, combed her hair, then sat on the edge of the bed and pulled up the black silk stockings which clung to her long, slender legs. She rolled the garters to her thighs and stepped into a sheer chemise. Dressed, she adjusted her black beret. "Voilà," she said, facing Rubin. "You see the transformation? It only proves fine clothes make a fine lady, yes? Come, Rubin Hack, now you will lead me to my very important day."

When the taxi stopped in front of Chanel's, Rubin helped Magda out. As he paid the fare she walked to the window and stood looking through it at the magnificent creation on the other side, draped in such studied perfection on the mannikin. For a moment she visualized herself standing there instead of the lifeless form so perfectly poised. Then her own image overpowered the fantasy, and all she saw was what she was, a shabby tart in a black clinging skirt and tight sweater revealing every curve of her body. All the anger, the pain and the hatred she kept carefully hidden away, deep inside her, rose to the surface. Swiftly, her mind moved to Bucharest, to death and war and poverty; to sweating bodies and filthy perverted men, to a twelve-year-old child. And at this moment she despised Rubin Hack more than the painful memories, for showing her a world she did not belong in; for evoking all the fears and self-hatred she thought she finally had overcome.

Rubin's reflection now replaced her own. She watched him pay the fare, mirrored in the glass window. He looked stately, impeccably dressed in his Bond Street suit, his black bowler hat on his head. She wanted to shriek with laughter at the two of them. It was a game of insanity. Did this stranger, this Rubin Hack, think a dress from Chanel would make her a lady? No, she was a lady only in her garret, from which they had just come. In the café, where she was admired, desired . . . She wanted to run back to where she felt safe. If she went along with this charade, she would lose the most important, the only, thing she owned, herself.

Turning abruptly, she faced Rubin, who now stood beside her. Her eyes were cold as they met his. "You're mad, completely out of your mind, if you think I'm going in there. *Look at me.* Look at you . . . We look like a pair of clowns."

Rubin at least recognized her vulnerability, and saw the fear in her eyes. He understood it more than Magda could possibly have realized. To him she looked like a fragile, heartbreaking child. Quietly he answered, "All I see is you, and what I see is beauty. Come, Magda."

She looked again at Rubin, debating with herself, then her eyes wandered back to the creation in the window. Could she look like that? Above all, could she feel beautiful inside? Rubin took her arm and opened the door. She walked in, her head high.

Rubin wanted Magda to model the clothes. Patiently, he waited for her to come out of the dressing room. When she did, he was genuinely speechless. Her beauty was now beyond anything he'd ever seen. Even her hair had been carefully arranged in a French twist. She stood before him, majestically, all her fears carefully guarded. Not even the tremor in her hands could be detected as her eyes met Rubin's.

"Do you like it?" he asked, smiling broadly.

"It's very pretty. Do you?"

"It's exquisite. Shall we order it?"

Her unrelenting pride would not allow her to plead or beg. Magda despised herself for not being able to say, "I want it . . . more than anything in the world." Instead she answered, as though it didn't really matter, "If you think so."

Rubin knew it was a façade that he could break through only with love. Someday she would leave it behind. Smiling, he said, "I think so. Now, try on the other things."

At five o'clock, Magda was rather fatigued. It wasn't easy to be a model—better a singer. After four hours the wardrobe had been selected, the colors and fabrics carefully chosen and the appointments for fittings made. In the luxurious dressing room, away from the condescending eyes of the saleswoman—who, Magda knew, was secretly laughing at her—she realized that a change had taken place inside her. All at once the idea had come: She was going to belong to herself . . . But she was also going to take everything Rubin would give her, and take it without guilt. Life owed her and life was in arrears. She was going to collect. As she slipped into the cheap black skirt and sweater (despising all they stood for) the three-week wait for her new wardrobe to be customed frustrated her. Why couldn't Rubin have bought ready-made clothes at the Marché de Lafayette? Taking out the hairpins from the French knot, she shook her hair loose and replaced the barrette, tilted her head to one side, and looked in the mirror once again. In spite of the shabby clothes a new person was already emerging.

It was a confident Magda who left the Chanel salon on the arm of Rubin Hack.

When the taxi stopped in front of 47 Rue Pierre Charron, an impressive building, Magda did not resist, not this time. After Rubin had paid the fare, they entered the building. In the entry they stood on the deep carpet waiting for the lift. When it came down Rubin opened the door, pressed the button for the fourth floor, swept Magda up in his arms, kissed her, watching her eyes as they slowly wandered over the foyer. She was overwhelmed. She had not known that anything like this existed. It was impossible to believe she would ever be surrounded by such splendor. She walked from room to room, as Rubin followed her.

The walls were muted rose, mauve silk, as were the damask draperies, tied back with heavy silk braided cords. They exposed the French doors from which could be seen the garden below and the Eiffel Tower beyond. The furnishings were all treasured French antiques. In the center of the floor lay a large Aubusson carpet. The oval walls of the dining room were painted with French pastel murals.

When Magda saw the bedroom she felt almost faint. She was so caught up in the magic that when she turned around and found Rubin standing there she was startled. In her eyes there was no gratitude, but she could no longer conceal her delight. It was there on her face, without words.

"You are pleased? You like it?"

I *love* it, I can't believe it. It can't be true. It will vanish . . . was what her eyes were answering back.

"These are yours." Cautiously she held out her hand as Rubin put the keys in her palm and closed her fingers around them.

Searching his face, still unable to comprehend what was happening, she said, "Why *are* you doing this for me? Truly why?"

"I've told you, Magda. I love you."

She shook her head. "Somehow I still can't believe you're doing this without . . . people want back, they don't give for nothing."

He led her back into the salon where they sat side by side on the small settee. "Of course, you're suspicious. You've been hurt and disillusioned. But people are not all the same, Magda. Human beings are unpredictable. Maybe once in our lives we're . . . well, tested. In the last few hours I've discovered a depth of feeling I didn't consider myself capable of."

She felt herself trembling inside.

"For the first time, I love someone else more than I love myself. I can't explain it, I've told you the truth. Please let that be enough."

Slowly, Magda walked to the window and stood with her back to Rubin. The room was in semi-darkness now, silent except for the sound of their breathing and the muted horn of a taxicab. No one had ever loved her . . . been kind to her . . . even respected her. When she turned again to face Rubin, there were tears in her eyes.

He took her in his arms, whispering, "Don't question it, Magda. Just accept what I have to give."

She could not say thank you, the words would not come, but cupping his face in her hands she looked into his eyes, then she kissed him with tenderness, and that was enough for him. Picking her up, he carried her into the bedroom.

Afterward, they lay quietly, warm against each other's body. The room was in total darkness. Languidly, lazily, she asked, "What time is it?"

Switching on the bedside lamp, Rubin picked up his watch. "Eight o'clock."

She slipped out of bed. "Well, it's time to go."

"Go where?"

She looked at him strangely. "I sing, I work, remember?"

She began to dress. Rubin got out of bed quickly and took the shoes from her hands. "No. You're not going back to that place."

Magda grabbed them away from him. "What do you mean, I'm not going back?" She had not gone to sing the night before. If she didn't show up tonight, she'd be fired. "You see, you don't own me, Rubin Hack. Not now, and not ever. You see, I was right. There are always strings attached." The last few hours had been a crazy dream, Magda thought angrily. *When will I learn not to trust?* "What do you expect me to do with my life? Sit here and wait for the clothes to arrive?"

"Darling, I'm not trying to dictate your life, I'm—"

"What you're trying to do is become my great benefactor. I don't know what other madness there is in your head, but—"

"Don't be angry, please. I have something to tell you . . ."

Her arms folded, Magda tapped her foot, breathing hard, but Rubin's look softened her defenses. "So tell me," she said . . .

"Come, lie down . . . I should have discussed it with you sooner," he said softly, leading her again to the bed. Placing her head against his shoulder, he felt her relax. She would not be owned, but still, she could not remain angry with him.

"Are you really angry?" He smiled, almost teasing.

"Yes," she answered, returning a half-smile.

"You're beautiful when you smile. It's the first time I've seen you do that."

"Don't get used to it. It isn't something I do too often." Then she asked quietly, "Rubin . . . what do I do with my life?"

"I want a great deal for you, and you're going to have it."

"How? Rubin, I'm going to tell you something. It's very hard to admit, but I'm . . . I'm frightened of all this. So much has changed since I met you. I had made a secure place for myself. Now, suddenly, I'm afraid of what's ahead. I don't even know who I am any longer. I don't know what you want me to be."

"I want you to be happy. I want you to be the lady I know you are—"

Magda laughed. "A lady? *Me?* You're a fool. People are what they are. You can't make just anyone a lady. That happens or doesn't happen, the minute you come out of your mother's belly."

"I don't agree with you, darling. There's an expression. 'Rosy O'Grady and the captain's lady are sisters under the skin.'"

Magda narrowed her eyes. "What the hell does that mean?"

"That basically people are pretty much the same. In spite of rank and position, we're all good *and* bad. Using the proper fork, and being privileged doesn't necessarily make a fine or virtuous lady."

"It helps, though, doesn't it?"

"Life, someone said, is like sleight of hand, now you see it, now you don't."

"Well, at the moment I don't exactly see—"

"If life had been kinder to you, there would have been no need for me in your life."

Suddenly, Magda's mind returned to Bucharest, when she was twelve . . . Rubin was right, life had played a dirty trick on her, and just possibly the deity who moved one's stars was now trying to make it up to her . . . After a moment she asked, "All right, Mr. Barrister, where do I begin?"

Rubin smiled, delighted. "There's a French lady, a countess, in fact . . . She's quite poor but she knows all the right people, is accepted into the best society. She's a friend I've known a long time. She's agreed to become your sponsor—"

"When did you talk to her?"

"I phoned her this morning. She'll live with you, teach you to speak English, teach you . . . and when you are ready, you'll become her niece from Bucharest. From then on, your life will be what I . . . we want for you."

"And what if I fail? Then all your efforts would have been for nothing—"

"You will not fail."

"How can you be so sure?"

"Because you're Magda."

And who is Magda, she wanted to scream. The tart . . . the Rumanian gypsy? She was terrified.

"Darling, please don't cry. Just trust me. I don't want to *change* you, only give you the chance to be what I sensed was in you from the moment I saw you."

"But how can I be sure that this will last? When you go, won't you forget me?"

"No. I won't forget you. Because I'm Rubin, who loves you." He wiped her tears and held her very close.

They clung together, and when he entered her, it was like the creation of a new world unknown to anyone except themselves.

Later, they lay still, overcome with feelings of peace broken only by the gentle breeze that invaded their privacy as the curtains billowed in and out through the French doors. Rubin looked at her. The Paris night, velvet, soft and fragrant, was barely a match for her.

He would paint her, oh, would he paint her! That way at least her face would never be forgotten, never be removed from his sight . . . But with the thought came the sudden pain . . . soon she would not be with him, and the feeling was too great to accept. Gently removing his arms from her, he got out of bed and walked to the French doors. He looked out beyond the small balcony to the lights of Paris. Whether or not he could share a paradise like this with Magda, at least this would be hers. He was brought back to reality at the sound of Magda's voice.

"Light me a cigarette. You see, you've already become tired of me, yes? And so soon." She laughed.

Handing her the lighted cigarette, he said, "Never, and by now you should know it."

"Then come back to bed, I want to talk to you."

He was quickly beside her again, taking her into his arms.

"How did you find this apartment so soon? You must have been a busy little man this morning."

"The truth is, it belongs to a very dear friend."

"Man or woman?"

"Would you be jealous if it belonged to a woman?"

"Don't be ridiculous. Don't be so damned conceited, I'm only asking. Now tell me about your friend."

Rubin laughed. "You do sound a little jealous. That pleases me."

"Why should I be jealous?"

"Because you love me just a little."

"*That*, Rubin Hack, is the most stupid thing you've said to me so far. I don't love you. I'm not even sure I like you . . . very much. Perhaps just a little. Now, about your friend. . . ." She moved closer, feeling the wonderful security of Rubin's body next to her, and waited, hoping it would be a male instead of a female friend. Not that it mattered, because she wasn't jealous. Not really. Besides, who was Rubin Hack really to her? *Nobody*. Soon he would be gone, and—

"His name is Emile Jonet." Magda heard Rubin's voice above her doubts. "We have been friends since boyhood. His family owns coffee plantations in Brazil. A good part of his childhood was spent there, but we met when he was sent to school in England. Last year, Emile's father suffered a stroke. Emile had to return to Brazil and take over the family interests. When I last spoke to him, he had no idea when he would be back in Paris. The apartment is at my disposal for as long as I like. In fact, it always has been. However, I prefer to stay on the Left Bank." Magda was only half listening. In her mind, Rubin was handing her the keys . . . "These are yours," he had said when he closed her fingers around them. She could still feel the sensation of cold metal touching her chilled hands. But they were *not* hers . . . nothing was hers. Rubin had lied . . .

Pushing him away, she sat upright. "And when he *returns?*" she said.

"What do you mean?"

"You know what I mean. This is not my home."

"It is yours, for as long as Emile is away—"

"You'll be in London."

"True, but I can trust Countess Boulard to find a *petite maison* for you. So please, please don't worry—"

"Don't worry? You will take care of everything . . . I'm to place my life in your hands . . . Wrong. You lied to me when you handed me the keys. 'These are yours,' you said . . ."

She wanted to go on yelling, fighting him, but looking at his eyes, somehow, in spite of herself, she did believe him, even though it was betrayal she was braced for. Why? Dear God, why was this man able to move her so with his kindness, convince her with his promises. She had never trusted anyone before, why him? His quiet gentleness disturbed her . . . The wall she'd built so carefully was crumbling . . . *Be careful, Magda, be careful, or you might find yourself falling in love. It's laughable. But you could love him, couldn't you?* Yes . . . Yes, Goddamn it, I could. *You're not so strong, are you?* No, but I never had anyone to fight this hard against. *But you mustn't fall in love. You must fight back. It will only destroy you. He's leaving . . . leaving . . .*

She jumped out of bed, started to dress. A bewildered Rubin watched for a moment, then said, "What are you doing?"

"I'm getting out of here. I've changed my mind. I don't want anything from you."

In a second, Rubin was out of bed and holding her in his arms. She pounded on his chest. "Leave me alone. I *hate* you," she cried as her hands went limp. She placed her head against his shoulder and he stroked her hair.

"Shhh, it's all right, darling."

Looking up at him she said, almost whispering, "Will it be all right, Rubin? Will it be?"

"Yes. And in time you and I will accept it. We have all our lives to remember now, more happiness than most people get in a lifetime."

She reached up and touched his face, then kissed him, surrendering, finally, her whole self to him.

* * *

The joy Rubin woke with the next morning was almost more than he could stand, or risk leaving. He looked at Magda, sleeping contentedly. He listened to her soft breathing, observed her fawnlike face in the dim shadows of dawn. She seemed even more beautiful than when awake.

Reluctantly he slipped out of bed and went into the bathroom. Seeing his reflection in the mirror he was shocked at the dark stubble that had grown in the last two days. After lathering his face vigorously, he picked up the straight razor, holding it deftly in his hand, and hummed one of the French songs Magda had sung that first night. That first night . . . had there been such a thing? It was as though she had been with him forever. Swiftly, he thought of Jocelyn. He actually could not recall her face. Unbelievable! Refusing to dwell on it, he quickly put the thought out of mind. Magda was an experience out of time, a gift. He would not allow anyone or anything to interfere with it. It belonged to him, only him. Later? He would do what was expected of him, but today this small corner of the universe belonged to *him*.

The haunting song came back as he stepped into the soothing water that almost reached the rim of the tub. He relaxed in its luxury. And allowed himself to dream.

Later, he walked softly into the bedroom and dressed. Magda still slept. Watching her, the same deep pleasure took him over.

He closed the bedroom door and went to the kitchen. He opened the cupboard where the staples were kept. The housekeeper who came in every day made certain that the larder was always stocked. He took down the coffee pot, filled it with water, added the fragrant coffee and turned on the gas beneath it. Then he left the apartment.

The *boulangerie* was fragrant with the exquisite aroma of yeast and cinnamon. There was no perfume quite comparable to the scent of French bakeries. Rubin was glad there was no other customer in the shop.

"*Bonjour*, monsieur." It was the first voice he'd heard that morning. A young, flaxen-haired, blue-eyed girl greeted him from behind the counter. Everything seemed special this day. The most mundane greeting took on special significance.

Smiling, he replied, "*Bonjour*, mademoiselle."

"What is your desire today?"

My desire, mademoiselle? To live each day like this one, but what he answered was, "I would like a dozen *croissants* and . . ." He observed the pastries, the delicately frosted butter cookies, as the girl returned his glance, enjoying the expression in the handsome young man's eyes. There was a sort of dreamlike quality in them. ". . . and two dozen assorted pastries, one pound of cookies—no, make that two pounds, and a pound of sugared almonds." Looking up to the shelves of cakes, he added, pointing, ". . . and the white cake with the white roses. Is it possible to have some silver leaves added?"

"*Oui*, monsieur," she responded, smiling broadly. As she adorned the cake, Rubin whistled softly. "*Voilà*, monsieur, is this the way you like it?"

"Oh yes, it's lovely. *Merci!* You're a genius."

She laughed. "And you, monsieur, are obviously a happy man."

"How do you know?"

"It's not so difficult to see when a man is in love."

"Is it so obvious?"

"*Oui*, monsieur. You have that certain look in your eyes."

"You, mademoiselle, are a most observant young woman."

"*Merci*. Are you just married?"

"Yes."

"Congratulations, and many years of happiness."

The lie did not bother Rubin. The days would become the years. "*Merci*, mademoiselle. What do I owe you?" He paid for the purchases and handed the girl a large tip. Before she could object, Rubin was almost outside the shop. She called out, "*Au revoir*, monsieur, and many children." He heard and wanted to answer, "Many," but stopped there. Today was too precious to waste a second on a dream that could never be. Never . . . ?

He walked to the *fromagerie*, where he ordered a quart of thick cream. He watched, fascinated, as the owner ladled it into the container. Indeed, Rubin was all eyes, watching everything. Then he told the woman to cut off a large slab of smooth creamery butter. Weighing it, she asked, "Will that be all, monsieur?"

"No, add a wheel of Camembert and a large slice of Brie."

At the street stall he bought a basket of lucious, long-stemmed strawberries. Passing a flower stand, he bought a single red rose which the vendor wrapped in newspaper, placing it on top of the cake box. Then Rubin walked back to the apartment.

Seeing Rubin's dilemma as he tried to reach the button of the lift, the concierge offered his assistance, which Rubin gratefully accepted. The rose teetered back and forth, nearly toppling off the boxes Rubin juggled as he entered the apartment. He went immediately to the kitchen and placed the perishables in the icebox. Pleased with himself, he walked to the bedroom, opened the door cautiously and peeked in. Magda still slept. The last few days had been filled with so much emotion, Rubin was grateful. Suddenly his mood changed, as he thought of what he knew would be so difficult, but he realized that the painful chore had to be done, and the quicker the better. Procrastinating would not accomplish it.

Going into the salon he seated himself behind the *Boule* desk, heavy with gold ormolu. From the letter holder he took a sheet of heavy parchment paper, dipped the pen in black ink and wrote to Jocelyn. It was hardly a love letter, but it was not cold or unfeeling either. It was phrased so that Jocelyn could interpret it according to her own needs. Without feeling any guilt, he sealed and addressed it, then wrote to his father asking for his understanding: Since these would be the last of his bachelor days, he felt the desire to remain several weeks longer. He wrote that this admitted whim in no way diminished his affection for Jocelyn, nor had it anything to do with his stability as a future husband. Ending the letter, he said he would cable prior to his return. As he attached the stamp, he felt fairly sure his father would smile. Rubin could almost hear him saying to his mother, "Sara, my dear, Rubin is being quite sensible. All young men, if they are to be faithful and contented husbands, must scatter a few wild oats. Fine boy, our Rubin. No need to worry there, my dear."

Rubin loved, adored, his father, a truly honest, honorable man. He could not remember a time when his father had gone back on his word, or done anything unjust or unkind. It was these very traits that especially endeared him to his sons: his sense of fair play and his understanding. These were the traits that Nathan believed he shared with his sons. Strangely Rubin didn't feel at all wicked or conscience-stricken over his deception. In fact, he felt rather pleased that he was up to it.

Slipping the letter into the inner pocket of his jacket (to be mailed later), he went back to the kitchen. As he opened the cupboard to take out the wicker bedtray, he heard the back door being opened and knew it was Mignon, the housekeeper.

Mignon was startled. Monsieur Jonet must have returned home without letting me know, she thought, as the aroma of coffee reached her nostrils. She walked rapidly through the pantry, but when she saw Rubin holding the tray, she gasped. "*Bonjour*, Monsieur Hack," she said with glad surprise. "I thought it was Monsieur Jonet. I am delighted to see you. It has been so long."

"*Merci*, Mignon. It has been a long time, and I'm happy to see you. I'm sorry I couldn't let you know I would be staying here, but I decided only yesterday."

"I trust it will be for a long time."

"Unfortunately, no. I will be here only a few weeks." He put the tray down to light his cigarette and give himself a moment to think. How should he tell her about Magda? Looking at the diminutive Mignon, her black hair streaked with gray and pulled back severely into a braided knot, he was embarrassed. After all, he thought, she had seen many a *fille de joie* of Emile's, so Magda would surely not shock her. Mignon was French, after all, and so was her master, but he, Rubin, was still afflicted by English propriety. But his desire to be emancipated managed to outweigh his English virtue, and without further delay he plunged on. . . . "However, Mignon, there will be a young woman living here in Monsieur Jonet's absence . . ."

Rubin silently applauded himself for his shameless courage. Mignon lowered her eyes, hiding her amusement, and her envy for the person fortunate enough to be loved by someone as attractive and virile as Rubin Hack.

Rubin looked at his watch; it was ten. Opening the door to the bedroom once again, having done so impatiently for the last few hours, he saw Magda's arms stretching above her head as she yawned away the last traces of sleep. He went to her, sat on the edge of the bed and drew her against him. She accepted his kisses, then pushed herself gently away. "Don't become too amorous, I haven't brushed my teeth."

Rubin laughed.

"What are you laughing at?"

"You."

"Why, am I so humorous?"

"Yes, and so practical."

"Practical?"

"Yes. How can you think of anything as unimportant as brushing your teeth at a moment like this? I've been up for hours waiting for you to wake up."

"That, dear Rubin, is your problem. Why weren't you here beside me, instead of wandering about?"

"I had things to do."

Magda went to the bathroom, leaving Rubin alone on the bed. Suddenly she turned and stood framed in the doorway. "How can I brush my teeth? I don't have a toothbrush."

"Use mine."

"How do I know you don't have a bad disease?"

"That's a risk you'll have to take."

Now Magda laughed.

"What's so funny?" Rubin asked, smiling.

"You, monsieur. Funny man."

Bowing theatrically, extending her arms, she spoke: "Let me present, ladies and gentlemen, Monsieur Rubin Hack, the clown of Paris, and his nude partner, the exquisite, the talented, the cultured Mademoiselle Magda Charascu, who will attempt to clean her teeth with her lover's brush . . . a feat attempted only by the famous Madam Fifi of the—" Quickly Rubin picked her up, circled the room with her in his arms, kissing her over and over again. "Darling, not now," he said, whispering, "not *now*. To hell with your teeth. I want you this moment." Biting his ear gently she whispered back, "Not till after I've gone to the . . . how do the English say? W.C.?"

When she returned, Rubin was already in bed, hardly able to control himself. She climbed in and lay on top of him, straddling his body. Her breath, smelling fragrantly of peppermint, mingled with the scent of French cologne quickly splashed under her arms, behind her knees and betweeen her legs. As he entered her, deeper and deeper, his only thought was for their love never to end.

When they finally lay spent, Magda abruptly sat up. "I'm starved," she said. "Do you never intend to feed me? We haven't eaten since early yesterday. Now I'm going to take a bath, and when I've finished you'd better find me something to eat, or tonight you sleep on the sofa. Don't laugh, that's a promise."

Imagine having a bath all one's own, Magda thought. She lathered her body with French bouquet of lavender soap, then immersed herself in the soothing water. As she relaxed, her eyes wandered around the large room, all mirrored and marbled. They came to rest on the tall stained glass window, each piece carefully put together like a mosaic. She was fascinated with the voluptuous figure of a girl dipping her toes gracefully into a lily pond. The flowers and trees around her were a profusion of muted colors, looking almost ethereal as the sun filtered through the colored glass. When Rubin bought her the *petite maison*, she would insist on such a window.

Rubin, Rubin . . . what god had brought him into her life? She hadn't meant to fall in love, but it was now far beyond her control. Except he would be gone soon . . . and after what they had shared . . . who could replace him? And with the thought came a deep pain and melancholy. Rubin had said, "It's more happiness than most people have in a lifetime." Why couldn't she find enough comfort in that? But she couldn't be so damn philosophical. It was Rubin she wanted, as well as the exquisite stained glass window, the *petite maison*, the clothes. Yes, damn him, above all she wanted to belong to Rubin forever.

Quickly she emerged from the tub, dried herself and, with the towel around her middle, ran back to bed. Soon Rubin brought in the breakfast tray and placed it across her legs. How beautiful the Lowestoff china, the small coffee pot, the monogrammed napkin, the silver, the place mat. She looked at the long-stemmed strawberries, the marmalade, butter, cream, the croissants. Rubin had forgotten nothing, even to the rose in the bud vase.

Kissing her gently, he poured the coffee into the cup

and said, "I didn't want to sleep on the sofa tonight. Drink it while it's hot."

"Thank you, it smells delicious . . . oh, Rubin, *thank you.*"

He kissed her lips. "I thank *you* . . . Now, drink your coffee." He buttered a croissant. He dipped a ruby-red strawberry into powdered sugar and put it to her mouth. She took a large bite.

She poured a cupful of half coffee, half cream, and handed it to Rubin. "You'd better build up your strength."

"Have no fears on that score, mademoiselle." They both laughed like conspirators.

When she'd finished she lay back contentedly and Rubin put the tray on the floor, then lay down alongside her. Slipping his arm around her shoulder he said, "Darling, I forgot to tell you, Emile's housekeeper is here. Her name is Mignon."

"Does she know about me?"

"Yes, I suspect she's quite pleased that there will be someone to fuss over."

Magda sighed. "Poor Henri must be out of his mind not knowing what happened to me."

"We should have notified him, but it was the last thing on my mind."

"Well . . . no matter. I'll have to go by today and see him."

"You're quite right."

"Rubin," Magda said, "I have to go back to my room and pick up my things."

"It's not necessary. We'll buy everything you need today at the Marché de Lafayette until your wardrobe arrives."

"No, Rubin, I still have to go back."

"I don't want you to. Let me get rid of the room—"

"You don't understand. There are things in that room that are important to me, the only possessions I have—"

"Such as what?"

"My pictures."

"You have paintings?"

"Just faded photographs of my mother and father . . . and Niko. Without them, I'm alone . . ."

"Then let me go."

"No, I always want to remember where I came from. If

I don't, I'll never feel right about . . . all this. Am I making sense, Rubin?"

"Yes, but we'll go together, you and I."

Magda smiled. "Rubin? Tell me about the countess."

"Well, she's rather extraordinary. When she was young she was the undisputed beauty of her time, really . . . the toast of Paris."

"Why does she have to . . . to sponsor me? Is that how she makes her living?"

"Yes. Although it's handled very delicately."

"But she's a countess . . . I thought all countesses were rich."

"Not all. Especially not in her case."

"Why?"

"Something happened a long time ago. She wouldn't want to be reminded of it. It was a very difficult period for her."

"You said she's accepted in the best society?"

"True . . . but right after her . . . well, she was pretty well shut out. Her family, though, was influential, and rich. With a large dowry she was forced to marry Count Boulard, who was not only on his uppers and thirty years older than she, but a fool who squandered her money. Still, with his title—never mind his disgusting behavior—she was once again reinstated, forgiven her transgressions, so-called, and accepted back into all the best French salons."

"Why did she stay with him?"

"According to French law, whatever a woman had became her husband's. And he outlived her parents. He died a few years ago, a crazy old man, leaving her broke. Fortunately, she's been able to hold on to a few valuables, a few jewels, which she laughs about, saying they'll protect her in her dotage from the poorhouse."

"Money is important, isn't it, Rubin?" she asked.

"Of course. But it has to be used in the right way."

"And what's the right way?"

"So it doesn't become an obsession—or a god."

"It can certainly help a lot."

"It can also corrupt."

"It can also buy respectability . . . Money seems to have such power."

"It does, Magda. It can do a lot of *good*."

Like a kaleidoscope, images of mannikins, stained glass windows and *petite maisons* swirled in her head. Then she thought of the Countess. Softly, she said, "It can also buy loneliness . . . don't you agree, Rubin?"

Full of the thought of what his life would be without her, he said, "Yes, Magda, endless loneliness."

She reached for his hand, held it tightly. "When will I meet the Countess?"

"She'll be here today at six."

"What should I do? I mean, how should I act?"

"Just be yourself."

"And if she doesn't like what I am, then what?"

"She can't help liking you. You don't have to pretend—"

"But, Rubin, I'm so . . . so—"

"So beautiful," he interrupted.

"To you, maybe . . . but I'm so uneducated, so common. I'm nothing but a singer in a—"

"That's enough, Magda. As of this moment, you're going to say, 'I'm beautiful. I'm worthy.' Don't demean yourself. An uneducated person is simply one who doesn't learn. And life is the best school. The Magda I see is a gracious, remarkable woman. That's what's important, the person you are. It's simple to become a lady—"

"Even with *my* temper?"

"Yes, even with your temper. That's part of your charm. Now get dressed. We've got a lot to do before six."

She looked at him, kissed him, tenderly at first, not so tenderly as she felt him respond.

Mignon was in her glory. She took out the Limoges china, polished the silver tea service and arranged the pastries on the Minton épergne. She had not been so excited since Monsieur Jonet left. Life had become dreary in Monsieur's absence. Folding the serviettes, she wondered if this *maîtresse* of Rubin Hack's would be able to handle the service at tea time. Mignon had her doubts. Men! There was simply no accounting for their tastes in women. This Mademoiselle Charascu was nothing but a common *souillon*. At least Monsieur Jonet's ladies had the breeding and training of courtesans, but this one! Oo-la-la. She had been shocked when Monsieur had summoned her earlier from the kitchen to meet his paramour, dressed in a black skirt and sweater so tight and revealing that nothing was left to the imagination. Mignon wondered where he had picked her up. Probably on the streets. Place Pigalle, undoubtedly. Ah, such a waste! But who could figure men out?

In the salon, standing at the window, Rubin looked at Paris, drinking in her beauty as he waited for Magda to finish dressing. Four times she'd changed, observing herself each time in the mirror. He could hear her exclamations of disgust. She hated every outfit.

Frustrated, she sat down heavily on the bed. She'd had her share of problems in life, but which dress to wear had never been one of them. Wasn't it stupid, she thought, looking at the boxes filled with lingerie, shoes, hats, scarves, even a French umbrella Rubin had insisted on, and it wasn't even raining. Tissue paper was strewn about the room. When she and Rubin had taken the dresses, suits, skirts and sweaters out, placing them on the enormous bed, she was so excited she hadn't realized the terrible responsibilities of decision-making . . . Wearing her new satin and lace slip, she quickly walked across the foyer to the salon.

"Rubin," she said, breathing hard.

He turned from the window, and looking at her expression of exasperation he smiled, then laughed.

Tapping her foot she said, "Stop *laughing* . . ." and then almost in tears, said, "Rubin, please . . . help. I don't know what to wear. I don't know what goes with what . . ."

Rubin took her by the hand and led her back to the bedroom. She watched as he carefully appraised each garment as though it were a matter of state. He picked up the simple mauve chiffon dress with the ruching around the neck. It was pretty, she thought, but so sweet and unadorned, especially to meet the Countess for the first time. As he spread the dress across the chair she looked at the full, bouffant sleeves, tight at the wrists, trimmed with the same ruching. Then she had second thoughts . . . Perhaps it was chic. After all, Rubin had selected it.

Opening a shoe box, he took out silk pumps in the same color and placed them on the floor. Next were the hose, soft, fawn-colored, and last the heavy strand of pearls with a diamond clasp, which Rubin had selected in only moments at Cartier. When the salesman had handed them to her for her approval, she thought they seemed no different from the ones sold at any cheap shop , . . except the price, which staggered her.

"Now, please dress. The Countess will be here in half an hour. And wear the pink satin slip."

"Oh, Rubin, what would I do without you?"

He smiled and thought, we won't think about that now.

She had just enough time to stand in front of him, hoping he would approve of her hair, carefully arranged now on top of her head, though she nervously toyed with the tendrils, which hung in front of her ears.

Holding her at arms' length he said, "You are *ravissante!*"

"Am I, Rubin? Oh, thank you, darling."

The sound of the bell almost went unheard. Only "darling" pealed joyously in Rubin's head. It was the first time she'd called him that, and it had seemed to come so spontaneously, so naturally.

Mignon was opening the door and saying, almost with reverence, *"Bon soir, Comtesse."* She curtsied. The Countess nodded and walked across the marble foyer to the salon, where a nervous Magda and delighted Rubin awaited the arrival of their distinguished guest. Rubin embraced her, kissing her on both cheeks. "You look better than ever, Solange."

"And you are the same enchanting rogue, dear Rubin, who almost makes a woman believe it." She smiled with a twinkle in her eye.

Magda watched these two old friends who were so at ease. The Countess was positively regal, though she had to be very old . . . at least forty-five. But her skin was so youthful, without a wrinkle or blemish, like pure porcelain. The whiteness was startling as Magda watched the ruby-red lips move in speech. Her cheekbones were high and delicately tinted with blush; one could scarcely detect that the color was not natural. Her sloe-shaped eyes, fringed with black lashes, could still affect men. What added to it all was the startlingly burnished red hair, above which sat a black silk turban trimmed with egret feathers. Around her long slender neck was carefully, yet casually, draped a scarf of sables. The black taffeta gown had a rich iridescent texture. The only adornment the Countess wore was a large diamond brooch.

When the Countess released the clasp of the sables, Magda watched fascinated as the skins fell softly to her side. Removing her long white kid gloves, the Countess did not take her eyes from this *petite poupée* of Rubin Hack's. Not one detail went unnoticed. Before Rubin could make the introductions, the Countess said, "Well, dear boy, your description was more than adequate, if nothing else. She is as you described."

"Darling, may I introduce Solange, Countess Boulard?"

"*Enchanté*," Magda answered softly. She felt as though she were being weighed by the pound.

"And you are Magda," the Countess responded. In their chat the day before, Rubin had said Magda's name over and over. She was incredible, more than the countess had expected . . . Men in love were always blind; the eye of the beholder dazzled . . . Bravo, Rubin, she thought. With this one you were quite accurate. What an exciting challenge she would be! This little sparrow could be turned into a radiant white swan. She had all the possibilities . . .

Solange sat in the *bergère,* facing Magda. Rubin seated himself on the settee across from them.

"You are from Bucharest?" the Countess said.

Her eyes direct, her voice steady, Magda answered, "Yes."

"A beautiful city, Bucharest."

"My recollections of it are otherwise," replied Magda. Rubin had said to be herself.

Solange moistened her lips . . . Ah, this one had spirit. She liked that. "Well, my dear Magda, you'd be surprised how a city can change in a very short time. Even Paris can be ugly. It all depends on the window you see it from . . ."

Rubin rang for tea. "Solange, would you care for sherry?"

"That would be nice, *merci.*"

"And you, Magda, dear?"

"Absinthe."

Rubin frowned. Magda was deliberately trying to be shocking. "I'm sorry, we have no absinthe," he said.

"Then I will have coffee. Sherry is much too mild."

A smile touched Solange's mouth. She understood every nuance in Magda's words, her voice. Magda did not like being patronized. Her insecurity was apparent. Solange, after all, was the enemy, and not a little bit threatening. Solange looked at Rubin and her eyes flashed a message: Patience, dear friend. All things worth achieving come with time and hard work. Sipping her sherry, the Countess said to Magda, "Rubin tells me you have an extraordinary voice."

"He's right," she answered, glaring at the Countess.

Solange was inwardly amused, and disregarded the rebuff. "He is about most things," she answered.

Magda took the words as an affront. She didn't like the Countess, and she would tell Rubin so later. She would not be treated like a stupid peasant. "Did he also tell you that I sang the lead at the opera in Bucharest? My last role was Carmen."

My God, Rubin thought, what is she doing? Why is she acting so belligerent . . . Solange couldn't be more kind.

Mignon wheeled in the tea cart, steering it to Magda, as her mouth fell open in shock. Was this the little strumpet who had gone off with Rubin earlier today? Impossible! Mignon left the room totally bewildered. Such a transformation!

But transformations had become a way of life for Magda during the last few days. She looked at her actions, her manners, as she'd never done before. No need to. Before she'd met Rubin, she'd been content with herself, satisfied with the café society that adored her. She had survived, after all, and reached the heights of her own tiny world. But now, suddenly, she could be a different Magda, detached from herself, scrutinizing her every emotion. What she felt toward the Countess at this moment was close to hatred . . . the Countess made her feel so inadequate, so ignorant. In fact, sitting here, even Rubin made her feel that way. The only time she felt herself his equal, in fact, his superior, was when they made love. But just wait, she thought. I'll give you a run for your money, Rubin Hack . . . And you, Countess. I'll show you how fast Magda Charascu of Bucharest can learn . . . I'm ready, teach me. Lesson one.

"Will you have tea or coffee, Countess?"

"Coffee, my dear." Chuckling inwardly, Solange thought, this little one learns quickly.

"Cream?"

"Please, and two lumps of sugar."

Magda handed the Countess her cup with a flourish. "Rubin," she said, "tea?"

"Yes, please." He answered with more annoyance than he intended.

But Magda pretended not to notice. Nothing, however, went unnoticed by the Countess. Magda was like a chameleon, cleverly changing her colors to camouflage her feelings, and the Countess was enjoying the performance.

There followed some light banter, mostly between Solange and Rubin. They discussed Emile, the years past, the fun and excitement they'd had. They exchanged little jokes between themselves. The conversation was scarcely heard by Magda, who had a headache. A real one.

Getting up, she asked to be excused, going directly to the bedroom. Once inside, she closed the door behind her and sat on the bed. How would she ever fit into *this* world? It was simply much too much. She ran into the bathroom and threw up. Then she reached into the medicine cabinet, took down the bottle of headache tablets, unscrewed the cap and popped two aspirins into her mouth, washing them down with a little water. God, but her head was pounding.

"Rubin, you mustn't be cross." Solange was grateful for Magda's absence. "She's swimming in a big sea, and she must feel as though she's drowning."

"I know. There are times I think she's happy, and just as suddenly it's as though a . . . well, a sort of cloud comes over her."

"Oh, dear boy, men are so foolish—"

"And women so wise?"

Solange smiled. "She's magnificent, Rubin, and she will grow. We will become good friends, so put your mind at rest. She's rebelling, not at you but at herself. Every woman needs the security of that one special man, and *you'll* be leaving her stranded. I do believe she loves you, Rubin. But when she gets frightened, she gets angry, and has to lash out."

"You're right, but what can I do? You know about my obligations . . . I can't just abandon my family and—"

"Then perhaps it would have been better if you had left her where she was. It might have been kinder."

"I couldn't. If I can't marry her, at least I can take care of her needs . . ."

"Rubin, I've often wondered what would have become of my life if I'd had the courage to—oh, well, that's long over . . . but if you love this girl as you seem to, why don't you marry her?"

"Do you think I haven't thought of that? . . . Maybe I'm a coward, too, but I can't hurt my family, go back on my word to a lovely girl . . . and I hardly need tell you, Solange, no matter what, Magda would never be welcome or even accepted. Do I have the right to subject her to that? And I repeat, I am engaged to a most lovely young woman—"

"But you don't love her . . ."

Rubin sat staring blankly for a moment. "Not in the way I love Magda . . . no one will be like that again for me, but Jocelyn is so decent—"

"*I'm* speaking about love."

"I love Jocelyn, too, but in a different way . . . *Please,* Solange, don't make it worse than it is—"

"You need to be honest with yourself, Rubin . . . did you ever truly *love* this other girl?"

"Yes, I think so . . . but Magda coming into my life has, to put it mildly, confused my feelings. I do still love Jocelyn but . . ."

"Rubin, I've no right to press you. No need to explain further. Whatever you do, you do and I am your friend . . . and I would suggest, with your permission, that I also try to be Magda's. Which at the moment means getting her to trust me."

Rubin nodded gratefully.

Solange left the room, crossed the hall and knocked on the bedroom door.

"Come in."

Magda was lying on the bed, staring at the ceiling.

"May I sit down?" Solange asked in a soft voice.

"If you like," Magda answered.

"Magda," Solange began, "if two people are to become friends, they must be completely honest with each other. I know you do not like me. In fact, you resent me. Is that not so?"

"Yes."

"I appreciate your frankness. Have you asked yourself why?"

"Yes."

"Tell me. My feelings are not fragile."

"You make me feel so . . . inferior."

"You mustn't feel that way, because you aren't. You are actually superior in many ways. You are also extraordinarily lovely. I want to be your friend. If you will accept my hand in friendship, you will find that I can be a very good friend indeed. Just remember one thing: You need not fear me, and you need not fear yourself." She took Magda's hand. "Now I'll go back to Rubin. Please believe what I have told you."

Magda looked around the silent room. You're a fool, Magda . . . a ridiculous, stupid fool. Here's a man who loves you. No matter how hard you try to twist it . . . defy it . . . fight him . . . he loves you. Why else would he be doing all this? And the Countess . . . why did you behave the way you did? . . . You know the answer. She was born a lady and in spite of what Rubin says, being born a lady is not like inventing one . . . and that is what poor Rubin is trying to do . . . You've embarrassed him in front of his friend, you acted like the stupid dunce that you are . . . I hate you, Magda. Instead of trying to learn from the Countess, she told herself, you antagonize her. She's trying to help you, not hurt you. Can't you understand that? Allow yourself to learn from her. Admit you're jealous . . . yes, jealous . . . You don't have to love her, but you can at least try to *act* like a lady.

Bracing herself, Magda returned. Standing contritely before the Countess and Rubin, she said, "Please forgive me, Countess. I was very rude."

Putting her finger to her lips, Solange pretended surprise. "Strange, I hadn't noticed . . ." Arranging the sables around her slender shoulders, she got up. "Well, my dears, I have to be going." She grasped Magda's hand warmly. "We will be in touch. Thank you for your gracious hospitality. You're a most beautiful young woman." She smiled, cupping Magda's face in her hand. "I can scarcely wait for Paris to meet my lovely niece from Bucharest. Now, *au revoir . . .*" She kissed Rubin lightly, and he walked with her to the door.

That one brief encounter with the Countess made a deep impression on Magda. She now wanted to emulate her in every way, to become the gracious lady Rubin had promised she could be. Instinctively, thereafter, Magda responded to every challenge. She began to handle Mignon with the kind of respect due a servant, and if Mignon resented having her position challenged, at least she knew her place. Painstakingly, Magda observed everything Mignon did. And after her duties were done and she had left, Magda rummaged through every cupboard, taking out pieces of china and turning them over to look at the hallmark. With the aid of a book, she soon knew the difference between Limoges, Sèvres and Dresden.

She discovered a ledger of menus, recorded over the years, with dates and the names of guests Emile had entertained. After certain names were checkmarks, indicating what Monsieur or Madam had not liked. Ah . . . so that was the way it was done! Very clever. It took a lot of skill and planning to be a hostess, and Magda was going to be perfect if it killed her. If she could become Rubin's equal, at least in such matters, he would be proud to introduce her to his family. And with all her new accomplishments, how could they not accept her? . . . She saw herself becoming a great hostess in London society. Why not? Why shouldn't she become capable of that? As the Countess's niece from Bucharest, wouldn't Rubin's family be proud of her? She would almost be royalty, after all. What if Rubin was engaged? So what? Engagements were broken all the time. . . . With the help of the Countess, she'd learn all the amenities. It wouldn't take a hundred years. Ladies were created, that was what Rubin had said. And Magda's confidence was being fortified each day with his compliments. She was on her way to becoming a woman of breeding.

Rubin had planned it all, the itinerary of her education. The books, the ballet lessons, the fencing, the voice training, that was all it took. The Countess was so wise. Bucharest, indeed, was becoming less and less ugly.

The days and nights were enchanted. Rubin showed her

a side of Paris she never knew existed. She visited the Louvre . . . Maxim's . . . the theater . . . the opera . . . the antique shops . . . Fontainbleu and Versailles. They drove out into the countryside for lunch. A whole new world had opened up for her. She was seeing it through different windows, different doors and different eyes. . . .

Rubin, she knew, would never be able to leave her, not when their nights were filled with such love. He seemed obsessed with wanting her. There was something almost spiritual in the way he loved her. A woman could tell. There seemed to be an urgency in him to live a lifetime within a few weeks. . . .

But the sands in Rubin's hourglass had run low. He was going home tomorrow, and the reality of that was suddenly more than he could face. He too had played the game of forgetfulness these last weeks. He too had lived in a world of fantasy.

That night Rubin had slept badly. Getting out of bed at dawn, he put on his bathrobe and went to the kitchen. Preparing his coffee, he looked out the window at the soft spring rain, as though it could ease his journey to London. He took his coffee into the dining room and seated himself at the window.

He could still hear Magda's voice, whispering I love you so . . . Oh, Rubin, I love only you . . . only you . . . you. But not once had she said I cannot live without you. Though he knew that was what she wanted to say; she wouldn't try to trap him. Solange's words came back hauntingly to him . . . she's swimming in a big sea. . . .

What was he leaving her with? Only material things. What had he really done for her? Taken her out of one hell into, perhaps, another. Yet when he'd first wanted to secure her future, it had all seemed so right, so simple, then to help her. But he knew she was reaching out for him without her having to say so. After all, he had helped create a new Magda . . . But Magda would marry . . . although he couldn't face the thought of her belonging to someone else. And quickly he told himself there was such a thing as honor. Remember, Rubin, he said to himself, you're an Englishman, brought up in a certain tradition.

And above all remember that you're a Jew, taught to honor your father and mother. It's a sacred commandment you can't forsake. . . . And Jocelyn, what about her? You can't find happiness built on the unhappiness of someone else whose suffering you're responsible for. . . .

He covered his face with his hands.

They stood facing one another in these last moments before Rubin was to board the train. Everything had been said, there was nothing left. Rubin held her very close as the final boarding call was heard. Then he disengaged himself quickly and walked off. Magda watched the train disappear into the mist of steam as the engine moved on slowly. Within seconds it was gone. She was heartsick but she knew that Rubin would return. She was so certain, she was able to smile as she left the station.

Two

The Hacks, the entire family, were seated around the table in the oak-paneled dining room. Nothing had changed. Only more chairs had been added as the Hack sons married and the number of grandchildren grew. Conversation was the same. Dinner, too, was the same formal yet convivial affair it had always been. Rubin alone felt alien. None of the other Hacks carried his burden of deception.

This morning he had come face to face with an excited, jubilant Jocelyn. She ran into his arms when he got off the train at Victoria Station. She held his face in her hands, kissing him tenderly. There was no other way—he had to respond, if not with the same pleasure, at least with a show of emotion. It was almost more than he could stand. His mother and father had stood by smiling broadly.

"I'm afraid you've lost weight," his mother had said. And his father had added, "Stop fussing so, Sara." He could not remember the banal amenities which had followed if his life depended on it. He vaguely recalled feeling Jocelyn's arm in his as the four of them walked out into the soft rain of London. In the silver-gray Rolls-Royce, they drove through the familiar streets . . . past Hyde Park, Marble Arch . . . but Rubin didn't see them. Instead he thought, When I left Paris it was raining, too. Is that a sign, an omen? A warning of what life is going to be like from now on?

As he lifted his napkin from his lap, he felt Jocelyn's hand on his. He was chilled with guilt at her touch. How could he do this to someone as tender and decent as Jocelyn . . . and how could he not? . . . should he have broken his word to her? . . . He had hardly been attentive to her all evening, but if Jocelyn noticed his lack of interest, she didn't make it apparent. Rubin had always been reserved.

For a moment Jocelyn felt somewhat embarrassed. Perhaps she had been too demonstrative when she saw Rubin get off the train. But she hadn't seen him for a month, and there had been only one brief note and a letter whose meaning she could only try to understand. But she refused to dwell on anything so negative. He was home, after all.

After dinner the men went off to the library to enjoy their cigars and brandy while the ladies retired to the solarium, where they talked about the new fashions: Queen Mary's turbans were becoming the rage of London . . . The upcoming charity ball had everyone selecting costumes. Sylvia Rothchild Hack was the chairman; the things she had planned were simply captivating. . . . She was too clever for words. Now what about Jocelyn? . . . Well, all the china had been selected, the silver, the crystal, the linen . . . The house was almost ready . . . And what about the wedding? Oh dear, so many details . . . She and Mother had a mild tiff about the style of her bridal cornet . . . Mother thought it should have been less modern, more in the Victorian tradition, but she finally relented and let Jocelyn have her way. . . .

In the library, Rubin looked at his watch. Dinner tonight had been in his honor, but now he could leave, having spent enough time with his father and brothers. He was very bored. He couldn't have cared less about the Prime Minister's position on colonial rule, or if the Thames overflowed. He wanted to be alone with his memories of Magda. The thought of sleeping in that oversized bed upstairs was too terrible to contemplate. His body ached for her.

"If you'll excuse me, Father," he said, "I'm very tired."

"Of course, dear boy. It's understandable after crossing the channel. Terribly choppy water."

Rubin said goodnight to his brothers and crossed the vast hall to do the same with Jocelyn and the others.

All evening Jocelyn had waited for Rubin to come to her so they could be alone and walk in the secluded garden, perhaps, since it had stopped raining, sit on the stone bench, discuss his trip . . . then kiss in the cool, crisp air of the London night. Instead she found herself being kissed perfunctorily on the cheek.

Rubin went upstairs to his room, closed the door, and sat down at the desk. He had always loved home, a fire glowing on the hearth, the portraits, the hunting scenes, the pictures of himself as a boy at Eton, then Oxford, all carefully mounted in heavy silver frames. But that Rubin no longer existed; he was lost . . . as lost as Magda Charascu. . . .

Downstairs, Phillip sat puffing on his cigar. "Our Rubin must have made the most of his last weeks of Paris bachelorhood. I think that, rather than crossing the channel, exhausted him." Nathan nodded, and everyone smiled except Leon, who had sensed a reserve in Rubin. Leon knew Rubin best. Since childhood they had been closest. Perhaps it was the two-year difference in their ages, but Leon had always understood Rubin, had known his sensitivities, his secret desire to paint. He also knew that Rubin was not in love with Jocelyn. Poor Rubin. Well, they would have a man-to-man talk, not tomorrow, but soon. To pry into his brother's personal life now would only result in making Rubin even more withdrawn. But when Rubin could no longer cope with the problem alone, Leon would be there to help him.

But as the weeks passed, Rubin still did not confide in his family. An enormous change had taken place in him. The whole family feared he was ill. Withdrawn into a shell, he couldn't eat. And his attitude toward Jocelyn was noticeably altered. At first the family rationalized; perhaps he was undergoing prenuptial jitters. Still, few men were *this* reluctant to relinquish their freedom. And though Jocelyn tried desperately to ignore his lack of interest, she was thoroughly miserable during what should have been the happiest time of her life.

Rubin's depression was almost unbearable. He had received no letter from Magda. Going each day to the post office box, where all her letters were supposed to be sent, he would take out the tiny key, open the metal door, and look inside in vain. Why hadn't she written? Was she ill? Surely Solange would have written if she was? Rubin became obsessed that she had found someone else. . . .

Finally, he went to the nearest phone and placed a call to Emile's apartment. When he reached it, the connection was bad, filled with static. "Where is she?" he shouted into the instrument, trying to be understood above the maddening noise. All he could hear were muffled sounds of a voice he believed was Mignon's. "In Cannes . . ." Those two words were the only ones which sounded distinct. Then the line went dead. Rubin held the receiver in his clenched hand for a long, very long time, then placed it carefully on the hook.

It was five when he returned home, after wandering around aimlessly. As he climbed the stairs to his room, he heard the voice of Martin, the butler. "Sir?" he said.

Rubin turned his head.

"Sir, your father has asked to see you in his study."

"Thank you, Martin."

Nathan was seated in the big leather chair at one side of the Georgian fireplace, a chair he had occupied for many years. He was shocked to see Rubin looking so distraught and disheveled.

"Sit down, Rubin . . ."

Rubin seated himself across from his father, gazing into the fire. Nathan poured two brandies, handed one to Rubin and kept the other himself. He took a sip.

"Rubin, the time has come when you and I must talk. Obviously something disturbs you. Please tell me what it is. You can speak freely, there are only the two of us here."

Rubin remained silent.

Nathan continued, "Rest assured, I will understand."

Rubin looked at his father as though he wanted to confide, then retreated into himself again.

"Since you returned from Paris, you're a different man. We no longer recognize you. Your mother is especially perturbed and you've made Jocelyn desperately unhappy. You don't have the right to hurt that dear loving child, who is, I remind you, soon to become your wife."

Rubin winced, in spite of himself.

"Are you that frightened of marriage?"

Rubin answered so softly Nathan had to strain to hear. "No . . . not marriage, exactly."

"Then it must be Jocelyn."

"I'm afraid it is, sir. A man can't love merely because it's . . . expedient."

Nathan got up and paced the floor, hands behind his back. "Expedient?" he said. "That's a strange word, Rubin. Are you implying that this marriage is only a merger between the Sassoons and the Hacks?"

Well, isn't it? Rubin wanted to answer but he couldn't, not when he saw the troubled look on his father's face.

"Do you feel that we've forced you into an arrangement?"

"We were certainly thrown together a lot. And suddenly, somehow, marriage seemed to be the next logical step. At the time, it all did, I admit, seem so right . . ."

"But everyone assumed that your affection for Jocelyn was real . . . in fact, no one was aware that you were anything less than deeply in love. This is what I find hardest to comprehend."

"My affection at the time was certainly genuine. Jocelyn is a lovely young woman—"

"But you've suddenly fallen out of love? How could that happen in so short a time?"

Rubin was silent.

"Rubin? . . . why did you stay in Paris so long?"

Running his hands through this thick black hair, Rubin looked at the vaulted ceiling while Nathan waited for an answer. Finally, he spoke. "Because . . . well, it happens I've fallen completely in love with a woman in Paris. . . ."

Nathan sighed deeply. Replenishing the brandy glasses, he handed one to his son, then seated himself again. "Is she going to have your child? Is that the problem?"

"I wish she was, it might be simpler."

"Is she in love with you?"

"Yes . . ."

"Still, you couldn't have known her for long."

"Is time the right barometer? I've known Jocelyn for a lifetime—"

"Forgive me, Rubin, but I always thought love was something that grew. Of course, I come from a different generation . . ."

"Forgive me, Father, but I suspect love hasn't changed so much—"

"I suppose you're right, Rubin. But the point is, what do you plan to do about this . . . woman?"

"Nothing."

Nathan nodded, and smiled for the first time. "You are right, Rubin . . . love has not changed so much from my generation to yours. . . ." And then he astonished his son as he told him for the first time . . . as though suddenly they were old confidants . . . how "when I was about your age, perhaps a little younger, I, too, thought I was completely in love . . . with a lovely young ballerina. Ludicrous when I look back on it now, of course, but at the time, believe me, I was inconsolable. . . . Marriage was out of the question, unthinkable, she could *never* have been accepted. . . . We have so much, but we can't always have what we want. When I think back . . . about how different my life would have been . . ."

And Rubin was hearing his father's last words merge with what Solange had said . . . What would have become of my life if I'd had the courage to run away with . . . ? Nathan's words brought him back. "I have my father, God rest his soul, to thank for setting *me* straight. I met your mother shortly afterward. And by then, Rubin, would you believe it, I could scarcely remember the girl's face. Loving your mother as I did, I understood the other was only a passing matter, a young man experiencing life, as they say, for the first time. Now, the most astonishing thing is . . . quite accidentally, I ran into this woman on the street a few years ago. I would have passed her by if she hadn't called out my name. When we spoke, briefly, it was like talking to a stranger. She had become, I'm afraid, a rather vain, unattractive woman. I walked away thinking, And for that I almost gave up my heritage, my life. So I know what you are going through, Rubin. I also know it will pass. Jocelyn is *right* for you. Once you're married, settled into your life, your affection for her will turn into the love and devotion I feel for your mother. There will be children . . . and before you know it, this woman in Paris will cease to exist. This, I promise . . ."

You're wrong, Father, our stories are not parallel . . . I won't forget Magda's face . . . I won't stop loving her . . . You can't promise me anything, it isn't yours to promise. . . . But I'll be your loving, obedient son, the son you respect. . . .

At least he would try. One thing, he was relieved he no longer had to go on deceiving his father. And for a moment, he felt almost rewarded in his misery as Nathan stood up and put his arms around his son's shoulders.

From that day, Rubin became a mechanical man, doing all the right things . . . saying what was expected. His conduct was exemplary. He was with Jocelyn constantly, working doggedly at the alchemy to change respect and affection into desire and love. He barely felt alive.

Two weeks before the wedding, Jocelyn showed Rubin through their new house, now completely furnished. Hand in hand she led him from room to room, in the fine mansion off Regents Park, the gift of her parents. Rubin found himself being led into the bedroom. He felt nothing as he looked at the large four-poster bed. He had to turn away and walk to the window. It was Magda he saw in that bed . . . Magda who—

"Are you pleased, darling?"

He looked at her. "Oh, yes, it's very nice, very . . ."

Jocelyn put her head on his shoulder. "We're going to be very happy here, Rubin . . . Darling, I do love you so."

He stroked her hair, honestly wishing he could feel the same, hating himself because he couldn't.

The days would not be held back. Nor the hours or minutes. It was his wedding day.

That morning he re-read his most recent letter from Magda—they'd finally begun to arrive after the wait he had thought meant she no longer cared. His eyes sped down to the very last sentence. . . . "And I can only wish you the greatest happiness with your Jocelyn . . . Love as always, Magda."

Oh, Magda, I want you . . . I need you . . .

And as Rubin sat alone reading her letter, Magda lay crying on Emile's bed in Paris. Solange tried to comfort her, but nothing could. "He doesn't love me, Solange. I was so sure . . . so sure he'd never be able to live without me—"

"That was a mistake . . . Your strategy . . . those lapses between letters to draw him back to you . . . But there are ties that can go beyond love, Magda . . . *Rubin* is being sacrificed, not you."

"But don't I count for anything?"

"Stop being ungrateful. Look at all Rubin *has* done for you—"

"But what have I *got?* Nothing but things . . . *things* . . ."

Solange shook her, then held her close, wiped away her tears. "Yes . . . things which make it possible for you to live like a princess. You should get down on your knees and pray that man finds some peace. He's the one who's going to have to spend the rest of his life in hell . . . Ask me. I know what it's like living with someone you feel nothing for . . ."

Magda turned over and buried her face in the pillow.

Jocelyn and her entourage were sequestered in the bridal room. The temple was filled with flowers. As the organ played softly, the guests were ushered into pews. The bride's mother was escorted down the aisle. The seat beside her was vacant, but soon it would be occupied by her husband, after he had led his daughter to the altar and relinquished her to Rubin Hack. Sara and Nathan Hack were next. What a handsome couple they made, Sara, so sedate, in a rose lace gown, and Nathan in his cutaway jacket and gray-striped trousers.

Sara glanced at the bride's mother, Annette Sassoon, who smiled with perfect decorum. The altar was breathtaking—the white satin canopy festooned with white roses, lilies of the valley, satin streamers and green maidenhair fern. The glowing candles in the candelabra made the sanctuary look ethereal. This was one of the most important weddings of the year. The Sassoons had outdone themselves.

Sara reached for Nathan's hand and held it tightly. The years had rushed by so rapidly . . . We never notice them slipping away. . . . Only yesterday Rubin was tugging at my skirts . . . And now he's a man, ready to take his place as husband and father . . . She sighed and looked at Nathan. Life had been good to them. They had brought four sons into the world. Soon there would be four daughters-in-law . . . daughters, really . . . and six grandchildren so far. No one could wish for more. . . .

The bridesmaids walked down the aisle dressed in soft tea-rose-yellow chiffon, carrying matching bouquets of roses. The ushers took their places. Rubin and Leon entered from a side door to wait for the bride.

Rubin literally felt as though he wasn't there. This was not happening to him . . . only to some stranger he didn't know. Leon, apprehensive, watched his brother's expression. He showed no signs of nervousness.

The temple became completely silent. Jocelyn, on the arm of her father, started slowly down the aisle. Yards and yards of tulle trimmed with heirloom lace trailed behind her, as she walked closer and closer to take her place next to Rubin.

The moment had closed in on him. Rubin felt like a spectator watching a young woman being kissed on the cheek by her father. Then the older man took his leave and seated himself beside his wife.

The play had begun, the actors were all onstage. The rabbi stood before them, preparing them for the solemn vows of union. Rubin scarcely heard. The words sounded like the echo of a distant chamber, ". . . Do you, Jocelyn, take Rubin to be your husband, to have and to hold from this day forward, forsaking all others . . . to love and obey . . . ?"

Jocelyn looked at Rubin through the gossamer veil covering her face, and answered, "I do."

". . . And do you, Rubin, take Jocelyn . . ."

Rubin's mind refused the question. The rabbi waited for his reply, but Rubin looked blankly back at the rabbi as though he hadn't heard. The rabbi repeated, ". . . 'til death do you part . . .?" The five-year-old ring-bearer handed the small white satin pillow to Leon, who held it out to Rubin. As he looked down at the two gold bands which would bind Jocelyn and himself forever, nausea came over him. He broke out in a cold sweat. Perspiration rolled down his back. His hand began to tremble as he reached for Jocelyn's ring . . . then the hand retreated. Something beyond his control had stopped him, as though he were no longer responsible for his actions. He looked at Jocelyn. Shaking his head, he said, "No . . . Forgive me, I can't . . ."

He turned and walked away, through the side door

from which he had entered and down the long passageway to the street.

It had all happened so quickly. The shock was so great that for a moment no one quite understood what had taken place. Then there were hushed gasps as Jocelyn collapsed against her father. Too stunned to cry, she shook her head in disbelief. She was quickly taken from the sanctuary to the waiting limousine. Her mother, dazed and near-incoherent, followed. Their car sped away.

The Hacks sat motionless, mute statues, as the guests quietly left them to their shame and embarrassment. What could anyone say?

Rubin had taken a taxi to the house. Outside, he got into his roadster, where his bags had been placed in the trunk for what should have been his honeymoon trip. He drove away, hoping to be gone before the family arrived. The consequences of what he had done would have to be dealt with later.

He went directly to Brown's Hotel. It was small and quiet. He wasn't likely to run into anyone he knew there.

In his bedroom, he immediately placed a call to Magda. The circuits were busy. He cursed. Impatiently he called room service and ordered a bottle of whiskey.

After the waiter left, Rubin poured himself a straight whiskey and swallowed it. Then another, which he sipped. What he had done today was cowardly. . . . He should at least have broken with Jocelyn when he came back from Paris. He should have faced it that his plan to live for but not with Magda was a hopeless one—

The ringing of the telephone made him jump. He picked it up.

"Rubin . . . ?"

"Thank God . . . Yes, darling . . ."

"Where are you?"

"In London . . ."

"Where is your bride . . . ?"

"I . . . I couldn't go through with it." He could almost see the look of disbelief.

Finally she answered. "I don't understand . . . what happened?"

"Darling, I want you to take the afternoon train to Calais. Pack only what you need, Solange can send the rest.

You should be here by nine o'clock tonight . . . Hello, hello! . . . Magda, are you there?"

"Yes, darling, I'm here . . . is it true, Rubin . . . ? I'm not dreaming? Tell me I'm not dreaming, tell me . . . Oh God, if you only knew how I've missed you . . . Rubin, I love you, Rubin. . . ."

Nathan Hack stood before the black marble mantle, and Sara's heart went out to her husband, knowing the anguish he was feeling, knowing the sense of failure that must be devastating him. . . .

It was Phillip who spoke first. "Well, Father . . . what should we do? Of course, Rubin's name will be taken off the door—"

"Never!" Nathan spoke in anger.

"What do you mean, Father?" Maurice said. "He can't continue with the firm. . . . It would be unthinkable."

"Unthinkable," echoed Sylvia, siding with her husband. But Nathan was adamant. "His name will remain."

"Father, I don't understand," said Phillip. "Rubin has brought shame on us for years to come—"

Nathan shook his head, his hands held behind him. Looking around the room at his children, he felt doubly sad at the rush to condemn one of their own . . . their own brother. He'd thought he knew his sons. . . .

"Perhaps you don't understand, Phillip . . . Don't you care, or realize, what this has cost Rubin? It's Rubin who will have to live with the consequences of what he has done."

That did not satisfy Matilda. "Indeed, Father, and *we* will have to live down what he has done." She started to cry, taking out her lace-trimmed handkerchief. "Chances are, I'll be asked to give up my chairmanship of the garden club tea—"

"Dear God," Deborah said, "how can you think of anything so superficial at a time like this? Father is right. We're only concerned with ourselves. . . ." Leon took her unsteady hand in his.

"Of course we're concerned with ourselves," said Sylvia in a righteous, indignant tone. "Why *shouldn't* we be? Why should we have to suffer because of Rubin?"

Matilda agreed. "We'll never be able to hold up our

heads again. The Sassoons will see to it. We'll be absolute social outcasts. . . ."

Nathan thought, They haven't heard a thing. No . . . I'm wrong. They heard, but they weren't listening.

"If you keep his name on the door, it'll be a sign that you condone what he's done. I'm sorry, Father, we are his family . . . regrettably, I must say . . . but Rubin has brought the worst kind of disgrace to our name." Maurice looked his father squarely in the eye.

Nathan sighed. "I will not argue with any of you. The debate is over. . . . You are entitled to your feelings, but Rubin's name will remain on the door as long as I am alive. . . ."

"I can't believe this, Father," Phillip said. "You, who always taught us honor . . ."

Nathan rocked back on his heels. "I cannot teach honor, Phillip, I can only try to be honorable. I will not remove Rubin's name because he is flesh of my flesh. No matter what Rubin has done, he is my son. If I remove his name, then I should wear a black armband. I will not hurt my son more than he has hurt himself. I would not wish for any of you to have his dreams at night. We don't have to punish him more than he has punished himself. Perhaps that does not comfort any of you, but that is my decision."

Leon spoke for the first time. "Father, why did Rubin do it? He's the most sensitive of us all. He never hurt anyone . . ."

Nathan told them then about the talk he'd had with Rubin. "I feel myself guilty," he said. "If only I'd known the extent of his . . . love, obsession, whatever, for this girl, I'd have perhaps been able to deal with it differently."

Sylvia finally found her voice. "A French girl . . . French? Oh, dear God! Did you ask him about her background? Who her family is . . . where she comes from?"

"No, regrettably I didn't."

"And Rubin didn't volunteer to tell you," Maurice said with unmistakable anger.

"No, he didn't."

"Well," said Sylvia, "it's clear enough what sort of woman she must be. Some . . . some . . ." She couldn't say "whore," but her inference was clear.

"You really shouldn't say such a thing," said Deborah. "We haven't even met her—"

"*Met* her?" Matilda said. "Have you taken leave of your senses? You're not naïve enough to imagine that she could ever be accepted . . . not in *my* house, at least. . . ."

"I'll reserve my judgment," said Deborah.

"Well, bully for you . . . but let's not forget that our dear brother jilted Jocelyn, and it will never be forgiven, not, at any rate, by me," Matilda responded with equal fervor.

"Well said," said Sylvia.

"Mother, you haven't said a word," Phillip put in.

Sara had indeed remained silent throughout her family's heated dialogue. "Listening can have its virtues . . . one sometimes learns something."

"But, Mother, please, what is your *opinion?*" Phillip said.

Standing up and going to Nathan, Sara answered, "The same as your father's. Now I think we should all go in to lunch."

In the home of the forsaken bride, bitter anger spewed from the mouth of Harry Sassoon. He would, he said, enjoy nothing more than to shoot Rubin Hack. And no court in the land would condemn him. If he stopped short of killing the man, he vowed to avenge his daughter's humiliation by seeing to it that not one single Hack would ever set foot again in a decent men's club. They would be banished from London society. He would blacken their name, sue for breach of promise . . .

In spite of Annette Sassoon's distress, she pleaded with her husband to calm himself, afraid that in his anxiety he would precipitate another heart attack. He had already had one, a few years back.

"Harry, please . . . sit down. This is not the way to deal with—"

"Imagine! Jocelyn having to go abroad. As though *she* were the culprit. The irony! Jocelyn has to leave, while that monster is free to go about as he pleases . . . that *bastard* . . ." He clutched his chest. Quickly Annette poured brandy into a glass and put it to his lips.

"Drink this, dear." She watched the anger drain from his face. "Harry, my dear, please do lie down on the sofa." She helped him as he obeyed. "Now, my dearest, we'll take Jocelyn away for a few months. She's spiritually strong, and youth is on her side—"

Harry spoke more calmly now. "Youth? Annette, she will never recover. This may damage her for life."

"I refuse to believe that, Harry. Given time, Jocelyn will recover. In her gentleness, she has much strength . . . but please, my dear, be careful. We both need you."

"Thank you. I'll try to do that. But I will have my revenge. I've got to—"

"Shh . . . shh . . . After we get back, then we'll have time to see what action should be taken. Now, if you are all right, I want to go upstairs and see how things are progressing. It's getting late, and if we are to catch the nine o'clock train for Dover . . ."

Three

June 27, 1914

Rubin paced back and forth in Victoria Station. He prayed for the time to pass. To divert his mind, he counted the seconds . . . ten . . . nine . . . eight . . . At last he heard the sound of the approaching train.

Impatiently, he waited on the platform until he saw her. They ran into each other's outstretched arms. He held her face in his hands. She was real . . . the only thing that made his life worth living. Whatever the cost would turn out to be, she was worth it. . . .

The Sassoons, too, were at the station, on a train bound for Dover. Harry Sassoon had relaxed for a moment, but the car was oppressively warm. He released the leather window strap, letting it down, and breathed in deeply. Looking outside, he gasped. Was that . . . could it be that bastard Hack? By God, he wished he had a gun. He reached for his glasses, fumbling in the inner pocket of his jacket. But by the time he'd got them on, Rubin and Magda had left, and in the exact spot stood another pair of lovers. Sitting down, Harry clutched his heart. Was he losing his mind? Every young man suddenly looked like Rubin Hack. . . .

When the bellboy left, Rubin said, "Do you know what an eternity is . . . ?"

"Yes, Rubin, a minute away from you."

The champagne bottle hissed as Rubin uncorked it, then poured the bubbling liquid into the glasses. . . . "To you, my love. May this be the beginning of a wonderful long life together . . . oh, God, Magda, just love me . . ."

"I do love you, Rubin." She touched his glass to hers. "To us, and all that lies ahead."

Afterward, when their at first frenzied and then deliciously fulfilling lovemaking was finished, they lay in each other's arms, savoring what had been missing for too long. Magda kissed him on the ear. "Rubin, why did you want to remain in London? Wouldn't it be simpler to live in Paris?"

"Perhaps . . . I'm not sure . . . I'm not sure, I'm afraid, about a lot of things—"

"About me?"

"Oh God, no . . . you're what I *am* sure of."

"Then, my darling, it must be your fine old English guilt."

"Yes . . . I suppose, but it's more than that. It would have been simpler, easier . . . but I ran away from my family once today. I can't keep running all my life."

"Would it be *running* to avoid a bad, a difficult situation? There will surely be a lot of unpleasantness, yes?"

"No doubt. I'll simply have to face it—"

"It does sound, darling, as though you're deliberately trying to punish yourself. Is loving me so bad . . . ? Is your precious family so—"

To silence her, and his own disturbing thoughts, he put his mouth to hers and they again entered the world that shut out, for a while at least, all the others . . . that belonged only to themselves.

The next morning's newspapers reported the scandal of the season: the Sassoon heiress had been left at the altar. There were pictures of the jilted bride taken in former days . . . her presentation at court . . . her coming out . . . at the races . . . dancing with the Prince of Wales at a ball in Mayfair . . . Rubin Hack was not ignored. There were pictures of him at Oxford, receiving his degree . . . standing with a broad smile as the captain of the Rugby team . . . as captain of the regatta . . .

Rubin was roasted. Not since Jack the Ripper had anyone appeared more vile. London loved its little scandals. And Londoners were lapping it up, like a cat with a bowl of cream.

Juicy as the scandal was, it didn't make the headlines. That spot was reserved for the Archduke Francis Ferdinand of Austria, who had been assassinated by a Serbian peasant.

Magda, drinking her coffee in bed, scarcely bothered to notice. She was too mesmerized by the news on page two. She, Magda Charascu, from the slums of Bucharest, had been able to depose the equivalent of royalty. The abandoned bride, she read, had been taken off to Europe by her family to recover from her ordeal. A jubilant Magda was pleased to glory in her triumph. Why not? You were wrong, Solange . . . It worked . . . I'm not Magda Charascu for nothing . . . anl his family will accept me . . . not today . . . not tomorrow . . . but some day, sooner than they know . . .

Quickly, she folded the paper as she heard the door open. Rubin came to her side and held out a jewel box. In it were two gold bands he had purchased that morning.

"I've seen the rabbi. He'll marry us today."

"Oh, Rubin, I can't believe it . . . I once said I could never love . . . Remember what you told me."

"Yes . . . because you'd never really been loved."

"I didn't believe it then, Rubin, but you were right. My beloved Rubin . . . I *will* make you happy."

"You've already done that . . ."

There was sadness in his eyes, but this time she was certain it was not because of her. She made a silent vow . . . It will be all right, Rubin. Your family will forgive you. I will see to it. . . .

Magda was less than impressed with the shabby synagogue in the East End of London. It was her wedding day, after all, a day she had secretly dreamed of for years. But this was not at all like her fantasies. No beautiful flowers adorned the chuppa. Instead, it was dismal, and the emptiness of unfilled pews dulled the words being said by the unkempt, bearded rabbi. Magda, in fact, could scarcely understand him. She comforted herself with the knowledge that at least she was dressed as she should be, a woman of respectability, of distinction, marrying a fine, important man.

She was wearing a powder-blue velvet Chanel suit. On top of her perfectly coiffed hair sat a matching small coronet hat with a veil covering her opulent, misty eyes. In her hand she held a sable muff, to which was pinned the fragrant violets Rubin had given her.

They pledged their vows, exchanged rings, and in ten minutes were husband and wife, to live together in sickness and in health, happiness and sorrow. . . . The rabbi blessed them.

In their absence, their suite had been filled with banks of white flowers in crystal vases. The perfume of roses, stock, and lilacs filled the rooms. A fire added to the enchantment. Candles made the crystal glasses gleam like iridescent prisms. Magda was more than impressed with the gold service, which, she decided, hotels must make available to very special guests only. There was still a lot to learn. Sitting across from Rubin, dressed in a flowing pink chiffon gown, she assumed the posture of a gracious lady, not only to practice her demeanor—which in the future would be important—but also to impress the waiter who stood to one side. After all, she was Mrs. Rubin Hack.

She watched the waiter carefully as he served a bowl of caviar in a bed of crushed ice . . . Magda loved caviar. And the champagne was Dom Perignon. It was marvelous; the bubbles tickled her nose, making her giddy. The whole dinner was perfection. Only at one point did she almost forget her posture—when the wedding cake was brought in. Each of the three tiers was separated by crystal posts. The roses were so well carved that Magda longed to cut them, and the two silver bells on top would ring, she knew, if she pulled the white satin ribbons. But what almost took her composure away was the music box beneath, which played "I Love You Truly."

Rubin dismissed the waiter. He placed the knife in Magda's hand, and with his covering hers they cut deep into the first layer. . . .

It had begun.

*   *   *

The next morning Rubin decided to drive to Brighton Beach rather than take the train, so Magda would be able to enjoy the English countryside.

From head to toe Magda was the image of *haute couture*. She was dressed in a beige tweed suit. The fabric, the style, the cut were obviously Chanel. Her accessories matched perfectly . . . the felt cloche . . . the brown alligator shoes and bag . . . the long, flowing chiffon scarf, persimmon-colored, tied casually around her neck. As she slipped on the soft cocoa kid gloves, Rubin shook his head in amazement. Her hair was pulled back under the hat; only the twisted chignon showed. She looked regal, as though truly born to the purple. Rubin beamed. "You're exquisite . . . really." She looked at him coquettishly, with those magnificent eyes that changed color; this morning they seemed, somehow, more green. "And did you think I would be less? Remember, I was taught by a master." She laughed delightedly. "However, if you noticed, I didn't require the maestro's help today . . . thank you." Indeed, she no longer required anyone's help. . . . Her thoughts shifted quickly to that day the countess was coming to meet her . . . the frustrations . . . the unsureness . . . the pleading with Rubin to help . . . "Please, I need your help". . . *That* Magda was gone. Today was the beginning of a new reign. . . .

Long live the Queen.

In Brighton, Rubin drove straight to the Regency.

Magda held her head high as Rubin registered. Nothing went unnoticed, everything impressed her. She had not only noticed the crest above the door, but also the date: 1812. Her eyes drank in everything.

On the way to their rooms, Rubin took her by the arm. Proudly, Magda walked through the lobby, aware that many eyes were on her . . . appraising . . . admiring. The Regency, she knew, was the height of elegance.

The suite was a symphony of color. The walls were covered in yellow damask. Above the gray marble mantel hung the ceiling-high mirror. The gold leaf chairs and settees were upholstered in petit point designs of roses and bows. Flower-filled vases were everywhere.

The moment Rubin dismissed the attendants, Magda led Rubin by the hand into the bedroom. The enormous canopy bed was covered in blue taffeta. The ivory draperies were held back with heavy tasseled cords. The walls were covered in rose silk. She could no longer wait to make love in such a bed. Her fingers slipped off Rubin's tie, unbuttoned his vest . . . shirt . . . slipped the suspenders over his shoulders. Nimbly, she unbuttoned his trousers, which fell on the exquisite carpet. She felt his hardness grow, as the last piece of underclothing was discarded. Quickly disrobing herself, they clung together, naked. Magda kissed the lobe of his ear, then his cheek. Opening her mouth, she gently touched his tongue . . . then more intensely. Now her kiss moved down slowly, unhurried, until it reached the place which made Rubin moan with ecstasy. Lifting her up from her knees, he carried her to the bed. The world was spinning as he entered her. Her pink distended nipples heightened his pleasure as he kissed and sucked them tenderly. Magda was now on him, they rolled over together without separating him from that deliciously warm, moist place. And finally it was as though the world had ceased to exist . . . and all that mattered was this moment. . . .

Rubin lay back now, with Magda curled up close to him . . . Suddenly she sat up in bed. "I'm starved." Rubin laughed. "It seems I've heard that before." Magda laughed. "In Paris, the first night at Emile's. You starved me then. Do you intend to make a habit of it?" she said, tickling him in the ribs.

"*Please* . . . don't . . . I'm afraid I'm ticklish—"

"Ah . . . now I'm getting to know your true weak points," and she continued remorselessly.

"Stop, I'll feed you, anything, just *stop*."

Slapping him gently on the bottom, she said as she jumped out of bed, "Then order the food . . . and it better be here by the time I'm through bathing and dressing. Do I make myself clear? Remember, this is your mistress speaking."

Laughing, he said, "What a fine combination, a mistress and a wife. I shall need to improve myself if—"

Going swiftly back to the bed, she bent over, kissed him into silence, then nibbled his ear lobe and whispered, "You, my lover, are the greatest lover. How in the world can you improve on that?"

Rubin woke up at four in the morning, trying to convince himself that it really wasn't raining. It didn't rain at

Brighton in June. Impossible! Then he looked over at the open window and saw the downpour coming in. Everything was soaking wet. He got up to close the window. As he got back into bed, he thought, it seems to rain a great deal in my life . . . the day I left Paris . . . the morning I arrived home . . . and now, on my honeymoon. Was it an omen? His last conscious thoughts before sleep were of his family. . . . Father . . . I've disappointed you . . . Mother . . . forgive me . . . I hurt you all, I know . . . Leon, my favorite brother . . . don't turn your back on me . . . and poor Jocelyn . . . Magda, love me . . . there are only the two of us now. . . .

It rained and stormed for the next five days. Magda was miserable. The only excitement she had was dressing four times a day. Eating in the dining room gave her a chance to show off her morning wardrobe. Then there was lunch, in a different outfit, then tea. Thank God for tea time . . . something to do and to wear. Of course, dinner was very formal, befitting the chamber music that was played as they ate. Otherwise, the days were very long. They knew almost no one, nor did anyone try to get friendly. It seemed that everyone else was acquainted. Magda was beginning to despise the Regency and Brighton Beach . . . what little she could see of it.

She hadn't been able to promenade or wear her bathing suit or dance or go out to the pier—and she wasn't too happy with Rubin just now either. What's more, she wasn't even going to the dining room today. Not after being ignored by . . . what was that bitch's name? Lady Pamela Pembroke . . . Magda hoped she would choke on her damned tea and crumpets . . . Imagine! The way Lord and Lady Pembroke passed Rubin in the dining room last night, drowning, looking daggers at him and then scrutinizing her. So this is the little strumpet Rubin had jilted the Sassoon heiress for . . . Well! Rubin had acknowledged them, but they walked on by without a word. Then, making sure they would hear, dear Lady Pembroke had said, "Come, Charles. I think our party is waiting." From that moment on whispers and glances were directed to their table. And by the time the Hacks left the dining room, the air was charged with hostility.

The sting of last night still remained. Magda turned from the window and went back to bed. She felt miserable, completely out of sorts with Rubin for making such a damned fool of himself by acknowledging the Pembrokes. To further add to her frustration, he now sat reading placidly in the living room as though it had never happened. And her menstrual cramps kept coming on stronger. Maybe if she had her period the tensions would subside. She sighed her discontent. When Rubin came into the bedroom to ask how she felt, she was near the point of screaming. "No . . . I don't want anything. Don't bother me."

He tried to take her hand, but she turned her back to him. "Magda," he said, "I'm *sorry* about the weather . . . I know it's miserable for you . . . Would you like some tea?"

Turning abruptly, she faced him. "I only want one thing, and that's to get the hell out of this damned place."

With more anger than he intended, Rubin said, "Don't talk to me like that. I didn't make this weather—"

"You told me it never rained in Brighton in June."

"You're acting like a child. I've done everything I could to please you. I'm going downstairs."

As he left she called out, "Please come back. I'm—"

But he had already shut the door.

Now her anger was replaced by embarrassment. She had lost her Rumanian temper. She would have to learn to control it. There was more to being a lady than just lovely dresses. . . . Ladies were restrained . . . Rubin must hate me . . . I did act like a spoiled little slut. Oh Rubin, I will learn . . . please have patience. . . .

Rubin went to the taproom, ordered a whiskey and water, and sipped it slowly. He was sorry, too . . . Magda was disappointed . . . Of course she was. She was young and spirited . . . Be tolerant, help her . . . love her . . . with all her tempestuousness . . . isn't that what attracted you to her in the first place?

Quickly, he got up and went back to the suite. Magda rushed into his arms, kissing him over and over as tears streamed down her cheeks. "I'm so sorry, Rubin. I've behaved like a spoiled, ungrateful—"

He placed his finger against her lips, stroking her hair. "Don't say any more, there's no need. It's been miserable for you. Forgive me for losing my temper. . . . We're leaving tomorrow."

"Then you're not angry with me?"

"How could I be, how could anybody be . . . ?"

"Thank you, Rubin . . . I love you, darling." And she proceeded to show him.

The next morning a subdued, dignified Magda sat at breakfast, brought to their rooms, serving her husband as a dutiful wife should. She was wearing an iridescent violet taffeta dressing gown. The ruffle around her neck, tied with a velvet bow, made her look positively angelic.

Rubin watched her as she broke the egg into the cup, buttered his toast, poured his coffee, and boned his kipper. She was feeling glorious this morning, thank God. During the night, after their lovemaking, she had gotten her period, and all the premenstrual tension seemed gone. . . .

"Rubin," she said, casually, "where are we going to live?"

"After you've seen a little of London, we can make up our minds."

"I don't know one place from another."

"You soon will."

"But Rubin, I'm going to have a terrible time with your language—"

"Nonsense, Magda, and I think you can speak it better than you pretend—"

She smiled. "Do you think I'm pretending . . . ?"

"Yes, my little actress, I do."

"Oh Rubin, you're too smart for me . . ."

"I don't think that for a minute."

"Yes you are, you see right through me—"

"Not true . . . you're a lady of many moods . . . I haven't even begun to discover you."

"No, Rubin, you are quite wrong. I'm exactly what I appear to be . . . when I'm happy I show it . . . when I'm not, unfortunately, I show that too. But I shall improve. I promise." She wondered if Rubin really believed her . . . or if she really believed herself. . . . She changed the subject. "What will you do when we get back?" A question which was inevitable, and this, she decided, was as good a time as any to ask it.

He spoke in obvious seriousness. "I'm going to *try* to paint. Of course I'll never sell in London, but there are other places—"

"But why shouldn't your work sell in London?"

"Because, my pet, I have committed the unpardonable sin of jilting an heiress and marrying for love."

Taking a deep breath she said softly, "I'm sorry, darling—"

"Well, please don't be . . . I'm not—"

"And your family? You have no regrets?"

"Not about marrying you."

"Will *they* ever forgive you?"

"I don't know, I hope so . . . although I suppose I'll always be the black sheep—"

"Because of me."

"No, because of *me*. The English don't mind adultery. It's run through our history from the beginning. As long as it's kept in its proper little closet, everything's fine. But once we flaunt our sins, they hold us up to ridicule. We must be punished. It's so very English. Anything for the sake of appearances . . . someday I'll tell you how Brighton Beach became famous . . ."

"Tell me now," Magda begged.

"Well . . . George the Fourth was considered a wicked young man. He was madly in love with a woman named Mrs. Fitzherbert, whom he'd been having an affair with for a long time. They came to Brighton to get away from the court and that's the way Brighton became fashionable. But he loved her so much he finally married her . . . though he eventually was forced to annul the marriage—"

"At least they can't make us do that. With such a history, you'd think the English would be more tolerant."

"No, the rules must be enforced at any cost. As long as our sins are kept within the bounds of propriety, we can do almost anything—except, of course, marry out of our class. But don't look so glum, darling . . . we won't, I assure you, starve. I do have some money saved from my practice as a barrister, my brothers and I share a legacy from my grandparents."

"Rubin, since you bring it up, how much *do* we have?"

"About . . . fifty thousand pounds."

"Oh, Rubin, I'll never understand your money. How much is that in francs?"

"About a million and a quarter, I'd say."

"My God, Rubin, that's impossible . . . so much . . ."

"The only thing impossible, my love, is to describe how much I love, and need you."

Magda waited by Rubin's side as he took care of the bill. Then he went on to see about the car. Walking through the lobby, she saw Lady Pembroke coming toward her. Magda's eyes narrowed . . . Nothing would have pleased her more than to spit in the *Lady's* eyes . . . But that would have been un-English . . . A woman of breeding did not act so vulgar. So Magda just smiled. A smile that said, Go to hell, your highness . . . or your ladyship. You'll drop dead before I ask for your approval . . . I'm Mrs. Rubin Hack, and don't you forget it. London will hear about me . . . Wait and see . . . Magda lifted her shoulders, her head held high . . . and walked to the waiting car. Comfortably seated, she adjusted her blue chiffon scarf.

"All right, Rubin Hack, let's go home."

Rubin lost no time in introducing Magda to London, showing her all the historical landmarks. From Canterbury to Haymarket . . . the buildings of Parliament . . . Piccadilly Circus . . . the Royal Mews . . . St. Paul's Cathedral . . . the tower of London . . . Trafalgar Square . . . Westminster Abbey . . . the Zoological Gardens . . . Hyde Park . . . the British Museum . . . Buckingham Palace . . .

When they returned from each trip, she'd take off her shoes and relax on the bed, but Rubin was like a man possessed. She was surprised to find that his desires were greater than hers. She would often be content to spend an evening in their rooms just relaxing, but Rubin wanted to keep on the go. They dined at Gatti's, the Dorchester, the Ritz. She loved the theaters, especially the music halls. It wasn't as though Rubin was deliberately trying to thumb his nose at London society. Rather, it seemed to Magda that he had decided not to hide, not to live like a leper on this snooty island. Naturally, she was pleased.

Although her English was improving—and she learned rapidly—still it wasn't always up to understanding all the humor, the nuances of the theater. But when she didn't understand a particular word she would ask what it was in French and Rubin, in turn, would repeat the English equivalent, which she would then repeat over and over to herself. She was determined to conquer the English language . . . well, if not conquer, at least insure that Rubin would not be embarrassed. At the same time, though, she made sure her French *accent* remained intact. She was actress enough to know how simply charming it was.

They looked for a flat, and finally found a perfect place on Wimpole Street.

"Only a few blocks from where Elizabeth Barrett Browning lived," Rubin said delightedly.

Who, Magda wondered, was *that?* She'd look it up. Imagine, she thought, the Hacks living so close to *her* . . .

The flat consisted of an oval central foyer which separated the drawing room from the dining room. Off the kitchen and pantry were the maids' rooms. The three bedrooms were huge. What impressed Magda most were the Victorian mantels. Two separate bathrooms had been installed by the former owners.

"It's going to be elegant, Rubin . . . Wait and see. I can hardly wait to move in. How long will it take?"

"A few weeks . . . if we have enough people working on the job."

"I want the dining room to have murals, like Emile's . . ."

"His are painted on the wall—"

"Why couldn't you do them?"

"It's not the kind of painting I do, darling, but we can select Zubbers."

"What are they?"

"Old murals done on canvas, very traditional and very attractive. Do you really like the flat, Magda?"

"I love it . . . I love you so, Rubin . . . let's celebrate. I feel like drinking champagne."

Taking the lift down, she said, "Just think of living so close to . . . Elizabeth Barrett Browning."

Rubin laughed.

"What's so funny, darling?"

"Magda, she's been dead for over fifty years."

"Really? . . . Well, I didn't know it was that long—"

Pulling her to him, Rubin laughed again. And this time she joined him.

* * *

Today was the end of a week's heavy shopping. When they got back, Magda quickly undressed and then soaked in a warm tub. Her feet were killing her. From the bedroom, about to call room service, Rubin asked what her pleasure would be for dinner.

"You . . ." she called back.

"A wise choice. But for the *entrée* . . . ?"

"Oh, make it Dover sole . . . for a complete English evening." She giggled, pleased with her small joke.

Rubin took the afternoon papers into the living room. He was more than a little interested in the news. The tensions in Europe were growing. He noted the date, July 28, 1914 . . . strange . . . one month ago today Magda and he had been married, and on that same day the Archduke Francis Ferdinand and his wife had been assassinated in Sarajevo. For a moment the coincidence startled him . . . Now, this morning, Austria had declared war on Serbia. True, the Archduke Ferdinand had been the heir apparent to the throne of the Austrian-Hungarian empire, but the great powers had seemed to take the assassination calmly. It was considered a local incident, a national problem which would obviously have to be dealt with. But no one would have thought that the major nations would become involved in war as the result of the carelessness of a chauffeur who had taken a wrong route. No one could have foreseen that a crime involving six unknown Serbian radicals would lead to open warfare.

Of course, the crime was shocking news, but nothing in the immediate aftermath suggested that further violence was inevitable. King George V offered seven days of mourning by the British court. Czar Nicholas II of Russia outdid Great Britain by declaring a mourning period of twelve days. And President Wilson of the United States cabled official sympathies.

The Serbians had immediately set themselves to the task of investigating and interrogating the conspirators, but their efforts were badly mishandled. The conspirators changed their stories, which caused a great deal of confusion. But finally the last of the culprits broke down and revealed the existence of a large terrorist organization in Serbia called the Black Hand.

Friedrich von Wiesner of Austria was dispatched to Sarajevo to see what could be uncovered. His findings—

whether true or not—were that the Serbian government was involved in the plot. Still, most European capitals continued to concern themselves very little with what was considered another Balkan conflict. Stress of that kind had been going on since 1912. No major crisis would grow out of the affair. But tension between Serbia and Austria intensified. In order to soothe Austria and play down the situation, which was becoming incendiary, the Serbian government forbade public assemblies, closed all theaters and dance halls, but made no attempt to censure the national press that raged against Austria. Austrian newspapers were no less violent in attacking Serbia.

On July 19, the Austrian council met in secret and decided that Serbia would have to be beaten into the dust. Austria demanded that the Serbian government formally condemn all anti-Austrian propaganda, expel from office anyone fomenting it and accept unequivocally the complete collaboration of Austrian agents on Serbian soil in the suppression of such propaganda. Belgrade was given forty-eight hours to comply or capitulate. The Serbian cabinet frantically contacted the Regent, Prince Alexander, to appeal for help from Czar Nicholas II. The answer was immediate: should Serbia be attacked, Russia would come to her aid at once.

Meanwhile, Vienna sent a secret communiqué to Kaiser Wilhelm II: If Serbia didn't comply with Austria's demands, could she count on Germany to sustain her as an ally? Germany's reply was an unequivocal yes.

Publication of the ultimatum was followed by two massive mobilizations. The Russian and German armies were ready. A shock wave was spreading across an unsuspecting Europe.

Rubin tried to absorb the latest developments. Wouldn't France have to take a stand, since France had an alliance with Russia? Germany had been hell-bent for some time on expansion, and her navy had already grown to greater proportions than Great Britain was comfortable with. Would Germany cross the borders into France? Would England feel compelled to aid her neighbor? The English navy lay off the coast of France, which placed Great Britain in a very awkward position.

Rubin sighed deeply, got up and poured himself a brandy. His own problems paled in the light of all these events. But if . . . and, dear God, it could only be conjecture . . . *if* England became involved, what would happen to Magda? He would have to enlist, and then she would be alone in a foreign country without a friend. . . . But why are you worrying, Rubin . . . Your imagination is working overtime . . . This whole mess will probably be over tomorrow. . . .

But something kept nudging him, and his anxiety persisted. It would not be dismissed lightly. And suddenly he thought of someone else who was vulnerable. *Solange* . . . Even if his fears were groundless, it would be good to see her. And if war did come, Solange would be here to look after Magda. Yes, he would insist that she come.

He went in to see Magda. She was studying a decorating magazine.

"Darling . . . I've been thinking," he said.

"Yes?" She had found an especially attractive fabric for the drawing room draperies.

"It might be good to ask Solange to come over for a while."

Magda froze. Why did Rubin want Solange in London? Wasn't she capable of standing alone, without the help of a countess? Did Rubin think she still needed her? Suddenly she felt the old insecurity about herself, and very angry. But just as quickly she checked her impulse to strike back, to blurt out her thoughts. Quietly she answered, "That would be a nice gesture, Rubin . . . after the flat is finished. The last of the furniture will be delivered tomorrow, and we're moving on August first. I want it to be perfect . . . and then we'll ask her."

"Solange won't mind if—"

"I'm not thinking of what she'd mind . . . *I* want to have our home looking proper before we entertain."

Rubin knew she was annoyed. The careful cadence of her speech made that clear enough, and, thinking about it, he understood why . . . He'd bring it up again in a couple of weeks, he thought, when the apartment was further along.

Suddenly, Magda realized that Solange in London was indeed something to think about . . . Solange could be a great asset to her . . . Why didn't I think of it sooner? Solange can bring me the kind of prestige the Hacks will acknowledge. . . . The niece of a countess . . . The English love titles. . . .

The idea was sheer genius.

"You're perfectly right, Rubin. I think we should ask her right away. You're very generous to think of it. I'm sorry not to have understood right away . . . of course I need a friend like Solange. . . . You'll phone her then?"

"First thing tomorrow."

Magda put her head against Rubin's shoulder. "I love Solange . . . in spite of the fact she said you'd never marry me."

"Solange didn't know how much I love you."

"No . . . but I did . . . I'm the smartest of the three." She gently nibbled his earlobe.

"Smartest, *and* prettiest. An unbeatable combination . . . Now get that pile of magazines off the bed."

Undressing quickly, he got into bed and waited for her. She joined him, pressing her body against his. She felt Rubin grow harder and larger and spread her legs to receive him.

There was no such thing as war, not tonight . . . not now . . . With an intensity that startled her, he said, "There's only you, only Magda."

four

On August 1 they moved to their Wimpole Street flat. The weather was perfect. Not a cloud on the horizon.

Rubin carried Magda over the threshold, kissed her and put her down. She stood, slowly turned around in the center of the oval foyer. It was all so beautiful . . . almost unreal. This was hers, the first real home she had ever had . . . The impact was overwhelming . . .

Gently she took his hand in hers as they walked from room to room. This was her homecoming. Mama . . . Papa . . . Niko . . . I'm home . . . *We're all home.*

Tears ran down her cheeks. "Rubin, I don't think there has ever been a woman quite as . . . as . . . fortunate . . . ? Is that the right word?"

"I hope so, my darling, I hope so . . ."

"Rubin, I want to go to the little synagogue where we were married . . . to say the *kaddish* for my parents . . . I believe the dead intervene for us. I believe that today I'm here because of them. I must share this with them. You do understand?"

He, of course, did.

That night Rubin lay awake in the dark, hands behind his head, staring up at the ceiling. The first night spent in his own home . . . and he could find no peace. A bride, a home that should have brought him complete joy, but it didn't . . . In spite of himself, he missed his family beyond belief. Without Magda he was nothing, still it was impossible not to feel regret. His dreams had been disturbing. Not quite nightmares, but painful . . . foreboding . . . Pretending not to care was difficult . . . The time the

78

Pembrokes had snubbed him at Brighton . . . the times he'd been ignored, despised, in London . . . they hurt . . .

He got out of bed and went into the drawing room without putting on the lights, unaware of the splendor that surrounded him. Standing at the window, he looked at the park across the street. The neat, cropped lawns, the trees silhouetted against the sky bathed in moonlight, made the cityscape so beautiful . . . so tranquil . . . so peaceful. Peace . . . he wanted that more than anything . . . in a world already mobilizing for war.

Earlier this evening when they had gone to the shabby little synagogue in the East End his emotions had come to the surface . . . all he'd lost . . . and gained, thanks to Magda . . . and he'd prayed for forgiveness, for having offended so many. He prayed too for a reunion . . . to become once again a member of his family. God, he did miss them . . . Leon . . . if only he could at least speak to Leon. . . .

The prayer book touched him deeply. It had so much meaning . . . as though it had been written for him alone, to explore his very soul. Still, when the service was over, he left the musty sanctuary with a feeling of even greater remorse. It hadn't cleansed his soul, but it had put him in touch with himself . . . with God . . . ?

Slowly he turned now from the window. If only he could bring the people he loved together . . . Getting back into bed, he shut his eyes and finally knew the relief of sleep.

Next morning, he felt a strange sense of peacefulness. Somehow, in daylight, everything seemed more hopeful. What couldn't be changed would have to be accepted. Magda had been up since six, wearing one of her many faces . . . no longer the Magda he had met in Paris . . . no longer a bitter, disillusioned young woman . . . and not the same Magda who had sat beside him in the synagogue last night, the Magda reciting the Hebrew prayer for *her* departed . . . Somehow, today, it was a jubilant, joyful Magda, ready to take on the challenges that lay ahead.

"Good morning, Rubin." She smiled and kissed him. She had set the dining table beautifully. The breakfast china was perfectly arranged, the linen snowy white, the monogramed napkins in their places . . .

"Good morning," he answered, resolutely putting aside his painful thoughts of the previous day and night.

"I've made a special breakfast for us." Dressed in a flowered voile morning gown, she went to the kitchen. Within minutes, she wheeled in the cart. Fresh juice . . . raspberries . . . kippers . . . kidneys . . . scrambled eggs . . . toast . . . butter . . . marmalade . . . coffee, cream and sugar. "*Voilà*," she said, filling a plate for Rubin.

Coating the berries with sugar, Rubin asked, "Why were you up so early?"

"I was getting ready for Solange . . . her bedroom . . . oh Rubin, it's . . . *divine* . . . I love that word . . . I used the divine blue sheets, remember the ones with the écru lace? And that divine"—she couldn't help but laugh at her own silliness—"that divine blue satin down comforter, which incidentally was made in France—"

He smiled, taking a spoonful of raspberries. "We do at least have enough taste to import things, you know . . ."

"Of course. You have only to look at me, an original Rumanian import . . . courtesy of France, which if mentioned I will deny . . . oh, Rubin, the room is simply div—"

"Magda, one more time and I will shut that *divine* little imported mouth . . ."

"First call Solange," she said, laughing and kissing him on the neck.

Solange was delighted and promptly got an early afternoon train for Calais. She stepped down from the car looking exactly as a countess should. She was dressed in a dove-gray velvet suit. The bow of her pink chiffon blouse billowed out. Her toque was small and feathered in shades of gray, and the sable scarf hung over her arm.

Magda and Rubin greeted her warmly. First she embraced Magda, then kissed Rubin on both cheeks and looked at him in her own sly way. Oh, the things I do for you, Rubin, her eyes were saying. And his responded, thank you. . . .

Later, after they'd settled Solange in, Magda said, "I'm so happy you're here, Solange." Magda lay across Solange's bed, on her stomach, her hands holding her face.

"Are you really? Two women in the same house with one man."

"What a question! You know I am."

"How are things going?"

"Very well."

"And Rubin is happy?"

Magda looked shocked. "Of course. Why shouldn't he be?"

"It isn't easy living so close to the past—"

"Well, I wanted him to come to Paris to live but he said he had to have roots."

"Yes, that's natural. Roots and family are very important—"

"He rarely thinks of them."

"Really? And what about running into people . . . ? He can scarcely avoid that."

"It doesn't bother him a bit . . . In fact, he says to hell with them."

"It's not so easy defying convention. Being shut out. Who knows that better than I?"

"It doesn't bother Rubin. And I believe you were taken back, and forgiven the *error* of your ways. Besides, I have a plan."

Solange began unpacking. Hanging up a dressing gown, she said, "My dear, you always have a plan . . ."

Magda disregarded the sardonic note. "Well, I *want* Rubin to be reconciled . . . I will never be happy until he's reunited with his family."

Solange looked at Magda . . . We don't fall in love with saints. She understood Magda all too well . . . liked her in spite of it, but there was more to this little suggestion than met the ear. "It means that much to you . . . his happiness . . . ?"

"Of course it does. Why are you being so . . . so difficult?"

Solange settled herself in the satin slipper chair. "The truth is, I've been annoyed with you."

"Why?"

"You took me around the flat like the Queen of Rumania, showing the palace to a serf. You certainly are pleased with the things you've acquired. No one is happier than I with your success, but I worry . . . Rubin loves you, Magda. He's vulnerable. Love always does that. He'll do anything to make you happy. This marriage must not fail. The price has been too great—"

"He can afford it . . ."

Solange sighed and bit her lower lip. "I don't think you've heard one word I've said. I wasn't talking about money. Is that why you married him?"

"No. Of course not. I happen to love him. But can't one have both? Is it a sin . . . ?"

"Of course not, but don't hurt him, Magda."

Magda began to cry. "I wish you hadn't come . . . I thought we were friends . . ."

"Rubin is a shattered man."

"How do you know?"

"I saw it in his eyes. If you have it to give, then love him, Magda."

"I *do*. You don't know the happiness I bring him—"

"I'm not talking about bed . . . I'm talking about the other Rubin . . ."

Magda was shocked. She hadn't seen any great change in Rubin. Wiping the tears from her eyes she said, "Why haven't I seen his sadness?"

"Because you're too absorbed in all this." Solange waved her hands about the room. "You haven't had time to *look* at Rubin . . ."

Magda was silent. Solange, in a way, was right . . . She hadn't looked at Rubin. She ran to Solange, knelt on the floor, and buried her head in Solange's lap. "You make me feel naked, Solange. You see right through me, you always have . . ."

Solange wiped away her tears. "You're selfish, but at least you're honest, and for that I do love you. But it would be best if I returned to Paris . . . I'll only upset you here."

"No, Solange," Magda said. "I need you."

"Why?"

"Because I'm lonely."

"And for what other reason . . . ?"

There was a pause.

"All right . . . There is another reason. I know Rubin is suffering because of what he's done. But I told you, I have a plan. I'm not going to lie to you about why I want Rubin to become united with his family . . . Yes, it is his wish, but by helping him I help myself to be accepted in the kind of society that once rejected you. You wanted it, Solange. Why shouldn't I? And I know it can be done, but I need your help."

"Was it your idea or Rubin's that I come?"

"It was his, I swear to you, Solange."

"But you knew I could help?"

"Yes . . . I knew you could be my champion."

"Well, at least that's honest."

"Don't be bitter, Solange. For whatever selfish reasons, I'm honestly happy you're with me. You do believe that . . . ?"

"Yes . . ."

"Does it make me wicked if what I want is to bring him together with his family? Wouldn't it make our marriage even better?"

Solange sighed. "Let me warn you, Magda, what you propose will not be easily accomplished."

"Once you said that Rubin would never marry me . . ."

"This is different. We're not dealing with a man in love but with a whole set of social rules that can't be reconciled so easily. Do you think that you're ready for such a task . . . ?"

"With you as my champion, I'm ready for anything."

"Ah," said Solange, "I may not do much good."

"Being your niece will help . . . being someone."

"Well . . ." she said at last, "we will try. For Rubin's sake, the effort is worth it."

Magda was weak with relief. She did not take offense that Solange's first thoughts were for Rubin. What did it matter, when victory would be for both of them?

The next morning's headlines were ominous: BELGIUM'S NEUTRALITY DISREGARDED. GERMANY DECLARES WAR ON FRANCE. Rubin's hand trembled as he picked up the paper. Solange had left just in time.

He poured a cup of coffee, took it into the dining room and read the latest reports. *Germany issued a declaration of war on France today . . . German troops have ignored Belgium's neutrality, crossed her borders and invaded the country . . . Although His Majesty's Government has attempted to be a conciliatory force, still nothing of any major significance has been forthcoming in the negotiations . . . This morning a stiff ultimatum was sent to the German High Command to withdraw her troops from Belgium immediately . . . Britain awaits the answer . . .*

*and must reconsider her position . . . her moral obligation
to aid a small and beleaguered country. Can she tolerate
this German aggression? Will any neutral country be
safe . . . ?*

It was eleven o'clock when Magda joined him, looking
like a vision in a pink mauve dressing gown. "Good morning, darling. Thank God the maid arrives today . . . the
house already needs a good cleaning . . . I detest house-
work." She looked at Rubin. He could not hide his concern.

"What's wrong, Rubin?"

"Germany is at war with France . . ."

She sat in total disbelief. After recovering from the
shock, she said, "Solange said nothing about trouble in
Paris . . . in France . . ."

"All of Europe may be affected, Magda. England may
be next."

Magda was close to tears . . . Why did countries have
to fight? Why did a stupid war have to spoil her happiness, just when everything was going so well . . . ?

"My Niko was killed in 1912 . . ." she said. "There
was a war then. There has always been a war . . . My
God, Rubin, won't it ever stop?"

Rubin told her of the Archduke's assassination, and
what had happened since. It broke his heart to see her so
unhappy.

"The Archduke's blood was more important than Niko's," Magda said bitterly, drying her eyes on a napkin.
"He gave his life for nothing . . . Just a body to be used
for fodder. We didn't even have a chance to bury him . . .
His body was never found."

"I wish I could spare you this, Magda."

The world was falling apart, and he wanted to shield
her. Indeed, today she did take a long look at Rubin. How
tender and good he was . . . "Will Solange have to go
back?"

"No. She must stay. I want her to stay."

"Rubin, why did you really want her to come just at
this time?"

"Call it a premonition . . . whatever . . . If England
should become involved . . ." He cleared his throat.
". . . I don't want you to . . . be alone."

"Alone . . . ? What are you talking about?"

"I may have to enlist, Magda."

Magda was stunned. She got up and paced the floor. Two days ago they had moved into their new home. My God, the plans she had . . . What good did it do to plan for a future. Only yesterday she had pleaded with Solange to help her become a great lady . . . to find a home in England . . . That was the most important thing in her life. But that was yesterday . . . Today was terrifying . . . How ludicrous all her ambitions seemed now, when her husband might have to go to war . . . and maybe die, like Niko.

"What will happen to us, Rubin?"

"I'll have to join the army—"

No, this simply can't be happening, she thought. We haven't even begun to know each other . . . Oh, God, I despise the world . . . I hate it . . . Rubin and I have done nothing worse than marry, and we are ostracized. But countries can destroy the lives of people, and that's accepted. *That* is quite proper. . . .

At dinner that evening Solange sat staring down at her food, unable to eat. The men of her country, of France, were being fitted for the uniforms of death. Some would never live to see the shine on their buttons turn dull . . . or return with the arms God gave them or the limbs to fill the legs of their trousers. . . . All that remained of her family's treasures had been left behind . . . Whenever she went back, *if* she went back, what would she find? Rubble and debris. . . .

"Poor Emile," said Solange. "Will he return to France?" Her eyes filled with tears.

"No doubt as quick as he can," said Rubin.

"I should have stayed, Rubin . . . My conscience bothers me so."

"Knowing you're with us brings us great comfort," said Rubin.

Magda broke her silence. "I've lived through wars, Solange, and I'm selfish enough to pray we all three survive. Dead heroes are soon forgotten . . ."

The next day all London waited. There was no hysteria, but Germany had not responded as the hours ticked away.

It was now eleven, and still no reply. Crowds had gathered at 10 Downing Street.

Finally there was a dispatch. Germany refused to yield its position.

The British Cabinet had been in session since early morning. At precisely midnight on August 4, 1914, His Majesty's Government and all its dominions declared war on Germany.

Ten thousand strong, the English people stood in front of Buckingham Palace waiting for their sovereign. . . . A cheer went up, as the King and Queen came to the balcony with the Prince of Wales and Princess Mary, waving at their devoted subjects. It was a moment in history. In a world filled with hate and dissolution, here, at least, there was a display of union and solidarity. The English stood arm-in-arm, shoulder-to-shoulder. Every able-bodied man would come to the aid of His Majesty. . . .

Magda roused herself from sleep and reached over to Rubin's side of the bed. He was gone. Getting out of bed quickly, she called out, hoping he was in the bathroom. When she found it empty, she slipped into her robe, tied a sash around her waist, and hurried across the foyer to the drawing room, and then from room to room. When she reached the kitchen she asked the maid: "Has Mr. Hack had breakfast?"

"No, madam. Just coffee. He didn't want to disturb you, but left a note."

Magda trembled as she took it. She went into the drawing room to read it: "I'll be back later today. I have to do a few things this morning. Eat lunch without me. Love, Rubin."

Quickly she went to Solange. "Where can he be, Solange? What could be so pressing it couldn't wait . . . ?"

"With the war going on, Magda, I'm sure he has arrangements to make. He has to think about your security. If anything should . . . don't get upset . . . please . . . He's probably seeing his solicitor."

Solange was right. Rubin was making plans for Magda's future. All monies were to be transferred to her name . . . Did Mr. Hack think that was wise . . . ? Why not invest the money in United States securities? No. There wasn't time for that . . . When he returned he would, he'd need the income . . . If on the other hand . . . Rubin instructed his solicitor to seek the advice of a certain firm that would wisely invest his estate.

Leaving the office he was wished Godspeed and personally escorted down the stairs. The street was filled with milling people, going in different directions. There was no panic. London seemed quiet and strangely sober this morning.

Rubin found a telephone and gave the operator the number. "Good morning, the Hack offices."

Rubin cleared his throat. "Mr. Leon Hack, please."

"May I ask who's calling?"

"Un . . . Mr. Emile Jonet."

"Will you kindly hold, sir?"

"Yes." Rubin's heart beat too fast . . . his pulse too hard. Was Leon there?

"Emile! How are you?"

"It's Rubin."

"Rubin . . ." Leon's voice was warm but subdued. "Where are you?"

"At the Bristol. Leon, I want to see you."

"Good. Where shall we meet?"

"John's Pub?"

"I always liked John's."

"Noon . . . ?"

"Noon."

Rubin hung up. The sound of Leon's steady voice was like a reprieve . . . even a pardon. . . .

Rubin arrived early and was seated in a corner. It pleased him. He and Leon had enjoyed so many quiet talks.

He got up as he watched Leon approach . . . It seemed like a hundred years since he'd seen him. All Rubin's worst fears seemed to vanish like smoke.

They shook hands. Then Leon drew his brother to him, putting his arm around Rubin's shoulder.

"How good it is to see you, Rubin."

"And you . . . I've missed you."

Leon ordered a Scotch.

"How's Deborah?" said Rubin.

Leon hesitated. "Not well, Rubin. We're all concerned about her—"

"But what's wrong?"

"The doctors aren't exactly sure. They've given her every test imaginable. Apparently she has a rare muscle disease, almost nothing is known about it."

"Did it happen recently?"

"Not really. I just wasn't aware of it . . . Deborah's always been fragile, but when I began to notice so much fatigue I got alarmed."

"I'm so sorry, Leon. Is she in much pain?"

"She never speaks of it . . . But from time to time, the last few weeks, she can scarcely walk. They tell us she may eventually be completely bedridden."

"How long will it take?" Rubin asked.

"The doctors won't predict."

"Does she know?"

"Yes."

"Could you have kept the truth from her?"

"I wanted to, but she insisted on knowing . . . She makes light of it all for our sakes, but I know she suffers . . . How are things going with you, Rubin? You got married?"

"Yes."

"Tell me about your wife."

"Well, I love her very much. She's everything I want . . . but I also love my family . . . I'd like to have you both."

Leon looked closely at his brother. "I want to be honest with you, Rubin."

"You always have been."

"It's strange, a family grows up and lives together, we think we all know each other. Then a crisis comes along and we find we don't."

"What does that mean?"

"We have, I'm afraid, a house divided. Maurice and Phillip have done all they could to turn Mother and Father against you. And their wives have kept the pot boiling. And I can say this without feeling at all disloyal to them . . . they're extreme. What you did was not so wrong . . . Deborah and I both feel that you at least were right not to marry someone you didn't love. Your mistake, I suppose, was the way you did it. It should have been done with discretion. I wish you had confided in me."

"So do I." Rubin spoke ruefully. "Does Father despise me?"

"Not at all. Strangely enough, he blames himself for not taking you more seriously."

"Do you think they would see me, Mother and Father?"

"Yes . . . I think they would."

"And Magda . . . ? Is that asking too much?"

Leon frowned. "I'm afraid so, Rubin. Father refuses to talk about it any more, but I know he would see you."

"Me . . . but not Magda . . . well, I can hardly blame him."

Leon took time out to summon the waiter. Then he shifted the subject somewhat. "At any rate, Jocelyn seems to be surviving nicely, which should give you some comfort. She does the town every night with any number of men."

"Tell me about her."

"You probably wouldn't recognize her, she changed so much. She's certainly not playing the part of a jilted bride . . . They only stayed abroad a week."

"Still, I did treat her shamefully. She'd be entitled to want to see me in hell—"

"She's had some help in that quarter. Harry Sassoon has done everything possible to harass our family."

"I'm truly sorry for that, Leon. I just wish he wouldn't hold the family accountable for my mistakes."

"Forget it, Rubin. Now, tell me about Magda instead. Lovely name . . . She's French, Father said."

"No, she's Rumanian, but she lived mostly in Paris."

"What's she like?"

"Beautiful . . . exciting . . . God, I don't know. She's everything I want, a mistress and wife . . . a woman of many moods—every one of which I love. I don't always understand her, but I assure you life is never dull."

"Would you do it again?"

"Yes . . ."

"I'm very happy for you, Rubin. You know, Father's refused to take your name off the roster."

"You mean my name is *still* on the door?"

"Yes."

Rubin shook his head. "Why?"

"Because Father thinks it's right."

"How remarkable he is."

"Yes . . . he is. But this war will take a toll on him."

"How is he?"

"Busy. He had the cabinet meeting last night. It was a great strain."

"Of course," said Rubin. "A man with four sons . . . I'm joining the army, Leon."

Leon was surprised. "Why the army? You could go into the admiralty as an officer."

"No, that would be rubbing salt on the wound. You and Maurice and Phillip will be attached to the navy. I'm joining the army today as a private."

"You'll be in the infantry, a foot soldier—"

"I know . . ."

"Then why?"

"Because . . . perhaps at least to this extent I'm my Father's son . . . I think it's right."

"Rubin, are you doing this to punish yourself?"

Rubin didn't answer. . . .

"Rubin, you'll be with those poor devils in the front line—"

"Someone has to, you know."

"Yes, but not my brother. There's no *reason* to put yourself in such danger."

"What about those who have no choice?"

"I'm sorry for them, but they're not you. You have an alternative. For God's sake, war is a time to survive—"

"I intend to do that."

"You're damned stubborn, Rubin."

Rubin smiled and leaned closer to his brother. "Leon, I must ask you a favor . . . Will you look in on Magda from time to time? It would mean a great deal to me."

"Yes, of course, when I'm in London. Of course I will . . ."

"God bless you, Leon . . . my dear brother . . . my dearest friend . . ."

He wondered if they would ever see each other again.

It was six o'clock that night when Martin opened the door of the Hack mansion. He was on the verge of saying, "I believe you have the wrong address, sir," when he recognized the caller.

"Mr. Rubin! . . . Sir . . . Good evening . . . I'm delighted to see you."

"And I you, Martin." Rubin was already in his uniform, khaki-colored, ill-fitting. His face was pale and strained.

He looked, Martin thought, old beyond his years. . . .

"Is Father in, Martin?"

Martin coughed nervously. "Yes, sir . . . he's in the study. Shall I tell him you're here?"

"Would you?"

"Indeed, sir."

Rubin stood in the foyer, his feelings a mixture of unease and pleasure . . . unease about the grief he'd caused his family, and pleasure at being home once again. . . .

"Your father is waiting to see you, sir."

Rubin followed Martin into the study.

Nathan sat in a large chair facing the door. As Rubin approached, his father examined him with tired if friendly eyes. As his son drew close, Nathan stood, reached out and drew Rubin to him, his ingrained British reserve no match for the welcome sight of his youngest child. Backing off after a moment, hands still on his son's arms, seeing Rubin in his uniform, the war had come home at last. It was terribly real now . . . And he had helped make the decision, he, Nathan Hack, perhaps only a cog in the enormous wheel called England, nonetheless helping to decide who should live and who should die by simply casting a vote . . . Nathan Hack, war-maker . . . *father* . . .

Neither man could speak for a moment. Finally Nathan released his son and sat down. "I knew you would come . . ."

"I've wanted to, Father, for a long time."

"Pity, the things we deprive ourselves of. Pride is a dreadful thing, Rubin."

"And the fear of being rejected . . ."

Nathan nodded. "We raise our children, think we know them, think we understand them, and they think they know us. But that's not so, Rubin. All our lives we're strangers to each other . . ."

"You're a wise man, Father. I wish *your* wisdom was for sale, I'd buy a gross, though I doubt they'd fit . . ."

Nathan waved his hand. "I'm only your father, Rubin—"

"Even after what I've done?"

"What *we* have done, Rubin. I am not so noble . . . I made my own fatherly mistake, trying to force my son into my own mold. I confused you with me . . . I thought you'd react as I did simply because you're my son . . . I was mistaken. You're not merely an extension of me, you're—"

"But you must have detested me for what I did—"

"No . . . I was disappointed, yes . . . Still, in the larger scheme of things, it doesn't really seem so important. I think you know I'm a religious man. But attendance at the synagogue is not the right test of that. The test is if we practice what we preach. The prodigal, after all, was more loved—"

"Maurice and Phillip apparently don't share your feelings."

"Well, they are misguided." Nathan sighed. "They also are not the extension of myself I once thought they were . . . When all is said and done, at such a crisis in our lives, I wanted my sons . . . and their wives . . . to stand together as one."

"Except I did hurt them, Father."

"In the face of a world that's about to annihilate itself, the episode becomes rather pale. At least no one was killed on that wedding day."

"Still, it was a painful time. And I deeply appreciate your understanding—"

"My feelings aren't all that fragile, Rubin. My concern is for you now. With the help of God, when this is over and sanity returns to the world, it might be easier if you lived abroad and started over."

"Perhaps I will, but I want my children to be English . . ." Rubin had come to the all-important question. "Father, would you meet her?"

Nathan moistened his lips with a sip of sherry. Then, carefully, he said, "Perhaps, Rubin, in time."

"But I may be away . . . I know I have no right, but I ask you to meet her, Father . . . She's had a very difficult life . . . She's motherless and fatherless, and she isn't, after all, to blame for my behavior—"

Martin entered then with a tray, which he set down on the table in front of them. "Don't bother, Martin," said

Nathan. "I'll take care of this, thank you." Nathan poured the tea, and Rubin held his breath.

Finally . . . "Yes, Rubin. Your mother and I will see
. . . your wife . . . Not here, however."

"Why not, Father?"

"It simply would be too awkward—for her, and all concerned."

Rubin was disappointed but understood.

"We have our disagreements," Nathan went on, "but the family at least still comes here. We remain a family. And your wife would be placed in an unpleasant position . . . It would be most unkind."

Rubin got up, went to his father and embraced him. "There are no words, Father, none at all, to thank you . . . for forgiving me—"

"Oh, my dear boy . . . it's only when we can forgive one another that we have the right to ask God to forgive us . . . That is our law . . . Yom Kippur, the message . . . Now then, I suggest we go up to your mother."

Magda looked at her husband in a state of shock. He had just come in wearing his uniform. She didn't know whether to faint, scream or break something. How could Rubin have done it . . . without talking to her? How dare he do such a thing without giving her notice? . . . Why hadn't he prepared her? She was not British . . . she would not be stoical . . . she was too angry. "Why have you done this?" she screamed in French, then ran into the bedroom and slammed the door.

Solange said, "Rubin, this is really brutal. At least you could have told Magda you were joining today—"

His angry look quieted her, and then he went to the bedroom, where, when he tried to explain to Magda, she slapped him. She immediately felt remorse, but at the moment she was too Rumanian to remember her cultivated manners. They were useful in the drawing room . . . but now she would not behave like a gracious lady. "Damn you, Rubin . . . why did you do this to me? Without a word of warning—"

He took hold of her firmly. "Magda, I was wrong, I should have told you, but—"

"You didn't even consider how this would affect me?

What it will do to our lives? Why couldn't you at least wait to be called up? Oh, don't bother to explain, I know the answer . . . you couldn't *wait* to be killed! How stupidly English—" She was crying, and Rubin pulled her against him. The hot anger gradually spent itself, and she relaxed in his arms.

"Listen to me . . . I did what I had to do—"

"You should have waited," she said, crying softly. "Why didn't you tell me?"

"And if I had? It would only have been an argument."

"But you might have avoided service altogether . . . Your family has influence—"

"Magda, darling, you may be right . . . I'm stupidly English, but this is my country and I can't desert it—"

"But you *can* desert me."

"Listen, darling, there is a war, you and I had nothing to do with starting it but we're in it now, along with millions of other people who didn't ask for it but must do their best with the reality of it."

She looked at him, kissed him impulsively, fiercely. "You and your damned English logic, you always win . . . I'm sorry I hit you, but sometimes you make me so mad . . ."

"I know . . ."

"In Rumania a man would beat a woman who did that."

"Well, this is not Rumania . . . and besides, you don't slap very hard." He smiled at her.

She glared back at him, unable to stifle a smile of her own. "Perhaps not, but you do make me mad, Rubin . . . mad enough to kill you sometimes. Does that shock you . . . ?"

"Beyond words . . . in fact, so much that I want you and Solange to dress, and I mean in your most elegant attire. We, my murderous love, are going out to dine."

Had he not been Private Rubin Hack he'd have been turned away by the captain at the Café Royal. Enlisted men were not encouraged, but the Hack party was seated at a table in the corner. Rubin refused it and forced the captain to reseat them at a prominent table.

"You're a snob," Solange chided.

"Of course. Why shouldn't I be, with two such beautiful women. I certainly don't want to hide you in a corner." . . .

That night Rubin lay back and watched Magda get

ready for bed. She sat on the slipper chair, rolling down her sheer stockings. His eyes never left her for a moment . . . Her slip fell to the carpeted floor . . . then the chemise. As she unhooked the front fastening, her delicately shaped breasts were exposed, showing the pink nipples, like small rosebuds . . . The scant panties were discarded, revealing the triangle of soft burnished hair between her slender, supple thighs. Slipping into a loose peignoir, she sat at the dressing table brushing her hair from its coiffed set. His eyes observed every movement, every motion . . . the way she took out the long hairpins and placed them in a china tray . . . the way she picked up the monogrammed silver brush . . . the way she removed the last traces of makeup. His eyes followed her until she was lost from his sight entering the bathroom.

They were really quite simple things . . . A woman did them every day . . . But whatever Magda did was distinctive . . . her delicacy of movement . . . her fragility . . . and yet her strength . . . Even her anger was unique in a way that made Rubin smile . . . Untamed, yet there was really no malice in it. She was such a paradox.

Oh, he was happy . . . With the world headed for war, he was happier tonight than he'd been in weeks. But now he knew that Leon was with him. His mother and father had forgiven him . . . Even more than that, they would protect Magda when she went away.

His eyes followed her as she came out of the bathroom, took off the peignoir, and walked toward the bed. As she got into bed and he turned off the light, he thought of his father. Nathan was right. After the war, they'd settle in Paris, where he would paint . . . He could still picture each and every preliminary gesture of hers tonight. He opened his arms to her . . . "Later, darling, I've got a surprise for you, but not right now," he said hungrily. "This moment is for me . . ."

The next morning Magda rushed into Solange's room. "What are you so happy about, Magda? Yesterday you were ready to—"

"That was yesterday. Solange, I couldn't wait . . . guess what!"

"You're going to have a baby?"

"Don't be foolish, no, no baby . . . no, *no* . . . Rubin's family is coming today."

Solange could only gasp, "My God. . . ."

"Well . . . they're coming today, Solange, do you *hear* me?"

"I hear you . . . I just don't seem to believe it."

"Believe it."

"His whole family?"

"No, his mother and father . . . and his brother Leon and his wife."

Shaking her head, Solange said, "God must love you a great deal. How and when did this happen?"

"Yesterday."

"*Soit tranquille,* be calm. Now tell me all about it."

"Well, Rubin met Leon at lunch yesterday . . . It all went well . . . Then he saw his parents."

"He saw his parents?"

"Yes, and they don't blame him for anything and they're coming to meet me. What shall I wear?"

Solange laughed. "Is that all you ever think of, what to *wear?*"

"What should I think of . . . I want to make the right—"

"One moment, please, Magda. Why are they coming *here?*"

"Because they want to meet Rubin's wife. You ask such . . . silly questions. I've been accepted, don't you see?"

"No, I don't see."

"Why do you always make me unhappy . . . ? You're so infuriating, Solange."

"You haven't yet been accepted, Duchess . . . not quite."

Magda was furious. "Sometimes I do hate you, Solange."

"I know. And it doesn't bother me in the least."

"Why are you trying to take away the—"

". . . the joy of being accepted?"

"Exactly."

"Because if they *had* accepted you, dear Duchess, you'd have been invited to their home."

Magda threw a pillow at Solange. "You're jealous. You're just trying to make me feel unsure of myself—"

"Sit down, Magda . . . Your foolish little tantrums may work with Rubin, but not with me."

Fuming, Magda obeyed. "All right, I'm sitting . . . Now, tell me . . . what are you talking about?"

"What I'm talking about is meeting a new member of the family. The invitation comes from them."

"I'm not particular about procedure."

"But they are, Magda. The Hacks are. I don't want you to read more into this visit than there is. You have not been accepted."

Magda narrowed her eyes. "Then why are they coming?"

"I'll tell you honestly and frankly."

"Please do. Let me hear your pearls of wisdom."

"They're coming because Rubin must have pleaded with them to come."

"That's certainly frank enough, dear Countess. Why do you insist on offending me so?"

The answer was swift. "Because I don't want you to be hurt. If you think the Hacks are doing you a great honor, you're in for a rude awakening. The other Hacks aren't coming, not today or any other day. Prepare yourself for that."

"That's how much you know. You said that Rubin wouldn't marry me and he did . . . You said his family would never talk to me and they are, so you can't be all that damned smart."

"His family are not merely his parents and a brother who'd lay his life down for Rubin in any case."

"Well, goddamn, it's a *start*," and she went into her bedroom, slamming the door.

By lunch time her temper had miraculously vanished. As though the morning's tantrum had never happened, Magda was now saying in her most winsome fashion: "Solange, don't you think the Royal Crown Derby would be appropriate . . . ? Your taste is so good. . . ."

Solange grimaced. "You think my taste is good, do you?"

"Yes . . . no one's better."

"Thank you, Your Highness. And do you know what should be served at high tea?"

"I do, dear Countess, my dearest aunt. Remember, I spent five most miserable afternoons gorging myself on high tea at Brighton. Now, seriously, Solange . . . what shall I wear?"

"Be understated, but elegant, and for God's sake, don't act like the Grand Duchess. Be gracious, be charming, and don't tell them how much you detested Brighton. *And*, don't be afraid of lessening up on the French accent. I know that we're allies, but I don't think that the Hacks want to feel that the Foreign Legion has landed. . . ."

Magda, taking Solange's counsel, was dressed well ahead of time. Nervously, she went back and forth from the kitchen to the drawing room. She examined the tea tray over and over again. She straightened the pictures, fluffed up the pillows, worried that the flowers weren't arranged just so.

She was satisfied with her gown. It was the same one she had worn when she met Solange. That time she had felt so plain, so underdressed, but today she knew it was exactly right. Besides, it should bring her luck. Putting on the strand of pearls, she appraised herself in the mirror . . . *Voilà*.

She looked at Rubin in his uniform, then coquettishly pirouetted around and around, finally dropping with an exaggerated swan into his arms. He promptly kissed her, and she could feel the rough weave of his uniform through her soft chiffon . . . Oh God, the damn war . . . even though it did help to bring his parents here . . . She shook off the threat of depression. Not tonight . . . "Will they like me, do you think?" she asked.

"They will love you."

A wistful smile played over her lips. "Love is a very strong word, Rubin. I only hope they'll like me and accept me as your wife—"

Then the bell was ringing. Taking a deep breath, she went with Rubin to the foyer. Anne opened the door. Nathan and Sara entered, followed by Deborah and Leon.

"Mother . . . Father . . . may I present Magda, my wife . . . ?"

Magda smiled, extending her hand to Sara. "I have hoped for so long that this day would come." And then to Nathan, "You have made Rubin and me so very happy. Thank you." To Deborah, "It's such a joy to meet you.

Rubin has told me so much about you." To Leon, "I would have recognized you on the street. The resemblance between you and Rubin is so great . . ." There was no strain, no awkwardness, as Rubin stood watching his wife. She was exactly as he had promised she would be. Now he said, "Shall we go into the drawing room?"

Solange got up as they entered. "Mother, Father, may I present Magda's aunt, Countess Boulard." Solange was totally charming as she greeted each guest in turn. When the introductions were over, the sherry poured and a toast made to a speedy end to the war, they talked about how things were going in London, and the rumors that came from France. Did the Countess enjoy England? Yes, enormously. There were the theaters . . . the shops . . . the museums . . . What glorious times she had had in London. And Magda? She loved it. Had she been here before? No, she had been raised in Rumania . . . her father had been attached to the French Embassy there, after which she had been sent to Paris to live with Tante Solange.

Solange dabbed her forehead with her lace handkerchief, then looked over at Magda, the cue that said, "time for tea." Magda rang and the cart was wheeled in by Anne. Magda performed to perfection.

Looking at Magda pouring the tea, Deborah never doubted for a moment that anyone Rubin would choose to be his wife could be anything but a perfect lady . . . How dare they . . . And when Leon looked at Rubin's happy face, he knew his brother's decision had been the right one. This was the woman he wanted to spend his life with, and Leon could understand his choice. Magda was indeed enchanting. It occurred to him that a Rumanian king had given up a throne because of another Magda. If a king could do it, then bravo, Rubin! he thought. English snobbery is nothing compared to having a woman you love. A woman like Magda.

When the Hacks finally were about to leave, Deborah said, "Magda, you and Rubin and Solange will be our guests at a nice quiet dinner." The implications were clear . . . "We'll make that very soon." She kissed Magda on the cheek. "It was most delightful, Magda."

"Welcome," said Leon.

"Good night, my dear, and thank you for a lovely tea," said Nathan.

"You're a most gracious young woman. Thank you for making Rubin so happy," Sara said, and meant it.

When the door had shut, Rubin swept Magda up in his arms and whirled her around and around.

"You were magnificent, Duchess," said Solange, when Rubin put her down.

"I beg your pardon, Countess. My name is Magda Hack of London, England. I'm not a duchess. I'm a commoner . . ."

"Bravo, Magda Hack of London! You've done us proud." Solange laughed happily to see her white swan.

"Did they really like me?" Magda asked, a plea in her voice.

"They loved you," said Rubin, "just as I promised you they would. . . ."

Rubin's orders came within the fortnight. He was to report the next day. That night he held Magda in the dark silence of their bedroom. Suddenly he whispered to her, "Darling, I want a child . . . that belongs to both of us, that *is* both of us . . ."

Magda was silent. This was something they'd never discussed, and she did *not* want a child. Not now. Why should she? To bring a child into a world at war . . . No. Rubin was enough for her . . . But how could she deny him . . . ?

She answered tentatively, "When you come home, darling—"

"No, Magda, please . . . I want a child now . . ." He might not come home . . . not leaving an heir was like never having lived. And Magda would at least have something of his, something of theirs to live for, care for. "Please, Magda . . . it would mean a great deal to me. . . ."

"Darling, I just don't think this is the right time to think of having a child—"

"It's the only time. Don't you want one?"

"Of course, but you're going away—"

"That's all the more reason . . ."

She hated herself for giving in . . . She had not even begun her new life and now Rubin wanted to saddle her with a child she didn't want. If, God forbid, he didn't come back she'd have another life to care for in this strange country . . . But to hear Rubin asking . . . well, it was more than she could bear. He *was* going away in the morning. The least she could do was try. But she prayed she would not succeed. . . .

The next day Magda, Leon and Nathan saw Rubin off at the station. They were not alone. Husbands . . . wives . . . children huddled together, kissed, cried, waved good-bye. Then the soldiers were aboard, and the troop train moved out.

Nathan seemed to be just a little more bent, a little more tired . . . a little more discouraged. He looked from the departing train to Leon, now in the uniform of an officer in His Majesty's Navy. Nathan didn't notice the impeccably tailored blue uniform with the gold braid on his cap. He only saw the man, his son. His sons would suffer more than he had in the Boer War . . . That was a gentlemen's war, complete with valet, luggage, silver military brushes, fine food and rare wines, tailored uniforms . . . Almost elegant, that war . . . a civilized war.

As the train pulled away, with Rubin hanging out of the window waving, Magda told herself to remember how he looked at that moment . . . remember the thin, warm smile . . . the color of his eyes . . . his hair. She wanted to imprint him indelibly on her mind. Because she was convinced she was never going to see him again. She held tight to Leon's arm as Rubin's face disappeared into the distance.

The Hack sons were now widely scattered. Maurice was attached to the admiralty, with the rank of captain, where he sometimes worked around the clock. Phillip was a commander on a battleship somewhere off the coast of France. And Leon was attached to a man-of-war in the middle of the Atlantic. Leon's leaving had taken a great emotional and physical toll on his wife Deborah. And despite her valiant attempts, she could scarcely hide the fact that her condition had worsened.

Nathan too had changed, almost overnight, from a vigorous man to a bent-over man who was almost gaunt. There was a vagueness about him, his mind seemed to wander in conversation as though it were some place in the Atlantic aboard a destroyer. His sons were his life.

Sara tried to shield and comfort Nathan as best she could. And she worked much too hard, spending long hours at the hospital doing the most menial tasks, which often were beyond her physical stamina. But she refused to be used for less strenuous duties.

Toward the end of November Rubin received his orders to leave for the front. At least the agony of waiting was over. Magda's reaction to his letter was at first terror, then a determination to play a role the family would appreciate. She would invite them to dinner, and in the middle of it she would give them the news . . . *her* news . . . that up to this moment nobody shared.

It was a fine dinner, and over coffee, Magda lifted a tall, slender champagne glass, "To my dear husband . . . and family. I wish to make an announcement." Everyone raised their glasses. "I have something that belongs to us all . . . a *child* . . ."

At first nobody moved . . . and then they were all around her and congratulating her. Only Solange looked bewildered . . . Magda had said nothing to her. . . .

Nathan sat holding Sara's hand. If one looked very closely, an uncharacteristic moisture might have been seen forming in the corner of one eye.

When they'd left, Magda wrote her letter to Rubin, telling him the news that she knew would make him deliriously happy, and telling him how delighted she was. She would be brave enough not to tell him the truth . . . the truth of her fear of being responsible for another life, when her own had barely started.

Martin was waiting when Nathan and Sara got home, all the color drained from his face.

"Sir, Miss Deborah just called . . ."

Nathan was confused. They had just dropped Deborah off, less than fifteen minutes ago. "Yes, Martin . . ."

"She asks that you and Madam come at once. . . ."

In the limousine, Sara prayed. Oh, dearest God, let me

not question your divine judgment . . . Give me strength to accept your will. She tried not to weep.

The door was opened by the butler. Quietly they went upstairs to Deborah's room. She did not speak as they approached the bed. Sara took Deborah's fragile hand in hers as Nathan looked down at her suffering eyes.

"I'm so sorry . . . to disturb you . . . When I got home I found a telegram from the War Office . . . It had been delivered shortly after I left . . ." She handed it to Sara. "The Lords of the admiralty regret to inform you that Captain Leon Hack is missing in action. The survivors have not all been accounted for . . . You will be . . ." Sara could not continue, the tears blinded her.

"Oh dear God, Nathan, do you think we might get more information from Maurice?" She was trembling; the telegram shook in her hand. Nathan held her in his arms. "Of course, my dearest, of course. You must not allow yourself to stop believing that he will be all right . . . You must believe that . . . We must all trust in the Almighty . . . If we don't, then we've lost our faith. And when we do that, we have nowhere left to go . . ." He looked closely at them, then added, "I think it would be best if we did not tell Rubin . . . for the time being. I will write him, Deborah. . . ."

She nodded, unable to speak.

CHAPTER

Five

Magda sat in the drawing room with Solange. It was dusk. Twilight was her favorite time of day. The French called it *l'heure bleu*, that hour when daylight is first struck through with the blue of evening.

Solange watched Magda's ashen face, locked into still-ness with the strain of events. "I think you have con-ducted yourself well. It's a tribute to your—"

"Dignity?"

"Yes . . ."

"Wise Solange, it had nothing to do with dignity. I feel like screaming, like tearing the world apart. How dare that German bastard sit in his palace and decide our lives. Rubin gone. Leon missing . . . I'm going to have a baby whose father may never live to see him . . ."

"Magda, don't . . ."

"Don't what . . . ? Be realistic?" She took a sip of port. "You see, Solange, nothing is ever really forgotten. We pretend, we try to fool ourselves that we've changed, that life is kind after all—"

"Please, Magda, try not to be bitter."

"And why not? There's supposed to be a deity who makes everything for the better. That's the worst lie of them all. Life makes us . . . *helpless*."

"Don't, Magda—"

"Why *not?* I'm having a child I don't want because of a situation that was forced on me . . . us. . . ."

"You owed that much to Rubin."

"*Owe?* I hate that word. You shouldn't have a child because you *owe.*"

"Magda, you're saying a great many things I know you don't mean."

"I mean every word."

"You can't say that. If there hadn't been a war, Rubin would still have wanted a child."

"That doesn't mean I'd have obliged him."

"You're too upset to know what you're saying."

"Solange . . . the one thing I'm not is stupid . . . Don't offer me fairy tales—"

"When the baby's born you'll feel differently."

"And how do you know?"

"Because it's natural for a woman to become a mother."

"You didn't . . . Do you miss not having a child?"

Solange stifled the cry that filled her throat. It was choking her. When she was finally able to speak, she said, "Yes . . . I miss my child. I would give my life to have him now."

Magda was stunned. "You didn't tell me."

"It isn't something I like to talk about . . . not because he was born of shame, but because I couldn't keep him. Illegitimacy is frowned upon, you know."

Magda went to Solange and knelt in front of her. Dear Solange, my dear Solange, as usual I think only of myself . . . And softly she said aloud, "So you won't think me as wicked as you thought, let me tell you why I don't want a baby . . . I'm not an innocent, as you know, Solange. I've seen too much ugliness . . . The thought of bringing a child into this world. . . ."

Solange sighed. "Come sit beside me, *cherie* . . . closer . . . You must forget what the world is like. You have Rubin, and with the help of God, when he comes back—and I know he will—the world will be better for all of us. All that will matter will be your husband and child."

The worldly Magda had become the child. "Oh, Solange, what would I have done without you?"

"Survive . . . You're a survivor, Magda. . . ."

Four months had passed. Magda began to show. She felt it with her hand . . . imagine, she was carrying a life inside her . . . If only Rubin were here to share it.

But Rubin was kneeling in a rain-drenched hole, his legs coated with mud. They called it a trench. To Rubin it looked like a grave that hadn't been covered over. If he lived a hundred years, he'd never stop hearing the sound of cannon shells exploding . . . One minute a man was alive, the next he lay bloody and lifeless. He should have listened to Leon . . . There are no heroes in trenches, they said, and they were right.

In his first action, Rubin was terrified, but when the Germans came at them, somehow he had managed to squeeze the trigger. Looking down at the youth, his dead blue eyes still open, his helmet askew, the blood already dried and matted on his body, Rubin vomited. The sour stench of death, mingled with the smoke of gunfire, made him double up in pain. He wanted to run, but a soldier shouted . . . "Move . . . Move out, you bloody fool, or you'll be blown to bits. . . ."

After the battle, Rubin crawled back into his trench and leaned against the now frozen earth. His bones ached . . . His mind was filled with the memory of dead bodies. There must have been hundreds. Were some of them alive? Who had time to find out . . . ? Why was *he* still alive . . . ? That was the question that plagued him . . . Who made those decisions?

Presumably the same deity who had decreed he was to be a father, and perhaps it did all somehow equal out. Perhaps . . . but in this stinking hell it was difficult to believe.

Winter had come to London, and with it a depression Magda couldn't shake off. There had been no letter from Rubin in more than six weeks . . . .At least Deborah knew where Leon was. His ship had been torpedoed by a submarine, but Leon had survived, floating for three days on a raft. When he was finally found and picked up, unconscious, it was by the Germans. But Leon didn't know that. He awoke one morning on a cot in a German prison camp. But at least he was alive, and that was more than Magda knew for certain about Rubin.

She was thinner than before her pregnancy. Except for the bulging stomach, no one would have suspected she was pregnant. As the freezing London weather peaked,

Magda became distraught. She called Nathan almost every day. "Can't you do something to find out where Rubin is? I'm beside myself."

"I know, Magda. Please try, if you can, to keep a good thought," he answered evenly. But of course his apprehension was as great as hers. The whereabouts of Rubin Hack was unknown.

She had to get out of the apartment . . . She had to get away from the gloom that hung over the house, even if only for a few hours.

She phoned Deborah.

"Has there been any word about Rubin?" asked Deborah.

"None. It's really too much, Deborah."

"I know . . . How well I know."

"But at least you got a letter from Leon last week."

"Hardly a letter . . . most of it was censored. I don't know how he's being treated."

At least he's alive, Magda thought. "Deborah, I've got to get out of here. Solange is driving me crazy . . ."

"She's worried about your condition, Magda, especially after your cold."

"I know, but I hate being smothered . . . ."

"Tell you what, come to lunch."

"Deborah, you're such an angel."

"Thank you, darling . . . Just be careful. It's seven above. I'll send the car around."

"Please don't bother, I'll take a cab."

"I don't think you should."

"What about the petrol?"

"We have enough. The car is seldom used."

Before leaving, Magda knocked on Solange's door. "And where do you think you're going in this weather?" Solange asked.

"Out."

"But where?"

"Lunch with my lover. You're always so full of curiosity."

"I'm trying to be civil, which is a great deal more than you've been the last week or so. One would think this war was only a problem for you."

"Well, I'm included." Her voice was at a dangerous level.

"So am I," Solange answered.

Magda suddenly felt like crying. Calming herself, she said, more softly, "I know I've been difficult and sullen—"

"Impossible is more like it."

"You're right, I've been impossible. When I get into one of my moods, I do and say things I don't really mean. Everything gets on my nerves. If I knew how Rubin was, I'd feel better." Going to Solange, she put her head on her shoulder. "I'm sorry, Solange. No matter how hard I try . . . Magda is . . . just . . . Magda."

Solange stroked her hair. "I don't know why I put up with you. I suppose it's because you're going to be the mother of my grand-nephew."

Magda smiled. "Are you sure it's going to be a grand-nephew?"

"Beyond a doubt. Rubin's first could only be a boy. Now take off that coat, it's too light . . . Use my sable. At least it will keep your knees from shaking. And where *are* you going?"

"To Deborah's. I'll give her your love. . . ."

Magda sat facing Deborah as she reclined against the large pillows. Except for a delicate tint of lipstick, her face was colorless and hollow-eyed, but she refused to be treated like an invalid. She spoke softly and slowly, as though measuring each word.

She had dismissed the nurse. The two women were alone, trying to comfort each other's miseries.

"Motherhood becomes you, Magda," Deborah said, without jealousy or bitterness.

"Thank you. If being big counts, I suppose I'm beautiful."

"You are, my dear. Imagine, it's only four months away. Unbelievable, how fast the time has gone."

An eternity, thought Magda, but she said, "It has gone fast. That dinner last November when I made my grand announcement seems like yesterday."

"I suppose all your shopping is done?"

"What shopping?"

"The layette."

"I haven't bought a thing."

"Really? I'd have thought you'd be through by now."

Magda wanted to say, I think of nothing but Rubin, but she didn't. "Now I am going to get started."

"Well, don't tax yourself too much, my dear. You have Solange to help you, and then there's always Mother Hack. I wish I were well enough, it would be such a joy to shop for this baby. Leon writes, and I agree, that she's almost ours."

Magda smiled. "You said *she*."

"Did I? Well, somehow I can see Rubin with a daughter."

Interesting, Magda thought. Earlier Solange had been sure Rubin would only have a boy. And now Deborah was seeing him the father of a girl . . . Rubin, the father . . . And what about her, the mother? How did they see *her*? Sometimes, it seemed, even the most friendly of Rubin's family forgot who was having this baby . . . Deborah, she noted, was getting very tired. She stood up and put on her sable coat. "Deborah, thank you. You've been so good to me. You've restored my spirits."

"Don't wait for an invitation. You're welcome any time . . ."

Magda bent over and kissed her fragile sister-in-law, saying she'd phone the minute there was news of Rubin.

Halfway down the winding staircase Magda paused. The front door was being opened by the maid.

"Good afternoon, Mrs. Hack. May I take your coat?"

Magda had stopped. She looked down into the large foyer. She could only see the top of a wide beaver hat, but not the face of whoever was wearing it. The woman walked regally across the foyer. About to ascend the stairs, she raised her head. Her mouth dropped. Magda knew the face from Rubin's description. And Sylvia Hack had no doubt whatsoever of Magda's identity. She glared at Magda with contempt. For the sake of this trollop, she'd been denied the chairmanship of the tea and the ball . . . Because of this whore she'd been dropped from the Orchid Society . . . Because of this foreign bitch Maurice was served formal notice that his membership would not be renewed in a club he had belonged to for years. Harry Sassoon had seen to that, and Sylvia didn't blame him. She would have done the same, painful though it might have been. Furthermore, she would never forgive Rubin. Never! If Deborah wasn't so ill—*and* a Mayer, daughter of a distinguished mother and father—Sylvia would have turned around and gone home. The way Deborah had defended this . . . *woman* . . . But she was, she reminded herself, a woman of compassion, which was why she was here now, to ask about Deborah's health, and spend a few moments cheering her up. Maurice had also been kind in visiting Deborah, which took a very big man indeed—especially considering the way Leon had defended Rubin's marriage to this . . . this prostitute.

Without further ado, Sylvia raised herself to her fullest height and walked slowly, sedately, up the stairs, ignoring Magda, as though she weren't there at all. Magda placed her hand on the banister, blocking the way, and stared. Blatantly stared. Sylvia was furious. How dare this *scum* of the earth dare to look at her that way? She eyed Magda up and down, then through clenched teeth said, "Get out of my *way* . . . you . . . you—"

"Mrs. Rubin Hack . . . Magda Hack."

"Not as far as I'm concerned. *How dare you—*"

She took Magda's hand, squeezing it hard, off the banister. "You're not fit to bear that name, much less be received in a decent home such as this. You should stay in the gutter, where you naturally belong. After all, it's where you came from—"

Recovering from the barrage, Magda slapped Sylvia's face with all the strength she had, almost losing her balance. But she steadied herself quickly and walked triumphantly down the stairs, across the marble foyer and out of the house, slamming the door behind her.

Arriving home at last, Magda told Solange what had happened. She hadn't felt so good in months. There was nothing like a good fight to free the emotions and clear the air.

Solange was rather sober. "I don't think you should have slapped her."

"Why? Was it all right for her to treat me like some slut? To tell me I'm not fit to live with decent people? That I belong in the gutter? I'll see her in hell first. That's rather bad language, especially from such a cultured lady, wouldn't you say?"

"I would, Magda, but behavior like that only makes things more difficult."

"More difficult than what?"

"Well, if you want so much to be accepted into London society . . . this isn't quite the way to go about it."

"My dear Solange, I'm going to make London society whether Mrs. Maurice Hack accepts me or not."

"Magda, stop being so childish. And stop this obsession."

"It's not an obsession. Rubin and I will be welcomed into the best houses in London, but for the time being that isn't my concern."

"Still, you shouldn't have antagonized Sylvia deliberately by blocking her way—"

"She could have walked around me . . . or crawled. In fact, if she hadn't glared at me the way she did, I was going to introduce myself politely . . . Now what do you think of that for ladylike behavior?"

"The French are no different."

"They probably learned it from the English. Now let's have dinner. I'm starved. And if I don't get a letter from Rubin before the end of the week, I'm going to the Foreign Office and sit there until they give me an answer."

That night Magda slept poorly. Her meeting with Sylvia had ignited her. She made up her mind that precious Sylvia was going to regret what she'd done.

In the morning she went straight to Solange's room. Solange was brushing her teeth. "I've got a lot of things to tell you," said Magda.

Sitting down in front of the dressing table, Solange looked at Magda's reflection in the Venetian mirror. She seemed more relaxed today, yet there was a look of determination that played around her eyes and mouth. Solange glanced back at her own image and said, "What do you have in mind?"

"A great deal. We're going shopping today for our baby. To the best and most expensive shop in town, the one that the Hacks patronize." Solange looked again at Magda's face reflected in the mirror. She knew that look . . . It meant man your battle stations.

"I think that's a good idea, and about time."

"I was afraid you'd say I shouldn't tempt the fates by shopping in the sacred places of the Hacks."

"You *are* a Hack."

"And I'm not going to let anyone forget it. Now just to show how much I love you, I'm going to let you ride in my new Rolls-Royce."

"In your what?"

"I've made an appointment with the agent at two o'clock."

"Sylvia Hack has affected your mind."

"Indeed she has, and it's about time. I'm not going to live like a poor relation . . . Also, I can't go on wearing your sable, so I'm buying one. The furrier will be here at five."

Solange shook her head and sighed. "I think you're being terribly extravagant. Remember, Rubin isn't made of money. I think a little restraint on your part is in order."

"If I couldn't afford it, I wouldn't do it."

"Well, I'll say one thing for you. If you joined Kitchener's forces, the war would be over tomorrow."

"I may suggest that to the war office." Magda laughed with delight.

"Any other plans, Magda?"

"No. That's about it for today. But tomorrow the painters are going to start on the nursery. This child of mine . . . ours . . . is going to be treated like the princess she is. After all, her great-aunt is a countess." Whereupon Magda got up and walked out of the room like an empress.

That morning the letter came, only the second since the one responding to the news of the baby.

Dearest Magda

My thoughts are always of you . . . Your beauty and love keep me going . . . The war is terrible, but probably much exaggerated in the papers. Don't believe everything you read . . . Take care of yourself, I beg you . . . We have so much life ahead of us . . . I hoped the war would be over by now but it seems there's a good deal of real estate to be taken. And I probably won't be with you when the baby is born . . . although I pray I will. Well, give my love to Solange and gratitude for all she's done . . . Tell her that France is on the right side . . . thank Mother for the cakes.

Love to all, Rubin.

Magda went straight to the phone and put through a call to the Hacks.

"Hello, Martin. This is Mrs. Hack . . . Mrs. Rubin Hack . . . Well, thank you, you're very kind to ask. Yes, I got a letter today. Is either Mr. or Mrs. Hack in . . . ? Would you be good enough to take a look at the post and see if there's anything from Mr. Rubin . . . ? Yes, I'll hang on . . . Two, you say . . . Oh, thank you, Martin. Please tell the Hacks I'll speak to them later. . . ."

Hanging up, she sighed deeply. At least it seemed Rubin was safe . . . for the time being.

No feelings stay the same, not pain, not boredom, not happiness. Emotions change, like circumstances, as life and events move forward.

In the weeks that followed, Magda and Solange finished the nursery and bought all the clothes, the toys. A nurse had been hired to live in. She would help with the birth, and take charge of the baby later.

Magda rarely went out. Her abdomen was so large she moved about only with a great deal of effort. Occasionally, they went for a drive in the gray Rolls-Royce. Magda loved it. It was just like Nathan's. But she wasn't happy with the chauffeur. He was much too old for service, but he was the only chauffeur she could find. And he looked presentable in his uniform. His manners were good, his credentials were not only excellent but many—he had outlived any number of employers. Still, Magda held her stomach each time he turned the corner a little too close to the curb, and was always grateful to get home in one piece.

She had dinner in bed, with Solange for company. Each night she wrote Rubin about the day's events . . . describing the nursery in great detail . . . the layette . . . the nurse. Rubin would like her. She was not what Magda expected an English nurse to be. She was jolly . . . reassuring, and a joy to have around.

"*July 12, 1915. Dearest Rubin,*" she began. "*Your bravery touches me deeply. You try to shield me, I know, but I want to share with you everything—*" She stopped writing and touched her abdomen. The first pain had started. Quickly she put down the letter and went to Solange. "I think it's started," she said joyfully.

"You've had a contraction?"

"Yes." Magda smiled. "By tomorrow Rubin will have his son."

Nurse Williams summoned the doctor. Methodically, she went about the business of bringing a new child into the world, a thing she'd never quite become matter-of-fact about. She still marveled at the miracle of each new baby born.

The birth was an easy one. Magda had been in labor less than five hours. The doctor slapped the child on the buttocks and a new cry was heard in the world.

Magda lay back, soaking wet. She smiled at Solange, who was holding her hand. "We did it!" she said. "We did it."

Stroking Magda's damp hair, laughing, Solange said, "*You* did it, my dear . . . You . . ."

Magda smiled up at her. "I want to see my son."

"I made a slight error, Magda . . . It's a beautiful little girl."

Magda cried, happily. "I *wanted* a daughter, Solange. I did. And I love this baby as you said I would . . . I hope God will forgive me for the things I said. . . ."

When the infant was placed in Magda's arms, she trembled with shock . . . The child was her . . . a small replica. At birth this baby was like no other child Magda had seen. Although she weighed only six and a half pounds, she was not red or scrawny or wrinkled as most newborns were. She was plump, delicately pink and white, with a perfect head of burnished light-brown down. Her tiny hands, which Magda held, were tapered as though they'd been sculptured. In awe, Magda said, "Did you ever see anything so marvelous? She's going to be a princess, the talk and envy of London society. She's a Hack. Her father is the son of respected barristers going back three hundred years. Her grandfather is a member of the House of Commons. Her grandmother is a great and revered lady. But most of all she is Magda Charascu's child. And . . . she's the godchild of her great-aunt, the Countess Boulard. Now what do you think of that?"

Solange smiled. Magda, my dear, naïve little Magda. We'll be fortunate if she's accepted into a good school. But today Magda was entitled to her dreams. "I think she's fortunate to be so loved."

"Oh, Solange, she is. You don't know how many nights I laid awake and felt her body moving and kicking."

"What will we name her? We never talked about a name."

"Jeanette," said Magda. "That was my mother's name."

Solange repeated, "Jeanette. Jeanette Hack, it's a beautiful name."

"Well," Magda said, "her namesake was a beautiful woman."

Miss Williams came in to take care of her charge. Reluctantly, Magda let her go.

"I'll bring her back when she's ready to be nursed," Miss Williams assured her.

Magda got ready to give her the news. The time was now. "Miss Williams, I'm not going to nurse."

"But you discussed nursing with Doctor Bemiss."

"I've changed my mind."

Solange frowned. "Magda, I know you're tired, but I think you should nurse."

"No, Solange. I've thought about it. When I'm up again, I want to do volunteer work for the war effort. Nursing would be very confining."

"But your first duty is to your child."

"You don't need to remind me of that, Solange." Magda spoke without anger. "Now, darling, I'm really very tired. . . ."

As Solange stood in the hall just outside Magda's closed door, she thought, Isn't it too bad not to have any illusions . . . ? To be blinded by love is better . . . Magda would love her child, of that Solange was certain, but on her own terms, as she loved Rubin . . . in her own fashion. Magda was a bundle of contradictions. She loved and hated with equal passion. She was restless, arrogant, compassionate, generous, selfish and kind. Solange wondered what there was about this girl, such a paradox of nature, that made her love her so much. She shook her head, unable to figure it out. But one thing she knew: Magda would always be a free, uncontrolled spirit.

She would always keep a part of herself that was only Magda's . . . and Magda's alone.

The battle at Verdun had been fought in the terrible

August heat. The men lay exhausted in the trenches, their lips parched dry and blistered. Listlessly, they talked of what kept them going. . . .

"Bloody well to survive, I'd say . . . Self-preservation, first bloody law of nature."

"I hope the next one doesn't miss me. . . ."

"If I can make it today, I'll live to be a hundred."

"For God's sake, why don't they blow up the whole bloody world and let the rats take over?"

"At least they're not killing us with gas."

"I'd like to ram a bayonet up the Kaiser's ass."

"Hell's got to be better than this."

"If I ever get back, I'm going to stay in bed with a girl for a whole bloody year and never take my pecker out. Of her, I mean!"

Rubin lay back against the wall of the trench, completely spent. His shirt clung to him like a second skin. Every day was the same, filled with carnage, the explosion of cannonfire, suffering, killing, dying. And for what . . . ? To gain a little more ground. Shutting his eyes he tried to go to sleep.

"Hack!"

"Yeah?"

Someone handed him a letter. It was from Magda, postmarked July 14. What was today? He'd lost all track of time.

"Hey, somebody, what's the date?"

"August 22."

My God, he'd completely misplaced July. He tore open the letter and began to read. . . .

"Hey!" he shouted, bolting upright and throwing his helmet in the air. "I'm a *father*. It happened yesterday, I mean, the day before this letter was sent." Jesus . . . For a moment it didn't seem possible. But somewhere in the world there was sanity. Somewhere there were beautiful things . . . like a beautiful new person named Jeanette . . . Jeanette Hack . . . a daughter . . .

Six

It was winter, again. And Sara Hack was busy in London. Daily, troop trains rolled in and out of Victoria Station . . . returning the sick and wounded. She was a Red Cross volunteer. She served biscuits and tea in all kinds of weather, snow . . . sleet . . . Aching with fatigue, still she served until she could no longer stand on her feet.

One night after she'd collapsed into bed, Nathan chastized her. "You know, Sara," he said, "you can't go on working this way. It's beyond your endurance."

Sara smiled at the face she had loved for so long. "Nathan . . . would you really have me not do my share?"

"You do more than your share . . . that's the trouble."

"But we're so fortunate. Our sons are still alive. And Phillip is home to stay."

"Yes, he's home . . . minus an arm."

"I work with a woman who's lost six sons, Nathan. Six. And still she never stops giving."

"I'm sorry for her," said Nathan, "but I must insist that you devote yourself to less strenuous efforts."

She smiled. "Like what?"

"Rolling bandages. Attending charity functions the way Matilda and Sylvia do. Work that's less demanding."

"We'll see, Nathan. We'll see. . . ."

"You're a very difficult woman, Sara. Very difficult." But her eyes were already closed in sleep.

That night, Sara's cough became so bad that Nathan summoned the doctor. He waited outside their room while the doctor examined Sara. Finally he came into the hall from the bedroom. Nathan could tell from the look on the doctor's face that Sara was seriously ill.

"She has pneumonia.".

Nathan had to lean against the wall for support. The doctor promised to try to send a nurse.

Nathan sat up with Sara through the night. Her condition worsened. By dawn she was coughing blood. The nurse arrived at nine.

At four that afternoon Sara was gone. Nathan sat at her bedside, alone in the silent room, bewildered . . . disbelieving, looking at Sara's uncovered face in repose. Incoherently, he spoke to her as though he expected an answer. "How could you leave me, my dearest Sara . . . ? Come back . . . come back . . ." On and on he grieved. He lay his head against her face, weeping uncontrollably, unaware that he was doing so.

The family had been summoned . . . They sat in somber silence. Nathan seemed to have the strength of a fortress in his bereavement. He wouldn't accept a word of consolation. This was a sorrow not to be shared . . . What comfort could mere words bring him . . . ? The sorrow was his alone to bear.

Maurice whispered in his father's ear. "Father . . . I leave it up to your discretion . . . but for the sake of Rubin's wife, wouldn't it be kinder if she didn't attend the service?"

Nathan shook his head in disbelief. Even in the face of death, Maurice's prejudices were in the forefront. Firmly, Nathan answered: "Magda is Rubin's wife. She will be respected as such . . . In my son's absence, Magda Hack will be present."

Maurice looked meaningfully at Phillip, a look they both understood. Neither wanted Nathan to think the suggestion had been made for anyone's sake except Magda's.

"You're quite right, Father. I'm sure Maurice realizes how thoughtless he was."

Maurice agreed. "Indeed I was. Please forgive me, Father."

Nathan did not answer . . . There was no need to.

* * *

The family crypt—home to the departed Hacks for many, many years—was opened to receive the last remains of Nathan's beloved Sara. Maurice and Phillip stood on either side of their father as Matilda, Sylvia, and the six grandchildren stood behind him. Magda and Solange stood to one side. In Nathan's grief, he realized that three of his loved ones were not present. Families should be together. Leon, Rubin, and Deborah were missed.

After the eulogy, the rabbi left the family alone and waited outside. Finally Maurice said quietly, "Father, I think it's time to go." Nathan looked at him vaguely, and nodded.

They left the small chapel, going out into the freezing December afternoon. Nathan lingered briefly, watching the heavy bronze doors being closed. He whispered, "Sleep well, my love . . . my life . . . my dearest Sara. I will lie with you each day and night until God wills that I be beside you."

Maurice, Phillip and their wives rode with Nathan in one limousine, the grandchildren in another. Solange and Magda were in Magda's Rolls-Royce as the funeral procession slowly drove off.

At sundown, after Magda had lit a memorial candle for Sara and said the traditional Hebrew prayer for the departed, she joined Solange in the drawing room. Sitting down, she looked at Solange's tear-stained face. "Solange, I don't know what to do."

"How to tell Rubin, you mean?"

"Yes . . . what should I do? How should I tell him about his mother's death?"

"I honestly don't know . . . Perhaps it would be better to hold off a while . . ."

"Would it be better if the letter came from his father?"

"How can one ask that broken man to write? Hold off for a little while, Magda."

"I suppose you're right. The mails are so bad anyway. Let Rubin have a small reprieve . . . Knowing won't bring his mother back."

In the days that followed, the only comfort Nathan found was with the baby in the flat on Wimpole Street, though secretly he wished her name was Sara. He held the child in his arms the same way he'd held Rubin so long ago.

Of all his present children, Magda was the most understanding, the most compassionate. Perhaps, Nathan thought, it was because she, too, had lost dear ones and understood the pain. They developed a friendship that went beyond the bond of blood.

At tea one day Magda said, "Do you remember the little synagogue on the East Side where Jeanette was blessed?"

"Yes, of course . . . Sara and I were there that day."

"If you don't mind, I'd like Jeanette to be named again. I've spoken with the rabbi."

Nathan was enormously pleased.

When they arrived at the synagogue Nathan held his youngest grandchild in front of the rabbi. He began with the blessing of naming this child, a name to be added to the book of life. From this day on, Jeanette would be known as Jeanette *Sara* Hack.

Nathan seemed to be rooted to the worn wooden floor, unable to move. Then, to Magda, with tears in his eyes: "Oh, my dearest child, that you would do this . . . I love you as Rubin does, but my thanks are beyond words that you have given me back my Sara. . . . She will live again through this child."

Sara had been gone a month, almost to the day, when Nathan was stricken with a massive coronary. Carried to his room, he was put to bed . . . the same bed in which Sara had conceived life, and known death. Lying against the pillows, he stared unseeing into the room. He had no fears. . . . What was there to fear . . . ? Death was only the absence of life, after all. . . . But looking at the whole expanse of it, he thought how strange the excursion was. . . . A man is born into the world with a veil of placenta; it is peeled away layer by layer and exposes him, scrawny and red. He takes a look at the world for the first time upside-down, held by the feet, and is swatted on the rump but he is told, "Don't cry, little one, this is only the beginning. You'll feel the sting of life's hand on your buttocks many times from the cradle to the grave." He lies in his crib, in his excrement, and waits for someone to attend him, and one day he discovers he has feet, stands up, wobbles back and forth unsteadily, takes his first step, falls flat on his bottom, gets up and tries again. One day he stands and waddles into someone's waiting arms, and he becomes a child, goes from puberty to adolescence, and the next day he's a man, young and vigorous, ready to scan the heights, except by the time he reaches middle age, halfway there he becomes tired of the dizzying heights he couldn't reach, sits back and awaits old age. His body bends over, his face wrinkles, his hair turns gray and sparse as it begins to expose the once-tiny baby head. He lies back, naked again in his excrement, and where once there were arms held out to help, now he finds there are none, and he falls asleep, never to awaken, and once again he becomes the infant, snug in the womb of the earth. . . .

The nurse was standing at his bedside, pulling him back from his dreamlike reverie. "Time for your medication, Mr. Hack."

Laughing inwardly, he thought, You foolish old woman, how long do you think that will keep off the inevitable? Pills are for the living. . . . He opened his mouth and swallowed the tablet.

When he awoke, Maurice and Phillip were seated near the bed. He looked at them. How wonderful to have children. One doesn't always approve of the things they do, but when all's said and done, they are of one flesh. . . . "Have you been here long?" he asked, his voice little more than a whisper.

"Not long, Father. The rest was good for you," Maurice said.

"Are you feeling better?" asked Phillip.

Nathan looked at the sleeve that was missing an arm. He sighed. My dear Phillip, it must have been so painful, and I was not there to comfort you, but here you are at my side, when I need you. . . . "Yes, feeling much better, thank you. . . ."

"Father," Maurice said uneasily, "Phillip and I need to talk to you—"

"Has anything happened to Leon or Rubin?"

"No . . . that's not why we're here."

Nathan sighed with relief. "Talk then."

Maurice ran his tongue over his dry lips. "Well . . .

according to our family tradition, the eldest son has always been the . . . executor. . . . Of course, we pray it won't be necessary for a very long time. . . ."

Nathan smiled to himself. It's much closer than you know. . . . "Continue. . . ." he said.

Maurice cleared his throat. "Well, Father, the will states that all living children must be present before the legacy can be apportioned. . . ." Maurice hesitated again, which was beginning to annoy Nathan.

"Go on, Maurice, say what has to be said, whatever it is."

Maurice swallowed. "Obviously, when the will was devised, you had no way of knowing that a situation such as the present one would prevent that from happening. . . . Leon and Rubin being away . . . We all pray the need won't arise, but in the event of . . ."

"My passing?"

"Yes . . . well . . . if they are not present, the will could be held up in probate indefinitely. . . ."

"You're quite right, Maurice. I should have taken care of that when the war broke out, but somehow it seemed unimportant compared to all the great issues of the world I imagined I was settling . . . go on, Maurice."

"Well . . . many things have taken place, Father. Now Rubin has a wife and a child, and should, God forbid, anything happen to him, they are not provided for according to this will—unless Rubin is home, or accounted for."

"Accounted for? You mean, should he die?"

"Well . . . yes."

"And that concerns you a great deal, Maurice?"

"Yes—"

"I'm happy to hear that."

"Well, Father, in spite of what my feelings were, I no longer feel that way. Nor does Phillip. . . . Rubin after all is our brother—"

"I am aware of that."

"Yes . . . well, I'll come to the point. . . . This is no time for you to redo a will. You're in no condition. Perhaps later. But for now, to insure the future of all concerned, we—Phillip and I—after long discussion, feel I should have power of attorney . . . to dispense the funds as I . . . as we see fit. The world is changing. Investments can be made in American industry and elsewhere which could bring substantial profits to the family estate—"

"Help me sit up," Nathan said, "so I can see you better. Ah . . . that's good. . . . Now, Maurice . . . I have no strength to debate the wisdom of this. . . . Much of what you say makes sense. However, that leaves you . . . in complete control. Money can be a dangerous thing. It has its . . . temptations. I've been aware of your . . . attitudes . . . toward Rubin and Magda. How can I be sure . . . that you are being . . . completely candid with me?"

"I'm sorry you feel called upon to ask that question, Father. No matter what my feelings might have been, this war has changed them. What seemed important yesterday is of no importance today. My main concern is with the family."

"Which is how it should always have been. . . . All right, on your honor, do you swear . . . you would not do anything . . . to hurt . . . I must lie back. . . . Thank you for helping me, Phillip. . . . Adjust the pillow . . . under my head."

Maurice quickly declared, "I give you my word, Father . . . my sacred word, and I do believe I'm a man of honor."

Nathan closed his eyes. Maurice and Phillip turned to one another . . . thinking as one that if Nathan died at this moment there would be no opportunity . . . Bending over the bed, Maurice whispered, "Are you all right, Father?"

"Yes . . . I think it's better with my eyes closed. . . . I can see more clearly."

Maurice cleared his throat.

"So this is a risk I shall have to take," Nathan continued, "because I need to believe in you, you're my son. . . ."

"Thank you, Father. And you needn't worry—"

"I suppose you've already prepared a document?"

"Yes, giving me power of attorney *only* until a new will can be drawn by you." He took out the document, reading it slowly.

"Is it dated?"

"Yes. Two days ago, January 9."

"That was very farsighted of you." And when Maurice didn't answer, "Now, you have witnesses?"

"Martin and the footman could—"

"Bring them in."

Phillip went to call them.

Maurice was the last to sign.

"Now, leave the document with me . . . tonight. . . . In the morning have our solicitor here by eight. I want to make a new will. Then, of course, this document becomes null and void. . . ."

Maurice tried to hold down his anger. "We'll be here in the morning, Father."

Nathan lay back. The color had left his face. His eyes were glassy. Maurice summoned the nurse. When she got there, Nathan gasped, his head rolled to one side. He was gone.

Phillip threw himself across Nathan and cried softly, as though no one else was in the room. "Forgive us, Father. I loved you and I betrayed you. . . ."

Maurice picked up the document and placed it in his inner coat pocket. Looking down at Nathan he said to himself, Father, you didn't agree but I honestly believe this is fair. Leon will get his share of everything, and Rubin will get what he deserves—a hundred pounds for life. He brought scandal and shame to our family, a shame we must forever live with—a whore who has the name of Hack. You were weak, Father . . . but I loved you . . . I loved you as much as the others, but what you thought was strength I felt was weakness. . . . Sympathy was hurtful to the loyal members of your family.

Still, no matter how hard he tried to convince himself— and only God knew how he tried to justify himself—when he looked at the death head of Nathan, his heart turned over. This man had been his father. No more. Maurice felt suddenly cold, and old. . . . Now he was no one's child. His mother and father were gone. He could cry for them. But what he felt for Rubin was a separate thing.

Nathan's illness had greatly worried Magda. In spite of the Hacks she wanted to go to see him. Her reasons for not doing so were not because she feared for herself. The hostile Hacks neither intimidated her nor threatened her peace of mind. In fact, she longed for a confrontation. It would clear the air once and for all. But she had felt that an unfortunate scene would only make Nathan worse. And so she stayed away.

It was Martin who gave her the news of Nathan's death. "Was he alone?" she asked.

"No, madam. The family had been with him constantly."

Well, I'm the family too, but I wasn't there. . . . If only Rubin had been here; he wouldn't have let them keep us away. "I'm coming over, Martin . . . I'm leaving right away."

"Madam"—he couldn't refer to Nathan as the body or the remains—"Mr. Hack has already been taken to the chapel."

At 7:00 A.M. Magda and Solange were led into the chapel by a very sober gentleman in a black cutaway jacket, striped trousers, a white shirt and black tie.

Magda placed the small gold baby ring in Nathan's hand. It was inscribed with the name of Sara . . . the ring Nathan had given his last grandchild. . . . Bending over the casket, she kissed the cold lips, then sat in the first pew alongside Solange, praying and reciting the mourning prayer.

"*Yis-gad-dal v'yis-kad-dash sh'meh rab-bo, b'ol'mo di'v-ro kir'-u-seh v'yam-lich mal-chu-seh, b'cha-ye-chon u-v'yo-me-chon u-v'cha-yeh d'chol bes yis-ro-el, ba-ago-lo u-viz-man ko-riv, v'rim-ru O-men.*"

How long they were there, she couldn't say. But she knew she had felt so great a loss only once before . . . for her brother, Niko. Obliging the usher, she signed the register and left.

At 11:00 Maurice and Phillip arrived with their families, taking the seats reserved beyond the casket, which could not be seen by the mourners since the small enclosure was hidden from view by the heavy, parted red velvet curtains. Other people were now arriving to pay their last respects. To a great man. To Nathan Hack.

Although the interment would be private, the chapel was filled with mourners filing past the bier. It was Maurice's duty to stand at the entrance and thank those who came to pay respects. When he glanced down at the register, he saw Magda's name. Straining his eyes, he saw her sitting in a back pew with that damn French countess . . .

courtesan would be more like it. . . . Well, for the time being he'd control himself, but when everyone left there'd be an opportunity to defend the family's dignity. . . .

The halls in the mortuary were now finally empty except for the Hacks. Nathan's casket had already been placed in the hearse. Slipping on one gray suede glove, Maurice saw Magda and Solange coming out of the chapel. Red-eyed, Magda noted Maurice's cold glare. Although they had never met, they were hardly strangers to each other.

Sylvia walked out, refusing to be in the same place with such a person. Phillip started to leave but stopped as Maurice stood in front of Magda, blocking her exit. She tried to go around him, to avoid a scene. . . . This wasn't a time for recriminations. Nathan wasn't cold in his grave. But Maurice persisted. Magda stood still, looking at him.

"You were not welcome in my father's house when he was alive," he said. "What makes you think you are any more welcome here now?"

"Because your father was also my father-in-law, and, more important, a man I loved and who loved me. He also was my *husband's* father. I have as much right to be here as any of you."

"You have *no* right. . . . Since we don't approve of whores—"

"How dare you!" Solange broke in. . . . "I think you must be mad. Since you've taken the saddest of all times to offend your brother's wife I can only say you're the cruelest, most ruthless human being I've ever had the misfortune of knowing."

Maurice raised his hand to slap her, but Phillip moved in. "Stop, Maurice, for God's sake." Then he ran out into the street, wanting to retch. Matilda and the children followed.

But Maurice stepped in front of Magda once again. Putting on his other glove he said, "I'd advise you to stay away from us . . . far away—"

"*You* don't frighten me, and you can't hurt me—"

"That's where you're wrong, Magda *Charascu*. I can do a great deal. It really wasn't too difficult to learn about your past . . . what you were before Rubin picked you out of the gutter. Now, once more, I tell you to stay out of our way."

Magda looked directly at him. "You need not be concerned. You'll see me only one more time—at your father's grave site," and taking Solange's arm, she turned and left.

Watching them go, Maurice decided to reconsider his promise to provide for Rubin . . . and his "countess." Poor Nathan, how soft, how naïve he'd been. . . .

CHAPTER
Seven

That evening after a very silent dinner, Solange sat with Magda in her room.

"Solange, I swear on my mother's grave, they are going to regret this."

"Yes . . . well, we've had enough of graves for one day. . . . Now try and get some rest."

The next day Magda reluctantly wrote Rubin about his parents' death. She withheld the details of his brother's behavior; Maurice had not even let her into the mortuary. She would not inflict that on Rubin. When the letter was written she showed it to Solange, who read:

> . . . All of us have had the sadness of facing the loss of dear ones, but you have been blessed with more love than most. You, dearest Rubin, can be sustained by the memory of a love and devotion few people have known. I ask you to forgive me for not having written about your mother at the time of her passing, but I wanted to spare you one more day of grief. Now that they are both gone, I can only pray that your memories will comfort you all your life, and that you will take strength from that, a gift to cherish. Come home to us soon.
>
> Love, Magda.

It was a cold crisp day in the trenches, and Rubin tried to will his mind to think of this as a field in summer after the snow had melted. In the midst of horror, it was necessary to develop the relief of fantasy. . . .

Yesterday the Germans had fought them with gas. The men had gagged, coughed, vomited. Some had doubled over and died. Others had gone insane. Rubin had urinated in his own torn, balled-up shirt and held it up to his nose, filtering the noxious fumes. The wind had finally shifted, and all the men who could had reported to sick bay.

This morning he had received Magda's letter, with the news of the death of his parents, and he cried, dry-eyed, deep down within himself, as he had never cried before.

In eight months, Jeanette's hair was just thick enough for Magda to tie a pink ribbon on top. What a beauty she was . . . a perfect smile, and sweet, innocent eyes. . . . She cooed and laughed at the things Magda told her. . . . My *petite poupée* . . . my little doll. Tossing her up in the air was a special delight. It made Jeanette shriek with laughter.

"Princess . . . that's right . . . you're a princess. . . . When your papa comes home, we'll have picnics in the park. . . . We'll buy all the toys in London. . . . But we're going to live in Paris and in the summer we'll live in a house in the country and you can have your own pony. . . . Now, young lady, if you behave you may sit on my bed while your mama goes through her wardrobe, which I must say is getting quite shabby. . . . Am I right? Of course, you say," and Magda tickled Jeanette's tummy and the child kicked her feet, giggling, and waved her hands. . . .

Afterward, Magda felt so good she decided to take herself and Solange to the Dorchester for lunch.

When they arrived, Magda was told that Mrs. Rubin Hack would not be seated. She looked at Solange. . . . Obviously the work of Maurice. Since Nathan's death the Hacks had become openly belligerent and clearly had given the word to certain restaurants and shops not to serve Magda or the Countess or the Hack patronage would be withdrawn. "Well," she said as they left the hotel, "they won't stop me. I've got a few cards up my sleeve. . . ."

They ate at a tea room and afterward Magda told the driver to go to Worth's. The doorman helped the two ladies out, then smartly opened the door to the salon.

The director of Worth's was most cordial to these, obviously, French expatriates . . . more than apparent from the cut of their clothes. . . . "Yes, Madam, what may I show you?"

"I'd like to see the full spring collection," said Magda.

"I'll have Miss Badden assist you."

Soon one model after another was showing the spring line. Magda liked everything. Solange was not quite so enthusiastic.

When her choices were made, Magda gave her name . . . Countess Magda Charascu. Who had referred the Countess? The Leon Hacks.

Colors and fabrics were selected. Appointments for fittings were made. . . . To what address should the wardrobe be sent? To Mrs. Rubin Hack. . . . Miss Badden turned putty gray. Excusing herself, she went at once to the director. He came immediately to Magda. "There seems to have been an error. We wish to apologize, but the items you have selected seem already to have been reserved. I'm sorry, Miss Badden erred, you will forgive us. . . ."

Quietly, Magda said, "Frankly, sir, you may take your spring, your fall and your winter collections and flush them down the W.C. along with your clients, the lovely lady Hacks and their lovely families." Turning, she pulled her sable grandly about her and departed in the fashion of mock stage royalty. She could still, by God, put on a show.

Magda's outrage reached its height when she volunteered to work for a charity dinner sponsored by the Belgian Minister, Count de Lalaing, and the Duchess of Vendôme. She received a brief note of rejection, no apologies included. That same day Magda received another letter— Jeanette was turned down for registration at Ramsgate, the exclusive school for girls where Solange said she should have been accepted at birth.

At dinner Magda fumed, "Those bitches aren't going to be happy until they see me drown in the Thames. Well, to hell with them. Somehow I'm going to make them wish they had. . . . And when this damned war is over we're going back to Paris. I despise London, the weather . . . the people. Especially the Hacks. But before I go, I'm going to leave *them* a legacy. . . ."

Eight

It was July, a week before Jeanette's birthday. Magda had photographs taken, alone, then with Magda, then with Solange, then the three of them together. Much to her surprise, she'd been able to hire Peter Scott, the finest photographer in London. Thank God the Hacks' and Sassoons' tentacles didn't reach out everywhere.

As Scott was gathering up his equipment he asked her matter-of-factly, "Have you ever thought of having your portrait painted, Mrs. Hack?"

"No . . . I haven't."

"If you'll forgive me for saying so, you are exquisite. . . . Do you mind?"

Before she could answer, he took her face in his hands, turning it from side to side. He felt the planes of her high cheekbones and the symmetry of her facial structure. Then he stood away, narrowed his eyes as though looking through a lens, and said, "Yes, Mrs. Hack, you really should think seriously of having your portrait done."

"And who should I get to do it?"

"I have a friend, perhaps the best portrait painter in the world."

Magda smiled. "That is impressive."

"He's a no-nonsense man, and he doesn't paint *just* pretty pictures. I know Camail will do you." He gestured toward a painting on the wall. "I admire your Picasso. . . ."

"Yes. It's exciting, isn't it? My husband bought that in Paris before the war."

"His works will be worth a fortune some day."

132

"I hope so. . . . Thank you for coming. I can't wait to see the pictures of Jeanette. I want to send them as quickly as possible to her father. . . ."

Two days later Peter had the proofs ready. He brought them by in time for tea. Although it was July there was a fire in the grate and the house was filled with flowers.

They looked at the proofs and afterward Peter Scott said, "I spoke to Camail yesterday. He'd like to see you. Would Thursday be convenient? Three o'clock at his house? We'll drive there from my studio."

Feeling far less calm than she appeared, Magda carefully nodded her agreement.

Magda stopped in front of Peter's studio at 2:15. He was waiting. Together they drove through the sandbagged streets of London. When they came to Regency Park, the Rolls halted in front of an imposing mansion.

A butler opened the door into a marble foyer. They were led to a large studio on the top floor, where the glass roof slanted almost to the floor. The painter continued to work as though they weren't present.

When he finally finished and turned around to face Magda, she was startled; she'd been so absorbed in watching him work. He was nothing at all like the bearded, unkempt painters she'd met in Paris. Camail was enormous; hard muscles showed below his rolled-up sleeves. His eyes were deep set, the color of a gray-blue ocean. The brows were thick, bushy and black, in contrast to his steel-gray hair. He didn't speak, but merely looked at Magda. What he thought was not revealed by any change in expression.

"Take off your hat."

She did so.

"Stand here, where I can see you in the harshest light." He examined her face. He looked at her hands. Giving her a damp cloth he said, "Take off your makeup."

When she had done so, he looked at her again, then walked around her, observing every curve, the length of her arms, her waist . . . nothing went unnoticed. It was as though his eyes could see through her clothes.

"She will do," Camail said, without looking at Peter. "Take the pins from your hair. Let it hang loose."

She did as he asked.

"Yes, she will do. Now you may go. I'll let you know when we can start."

"What do you plan, Monsieur Camail?"

His eyes were, truly, penetrating. "I never talk about my subject in advance. I also don't allow my clients to see the work in progress, or question me about it. Is that all understood?"

"Yes," she said. She wasn't intimidated, although Peter had told her Camail's paintings were on display in the most prestigious galleries of London, Paris, Holland and America.

"And don't call me 'monsieur.' My name is Camail."

"My name is Magda."

He looked at her as though he hadn't heard.

Smiling to herself, she thought him fascinating, and suddenly, she decided to do it. "I have one request to make. . . ."

"Yes?" His tone was impatient. He returned to his painting.

"I want to be painted in the nude."

"Why?" Camail added a dab of yellow to the canvas in front of him.

"It's a long story. . . ."

Wiping his hands on a rag, Camail said, "Sit down. . . . Would you care for an aperitif?" When he had served his guests, he said, "Why do you want a nude? Please be honest or I will not paint you at all. . . . I can only capture truth."

Briefly Magda then told him the whole story . . . from her days in Bucharest through the years in Paris, until this very moment. She didn't prolong the story. She told the facts. Yes, she wanted to embarrass Maurice and Sylvia and Phillip as they had offended her. Had Sara and Nathan been living, she most emphatically would never agree to such a thing. But they were gone, and she had a right, an obligation, to return some bitter medicine. . . .

Camail was caught up in the drama of Magda's story and obviously sympathetic. She was exquisite. Even before she'd finished talking he knew how the painting would be done. Not one of those vulgar nudes reclining on a red velvet sofa, not a demure nymph standing near a lily pond, a piece of netting draped over her shoulder flying in the wind. No, he saw the painting of Magda clearly, as though the canvas were dry and ready to be hung. She would be seated on a gold-leaf cane bench in front of a triple baroque-framed mirror, dressed in a sheer pink-mauve peignoir which billowed out, away from her body. Not a curve, not a contour would be missed. Although her back would be toward the viewer, her image would be seen from all angles, the two profiles reflected in the side panels, her torso facing the center one, thereby revealing her breasts, exposing the nipples through the thin gauze of chiffon. Only her slim thighs and her legs, crossed at the ankles, would be exposed provocatively, the peignoir draped just so. Her feet would be bare. Her thick mane of hair would hang loose. Her eyes would reveal only what the viewer wanted to see in them. A deep gray background, warmed with vermilion, would make the painting sensual but not somber. It would be the subject in her most intimate, unguarded moment, the viewer feeling as though he were intruding on the lady's privacy. He wanted to begin at once.

"We'll start tomorrow at ten," he said.

They worked six days a week. And during the four months they worked together, Camail grew to admire Magda more and more.

Camail was not especially given to liking women. When his work failed to exhaust his energies, he usually made commercial arrangements with a number of women. Transactions, actually. What he admired most about Magda was her strength of conviction, her air of emancipation. She spoke little, was never temperamental, never late. She took directions as though she had modeled all her life.

One day he said, "The canvas is almost done. Will you come for supper tonight?"

"Yes." She said it at once.

She arrived not one moment early, not one moment late. She was filled with curiosity as he led her into the salon. It was the first time she'd seen it. The grandeur took her breath away. It was filled with treasures from all over the world. The furniture was covered in silk and velvet, in a variety of colors, from cyclamen-pinks to light lemon-yellows. . . . Aubusson rugs . . . the ivories, jades, porcelains. . . . It was a fabulous room, a fabulous house. . . . Her eyes took in every object. From time to time her hands gently touched the surface of some object she found irresistible.

"I love it," she said finally.

"You have good taste, Magda."

"And the bad manners to admit it. . . ."

"Shall we have dinner first, or shall we make love?"

"Dinner first . . . I'm usually very hungry after."

Magda lay back against the pillows and sighed with content. Camil outlined her cheeks . . . her nose . . . her lips, with the tip of his finger.

"You're painting, Camail. Lie back and relax. . . ."

He obeyed. "Did you know I'd make love to you?"

Magda's smile was borrowed from the Mona Lisa. "Did you think I'd resist?"

"Do you also read minds?"

"When they're transparent."

"But you love your husband . . . ?"

"With *all* my heart."

"Yet you'd still sleep with me?"

"What does one have to do with the other . . . ? I have an affection for you. . . . But this is the first time I've slept with anyone since Rubin went away. . . . If he were home I would not be in your bed."

"How can you be so certain?"

"Because my husband happens to be a very good lover who satisfies me. . . . Why should I look elsewhere? I'm a very sensual woman who has been without a husband for over a year."

"And you've been able to abstain for that long?"

"Yes. I admit it hasn't been easy. . . ." Magda started to the bathroom.

Camail continued. "This will be the beginning of a new—"

"This will be the beginning of nothing. But at least I had the *good taste* to choose you for my one infidelity. . . ." She closed the bathroom door. Camail laughed at and appreciated her candor—not to mention, damn it, her good sense.

CHAPTER

Nine

It was the night Magda had waited for . . . a night to be
savored like honey in the comb. She took one last look at
herself in the triple mirror Camail had given her as a souvenir. . . . What she saw more than pleased her. The
black satin coat was long and flowing but the dress beneath was strapless . . . molded to her body, eight inches
off the floor. She and Mademoiselle Françoise had secretly plotted what a sensation it would be . . . perhaps
beginning a new trend. Attaching the pearl choker around
her neck, adjusting the diamond and emerald clip, Magda
could scarcely take her eyes away from the elegant simplicity. Onto her wrist she slipped a diamond band, an
emerald, then another diamond. She wore the large emerald ring, surrounded by diamonds, on her right hand, and
on her left, below the gold wedding band, she placed the
diamond and platinum band Rubin had bought her after
their marriage. But the crowning glory was the black
toque, encrusted with crystal beads in various sizes, which
covered her hair completely. Each bead had been hand-
sewn. As she shook her head gently from side to side, they
seemed to dance with excitement.

She looked at herself once again. She'd never quite felt
this way before. . . . Taking out the jeweled case from
her evening bag, she filled it with gold-tipped cigarettes.

"Magda, you are *divine*." It was Solange, in her four-
year-old Mainbocher. She had refused to try to outshine
Magda, knowing it was impossible in any case.

Before leaving, Magda went into the nursery and kissed

137

her *petite poupée*. She held the child above her head as Jeanette kicked her legs. And as Magda lowered her back into the crib, she looked at the innocent eyes of her child. "Your mother, darling, is going to let all of London know we're here. . . ."

Invitations to Camail's private showing had been sent to the most important patrons and buyers in the art world, including royalty. The guest list was not as long as it was selective. And, of course, included were Hacks and Sassoons.

The Sassoons, however, could not attend. Harry Sassoon had died only a week before. Strangely enough, it wasn't his heart; a chicken bone had lodged in his trachea. The Hacks, though, were not only eager to go to Camail's showing but also genuinely wanted to see his latest works—they already owned four of his paintings. It was a gala affair.

No one knew the real Camail. He was many things to many people. He was in turn flamboyant . . . a man of mystery . . . a private person . . . a public person . . . an eccentric . . . an aristocrat. . . . He made shocking statements about art . . . and insulting statements about the people who bought it. He could be charming . . . unaffected. . . . No one seemed to know when he was pretending and when he wasn't.

Camail had begun his career as a pauper from Belgium, with barely enough money to study in Paris. He was a renegade. He did things most artists wouldn't do, both in his art and in his private life as well. Camail did not feel it was necessary to starve and suffer in order to create. Just the opposite . . .

God smiled upon some artists, and Camail was one of them. He wanted to be a fine painter, but he also wanted to be rich and famous, so he decided to live in London. His charm and ambition brought him into the most important homes. His sponsors were the old, influential dowagers of London. If he had to oblige them with a brief *affaire de coeur* he was only too happy to do so—so long as they supported his work. In a reasonably short time Camail was in demand. His work proved him a man of great talent; his fortitude made it pay off. Paintings by

Camail brought enormous prices. He had become a master showman. He would sell only to those people who loved his work, thereby raising his price ever higher.

Yes, this affair was indeed fashionable. The white-gloved waiters moved among the guests with trays of champagne. One could almost forget the war. . . . All the paintings were splendid. However, one painting, not mentioned in the catalog, was shrouded in mystery. As the guests circulated, it was hidden from view by curtains.

The director of the gallery stood on a small platform and clapped his hands. "Ladies and gentlemen, we welcome you to this show of paintings by Camail. One painting, however, was completed too late to be listed in the catalog. May I direct your attention to the artist, who will unveil it now . . . ?"

Dressed in formal cutaway and white tie, Camail stepped onto the platform, smiling and bowing to his patrons. It was the moment everyone had been waiting for, the unveiling of a treasure. For one long moment, he paused, heightening the tension. The gallery was absolutely still. Then he pulled the silken cord. The blue satin draperies were drawn apart. In a simple gold-leaf frame, Magda's perfect likeness came to life in the triple mirror, her back to the viewers. A collective gasp came from the spectators. . . . It was, quite simply, the most beautiful portrait in London. The audience was dazzled, stunned.

Then everyone began to talk at once. "She's mine!" shouted a wealthy baron. "I'll have her at any cost!" Other prospective buyers spoke up.

With perfect timing, Camail gestured for the real Magda to step out of the shadows, and she came proudly to Camail's side. Taking her hand in his, he announced, "This is my model . . . the real Magda. . . ."

The spectators applauded, gasping once more. There could be no doubt Magda was sensational, in life and in art. The other Hacks were in shock. Sylvia had fainted. She was carried out by Maurice, followed by Matilda and Phillip.

Magda smiled at Solange. This is my revenge . . . my triumph, her eyes seemed to say. The painting is magnificent, it can hang in the Louvre. . . . But Solange wondered for a moment what Rubin's reaction would be had he been there . . . except, of course, he wasn't . . . and

Magda had surely endured enough to be entitled to her triumph. Revenge. . .

The picture was to be placed in the window; the name-plate beneath it would read "MAGDA." A spotlight would illumine it perfectly.

Camail was giving a small party at the Savoy. Tonight Magda was certain she would not be turned away . . . neither tonight nor any other night. She had not made "high" society, but the society she had made was good enough for her. She was seated between Camail and Count Alexis Maximov.

". . . Camail and I met in Paris, more years ago than I care to remember."

"Why are people so sensitive about age? How can a man be exciting and under forty?"

The count beamed; he was forty-six. "You are too young to know," he said.

"I'm twenty. Why should I deny it?" She smiled back.

"When you're . . . say . . . forty, then we'll see."

"When I'm forty, I'll improve with age, like wine. Look at my aunt, the Countess."

"You're the only woman in this room."

"Thank you. You're very kind. . . . Tell me about your meeting with Camail."

"We met at a ball in Paris. But let me take you to lunch tomorrow and I'll tell you all about it."

"No, I think not. But thank you for the invitation."

"Will you forgive a very personal question?"

"Perhaps . . ."

"Are you Camail's lady?"

"No. I am my husband's lady."

"I see. . . . You will forgive my boldness?"

"You're forgiven. . . . Would you like to come to tea tomorrow?"

The Count beamed again. "Yes. Thank you."

"Four o'clock?"

"Four o'clock."

That night Magda lay awake and dreamed. . . . A whole new life had begun. . . .

The next morning the most important critic called *Magda* a masterpiece. The second most important critic called it a piece of pornography. The other critics were about equally divided.

Camail's telephone rang early. It was Maurice Hack. He wanted to buy the picture. Price was no object. Quite simply, he had to have it. Camail was amused. He knew Maurice Hack would burn it. He assured Mr. Hack that this was one piece of art no one could buy.

Maurice persisted. "Everything has a price."

"You're mistaken, sir. . . . The truth is, I no longer own the painting."

There was a long, long pause.

"To whom was it sold?"

"It wasn't sold. . . . It was given away."

"To whom? Perhaps the party would be willing to sell it . . . for a large profit. . . ."

"Would you sell a gift?"

Maurice responded quickly, "You're right, of course. It's just that my wife wants it so much—"

I'll bet she does. . . . "The painting I call *Magda* is a painting every woman would want . . . and every man. . . . Women will see themselves reflected in the portrait. . . . Don't you agree?"

Maurice was not in a position to disagree, but he swore he would never buy another Camail painting. "I hope the recipient is deserving?"

"Oh, quite deserving . . . I gave the painting to my model. It was the least I could do. . . . Don't you agree?"

But Maurice didn't answer. He had turned white.

Camail hung up, laughing.

Ten

Magda sat with Camaïl to her right, Alexis to her left and Solange next to him. Across the table, Peter Scott's mistress Pamela was seated between Camaïl and Peter. No one sat in Rubin's chair at the head of the table. His name card was placed in front of the service plate, as were the others. It was New Year's Eve, 1916.

Magda had received a letter from Rubin that morning. It had upset her so much her mind was still distracted.

"Delicious salmon, Magda," said Alexis.

She saw him through a haze, having drunk more than usual.

"What's delicious?" She started to get up.

"What can I do for you, Magda?"

She looked at him blankly, then intently. She was having trouble focusing her eyes. "What can you do for me? Can you bring my husband back, Alexis?"

He almost whispered, "I wish I had that power."

"Then you can't help me, but thank you for the offer. . . . Here, Alexis, let's drink to your health."

"To being your friend . . . when you have need of one."

"I'll drink to that," she said, clinking glasses. "One always needs a friend."

The mantel clock rang in the New Year . . . 1917. They hugged one another, kissed and wished each other the best of everything and a speedy end to the war.

Magda went in to see Jeanette. She whispered, "Happy New Year, my precious. . . ." When would Rubin ever get to see her? She lingered for a moment, then walked out to join her guests.

They listened to music on the victrola and drank champagne until three. Solange was the first to excuse herself. Then, gradually, the other guests left. Magda was hardly aware of what she said as she wished them all good night.

She shut the door and leaned against it, staring up at the ceiling. Then she took off her shoes and went to the kitchen to get a new bottle of champagne and a glass to take back to her room. On her way, she saw Alexis. For a moment, she couldn't remember. Why was he still here? Hadn't he left with the others . . . ?

"I hope you don't mind my staying on?" Alexis said.

"No . . . I'm grateful not to be alone. You're my friend, and I need . . . Fix up the fire while I change. . . ."

"Would you like me to come to you?"

She looked at him. "No, that's not necessary. You're already here."

She changed into a loose-fitting peignoir. Barefooted, she came back into the drawing room. Alexis was seated by the fireplace in the large brocade chair. Magda sat down on the floor beside him. "Tell me about your father and his boyhood friend, Count Leo Tolstoy. I love to hear stories about royalty. . . ."

She rested her head on his lap as he began. Alexis had been born in Moscow. His father was second cousin to the Czar. His mother had been of royal French blood. They lived in a very grand house in the country. . . .

As Alexis talked, Magda got more and more sleepy. "They met at the university. Papa said Tolstoy was a great writer. . . ."

"Yes . . ." said Magda, her eyes closed, ". . . a very great writer indeed . . . but all this royalty business . . . truth is, I don't understand a damn about royalty. . . . The English King is a cousin to the Czar and that bastard the Kaiser is a cousin of both and would you think a family could be so cruel to one another? Yes, you would, I would . . . I ought to know. . . ." And she put her head down on Alexis' lap and passed out cold. He carried her into the bedroom, put her under the covers and looked at her for a very long time. He kissed her lightly on the cheek, turned off the light and walked out slowly, closing the door behind him.

Magda spent the next day in bed. She was not only hung over, but also depressed. She even refused to see Jeanette. From time to time Solange came in. Magda hardly knew she was there.

The phone rang. "I don't know what to say, Alexis. Magda is quite depressed. I can't seem to reach her."

"Would it do any good if I came over?"

"It might. . . ."

Alexis sat by the bed and spoke softly, asking if she'd like to talk about what was troubling her, though he of course had a rather good idea.

Magda shook her head, then managed . . . "My husband's been away for over two years, in all kinds of hell. How can you expect me to feel?"

"Perhaps it would help him if you committed suicide, or had a nervous collapse?"

"Don't laugh at me!"

"I'm not. I'm going to make a suggestion. Starting tomorrow, we're going to find you something to do that will keep you occupied, so you at least won't have so much time to brood."

"What? Rolling bandages? Nobody even wants me as a volunteer. Let's face it, I'm an outcast. And besides, I'm not English and stiff-upper-lip enough. I don't think the English are real."

"They're real. And they suffer as much as you do, but they show it differently."

"I suppose you're right. My knowledge of the English is somewhat distorted by certain members of the Hack family." She started to cry. Alexis put his arms around her shoulders. "I'm so damned lonely, Alexis. I miss my husband. It's not natural to be parted for so long. We were together such a short time after our marriage. . . . How can I be brave?"

"Well, crying isn't the answer—"

"What is?"

"We'll begin with dinner. . . ."

They went to the Ritz.

"Now," said Alexis, once they were settled. "What would you *like* to do?"

"You know, it's strange," said Magda, "your asking me that. All day I've been thinking I'd like to be an actress." She smiled. "I used to do a little singing. . . ."

"Then why not do it?" said Alexis. "*Be* an actress."

"Do you really think I could?"

"I know it. Magda, you can do anything you want to do. . . ."

Alexis arranged for her to see Edward Goldstein, the impresario—and also the most important agent in London. When Magda came in to see him, he was enchanted with her. Physically, she was what Alexis had promised, but could she act? He handed her the script of *Camille* and asked her to read from it cold.

"You know the way it ends," said Edward. "Camille is very sick and Armand comes to see her. . . . She knows she's dying, but her courage is tremendous. . . . Armand must never find out, so she sends him away."

Magda knew that the play was based on *La Dame aux Camélias* by Dumas *fils*. She concentrated on the character of Camille, the beautiful courtesan, trying to protect the man she loved. In her mind, Magda tried to become Camille . . . feeling all the things she must have felt. . . . Then, simply, she read Camille's lines as though they were hers. Edward played the part of her lover.

When the reading was over and Magda had spoken the last tragic words, both men had tears in their eyes. And Edward Goldstein knew one thing: although Magda had never had an acting lesson and didn't know stage left from stage right, she knew exactly where she was. She knew center stage.

"Was I all right?" Magda herself broke the silence she had created.

"You . . . were . . . wonderful," said Edward.

"And you'll help me . . . ?"

"I will help you . . . though I must warn you not to expect too much. The theater is hard to gain a foothold in . . . and once you're in, she's a tough mistress. Even with my help, you may not succeed."

"Have no fear, Edward." It was Alexis who spoke. "When Magda Charascu makes up her mind to do something, she does not fail."

"Magda Charascu . . . is that the name you want to use?"

"Yes . . . for on the stage, that's who I am. . . ."

She was cast as a maid in a play called *London Town*, understudying the ingenue. It was a modest hit. In the third week of the run, she got a chance to play the ingenue. A young critic, Aleister Comfort, happened to see that performance and wrote a glowing review of a new, unknown young actress named . . . what was it again . . . ? Magda Charascu. . . .

When the actress she understudied was forced to leave the play because of illness, Magda was given the role.

Items began to appear in the newspapers about her. She was called "glorious," "radiant," "divine." Her past as an artist's model was publicized . . . her career as a singer in Paris . . . her relationship with the Count. . . .

The Maurice and Phillip Hacks were scandalized. Her lurid past was bound to affect their social standing even more. Her escapades would ruin them. Why, the brazen little witch even smoked in public! The Hacks devoutly wished that the dear Lord in his wisdom and justice would do something to alleviate their painful embarrassment, like having Magda fall off the Tower of London. . . . That was their fervent prayer.

But their prayers went unheeded. Magda Charascu flourished.

July of this year, 1917, would soon be upon them, and with it Jeanette's second birthday. She was a beauty, and so attended by Camail, Peter, Pamela, Alexis and Deborah that one would have imagined she would be positively intolerable, this diminutive Magda; but she was not in the least spoiled, perhaps in part because she had never really been treated, or spoken to, as a baby. . . . Not from the day she was born had anyone spoken baby talk to her. . . . She was a person, and was treated as such. She was never punished, but was told there were things she could do, things she could not do, and the reasons were explained to her. Her temperament was more Rubin's than Magda's.

On Sundays Alexis would call for the three of them, Solange, Jeanette, Magda. He would hold Jeanette on his lap as they drove to lunch. She adored him. . . . He bought her lollipops and balloons and ice cream. They romped in the park and rolled in the grass . . . they took drives in the country . . . they rode on the ponies and the carousel. Alexis was her favorite person, next to Mama and Aunt Solange. . . .

Eleven

In April 1917 America had declared war on Germany. To England and France, it was as though the Messiah had come. "The Yanks are coming, the Yanks are coming . . . and we won't be back till it's over, over there."

The song was in everyone's heart, that and "Keep the Home Fires Burning." And the war took a decisive turn for the better. With Germany on the defensive, a new hope was born.

Rubin's letters, however, had become more pessimistic. He wrote Magda that he sometimes despaired of the war ever ending, despaired at such vivid proof of man's inhumanity to man. Magda tried to cheer him up with news of Jeanette and her new success as an actress. She so much wanted Rubin to be proud of her. . . .

She was more dependent on Alexis, who was now the most influential force in her life. Her love for him, though platonic, was greater than for any other man with whom she had shared herself. Their relationship had a special quality that went beyond the flesh, because Alexis never stepped beyond the boundaries Magda imposed. . . . They had a deep and abiding friendship. She knew he had a mistress here and there, but they never discussed it.

Magda was most shocked at herself. Although she had tremendous desires, she hadn't slept with anyone since that night with Camail . . . it would be a year ago in November. . . .

* * *

In November Magda was to star in her own one-woman show. Alexis had put up the largest amount of money, and the balance was raised from Camail and a few other people, including Edward Goldstein—who had never before invested in a show.

The show was booked for a two-week run. By now Magda's name was no longer unknown, and all of London waited to see how she would handle her own show. . . . The finest director was hired . . . the best musicians . . . no expense was spared. . . . The proceeds of the first performance would go to the widow's and orphan's fund. And in fact, most of the money Magda made was donated to charity.

That night Magda sat at her dressing table, smoking one cigarette after another. She had asked that no flowers be sent in advance. Being Rumanian, she was a little superstitious. . . . Tonight could be so important.

When the first call came, Magda's heart beat painfully, though outwardly she was calm. She waited for her cue . . . a certain crescendo in the music. Suddenly she panicked; she had forgotten the lyrics to her first song. Nonetheless, she took her place. . . .

The curtain was raised on a blacked-out stage, as the music began to swell. Then a spotlight picked up Magda's face, her hair in studied disarray.

When she opened her mouth to sing, the lyrics came forth without effort, the lyrics she thought she'd forgotten. And from that moment on she sang to Rubin, to her memories of him. He had discovered her as she looked now, in the days when she'd literally had to sing for her supper. Her costume had cost a fortune, yet it looked like the same peasant blouse and tight skirt she'd been wearing when she met him, even to the slit on the left side, revealing her slender legs as she sat on a stool. . . .

She sang a song in French about a young man going off to war and leaving behind a girl who would become the mother of his child . . . if he didn't return, she'd keep her child as a symbol that he'd once walked on the earth.

She sang in Spanish, in Greek, in Russian. And because music is the universal language, the audience understood. Her eloquence only added to the meaning of the words. She sang as she had never sung before.

During the intermission, she was keyed up and excited.

Did the audience like her? Was their applause a sign of genuine enthusiasm? Alexis assured her that the answer to both questions was yes. And finally she sang a medley of English and American songs, her voice an instrument of love, of pathos, her face, with the incredible mane of hair, the face of women everywhere.

The applause was tumultuous. First one man, then another, stood, then a woman, until the whole house was on its feet, clapping, shouting their approval. Magda—spent and drained, she feared, of all emotion—took one curtain call after another.

She hurried back to her dressing room, truly surprised by the warmth of her reception. How kind they were to her, how generous. Alexis and Camail were waiting.

"Isn't it crazy?" she said. "I used to do the very same act in the dingiest café on the Left Bank . . . and you know what I got? My supper . . . and five francs a week."

"Life changes. . . ." said Alexis. "And thank God it does."

They waited while she changed behind a screen, chattering all the while.

"You've taken London by storm," said Camail.

"Have I?"

"You can have any role you want," said Alexis.

"But that's not what I want, Alexis."

"You can be a great actress. Other women would give their lives to have your beauty and talent."

She shrugged. "Perhaps. But I'm not sure I want a career on the stage. . . ."

"Aren't you thrilled with the sound of applause?"

"Of course; I'm human. But that's not *all* I want. Try to understand, Alexis. I want what I never had."

Alexis grimaced. "Tell me about your deprivations."

"All right. I want Rubin. I want my *petite* to have what I didn't. When she grows up I want her to be accepted in the best homes by the best people. I'm very ambitious for her—and for myself. . . . I love performing, but not as a career."

Alexis sighed. "Such a waste of talent. You're young, you'll get stardust in your eyes. This is not a little café in Paris."

"You're wrong," said Magda. "I was never young. I was

never a child. So don't tell me about stardust, I know what I want."

When she appeared again, she looked like Magda Hack . . . the elegant, patrician Magda. She was wearing a heavy silk gown, completely encrusted with iridescent beads. The high oval neckline receded to the back, plunging down to reveal her slim waist.

"You always amaze me, Magda. I can barely take my eyes from you."

"Thank you, Alexis. You've made the world smile for me. I've been gifted with many blessings, but you have been my true savior. And furthermore," she added, kissing him lightly, "you never demand anything in return."

It was less than he wanted, but he would settle for the crumbs. From her. That was the compromise he'd made when he fell in love with her.

Camail was almost as excited as Magda. He had seen his protégé become the toast of the city. "Magda," he said, "you were wonderful. I've finally decided that you must be a genius."

"It takes one genius, dear friend, to know another. . . ." They both had the wit to laugh.

She loved being the center of attention. . . . This was the life she wanted. To be needed, to be admired, to be *seen*. She'd come a long way, and she knew one thing: Magda Charascu of Bucharest—against an array of obstacles—had finally conquered London. . . .

CHAPTER

Twelve

What began as a two-week engagement became an extended run. The critics had outdone themselves in praising Magda's talent.

When April came, Magda thought of Paris in the spring, the daffodils in bloom, the chestnut tree-lined boulevards. . . . The war, it seemed, would never end. Though Rubin's letters still tried to make light of it, she knew he was suffering greatly. And she was right. . . .

He was fighting in the knee-deep mud of Verdun. The Germans were leaving their corpses on the field to disintegrate. Yesterday he had passed by the body of a German still in uniform, the hands and face were fleshless, the skeleton exposed. . . . He had seen a group of French soldiers devouring the flesh of a horse. God, oh God, strike us dead and be done with it . . . we've turned into savages.

In May of 1918 his unit moved on to another hell. . . . June was no different. July was unbearably hot. Soldiers fainted in the fields, their faces sunburned and raw. Rubin's only joy was the letter written by the hand of his daughter, her fingers guided by Magda:

"Dearest Papa, I'm three years old today. Mama shows me your picture. I love you, Papa. Your daughter, Jeanette Hack."

Then he read Magda's letter, "Dearest Rubin, It's impossible for us to realize what you're going through. . . . We pray for the end of the war. . . . I dream of you and

miss you every moment. . . . Solange sends her love. . . .
As always, Magda."

In August Edward Goldstein found a comedy Magda
was interested in.

On November 9, the first day of rehearsal, the Kaiser
abdicated. Two days later the Armistice was declared.
London was filled with people celebrating as the whole
free world rejoiced.

"How long will it be before Rubin comes home?"
Magda asked Alexis at dinner that night.

"It may take some time."

"Why?"

"There are always mopping-up operations, Magda. The
soldiers don't just head for home."

"I can't stand it . . . if that bastard Maurice gave a
damn, he'd see to it that Rubin came home at once."

"That wouldn't happen even if they were on good
terms."

"Why?"

"Because the wounded usually return first. Then the
prisoners of war have to be relocated. Many men are
needed for disbursements. . . ."

"What you're saying is Rubin might not be home for
months—"

"It's possible, I'm afraid. . . ."

In her room that night, Magda cried out her frustration . . . and her gratitude . . . for Alexis. . . .

January 1919

Opening night was tense, as usual. There were all the
chronic fears. . . . Would the actors remember their
lines? Would the audience laugh at the right times?
Would there be jeers . . . or cheers?

Tonight would be her real test as an actress. Magda
Charascu was to star in a play for the first time. After
tonight, she'd know for sure. . . .

But everything that could go wrong did. When the curtain rose she tripped on her way from the desk to the
window where she was supposed to be looking out, awaiting her lover. As she leaned against the window pane it

fell over into the snow, with her following it. When she finally climbed back into the room, she was covered with fake snow. She brushed herself off, angrily, but she did it with such a comic flare the audience thought it was intended, and a roar went up. Next the leading man had forgotten—incredibly but true—to button the front of his trousers, and when he bent down to propose marriage . . . well, the audience was in hysterics. Getting up, a lamp fell over . . . again laughter. The maid brought in a box of roses sent from another suitor and when Magda read the note she fluffed the lines in such a way the audience was convinced she was the best comedienne to come along since . . . heaven knew when.

When the play was over, Magda was in a state of shock. She had, she was certain, made an ass of herself. But the cheers continued as the curtain rose once again. The cast bowed in unison, but when Magda came out alone the bravos were ridiculous.

Back in her dressing room, exhausted, she said, "I think we played to an audience of idiots."

Alexis laughed. "You were brilliant. If you can only remember what you did and said, this is going to be the comedy of the season."

Magda looked back at him, then back over what had happened, and back at the performance, and began to laugh. And every time she tried to say something to Alexis, she doubled over; she couldn't stop. Finally, holding her stomach, she said, gasping for breath, "I couldn't possibly have done it if I'd tried. . . . I was so awful, I was funny. And all the time I thought they were laughing at me. Once I was so angry I wanted to walk off the stage or scream back at them . . . but they were laughing *with* me."

"Of course, because you did everything with such finesse. You were so serious they thought it was part of the act."

"Oh, Alexis, what would I do without you?"

He tried not to think about that, because when Rubin returned . . .

That night Magda gave the cast a party at the Savoy. She never allowed Alexis to pay for her parties. For Magda it was a thrill to spend the money. She spent it faster than she received it. There were charities, gifts for

Solange and Jeanette . . . a new jewel . . . a new fur. She threw money around like confetti on New Year's Eve. She seemed to live to be extravagant. Tonight she wore a dazzling white full-length Russian ermine. She was, after all, a full-fledged celebrity. She had earned her status, her fame.

The newspapers reported everything she wore . . . everything she did. . . . Invitations to her parties were a sure sign of status. Her companionship with Count Alexis Maximov was always played up, and Alexis thought, if only what the gossip-mongers hinted at were in fact true . . . what a happy man he would be.

The Maurice and Phillip Hacks were furious. What an everlasting curse she was, this Magda Charascu who had come into their lives. . . . There was no choice but to try to ignore her flagrant exhibitionism. . . . There was nothing else they could do. Each one of her triumphs brought new lines of worry to their faces. How long . . . ?

By March Rubin still hadn't returned. His letters seemed stilted and evasive, and Magda was frantic with worry. Everyone else was coming home. Why wasn't Rubin?

One day she found out. Anne excitedly handed her a letter from him.

"Thank you," she said, ripping it open.

My dearest Magda,

Please don't be upset, but I am in Calais. If I sound inarticulate, it's because I still can't believe the war is over. A week has past since I received orders that I could go home. Forgive me for not letting you know sooner, but I think I was afraid at the last moment something might go wrong and my orders would change. The army does that to you.

There was something else too. . . . I'm afraid I've withheld the truth from you, but now I must tell you what's happened. On November 10 I was wounded by a piece of shrapnel. I deliberately asked not to be sent home then because I looked so awful. For months my head was in bandages. I've lost about twenty percent of the vision in my left eye, and my upper lid is paralyzed and partially closed. There is a scar on my cheek which has faded, but

*not entirely. It has taken a long time, but now I've
learned to live with these injuries. I am, after all,
one of the fortunate ones. What's so strange is that I
survived the worst battles, but the day before the
Armistice I was wounded. But, my dearest, the
worst of my illness is now behind me, and I should
finally get to London within the next few days. I'll
be sent to the out-processing center near London before being discharged.*

With all my love, Rubin.

Trembling, Magda started to cry. All she could think
about was Rubin coming home. His wounds were forgotten; her mind refused to believe that Rubin could be
changed. He still had his vision. And a scar made a man
more attractive, more exciting. Still . . . she cried for his
pain . . . and out of relief. He was finally coming home.

She jumped out of bed and ran to Jeanette, picking her
up, smothering her with kisses. "Your papa's coming
home, *ma petite* . . . your papa . . ." She carried Jeanette into Solange's room. "Rubin's coming home. . . . I
can't believe it." She handed the letter to Solange, who
read it, tears of gratitude in her eyes.

"Thank God," she said, "he's coming back to us at last."

That night Alexis looked at the face of Magda with special love. The long years of waiting were written in her
eyes, and her face was radiant with anticipation. But for
Alexis, it was hardly a night for rejoicing. Rubin was coming home and he was losing the only thing he'd really ever
wanted. . . . But Magda had never belonged to him and
perhaps that made the parting even more painful than the
end of a physical love affair. In the years since he'd
known her, he had pretended each woman he'd slept with
was she.

Taking up his glass of wine he said, "I have an announcement to make. Tomorrow I shall leave on a much
deserved holiday."

Magda looked at him. She knew how much he felt
about her, and now he was sending himself into self-
imposed exile. Trying to keep her voice matter-of-fact, she
said, "You do indeed, my dear Alexis, certainly after what

you've put up with from me for so long. . . . Where will you be going?"

"To my villa in Cannes for a while and then on to Monte Carlo. . . . After that, who knows?"

"There's no place like Monte Carlo," Solange said lightly. "I used to love it. . . . When will you be leaving?"

"In a few weeks, I expect, or sooner. . . ."

Magda nodded, swallowed, and said, "Yes, well, I'm giving my notice to the producer tomorrow. . . . I want to give all my time to Rubin—"

"That's very sensible. . . . I know he'll be pleased with your decision. . . ."

Solange put in quickly, "I think we should all drink to . . . to new beginnings."

Rubin's train was due. Magda walked nervously back and forth at Victoria Station. Solange sat, holding Jeanette on her lap.

"Magda!"

It was Rubin's voice. Magda turned. . . .

A stranger was coming toward her. He was holding out his arms. It couldn't be Rubin, could it? Was this the man she had said good-bye to back in 1914? It didn't seem possible. He had changed completely. Magda couldn't hide the shock she felt. He was so thin, his uniform hung from his body. Lines of pain and suffering were permanently engraved on his face. The scar was deep; the damaged eye made her feel ill. His hairline had receded. . . .

In spite of his letter, Magda was totally unprepared. Still, his joy at seeing her was so affecting she began to weep. He kissed her over and over again, whispering, "Magda, Magda . . . how I've waited for this day. . . ."

She clung to this stranger, responding numbly . . . and thinking, in spite of herself, Dear God, is this the man I married? . . . the wonderful lover I met in Paris . . . ? the Rubin I hoped and prayed would come back . . . ?

Calling on all her acting abilities, she tried to rally to the occasion. "Welcome home, Rubin. . . . Darling, it's been so long." Taking him by the hand, she took a deep breath and said, "Now come and meet your daughter!"

"Give your papa the flowers, *ma petite*. . . . Go to

papa," Solange urged. The child knew and loved only the *word* "papa."

Holding out the bouquet, Jeanette walked toward the stranger . . . her "papa." "Welcome home, Papa. These are for you."

Bending down, Rubin drew her to him and held her close against him. In all his life there had never been a moment like this, nor would there ever be again. God had surely spared him to know this joy . . . this gift of love. . . .

"We've missed you, Papa . . . we've got a surprise for you. . . . Why are you crying . . . ? Are you sad?"

Rubin fought the tears as he looked at this tiny Magda . . . his daughter. . . . "No, my darling. I'm crying because I'm very, very happy." Kissing her, he turned to Solange. "Still slim and beautiful as ever, Countess. . . ."

"And you, Rubin Hack, are the most beautiful sight in the world." She could say no more.

Quickly, then, they walked to the Rolls and drove home.

Rubin could not believe it. Home. He was *home*. Slowly he went from room to room, holding Jeanette's tiny hand in his. It was as though he were seeing it for the first time. There was so much he couldn't remember . . . so much of what he had left. The paintings seemed more brilliant, the flowers more beautiful. He had forgotten what comfort was. A bath seemed a luxury he'd never known.

His old suits hung on his body like sacks. And when he looked at himself in the mirror, the face of a frightened stranger stared back. He was freshly shocked at his image. The scar looked even deeper and more discolored. He wanted to bury his reflection.

Then came the surprise—Deborah and Leon. The two brothers embraced like children who'd been apart for a very long time.

"Well, Leon, we survived."

"Yes, Rubin . . . we were the lucky ones."

Leon had been home only a week, after four long years of internment.

To Rubin the whole evening seemed unreal. The homecoming seemed more than he was prepared for. He couldn't adjust; even ordinary things seemed foreign. To sit at the head of his table, near his child, and look across at his wife . . . to taste the flavor of good food . . . to be with Leon and Deborah. . . . Everything good seemed to be a mirage, which would vanish in the night . . . disappear like a vision of heaven . . . or hell. . . .

Later, when Leon and Deborah had left, Rubin's feelings of alienation increased. The gentleness of the night seemed intimidating. As he lay in bed, he felt that he would never take anything for granted again.

Soon Magda was beside him . . . a moment he had dreamed of . . . yet somehow dreaded. . . . He was embarrassed by his body. . . . He felt that it was no longer an instrument for love-making. . . . The reflection of his face stared back at him . . . mocking him, taunting him. Now, at last, he was afraid to touch Magda for fear he would fail. He turned, took her in his arms . . . but it was no good. . . . Quickly he got out of bed and went into the bathroom, where he sat wiping away the perspiration. Face it. He was impotent.

Magda lay alone in the dark. She realized that the man she had waited for had been left somewhere on the fields of Flanders. Rubin Hack was as lost to her as if he were dead. She had seen the change today . . . tonight only confirmed it. . . . Even with Leon, Rubin had seemed vague and withdrawn, as though his mind was in another place.

When he got back into bed, he said, "I'm sorry, darling . . . coming home today was more than I was prepared for—"

"I understand, Rubin . . . believe me, I understand."

He was grateful that she couldn't see his face.

Eventually, they managed to fall asleep, each body a stranger to the other.

The next morning Magda went in to see Solange. She sat down on a blue satin chair.

Arranging herself against the pillows, Solange took a long look at Magda. "You've come to tell me something, yes?"

"Wise Solange . . ."

"And what is it?"

"I've waited five years for a man that I invented."

"What does that mean?"

"There is no Rubin Hack."

"Did you actually expect him to come back unchanged?"

"No . . . but I didn't expect this . . . this shell, this stranger. . . . No, I didn't expect that. . . ."

"Is it his looks that upset you?"

"Solange, Rubin is impotent. . . ."

"I take it you mean he was less than amorous last night."

"He couldn't even touch me."

"That sometimes happens to men who've been in battle."

"And what am I supposed to do until he recovers . . . *if* he recovers?"

"You sound angry, as if Rubin were to blame."

"I am angry, I admit it . . . we waited five years to say hello to a ghost."

"Do you love Rubin enough to help him through this . . . perhaps the worst time of all?"

Magda got up and paced the floor. "I'm human too, Solange. I've waited so long for a husband to come home and love me—"

"Rubin certainly loves you. Are you confusing sex with love?"

"But sex is part of loving—"

"Of course it is, but Rubin needs your help. . . . Are you willing to give it?"

Magda felt like screaming. "What do you want from me, Solange?"

"I want you to be a woman. I told you that once before. Maybe you no longer love Rubin because he's not quite so handsome. Maybe his scars repulse you."

"I'm so *confused* . . . maybe it's because we weren't together enough before Rubin enlisted. . . ."

"I think it would do you a great deal of good to think of your memories of Paris *before* Rubin found you."

Magda did not want to be reminded of those days, which, of course, was what Solange meant. "I resent your bringing that up, Solange. It isn't fair . . . I've been faithful to Rubin." She blocked out of her mind the one time with Camail. "I've been a good mother . . . I have."

"You've also been a pretty selfish and self-centered person who's very good when you get what you want. But when things aren't to your liking, I'm afraid you're capable of being just a bit ruthless. Rubin has changed physically, but he's still the fine human being he always was."

Magda seemed to be rooted to the floor. *"How dare you say such things to me?"*

"Because, my dear Magda, I think you lack gratitude, compassion. No one knows you as I do. . . . At this moment there are wives all over the world who will have to live with men who have lost their limbs . . . their eyesight. . . . Do you think that God has singled you out? You live too much in a world of make-believe, Magda. You wanted Rubin to come back to you exactly as he left. . . ."

"You've said quite enough, Solange. We can no longer be friends, not ever . . . not after this. . . ." And she rushed out of the room, slamming the door behind her.

Solange rang for Anne to get her suitcases. The time to leave the Hack household had come. She had wanted to go back to Paris the day the war was over, but she'd promised Rubin she wouldn't leave Magda until he returned. Well, he was back now, and she could go home, a place she longed to see again, no matter what she found there. It would be better than staying.

Rubin didn't seriously try to change her mind. She was, after all, French. She had been away a long time. But he hated to see her go. She had been a wonderful friend to him . . . and to Magda. He could never replace Solange.

Her parting from Jeanette was especially difficult. . . . *"Tante* Solange, please you can't go, I won't let you." It had been *Tante* Solange, after all, who had been there the night she was so sick and mama was at the theater . . . *Tante* Solange, and Uncle Alexis, who had brought her balloons, taken her to the Punch and Judy Show, the carousel. . . . She asked if she couldn't go with her aunt. . . . After all, she knew her better than she did her father, who could keep her mother company . . . and Solange had to tell her, try to tell her, how much her father needed her too, how very special fathers were for daughters . . . more than aunts . . . and daughters were for fathers. She told her that they would write one another and remember each other on their birthdays and on Christmas. . . . "There, now, isn't that a fine plan?" and Jeanette said, not very enthusiastically, that she guessed it was. . . .

And then there was Magda who in her fashion had surely loved Solange. And now she would have the full responsibility of her daughter, which she had feared even before her birth, which had made her resist having a child at all and might well have continued to if it had not been for the war and Rubin's imminent departure. "I'm truly sorry for the things I said, for the way I behaved," she said to Solange as they walked arm-in-arm toward the foyer just before Solange's departure. "I will miss you terribly, you must know that," and Solange thought, yes, for a time, but life goes on, and she thought too that she did love this strange, difficult, marvelous girl-woman, and wished devoutly that she had a little more wisdom, but corrected herself quickly, reminding herself that perfection had nothing to do with life. . . .

Magda stood now looking at her for what she was certain would be the last time. Her eyes were full of tears. "I love you, Solange. . . . I always will."

"Thank you, Magda, and I you, but there are others who also need your love. Give it with all your heart."

And then she was walking out to meet Rubin, who would see her to Victoria Station where she would leave for home . . . and, to his regret, out of his and Magda's immediate life. . . .

In the days that followed, Rubin's strength began to return. As life once again took on a semblance of sanity, his spirits began to lift.

He gloried in Jeanette. She gave him a sense of purpose he had thought was lost. He no longer felt so useless. They took long walks together, and the familiar London streets and parks did much to raise his spirits.

Magda noticed the changes. Thank God, she thought, at least he no longer sat for hours gazing into space. Their nights, however, were still the same. Loveless. Rubin's slight rally from his earlier depression seemed to have an inverse effect on Magda . . . perhaps because she could afford at last to allow herself some of her own true feelings without the awful guilt Solange had made her feel when she first voiced them. The facts were she was still rejected by the family except for Leon and Deborah, and even Leon seemed cooler of late. Rubin was an object of sympathy, but sympathy was not love or even strong affection. It was nobody's *fault* . . . damn it . . . but it was the way it was. And then there was Jeanette, constantly with Rubin now, almost as though Magda didn't exist. All right . . . she was his daughter and it was natural he should want to make up for lost time . . . but *she* had lost time to be made up for too. . . . God, to resent one's own child . . . and yet in a way she did—admit it. From the first, wasn't she more Rubin's than hers . . . his desire, not hers . . . ?

There were days when she felt she was breaking apart, and this was one of them. She decided to try to make some conversation with Rubin. "Have you seen Leon this week?"

"No, but I spoke to him."

"What did he have to say?"

"He wants to talk to me about some legal matters. . . ."

"Legal matters?"

"Yes. It's probably about the estate. . . ."

She had something important to talk about too, and she might as well bring it up now. "Rubin . . . ? I don't want to upset you . . . but . . . well, you know I never wanted to live here . . . and now that you're home . . . Rubin, please, let's go back to Paris. We'll be happier. You said you wanted to paint. . . ."

She waited for his reply. When there was none, she said, "Rubin, you seem to have left me."

"No," he said, "I haven't left you, but you're asking me to do something I simply can't do."

"I thought, eventually, that that was what you wanted to do. . . . In fact, you once told me your father advised it—"

"*He* advised, and besides, that was before the war. . . . I can never leave London, Magda. This is my home. I never realized before now how much I love it."

"And what about me?" she asked softly. "Don't I matter?"

He came to her, holding her. "You are my life, Magda . . . you and our child . . . but the past is over. No, dearest, I can't leave this place, it's like a safe port after all the—"

"But for me it's like a hell. I've nothing here, I've been ostracized. Even Leon seems to have changed toward me—"

"No, darling, that isn't true, it's your imagination. You've had a very difficult time, God knows, but now I'm home. . . ."

That night Rubin reached out for her. He held her close and kissed her . . . felt her . . . explored her. . . . And at last she felt him grow hard. She helped him find his way as he entered her. It was something less than fulfilling, but at least she felt some release. . . .

Later, Rubin said, "It will be better, Magda . . . I promise it will. You've been very patient. . . . I love you. . . ."

She was asleep before he finished talking.

In the morning, lying there beside him, she felt on the edge of tears. His well-meaning solicitude was more than she could bear. She could still feel the touch of his body . . . his near-fleshless ribs, his bony thin legs stretched across her. . . . Oh God, he was like a cadaver.

But Rubin was comparatively cheerful . . . at least he'd regained some of his self-esteem as a man . . . as he chatted about going to see Leon and then they'd all go for a walk in the park. . . .

Magda begged off. A headache.

As Rubin waited at the door of Leon's house, he wondered briefly why Leon had seemed to make a point of suggesting he come alone. He'd hardly have brought Magda along to a discussion of business matters in any case. . . . Magda had mentioned that Leon had been slightly aloof, but he was certain she, and he, were reading something into nothing.

It was the first time he'd been in Leon's house in years, he realized, as Leon now came forward to greet him.

"Rubin," he said, "how are you getting along?"

"I feel better every day. It's good to be back in London."

"Yes," said Leon, "isn't it . . . ? Sit down, Rubin, and let me tell you straight off the situation we're faced with."

Rubin sat down.

"Rubin, I'm afraid you're in for a rather bad shock, but I just don't know how I can delay telling you any longer—"

"What is it?"

"Our solicitor came round a few days ago to speak to me about you."

"Why didn't he call me?"

"Because I told him how ill you've been. The truth is . . . Magda has spent almost all of your inheritance. . . . In fact, there isn't enough money to pay your creditors."

Rubin was stunned. He shook his head in disbelief. "That can't be true. . . . When I left London there was fifty thousand pounds. How could she possibly have spent so much in less than five years?"

"She's been very extravagant, I'm afraid."

"Still, fifty thousand pounds? I don't believe it. . . . There must be a mistake."

"There's no mistake. I've been over all the accounts."

Rubin was completely bewildered. "That was all the money we had . . . she *knew* that. . . . Still, with the money from Father's estate, we should be all right."

"Unfortunately," Leon continued, taking a deep breath, "you and I were not here when Father was dying, and it seems Maurice talked Father into giving him power of attorney, since you and I were not here, in case Father died before he could make a new will. Which is exactly what happened."

"What does that mean . . . in concrete terms?"

"Father's will is null and void."

Rubin went white. "I don't understand. Is Maurice withholding my share? Where do I stand in terms of the estate?"

Leon finally answered. "Without, I'm afraid, a shilling."

"And Maurice has done this?"

"Before Father died, Maurice convinced Father that there should be someone to provide for the family and invest the money, in case we didn't return . . . especially for the sake of the children."

Rubin laughed. "You have no children at all, and I have one, so that means Maurice and Phillip."

"That's right."

"How did you find out about all this?"

"Shortly after I came home Maurice and Phillip called me into the conference room. Maurice did all the talking. He told me his side of the story."

"And how are you to be treated, Leon?"

Leon hesitated. ". . . The same as Phillip and Maurice."

"But not me . . . and you allowed them to do this to me?"

"Rubin, I fought with them. I said things I never thought I'd say to a brother. But Maurice will not give an inch."

"And what about Phillip?"

"Phillip is on your side, but Maurice has the power of attorney and, believe me, he will not budge. Worse, he's convinced that he's justified."

"But why? What have I—"

"It's his hatred for . . . Magda. It's become an obsession. . . . He's punishing you for her. He even had Magda investigated right after your marriage. He . . . they . . . know about her past—"

"I see. . . ." said Rubin. "Is there anything else?"

Leon gave Rubin an envelope containing a record of Magda's extravagances. "Try not to be bitter, Rubin. I'm going to help you. We'll work out something. . . ."

Rubin hardly heard him. He was trying to think about how to tell Magda, how to sort out his feelings. How could Maurice, his own flesh and blood . . . and Magda . . . In the car on the way home he berated himself for having been an incredibly stupid ass, for being so irresponsible as to expect a young woman, a girl, really—who knew nothing about the value of money—to take over control of so much. At first he was staggered by the contents of the envelope Leon had given him from their solicitor, a record of expenditures for parties, jewels, gowns and gifts, and then once again he tried to remain calm as he reminded himself that she had been left as abruptly on her own, in her fashion, as so many millions of others at the outbreak of war. Her life had been wrenched, too. . . . Still, he thought as he put the records back into the envelope and took up the package that Leon had also given him—somewhat reluctantly, he'd thought at the time—and tore it open to examine its contents, as much as he could justify or at least explain her spending—he'd try not to think of it as extravagances—he couldn't help feeling a resentment, even an anger. . . . Who, after all, wanted to come home to find himself without resources, stripped by his own brother, spent to the bottom by his young wife . . . ?

And now his nagging anger gave way to an eruption as his attention turned to the contents of the package . . . to pictures of Magda with Camail, of Magda with Alexis at her side after the opening of the one-woman show, and the newspaper caption about "LONELY WIVES LIVING OUT THE WAR IN THE ABSENCE OF HUSBANDS AT THE FRONT" (a headline that had infuriated Magda and Alexis both, at the time, but which, of course, they'd had no control over). Oh yes, he thought, she'd written him about her wonderful success on the stage and her new source of income, although apparently she'd squandered even that—but this was something else. . . .

He decided not to waste any time, and when he got home immediately confronted her with the contents of the envelope and package. The clippings caught her eye first, and she realized how they distorted the truth . . . those charming, so civilized and well-born gentlemen Maurice and Phillip Hack, and their charming and so civilized ladies had done their job well. Looking at Rubin, at the anger . . . anguish . . . in his eyes, she was for the moment panicked, terrified of him. . . . His cheeks were sunken, his eyes seemed never to leave her face. . . . She tried to explain about Peter Scott and how he introduced her to Camail, and how there had never been anything between her and Alexis, but the more she talked the worse it sounded, and the less he seemed able to believe her. . . . And then when he told her the truth of their finances, she was dumbfounded. How was that possible? Surely he was joking, though the look on his face clearly said he was not. It was, at that moment, a look of anger on the edge of rage, and rage on the edge of . . . hate? My God, yes, she'd spent money, but he'd told her they had a fortune, and most of what she'd earned herself she'd given to the war effort, thinking in some way it would help bring Rubin back to her sooner. . . .

Abruptly he seemed to subside, to look at her like a defeated man, which frightened and, frankly, disgusted her some. She listened without hearing as he repeated that there was no inheritance, that they could no longer go on living where they were, that he'd need her jewels to appraise and sell.

Feeling numb, she went to the safe and took out everything. She put the jewels on the table in front of him. Then, without a word, she left the room, walked down the stairs and out into the brisk afternoon air, forgetting to shut the door behind her.

She needed to think, to collect her thoughts, she told herself, but actually she had only one thought, intrusive, overwhelming. She located a public phone and called Alexis. The phone rang an eternity before . . .

". . . Hello."

Thank God he was home. "Alexis? This is Magda. I have to see you—"

"Speak up, Magda, I can barely hear you. Is everything all right—?"

"I wouldn't be calling this way if everything were all right. . . . Alexis . . . I must see you, I need you . . . now. . . ."

"Shall I send a car for you?" Clearly she was in no condition to explain at the moment.

"Yes, I mean no, tomorrow . . . at ten. Alexis—"

"I'll be there, Magda. Now, please try—" But she'd hung up.

When she got home she learned that Rubin was out, which she was thankful for. She tried to stay calm, not to think too much about what she was doing, had done, and was grateful for Jeanette's interruption with some talk about her day in the park with Miss Williams. Magda nodded, smiled and then told her to run along, that mama was tired, needed a rest. Oh my God, how she needed a rest . . . escape. . . .

At five o'clock Rubin came home, completely deflated, not a trace of the earlier flare-up. He even took complete responsibility for the fix they were in. He should have taught her more about the value of money before he went off. He told her that he'd sold the jewelry, and added, "Perhaps if we sell some of our other things there will be enough to take a small place. . . ."

She couldn't bring herself to answer him.

"And if we pull together—and with Leon's help, which he's promised—I can buy a small business or even get started again as a solicitor. . . . What do you think, Magda?"

She drew in her breath. "Whatever you feel is best. . . ."

* * *

The next morning at ten she was waiting for Alexis' car. When she reached his house his joy was apparent, though he did his best to control it until he'd heard her out.

She didn't keep him waiting. "Alexis, I'm leaving him."

His face masked his delight. "And when did you decide that?"

"I think from the moment I saw him . . . the day he returned—"

"How does one fall in and out of love so quickly, Magda?"

She looked at him, not realizing he wasn't so much asking a question as testing her . . . as she was herself. "I honestly believed I did love him. He took me out of one world and put me into another . . . and I liked the world he seemed to offer me. . . . When I met Rubin, you know what I was . . . I've kept no secrets from you. But when he got back . . . well, I finally realized it wasn't love at all. . . . I'd fallen in love with the physical part of a man . . . and his world . . . I really didn't even know at all." She took a sip of wine. "You and I, Alexis, have shared more together . . . without sex, though I must admit that I did confuse that with love, in fact I thought it was love. Maybe, if he hadn't gone away it might have grown, deepened, but who can say?"

"In other words, you've lived in a make-believe world?"

"Yes."

"And there isn't anything to be salvaged?"

"No . . . I'm sorry, but I simply can't stand him. I know that sounds cruel, but there's been cruelty on both sides. . . ." And she told him about the family, and how Maurice had swindled Rubin, how really cruel they'd been to her, worked from the beginning to destroy the marriage and drive her away. . . . And how she'd wanted to live in Paris but he'd insisted on staying in London for the family . . . the damned family that was destroying him too. . . . "I keep telling myself we'll both be better off, that with me gone maybe Maurice will change his mind about the money and—"

"And isn't the money also one of the reasons you want to leave?"

She stopped short, and looked directly at him. "Yes,

that's true, Alexis. I will not lie to you. I'm not going to live without love *and* money. I've been through poverty, I'm not going to be poor again."

"I admire your candor. . . . And what now?" he said, hoping her answer would be the one he'd waited years to hear.

"I want to live in Paris . . . I don't want a special bench in heaven as a martyr . . . I want to go away with *you*, if you want me. . . . If you don't, I'll go alone—"

"I want you, Magda. I always have, you know that. . . . But what about your child?"

She hesitated, thinking for a moment that he might properly have been referring to Rubin, who certainly wasn't a man, not any longer, and she was sorry but, as she'd said, heaven had enough martyrs. . . . But yes, what about Jeanette, her darling, Jeanette whom she loved but had to separate from before they were all destroyed. Damn it, she was no monstrous, unfeeling mother, but she was a woman and there was no way to preserve the woman and stay as the mother. . . . She couldn't really explain all this to Alexis now, not now, and so what she managed to get out sounded cold, colder than she felt or meant. . . . "Jeanette," she told him, "will get along without me, better, I suspect, than with me. She loves her father. And somehow, I'm not sure how yet, but somehow I'll manage to keep track of her, to watch over her . . . although I'm sure she'll come to hate me in time, the terrible mother who deserted her and her father. . . ."

Magda poured herself another port and drank it quickly. "Listen to me, Alexis. I didn't pursue Rubin. Believe me, it was the other way around. So do me the favor of not making me feel guilty. . . . And I repeat, once I'm out of his life I'm sure his precious family will reinstate him, he'll be forgiven his transgressions. This could turn out very well for him. . . ."

Alexis smiled. "Magda . . . you don't need to justify yourself . . . not to me. I love you, Magda. I want you. But I'm not Rubin. I'll indulge you, take care of you, love you. But understand this too . . . if you ever betray me I'll kill you." He said it so matter-of-factly that it almost sounded as though he might be joking, but Magda knew Alexis too well for that. He would do as he said. It was not a threat, it was a promise.

When their eyes met again, they had made their pact. "Now . . . you'll need a passport, which we'll get today. When would you like to leave?"

"As soon as possible."

"I'll make arrangements for tomorrow. First, we'll go to my villa in Cannes."

"Why not Paris?"

"Don't you suppose Rubin will wonder what's happened to you?"

"And Paris will be the first place he'll look?"

"I should think so. We can do without scenes . . . besides, it might be just the thing for you. . . . Life's been very difficult for you. . . ."

"Are you laughing at me, Alexis?"

"No, but I was thinking . . . it pays not to start a new life with illusions. When a man gambles, he should consider all the odds. Rubin didn't."

Somehow, she got through the night. The next morning, Rubin left early. She thanked God for that. She went in to see her daughter, hoping she would be as strong as she needed to be.

Jeanette was reading aloud to herself. For one long moment, Magda's determination wavered. This was the child to whom she had given life . . . a part of herself she was leaving behind. A tight knot formed in the pit of her stomach as she sat beside her daughter and took her hand. "*Petite* . . . Mama has something to tell you, and you must not cry. . . . Can you do that for me? Good. Now, Mama is going away for a little while. . . ."

"Can Daddy and I go with you?"

It was Magda, not the child, who was showing tears. "No, my love, Mama needs to rest, to go off for a while by herself. . . ."

"But when will you come back?"

Magda felt herself wavering, and for a moment actually thought of taking Jeanette with her, and then quickly realized how impossible that would be. My God, she didn't hate Rubin, and only if she wanted to kill him would she take the last remaining possession he had. Besides, once the infamous Rumanian had departed their sacred precincts, the Hacks would take her in completely, wipe out the memory, the existence, of her mother and she would at least be raised as a Hack, with all the advantages *that* would have. She would be legitimate, not an ersatz made-up lady like the girl from the Parisian gutter. . . . And, of course, they would never ever let her alone if she should be so foolish as to take their child away. They'd find her, and bring her back, and . . . She hugged her daughter, kissed her, told her that she'd soon be back home and that she'd send her postcards like Tante Solange, and quickly rang for Miss Williams to come and take her off for a nice long walk in the park, helping her on with her coat, buttoning it with unsteady fingers.

But just before going off with Miss Williams the child hesitated, stopped and came back to Magda. She put her arms around her and said, "I love you, Mama," almost as though she knew right along the truth behind the play-acting of adults.

"I love you too, *Petite*," Magda said, fighting back the tears, "and, now you must run along, mustn't keep Miss Williams waiting. . . ."

When Magda heard the footsteps disappear and the door close, she remained sitting on her daughter's small chair and looked about the room at the child's crayon drawings attached to the wall. This was Mama . . . this was Papa. . . . And this was Tante Solange. . . . They were all alike, except that Mama's hair was amber and brown, Papa's hair was thin and black, and Tante Solange's was gray and black. Their eyes were all very round, their lips thin and smiling. Their cheeks were all circles of red, and they all looked very happy. The sun was shining and the sky was blue and the grass was green . . . and . . . oh, God. . . .

The doorbell was ringing. Magda wiped away her tears. Good-bye, Jeanette Sara, she said to the empty room. She picked up the sable coat and left a note for Rubin on the bed. Then she went to the front door, opened it, shut it quickly, and went down the steps to Alexis' waiting car.

She did not allow herself to look back.

Rubin returned home a little before three. He took off his hat and hung it in the hall closet. The house was very still. Perhaps Magda was in Solange's room. He knocked softly and waited. When there was no response he gently opened the door and found the room empty. Then he went to his room. Magda was not there either. He rang for Anne.

He looked at the things they had so carefully bought . . . possessions. Now many of them would have to be sold. But they were only material things, after all. Thank God he still had his wife and child. Soon he'd perhaps have a small business. In time things would adjust themselves; he and Magda would soon be as close as they used to be. It was just a matter of time.

"Yes, sir?" Anne interrupted his thoughts.

"When will my wife be back?"

"I don't know, sir. She didn't tell me."

"And Jeanette? Miss Williams?"

"I don't know that either, sir. . . ."

"Thank you, Anne."

Tomorrow he would have to give the servants notice. Tonight he'd tell Magda about the tobacco shop he planned to buy, with the help of Leon. It was old and established, and the figures looked good. With a little thrift, and a little luck, things would work out all right. . . .

When Jeanette came in, he was making out a list of the heirlooms he hoped to save.

"Hello, my darling," he said when she ran into his arms, hugging her tight against him. "Was Mama with you?"

"No," said Jeanette. "She's gone away. . . ."

"What? Where?"

"She's gone away," said Jeanette, "for a little while. That's what she said, Papa."

"When?" Was it possible? His heart began to pound.

"This morning . . ."

Rubin didn't hear the rest of what Jeanette said as he rushed into the bedroom and looked in the closet. Almost all her clothes were gone. He went through the dresser drawers. They, too, were almost empty. Then he saw the letter on the bed. Taking it out of the envelope, he dropped heavily into a chair and began to read.

Dear Rubin:

You must believe this has not been an easy decision for me to make, but there was no way to go on pretending. We could not go on living together. I hate

*London. It never was, never could be, home to me
. . . any more than Paris could be home to you.
Maybe the war was responsible. I don't know who
or what is to blame, or how it happened, but we
simply are wrong for each other. Both of us went
through too many changes, or maybe not enough. . . .
I hope you find some happiness and peace in
your life, Rubin, but it's better to part while we're
still young enough to make a new start. I truly am
sorry for anything I did in your absence that has
caused you pain. I hope you can forgive me. I leave
you our daughter. Please try not to hate me.*

Magda.

He cried out like a wounded animal. Jeanette was terrified. He tore what was left of Magda's clothes into shreds.
With one sweep of his hand, he knocked everything off
the dressing table. The crystal perfume bottles went crash-
ing to the floor . . . the mirror tilted over and broke into
fragments, distorting his image as he looked at himself. He
ran through the foyer, and Jeanette cried out, "What's
wrong, Papa?" He neither saw nor heard. Miss Williams
picked up the sobbing child and held her. . . .

"Magda . . . Magda . . . why have you done this to
me?" Over and over, he asked the same question. He ran
out of the apartment, down the stairs and into the street,
screaming her name.

When they finally caught up with him, it took three
bobbies to subdue Rubin. He continued to scream out
Magda's name. He began to have delusions. He tried to
free himself from the enemies holding him. . . . He had
killed before and he could again. . . .

A crowd had gathered to watch this crazy, insane man
struggling to free himself as a fourth bobbie came running
up. Finally, the ambulance came and, with the aid of the
attendants, they were able to get Rubin into it and strap
him down inside. By the time the ambulance reached the
hospital, Rubin had already been sedated. . . .

When he woke up, he was looking into the eyes of
strangers.

"Rubin, Rubin, it's Leon. . . ."

They were trying to fool him. . . . He knew Leon was

in a prison camp, and now so was he. . . . Ssh, play
dead. Don't let them know you're alive. . . .

"Rubin, they told us you were here. They found your
identification. That was how they knew to call. . . ."

They were lying . . . Get out of here you damned
Krauts . . . The doctor gave Rubin another injection to
calm him, and finally he was asleep again.

Leon was ashen white as he and Phillip left the room.

"As though Rubin hadn't been through enough already,
now this. . . ." Phillip held up his hands in a gesture of
despair. He knew what he'd done to hurt Rubin . . . he
despised himself. But then he'd had Matilda to contend
with. She'd even tried to stop him from seeing Rubin.

"I must go and look after Jeanette," Leon said. "Do you
want to come with me?"

"I'd go if I thought it would do any good, but perhaps
it's better if you go alone. There'll be less confusion that
way. But if there's anything I can do, please call."

"Thanks, at least for coming, Phillip."

"I am Rubin's brother, after all."

Leon shook his head. "A shame you didn't remember
that when Father was dying." And then he was walking
down the dimly lit hall, casting a long shadow on the wall.

Miss Williams had seen Magda leave in Alexis' car. She
had been watching from a window. She gave Leon all the
details, including Rubin's behavior. It was, after all, her
duty.

Leon thanked her, shaking his head in disbelief. What
kind of human being could have done such a thing . . .
could have literally abandoned her child, her husband . . . ? He and Deborah would have given anything
to know the blessing of a child, and Magda had given Jeanette up for a man. My God, he thought, like Medea, except
she did a complete job . . . she killed her children. . . .

He saw the carnage in the bedroom. He saw the open
letter from Magda, which he picked up and read. When
he finished reading he felt ill. Rubin had been willing to
give up his life, and for this?

Jeanette was sleeping. Leon instructed Miss Williams to
get both the child's things and her own ready to move to

the Leon Hacks'. "She, and you, will live with us until we decide what to do. . . ."

He picked up Jeanette and carried her down. In her sleep she called out, "Papa." Leon, getting into the car, said, "Yes, my baby . . . yes."

"Are you up to talking about what happened?" Deborah was saying to Leon in their bedroom.

"Yes, but I don't know where to begin, the story is so incredible. The fact is, Magda has gone off, she's left Rubin."

Deborah was speechless. It was indeed incredible. Finally, she found her voice. "Leon, I don't understand—"

"Neither do I, but the shock of her leaving must have been too great for him. He's gone . . . well, a little mad." He would not describe the terrifying scene at the hospital.

"You mean he's had a . . . a nervous breakdown?"

"Yes."

"Oh, dear God . . . how serious is it?"

"We don't really know, but he seems to be quite ill." And then he did tell her about the letter Magda had left and about Alexis.

"Oh, yes," said Deborah. "I met him once with Magda, he helped her go on the stage. . . . Well, you did the right thing bringing the child here. We'll care for her like our own till Rubin's better. . . ."

"Yes . . . tomorrow Phillip and I are going to have Rubin taken to a private sanatorium. I'll look after the apartment while he's away. This is the time Rubin needs all the love and understanding we can give him. . . ."

Poor Rubin. Who can really console him . . . ? I used to like Magda, I really did . . . I defended her to the family, and I refused to speak against her. After all, she was Rubin's wife. But I must say this changes my feelings. . . . I'm not blaming her for taking a tremendous dislike to Maurice and the rest of the family, she was treated so shabbily. But on the other hand . . . a husband, and a child . . .

In the three months Rubin had been at the sanatorium, his behavior had changed. He no longer lived in a world of delirium. He recognized Leon, but sometimes Leon almost wished that Rubin had never left his world of fantasy, because his depressions seemed even worse than his delusions. He sat for hours in a chair, without moving or speaking. Leon tried to cheer him up. . . . He told Rubin about Jeanette, about how much she missed him, and how she constantly spoke of "Papa." But Rubin just stared into space as though nothing mattered. . . .

Leon shielded Rubin from the fact that he and Deborah had encountered much pressure and criticism from the family for taking Jeanette in. Magda's scandalous behavior only reinforced their distaste for the child . . . Magda's child. Sylvia and Matilda pointed out to Deborah that fact of life.

Phillip, to his credit, argued with Matilda that Jeanette was hardly responsible for her mother, but Matilda would have none of it. "I don't understand you, Phillip. This child is as great an embarrassment to us as her dreadful mother was. She's a constant reminder. And if Deborah sends her to Ramsgate, our children will not attend."

"You're being very unkind. Jeanette has neither a father nor a mother, and if it weren't for Deborah and Leon, God only knows what would have become of her."

"I find all this very touching," said Matilda, "but may I remind you of a few things? To start with, if Rubin hadn't married that slut, none of this would have happened. But he did, and it's for him to take the full responsibility for the girl, and not force her down our throats. Our children should not have to grow up with such a stigma. And while we're on the subject, would you explain to me this sudden about-face in your attitude toward your brother?"

"What he did no longer matters . . . I remember Father saying that we wouldn't like to suffer his dreams. Rubin's already been through enough hell, and I'm not going on with this vendetta."

"Well, you lost an arm. What did Rubin go through that a million others didn't? And you weren't too opposed to Maurice's plan at the time. You certainly went along with him."

"I did, and I've despised myself for it ever since. I did a terrible thing to Rubin, but I won't hurt him any more—"

"That's very noble, Phillip. But let me tell you something. If you want me to be your wife . . . I mean, in the true sense of the word, then I would caution you. I won't accept this child in my house any more than I would have accepted her deplorable mother. I hope we understand each other." Matilda walked out and slammed the door.

Phillip buried his face in his hands. It seemed to him that Matilda's righteous indignation was just as callous and calculating as any behavior of Magda's. How could Matilda—or anyone—reject this child so totally on grounds that had nothing to do with the child? Where was his wife's compassion, her maternal instinct? Still, she was his wife, and in spite of it all she would have to come first.

He remembered going to see Rubin with Leon when he'd been in the sanatorium only a month. The only time Rubin had spoken was when he saw Phillip come in. Rubin had gotten up from his chair and had actually lunged at Phillip, screaming, "Get out! I don't want to see you again . . . you made me lose my wife. . . ." It took an injection to calm him down, to provide Phillip with *his* escape.

Tonight, Phillip could find no place to hide.

Life for the Hacks had indeed changed. When the holidays came, the family was divided. At the Rosh Hashana and Yom Kippur services, Deborah, Leon and Jeanette sat in a separate pew. The other Hacks sat in their customary places. Deborah and Leon were excluded from all family dinners and functions. They had taken over, in a way, the old roles of Rubin and Magda as family pariahs. However painful Deborah found this situation, she accepted it. Except for Leon, Jeanette had become the most important person in the world to her. As the months passed, Deborah came to love Jeanette as though she was her own. Jeanette, however, did not go to Ramsgate. Not because of the threats, but because Deborah refused to send her to a school where Magda's reputation would be an indirect factor. What pleased Deborah most, though, was the way Jeanette seemed to have adjusted to her new environment.

What Deborah did not know was how Jeanette secretly cried herself to sleep at night. She could not forget Magda. She dreamed about her mother. In her mind, she could still see her getting dressed to go out, remember the smell of her perfume. Life had become very confusing.

She loved her mother, and yet she could not understand why Mama had never kept her promise to send her the postcards. And why was Mama gone for so long? Whenever she asked Uncle Leon or Aunt Deborah they gave her some vague, funny answer and changed the subject. She also missed Papa, desperately. And she couldn't understand why her other relatives passed her by on their way to and from temple. When she attended Sunday School, her cousins wouldn't speak to her, although she longed to know them.

One night at dinner Jeanette asked, "Uncle Leon, when am I going to see Papa?"

"Soon, darling."

"But you've been saying that for such a long time."

"But this time, it's sooner than you think. This time, it's next week."

Jeanette counted the days. When the right day finally came, she stood at the window until she saw the car. Then she ran to the front door and opened it. Leon got out first, followed by Rubin, who was very weak and unsure of himself. He had recovered to the point that the doctors wanted him to live in a more natural atmosphere, but he was far from well. Leon had been warned that Rubin would have lapses into depression from time to time. The best therapy would be being occupied, and during the last few months Rubin had taken up painting again.

"Papa . . . Papa!" Jeanette ran outdoors and into Rubin's arms. At first he couldn't respond. She looked exactly like Magda. Then, suddenly he lifted her high off the ground and held her tight against him. After that, Jeanette wouldn't leave her father's side for a moment. She loved Aunt Deborah and Uncle Leon, but not like Papa. With him she felt so safe that it didn't even matter if her cousins or her aunts and uncles didn't like her. Papa wouldn't let them be mean to her. . . .

As the weeks went by, Rubin began to think about the future and decided to have a talk with Leon. He waited until the two of them were alone. "Leon, I've been thinking . . . the time's coming when I must find a place for myself and Jeanette."

Leon was shocked. Rubin wasn't ready to take care of

Jeanette. He was scarcely able to take care of his own needs. "I'm happy you feel strong enough, Rubin, but I would suggest that you stay with us a little longer—"

"No, Leon. I've thought this out carefully. I must get on with making a home for Jeanette."

"How would you earn a living?"

"Well, I have always loved to paint and I believe I could make a fair living at that. Some of my recent canvasses are good enough to sell, and I believe someone would be willing to handle my work. . . ."

Leon got up and walked to the window. Who would handle Rubin, much less buy his work, he thought, but he answered quietly, "In the meantime, though, how could you support yourself and the child? I'm more than willing to help out, but you've rejected my offer to help—"

"I've got the money left from the sale of the furnishings."

"But that's not enough to last you for any length of time. And, painful as this might be for you, Jeanette needs the comfort of a mother. Deborah's been able to provide that. Jeanette is only five now, but soon she'll be growing up. Why not stay here a little while? When you're feeling yourself again and not so tired we'll look for another small business—"

"No, I don't want to go into business, Leon. I don't want to be with people. What I want to do is *paint*."

"All right, Rubin. We'll have the top floor made into a studio and you can paint there."

"*No*, I want my own home—"

"But how would you cook . . . clean? You have a child, after all."

"I know. And I have the need to try to find my self-respect."

How could one argue with that? "All right . . . we'll find a place for you. But will you agree to this? Will you leave Jeanette with us until you're settled?" He was asking *until*, but he meant *forever*.

Rubin thought carefully about the child his life now revolved around, and he knew he couldn't reasonably disagree with what Leon proposed. And he would, after all, be near her, even though she lived with Deborah and Leon. . . . At least he could see her and spend time with her. They could go to synagogue on Saturdays and spend the day . . . on Sunday they could go out to the country on picnics . . . there was the theater. . . . If he truly loved her as he said he did, then she must continue to stay with Deborah and Leon.

The next day Rubin found a shabby attic room. When Leon complained that it wasn't adequate, Rubin said he felt thoroughly comfortable there and that the light was good for his work. Leon said no more. . . .

CHAPTER

Thirteen

It was dawn. Magda stood at the French doors in her bedroom, looking out. Even the Seine, which could be seen from her window, seemed restive. Hers was a restlessness she was familiar with. . . . Her dreams had been turbulent, angry . . . she tried to clear her head.

Magda, why do you stand in the way of your own happiness . . . ? Alexis has, after all, given you everything. . . . You hadn't even known the Isle of Saint Louis existed until he brought you to this place. . . . You've become a successful Parisian hostess, as Alexis promised you'd be, as the Hacks never wanted you to be in London. . . . You live in one of the great houses of Paris, a house Alexis' own mother and father lived in . . . it was his legacy, and now you're chatelaine, replacing a mistress born to the aristocracy . . . and still you aren't content. . . . Alexis even arranged to change your name legally to Margot Maximov so that no one would question you, so that you would be free from your past . . . the *Countess* Margot Maximov. . . . He's been so clever in covering your tracks that no one in Paris questions your marital status . . . he not only invented a past, but paid to have it documented. . . . You entertain royalty . . . you're accepted in the most distinguished salons in Paris. There's nothing Alexis hasn't done to make you happy. And *still* you're the most wretched woman on the face of the earth . . . because he can't give you the thing you want most in all the world . . . your child. . . .

"Good morning, *cherie*."

She was brought back to reality by the sound of Alexis' voice and turned to face him. How handsome he was, even better looking, if possible, than that first night when Camail had introduced them . . . at the Savoy after the showing of that unfortunate painting. She cringed now when she thought of how she had embarrassed Rubin, although at the time it was to embarrass his family, not him. . . .

"Why are you up so early?" she said.

"I never can sleep when I find you're missing. Now, why are you standing there in that flimsy gown with the windows open . . . ? Get back into bed, or you'll catch cold."

She kissed him, then got under the covers as he closed the French doors.

Soon they were snug in bed together. Being held by him seemed to comfort her. Pretending not to show her discontent was not easy, but she would never let him guess her secret longings. He was more than entitled to be spared that. . . .

"Alexis, darling, you've been so good to me. . . ."

"You're quite right, my dear," and he squeezed her. "By the way, don't forget, we're lunching today with the Eaubonnes . . . then we're going to the auction. I want to bid on that large bronze for you—"

"For *me*? For you, darling. When we finally finished doing this castle of a house I remember your saying you couldn't look at another antique or objet d'art."

"Quite true, but I have the prerogative of changing my mind, no less than a woman. When I saw that bronze at the preview showing last week, I knew I was going to have it."

"And, my dear Count, do you *always* get what you want?"

"Usually . . . if I wait long enough. Now come over here and kiss me."

"Oh, Alexis," she said with an elaborate sigh, "you're all I need."

"Are you sure . . . ?"

For a moment there was a look in his eyes—she'd seen it before—that made her feel he could see into the depths of her thoughts . . . into her very being . . . that she could really hide nothing from him. She drew him against her and answered softly, "I'm sure, Alexis . . . I'm sure," trying—but not succeeding—to convince herself.

At breakfast, she said, "Alexis, I'm going to see Solange."

Alexis continued to scoop out his egg from its shell. "How do you know she'll see you? She's very loyal, you know, to Rubin. . . ."

"True . . . but I have such a deep fondness for her. We went through a great deal together. . . . And if she refuses to see me, well, *c'est la vie*. . . ." The bravado was somewhat more obvious than she'd intended.

"That's very mature, dear."

"Thank you, Alexis. You make things so easy for me . . . but when everything is said and done, you're all that matters. As I said . . ."

"Am I . . . ?"

Magda placed the call herself. Finally a voice answered. "Hello?"

"Solange? This is . . ."

"Yes, I recognize the voice."

"Solange, there's no need for us to play games. I want very much to see you."

There was no immediate answer. . . . Then: "Please come around any time, I'll be here."

"Later today then?"

"Yes, any time . . ."

Magda sat with the silent receiver in her hand, her heart pounding so hard she thought she might faint.

Solange lived on the other side of Paris, in the Arrondissement on the Avenue Foch. As the Rolls crossed over the Pont Sully, then sped along the Champs Elysées, Magda directed Pierre through the tube to stop at the perfumery. There she bought a bottle of Solange's favorite scent.

As she stood at Solange's front door, it took a few minutes for Magda to summon the courage to ring. When Solange opened the door, Magda was afraid her knees would buckle.

"Solange," she said, "I'm so happy to see you. . . . May I come in?"

"Please do. . . . I told you when we said good-bye in London you would always be welcome."

Seating herself on the large bergère, Magda waited.

"Do you still take port?"

"Please."

As Solange poured the wine, Magda placed her gift on the coffee table and looked around. The furnishings were still in impeccable taste, but everything seemed to be worn with age. A stale, musty odor of liniment hung in the air. The brocade on the chairs was threadbare, and on one wall there was evidence that a painting had recently been removed. Poor Solange, she must have had to sell it. . . .

Over port, the two women sized each other up. Solange looked down at the gift-wrapped box on the table. She picked it up and took off the wrapping.

"Thank you for remembering," she said.

Magda felt stupid and ridiculous . . . embarrassed now. . . . Perfume was probably the least of Solange's needs. "How are you getting along?" she said.

"My arthritis is worse," said Solange, "but somehow I seem to manage."

"I'm living in Paris now," said Magda.

"My dear, I know. Your arrival hardly went unnoticed by the press . . . Count and Countess Alexis Maximov in front of their mansion on their own little Isle of Saint Louis, in the heart of Paris . . . Count and Countess Maximov at home, entertaining their guests at a lawn party . . . the Count and Countess at the opera . . . at the races. . . ."

"Please stop, Solange. I didn't come here in anger."

"Why did you come? You've been in Paris for months. Why now?"

"Because I had to see you."

"I've been here since I left England."

"I know. I should have come sooner."

"What kept you from doing so?"

Magda swallowed. "Fear, I suppose . . . and guilt. . . ."

"But suddenly you've summoned up the courage and overcome the guilt?"

"It didn't just happen today . . . I've thought of you often, and wanted very much to see you."

"Why? Are your new friends so boring?"

"It wasn't boredom that brought me. . . . But I need

something from the past. Friends . . . reminders. I'm not complaining, Solange, but it's almost as though I no longer exist. My name is gone . . . my roots. . . . Now I even come from a noble Polish family, isn't that wonderful? Please don't laugh, though God knows nobody is more entitled to. . . . I know how you feel about me, Solange, and I can't blame you. But we've shared so much together, and I suppose I really came here today to try and . . . how do you put it . . . ? bind up the wounds. . . ."

"I must tell you, Magda, I find it very difficult to forgive what you've done. Aren't you happy with Alexis?"

"I could be . . ."

"*Could* be? My God, Magda, how much do you want? He's given you everything."

"Not everything, Solange. I want my child."

"But that was the choice you made when you left Rubin. You must learn, Magda, that you can't have the world."

"I know . . . but . . . oh, Solange, how do I live with it?"

"I find no comfort in your grief, Magda . . . quite the contrary . . . but the *way* you left Rubin, regardless of your reasons . . . he has been very ill, you know."

"How do you know that?"

"I've been in touch with Leon, as you might imagine."

"Tell me, *everything.*"

"Are you sure you want to know?"

"It will be worse if I don't."

"Well, then . . . after you left, Rubin went berserk . . . in fact, he was in a sanatorium for a year. Recently he's been living with Leon, but now he's taken a garret in the East End of London, where I suppose he hopes to paint. No one knows for sure that he's recovered, I'm afraid. . . ."

Magda wept softly. "What about . . . my daughter Jeanette?"

"She's living with Deborah and Leon . . . and has been since Rubin's illness. . . ."

"Dear God, she'll be seven this July. . . . I suppose she writes to you?"

"Yes, in a most delightful scrawl. She's very bright."

"Oh, Solange, tell me what I can do to get her back."

"I don't want to be unkind, Magda, or overly harsh, but you must face it . . . you gave up your right to any claim when you abandoned her and Rubin. If you try to get her back, Leon will certainly fight you . . . and how would such notoriety affect Jeanette . . . ?"

Magda was trembling, although she knew Solange was right. "May I see the letters from Jeanette?"

Solange got up, opened a large boule box on the desk and took out a packet of letters. Magda selected one at random. . . .

Dear Tante Solange,

I miss you so much. I love Aunt Deborah, but she's so sick, I have to be quiet. At night I dream that Papa will get well and Mama will come back from her long holiday so we can go home. Then you could live with us the way you used to. It would be such fun. Please send me another postcard. I love the pictures. Good night, dear Tante Solange. Your niece,

Jeanette Sara Hack.

There was nothing more to say. Magda put the letter back in its envelope, stood, and handed the packet to Solange. "Thank you for your kindness. I do love you, Solange . . . I hope you'll see me again."

"Of course, my dear. The problem is not between us. . . ."

Alexis was not there when she arrived home. She was grateful for that. She didn't want to face him, or anybody else. She went to the wine cellar and fetched a bottle of vintage champagne. On her way to the salon, she took a crystal goblet from the cupboard. She collapsed into the large wing chair before the fireplace, uncorked the unchilled bottle and watched as the bubbles danced in the liquid poured into the glass. She took a long sip, almost draining the glass, then another, and another. . . .

The reception that night at the Embassy was festive. Magda was exquisitely gowned in black velvet trimmed with ermine. Her diamonds and pearls dazzled. She was flushed with too much champagne, but no one could have guessed the reason.

As they danced, Alexis said, "You're very gay this evening, my love."

"And why shouldn't I be?" Her voice was somewhat slurred. "I'm with a most unusual man. In fact, Alexis, I believe you're the handsomest man here. Please hold me a little tighter. . . ."

Supper was served and as they stood holding their plates in their hands an unusually handsome young man approached Alexis.

"Count Maximov, I'm delighted to see you."

"And I, you, Monsieur Dupré. May I introduce my wife, Countess Maximov? My dear, this is Monsieur Jean-Paul Dupré."

Magda extended her hand. *"Enchanté,* monsieur."

The countess, Jean-Paul decided, was a remarkable beauty. Imagine a man the age of Count Maximov possessing this creature. But before he could speak to her, his partner claimed him for the next dance.

"May I have some more champagne?" said Magda.

"I think you've already had enough."

"Now, Alexis, I always know when I've had enough . . . be a dear and find a waiter. . . ."

Alexis noted the dark circles under her eyes, despite her expert camouflage. He summoned the waiter.

"Who is Monsieur Dupré?" she said, "and why do they invite children to diplomatic functions?"

"For your information, my dear, Dupré is a member of the diplomatic corps—"

"He can't be more than seventeen or so. . . ."

"I don't know his age, but all diplomats are not necessarily white-bearded old men."

"Whatever you say, Alexis . . . and now will a real man please take me home and make love to me?"

The next day Magda put through a call to Camail. When he answered, she tried, with an effort, to assume her old light-hearted, teasing Magda role. "Do you know who this is?"

"Of course I do . . . her highness the Countess Maximov—"

"Camail, stop your jokes. This is *Magda.*"

"Oh, Magda! How silly of me. But since you left without saying a word, you must forgive me my faulty memory. What can I do for you . . . this time?"

"I don't blame you for being angry with me, Camail. I know I was inconsiderate. . . . It's unforgivable that I haven't been in touch. Sometimes I seem to do all the wrong things . . . or not do the right ones—"

"Why, Magda, how contrite you sound. I'm not sure I like you this way. It isn't your customary role. I prefer the tempestuous, willful Magda. But forgive me, you called . . . for a favor, yes?"

"Yes."

"Well, at least that sounds like the old Magda."

"Camail, *please* . . . I want you to do a portrait of my child."

"Well, well, it just shows how wrong one can be. Somehow I don't quite connect you with the role of motherhood, but of course life has its surprises—"

"Please, Camail, *please* let's stop all this fencing about. I'm sorry you're angry with me, and I understand . . . but, please, Camail, I want a portrait of my child. Very much . . ."

"And how do you suggest I get her to sit for me? By kidnapping her? I assure you her aunt and uncle, decent souls though they are, aren't likely to be cooperative. What should I tell them, the Countess is having her many regrets . . . ?"

Magda was on the edge of tears. "Camail, stop punishing me. It will do neither of us any good. I've thought about it carefully, Camail. . . . Couldn't Peter Scott take a picture of her while she's in the park, say, that you could use for a model?"

"Well, that's the old Magda—the one with the great imagination. I'll tell you what—I shouldn't but I'll see what I can do—"

"Thank you, Camail. From my heart . . ."

"From where . . . ?"

"That's unkind, Camail. I'm sorry you're still so angry with me. But what really matters is that you're willing to help. I'm grateful, Camail, even if you find it difficult to believe I'm capable of such an emotion." And then she quickly told him where to send the portrait and hung up.

On the other end of the phone, Camail, a half smile on his face, shook his head and slowly replaced the phone on its hook. Magda was a difficult woman to forget. One of the very few such in his life. . . .

Through his chauffeur, a retired private investigator, delighted now with his unofficial though familiar assignment of surveillance, Camail learned that the little Hack girl spent the time with her father in Kensington Gardens on Saturdays and Sundays from about eleven in the morning until mid-afternoon. Camail immediately gave this information to his photographer friend Peter Scott, who the following Saturday provided Camail with a roll of excellent film.

A month later Magda received a large package. When she opened it up and looked at the painting she thought she would faint. The canvas was done in somber grays. A man, slightly bent, held the hand of a small girl, their backs to the viewer. The frame and the velvet mat were black. Magda sat down heavily. Camail has done this to punish me. Dear God, when will it stop? The Hacks despise me, and rightly. And this is Camail's way of telling me. . . . Oh, Camail, I could kill you . . . I could kill you for doing this to me.

It took her weeks to recover.

One morning, as she lay in bed, her maid brought a package to her. Somehow without even looking she knew it was from Camail. With trembling hands, she opened it.

This time she saw the face of her child, the lovely dark hair framing a tender, innocent face. The colors were soft pastels. And although the eyes were Magda's . . . the overall resemblance was to Rubin . . . the handsome Rubin of past years. Magda took in every light and shadow, every contour of the sweet face. Hugging it, she wept tears of love and longing. . . . At least she had this.

She went to her desk, propped the painting up against the desk lamp and called Camail to thank him for giving, in a way, a part of her child back to her.

Fourteen

Not a day went by that Leon didn't see his brother. With the passing of the years, Rubin seemed to be mostly content. Watching his daughter grow up was the one great joy in his life. If time had any meaning at all, it was on her birthdays. Once a year he could forget himself, seeing her eyes gleam in the candles' light just before she blew them out. . . . How many had there been? Eleven? Twelve? Yes, twelve. Childhood's end. . . .

Rubin sat in the park on his small canvas chair, his painting before him on an easel, chatting with Leon. From time to time, as he and Leon talked, he glanced at Jeanette. She caught his eye and smiled, then returned to her letter writing.

> *Dear Tante Solange:*
>
> *Tomorrow I'll be thirteen. Papa and I are going to Scarborough. Aunt Deborah and Uncle Leon have given their permission. It will be my birthday gift. I feel quite grown up today. Thank you so much for the presents, especially the pearls. . . .*

As always, Solange called Magda the morning the letter came. Magda stopped in during the afternoon to read it. She sat in Solange's bedroom. Solange had spent the last few days in bed, her arthritis so painful she could barely walk.

When she finished reading, Magda put the letter back

into its envelope. She pressed it to her bosom, as though by doing so she was holding Jeanette close. She looked up, tears in her eyes. "Where have the years gone, Solange? Imagine, our little doll is already thirteen. . . . She loves the pearls . . . if only she knew they came from me. . . . But at least she has something of mine. . . ."

Magda took a deep breath and changed the subject. "Dearest Solange, I know how proud you are . . . but please, let me send you on a holiday. . . ."

"Thank you, Magda. And it isn't pride. Believe me, I'd accept your generous offer without protest, but I'm afraid this awful arthritis . . . just makes things too difficult."

Once again Magda felt the tears, remembering, in spite of her determination not to dwell in the past, the exquisite Solange she'd met at Emile Jonet's so long ago . . . the startling red hair . . . the black toque with egrets . . . how gracious, how kind she'd been. And now to see the deep lines etched on that lovely face, the gnarled hands, the bent back. . . .

"All right, dearest friend, but this I do insist on. . . . You are coming to live with me. I insist—"

"That, I can't do, Magda. This is home to me—"

"But you can't go on living as you are, alone . . . with no help. . . . You must let me take care of you."

"I'm sorry, Magda. . . ."

Magda suspected, but did not say, that there were other compelling reasons for her refusal . . . her feelings about Magda and Alexis living as they did was perhaps one, but far more important, she was sure, was that to do so would, for her, be an act of disloyalty to Rubin. . . .

The two women looked at each other. Close friends, lifelong antagonists . . .

Rubin continued to see his child grow closer and closer to him. Her attachment to him was almost motherly, their roles seemingly reversed. He was the child, she the parent. Jeanette was becoming a young woman, nearly sixteen now.

She did seem to be happy, which greatly pleased Rubin. If anyone had the right to be morose and disheartened it was Jeanette, but it was not so and he thanked God for that.

Today, though, his heart would have broken had he seen her as Leon sat trying to comfort her in her grief. She had received a letter this morning from Magda though sent anonymously. It ended simply with . . . "I have been a friend of your Tante Solange." For Magda it meant the loss of her last contact with her child. For Jeanette it was like the death of her second mother.

Solange, with characteristic grace, had died quietly, without fuss, in her sleep.

On Jeanette's eighteenth birthday Deborah arranged a small party for just the four of them. When Rubin saw his child sitting across from him at the table, he knew that in spite of his loneliness, in spite of the depressions he suffered, the decision to let her live with Leon and Deborah had surely been the right one. His daughter was cultured . . . educated . . . and so accomplished on the piano that she could have become a concert pianist. However, that wasn't her inclination. She had been given the advantages the daughter of a Hack should have been born to. God had, finally, been merciful and kind. . . .

Jeanette was pleased to see her father so happy. Since Tante Solange had died, she needed him even more. She tried to spare him her longings . . . her disappointments. . . . Life was not nearly as serene as she pretended. She still couldn't understand why her mother had left her, or her father. Secretly she prayed for only one thing—to graduate from school and take care of her father. She lived for that time. She wanted to make a home for the two of them. . . . She was well prepared to be a teacher in both French and music. She would make up to her father for all that life had denied him. She loved Deborah and Leon. They could never be her parents, no matter how hard they tried, but she would never let them know her feelings. As Jeanette looked back, she realized that she'd been deprived of the one thing most children take for granted. The house she lived in was not really her home. . . . Home meant a mother and father. Home also meant being accepted, and the other Hacks had never accepted her. If she happened to be home when the other Hacks came to call, she was completely ignored. . . . She had become aware of the stigma in her life when she was eleven. Her cousin Julien, who usually avoided her, had interrupted her piano practice.

"I suppose you're going to be an actress like your mother," he had said. Julien's smirking, arrogant face was filled with hatred; his voice sounded accusing . . . sinister. Jeanette couldn't understand why. Still, she felt ashamed. . . . But ashamed of what?

"There's nothing wrong with being an actress," she said.

Julien smiled, a mean glint in his eye. "I'm sorry, I should have said 'adulteress.' That's what your mother was, after all."

Jeanette had slapped him. Then she left him standing there without shedding a tear, holding her head very high. Julien had called after her, "Like mother, like daughter." But not until she reached her room did she allow herself to break down and cry. And what was foremost in her mind was . . . "Poor Papa. She'd take care of him . . . she'd make up for all the hurt. . . ."

She was, after all, a grown woman now. In July she'd be nineteen, and soon she'd be able to take Papa away. She had already decided where they would go. She only hoped she would be in time, for recently he seemed to be worse. Much worse.

Rubin sat at the window, watching the torrential rain. For days he had sat in the same chair, in the same place, in the attic which had become his refuge, his exile, his prison. . . .

Suddenly he turned away from the window. Overpoweringly, he felt the futility of his existence . . . the failure of his life. He looked at his canvas in progress. . . . After all these years, any woman he painted still became Magda. The bodies . . . the forms . . . were all different, but what did it matter? The face was always Magda's.

Why was he fooling himself? He couldn't paint. . . . The occasional pieces he sold were bought out of charity. Nobody really wanted his work . . . except Jeanette. His daughter. Who would destroy her life to take care of him, to take the place of her mother. . . . That, by God, he would not allow. Not that too, Magda. . . .

He searched out a piece of paper, took up a pencil, sat down at the wooden table, and wrote:

My dearest daughter,

*Without you my life would already have ended
. . . I have nothing to give you except a trade . . .
my unfortunate life for the promise of yours. I can't
allow you to sacrifice your youth and your beauty
on a man who is already dead. I cannot let you do
this. I want you to get away from London. You've
suffered enough for all of us. You can't have a decent life here. Please go away before we all destroy
you. Please believe in my love . . . it is everlasting. . . .*

Papa

Leon found him the next day, hanging by a cord. For a
long, stricken moment, Leon could not move. Then, without thought, he got a chair and cut the cord, and Rubin's
body fell to the floor. He called out to the landlord, who,
when he saw Rubin, turned ashen white. "Oh, bloody hell,
what a sight," and he fled from the room. Bending over
his brother's body, so cold, so thin, Leon wept. . . .

The most difficult part was telling Jeanette. She kept
repeating over and over again, "Why . . . ? *Why* . . . ?
I would have given him the love he needed. He lived his
life without a moment's peace . . . oh, why . . . ?"

Leon and Deborah couldn't console her. There were no
words. When Phillip came by to pay his respects, Jeanette
refused to see him. In fact, she told Leon that Phillip was
not to attend the funeral. She knew the other Hacks
wouldn't even want to be there.

The next day Rubin was put to rest in the family tomb,
with just the three of them standing by, watching the cof-
fin reach its final resting place.

At long last Papa was home. Sleep well, Papa, near your
mother and father, who loved you as I did. Sleep well.

It was not until that evening that Leon could bring himself to show Jeanette her father's letter, and he turned
away so not to intrude on the awful pain and shock in her
eyes as she read, and reread, the words that had earlier
torn out his heart as well.

Finally, tears on her cheeks, shaking her head to deny

the reality of what she'd just read, she asked her uncle to at long last tell her about her mother.

"Darling, why pain yourself needlessly . . . especially now. . . ."

"No, this *is* the time. All I know is what I've gathered for myself, bits and pieces . . . partial truths. I think I have a right to know what happened."

Leon looked at this lovely girl who already wore such deep scars. He hesitated.

"Uncle Leon, I must know. I don't want to be protected any longer."

He started from the beginning, leaving nothing out that he was aware of. When he had finished, Jeanette stood up, went to the window and looked out. "Uncle Leon," she said, "do you think traits are inherited?"

"No," he answered quickly. "Have no fear on that score. You're in no way like your mother—"

"I wonder. . . . You know what I want now more than anything else in the world? I want to be loved . . . at least to be accepted . . . for what I am or am not—not for what my mother may have done. When I was very young, I never understood why all my relatives didn't like me. Well, I hope the other Hacks rest easy. I'll no longer be an embarrassment to them. I'm leaving London. That's what my father wanted, what he gave his life for . . . so I could find a place where *I* belong. . . ."

"Jeanette, dearest, please listen to me. Try to understand. Your father's mind was confused, I truly don't believe he realized what he was saying—"

"I'm sorry, Uncle, but I believe he did. I ask you, what chance do I have here? Who would marry me? I love you and Aunt Deborah, you've both sacrificed enough because of me"—she shook her head energetically to cut off his protest—"I've been responsible for the breach in the family. It's been years since you have accepted an invitation. When Elise married you didn't even go to the wedding because of me."

"That's not true. Aunt Deborah was not up to it—"

"Thank you, but that's not all of it. I remember how your brother Maurice said I was responsible for your offending him by not accepting the invitation—"

"How in the world do you know that?"

"How? Julien was very kind and kept me posted on all

important details. Perhaps I am like my mother . . . but I truly despise them beyond words. I thank you for your love and goodness to me, but I will no longer live here. I want to go to Paris."

"But why Paris?"

"Because in a way I think I am a child of two worlds. . . . I don't ever want to see my mother, not as long as I live. I'm sorry, but I just can't forgive her for what she did, even though I think I understand some of it. It may be that she lives there, she did once before . . . but I will make no attempt to find her. Still, something draws me there. Perhaps because of the brief happiness my father had there before the war. I remember times when we were together, he would look back to the Paris of his youth with real fondness. And *Tante* Solange lived. there. . . . I've kept all her letters and the postcards she sent me. She kept her promises."

Leon sat quietly. Finally he answered. "Well, so be it. If that is what you really wish, I will provide for—"

"I'm most grateful, Uncle, but I do have a bit of my father in me. I just cannot accept your generous offer. You supported me and my father all these years, and now it is time I began for myself. After all, I'm qualified to teach. I have credentials in music, and there must be a demand for English tutoring in Paris."

"Jeanette, please, my dearest, you are very hurt and angry, but you are like our child. Be sensible—"

"I'm trying to be, Uncle . . . and you are right. I am angry and hurt, but I will have to solve that myself."

Finally he saw there was no point in arguing further. "At least, let me give you enough money to see you settled."

"Only on one condition, that it be a loan."

He shrugged, nodded. "I have a barrister friend in Paris. Charles Dryfus. I'll write to him that you're coming. At least I'll know that someone is looking after you."

Jeanette went to him and put her head on his shoulder. "Oh, Uncle, I know I sound stubborn and ungrateful, but you know how much I love you and Aunt Deborah. I don't know how I can really thank you . . . for being my comfort, the way you were my father's. . . ."

"We loved you both very much. . . . When will you go?"

"I would like to stay until after the first of the year, February, March perhaps. I need the time to be close to my father and visit his grave. . . . You know I remember once my father looking out through the window here, and talking as though he were seeing Paris. He said he loved Paris, especially in the spring. The last time he'd been there, he told me, was in April of 1914. He was so . . . well, poetic and carried away that I remember crying. . . . I want to be there, in Paris, by April."

Leon looked at his niece, and then held her close. Together they shed tears for the past. Pray God, he thought, she would have a kinder future. . . .

Jeanette

Fifteen

The pension Jardin de Neuilly had been a family dwelling in one of the best parts of Paris in the 1800s. It was a large mansion with a formal salon, a dining room, a small, charming sitting room, and a large kitchen on the first floor. The imposing circular staircase led to the second floor where there was a master suite, replete with a bedroom, a bathroom and a dressing room. For many years, this suite had been occupied by an elderly couple. In addition, there were seven other bedrooms and a central bathroom. The old servants' quarters on the third floor had been converted into guest rooms. Jeanette was fortunate; hers was the only room with a private bath. Other guests had to trudge to the toilet down the hall in the middle of the night, if need be. A shower had been installed in one of the hall closets by the present owners.

Jeanette had loved the spacious, light room the moment she saw it. The walls were soft pink-mauve, and the double brass bed was covered with a blue velvet spread. But, best of all, the French windows looked down on a garden below. The first thing Jeanette did after unpacking was write a letter to her aunt and uncle. It was a cheerful letter, but a short one. Then she took out the journal she'd been keeping since her father's death. She began to write:

February 3rd . . . Dearest Papa,

I arrived in Paris this afternoon and stood in front of the station San La Gare for a long time, with so many thoughts, and most of them were of you. It was as though you were beside me. . . . I couldn't see your Paris, or remember its first embrace, because tears blurred my vision. Then I took a taxi to Monsieur Dryfus' office. They greeted me warmly, and surely not as a stranger. You would have been proud. Monsieur Dryfus is a charming man with three sons . . . two are barristers and one is in banking. It was he who found my lodgings.

A strange thought occurred to me, Papa, as I waited to be seen. You were once a barrister . . . but, imagine, I've never even seen the inside of the Hack office where you used to work. Isn't it strange what we think of sometimes. . . . Monsieur Dryfus offered me little encouragement so far as teaching piano is concerned. Paris, he says, is full of starving musicians. He was more encouraging about tutoring English. Somehow, dearest Papa, the bravado I started out with seems to be crumbling a little . . . but big adjustments aren't easy to make, are they? Who understood that better than you? Monsieur Dryfus was so kind, I could almost imagine he was you. On his desk was a portrait of his children as small boys. . . . I often feel that I never had a childhood . . . my mother came to my mind. . . . Why did she discard us so easily . . . ?

I don't need to pretend with you, Papa. I miss you terribly. I'm unsure of myself, but with your inspiration to guide me I will conquer myself. And now I say good night . . . and sleep well.

Jeanette closed the journal slowly, put it back into the desk drawer, and sat for a moment.

Taking her purse and keys, she went downstairs to post the letter to Leon and Deborah. Two blocks away were shops and vending stalls. She went to the tobacconist's to buy stamps, attached one to the letter, kissed it and posted it. Then she bought a small slice of cheese, a loaf of French bread, a can of sardines and a crocheted shopping bag into which she put two of her purchases. In the French style, she carried the thin loaf of bread under her arm. Tonight she wouldn't have dinner with the other guests; she was afraid all eyes would be on her. Tonight she would eat at a table for one.

After eating she tried to read. But her thoughts wandered back to the past. At ten o'clock she turned out the bedside lamp and waited for sleep, but sleep eluded her. She gazed out at the moonlight. When she turned on the lamp and looked at the travel clock Uncle Leon had given her, it was one o'clock. Impulsively, she decided to take a walk. Quietly she dressed, went outside and walked toward the Seine.

After an hour or so, she sat down on a bench to watch the moonlight play on the waters.

"Mademoiselle?" It was a gendarme. "Can I help you?"

She was startled, not knowing what to say. "No . . . no, thank you. I'm just on my way home."

"I think that's a good idea. It's much too late for a young lady to walk the streets of Paris alone."

"You're quite right. . . . Thank you."

She got up and hurried away. When she let herself back into her room it was almost four o'cock in the morning. She went to bed without undressing, and this time fell quickly asleep.

She woke up at ten, feeling curiously refreshed. A feeling of spiritual strength coursed through her. . . . Thank you, Papa. Today is the day I begin the rest of my life here in Paris. And for both our sakes, I'll try to accept the past. . . . No more indulging in self-pity. Whatever happens, we'll face it together. . . .

She asked the concierge to have breakfast sent up. She undressed, brushed her teeth and bathed. As she finished drying, there was a knock on the door. "One moment, please." She slipped into her robe, tying the sash around her waist. When she opened the door, she was greeted by a smiling young girl, about the same age as herself.

"Good morning, mademoiselle. My name is Madeleine. I hope you slept well."

"Thank you, yes."

Madeleine placed the tray on the table. On her way out, she said, "Enjoy your breakfast."

"Thank you."

Under a white napkin, Jeanette found two warm, fresh croissants, sweet rolls that smelled of cinnamon and walnuts, a bowl of fresh churned butter, marmalade, a pot of coffee and a pitcher of cream. Since she had eaten little the night before, she took a large bite from a croissant, poured a cup of café au lait and walked to the window.

Below, the gardener was on his knees, spading the rich, black earth between daffodil bulbs. As he got up to stretch, throwing back his shoulders, he happened to glance up and saw Jeanette. "Good morning, mademoiselle," he called out, smiling.

"Good morning, monsieur."

"Beautiful morning, is it not?"

"Oh, yes, it is, it *is*. . . ."

She was going to wear her tweed suit; it was warm and simple. She chose her navy shoes and bag, and short white cotton gloves. She made sure to button the jacket, and adjusted her hair under the pink felt cloche. Then she appraised herself. She approved.

She decided to take a taxi, since cabbies were often a storehouse of information. She asked her driver for the name of the most likely newspaper in which to advertise for a position. He was most helpful. He drove her there—going twelve blocks out of his way to insure a big fare. Jeanette thanked him and tipped him generously.

She placed an ad in the classified section, offering both tutoring and piano instruction. Then she decided to be a tourist and walk the streets of Paris.

It seemed that all of Paris was alive. . . . She soaked up the sounds, the smells and the sights. In bakers' shops queues of people waited to buy bread. On the Rue de la Paix women went in and out of dress shops. Jeanette looked at the jewelry stores . . . they were magnificent, especially Cartier's. She admired the petite lingerie shops, all soft lace and silk. Her heart beat faster with excitement as her pace quickened. She turned into the Avenue de l'Opéra and watched the people at sidewalk cafés. Seating herself at a table, she fantasized about the people around her. She gazed at the opera house. How beautiful it was. And how incredible to be so close to the source of such wonderful music. . . . She had a demitasse.

Next she went to a bookstore, where she bought a map of Paris, a guide to the metro system (which she had been told was the greatest in the world) and a guide to the Louvre. Then she registered with three employment agencies.

That night, after first considering eating alone in her room, she decided to go down to the dining room. Dinner was served from seven-thirty to nine. By the time she got there, many guests were already seated. Most were widows on small pensions who had lived in the same room for years. They were hardly friendly. The only welcome sight was Madeleine, who had been questioned endlessly by the dowagers about the new tenant, and pretended by evasion that she knew a great deal more than she was willing to divulge. She greeted Jeanette warmly, and with a true native Parisian's love of the city told Jeanette she hoped she was enjoying her first view of the sights.

Later, alone in her room, Jeanette told herself to be patient in her search for a job. Things were bound to work out. She was in the city where Mama and Papa had first met. Surely good things would happen here, where they had fallen in love, before the bad times. . . .

For a moment she stood staring at her reflection in the bathroom mirror. . . . Well, face it, Jeanette Hack, you are not your mother, with her strength, are you? You don't *want* to be like her, but still you would like to share the part of her that was strong enough to let go, to walk away from what she could not live with. . . . You despise her, and yet you do admire that. She was fourteen when she came to Paris, fatherless, motherless and penniless, but she *survived*. . . .

The next morning Jeanette arose early. Today held the promise of something she had dreamed of doing since she had been a little girl. As she walked along the Seine, she could almost hear her father telling her the story, before his bitterness had set in. She followed the route up the steep stone stairs to Nôtre Dame, and paused at the lonely café where Rubin had met Magda. Then on to 27 Rue de Fleures . . . she tried without success to find Sylvia Beach's shop, but it was gone. She walked the crooked streets of Montmartre, hoping her footsteps might fall in exactly the same places as her father's once had. Finally she stood at the stone railing along the Seine, once again watching the boats glide up and down. But her thoughts were in another place. . . . Should I stand before the door, dearest Tante Solange, where you lived, or should I leave that in the past, where it belongs . . . ? You are all gone . . . your world is gone. . . . Dear Papa, only the ghosts of your memories remain through me. May they all rest in peace. . . .

On Saturday morning she went to the synagogue for memorial services, and wept during the Kaddish. But she was filled with gratitude that the depth of her loss could be faced with quiet bereavement. . . . Later, she went to the Tuileries, remembering the happy times when she and her father, Rubin, had gone on Saturdays to the synagogue and then to Hyde Park. Her thoughts were interrupted by a small boy who asked if she could reach his ball, which had rolled under her bench. She handed the ball to him, impulsively kissing his cheek, and watched him run back to his mother. What a beautiful sight . . . mother and child. Suddenly she was so happy. . . . Tomorrow was Sunday, her first Sunday in France, and she would be spending it with the Dryfuses and their children, her very first invitation. . . .

The Dryfuses lived on the outskirts of Paris, near Versailles, in a house three hundred years old. Although Madame Dryfus was twenty years younger than her husband, and a head taller, it seemed not at all odd. There was an unmistakable bond of love between these two, which greatly impressed Jeanette. Devotion was so rare. Most people seemed to tolerate each other . . . if they stayed together at all. . . .

"The children are so eager to meet you," said Madame Dryfus as she led Jeanette out into the garden. She introduced Jeanette to Berton, who was five, and Meirer, who was eight.

They ate lunch in the garden under a huge chestnut tree. Monsieur Dryfus observed Jeanette's pleasure with the children. What an extraordinary young woman, he thought . . . not only beautiful but poised and perfectly charming. She seemed far too mature to be only nineteen . . . but there was such sadness in her eyes. . . . Of course, how could it be different? A father who had gone mad, and a mother who had abandoned her when she was only a small child. . . .

"Tell me, Jeanette, are you satisfied with your lodgings?"

"Yes, thank you. I'm very pleased."

"And Paris . . . ?"

"Oh, monsieur, how could anyone not fall in love with Paris?"

Her only problem, she added, was in finding a job, but he told her not to worry, sooner or later something would turn up, and meanwhile, she should enjoy the city.

When it was time to leave, Madame Dryfus told her how very welcome she was. She hoped Jeanette would visit frequently. Monsieur Dryfus took both her hands in his. "I want you to know that your happiness is ours, that you can call upon my dear wife for *any* reason . . . and consider me as an uncle in the absence of your own. . . . Will you do that?"

"Oh yes, monsieur. How kind you've been to me. I don't know how to thank you—"

"There are no thanks needed, my dear. Paris and ourselves will be better for having you amongst us. I mean that."

Looking at him, she knew he did. It was the end of a rare and beautiful day.

The next weeks passed swiftly. Jeanette, taking Monsieur Dryfus' advice, did everything that tourists do. She went to the top of the Eiffel Tower . . . she wandered through the Left Bank . . . she took a boat ride on the Seine . . . she ate *escargots* . . . she loved the onion soup with the thick crust of cheese on top. . . . She fell hopelessly in love with Paris, every worn cobblestone . . . every crooked street. . . . At last she was home. Oh, Papa, if only we could have shared this together. . . . Everywhere I go I wonder if maybe you and Mama have been here before.

But no one, it seemed, wanted to hire her. No one answered her ads. None of the agencies sent her out on interviews. She didn't want to go deeper in debt to Uncle Leon than she was already. Surely *someone* would need her soon. But in the midst of a world-wide depression, there seemed no call for an English tutor or practical young lady pianist. . . .

One morning when Madeleine brought her breakfast, Jeanette was still in bed, the blinds drawn. "Good morning, mademoiselle."

"Good morning, Madeleine," Jeanette answered dully.

"Are you feeling ill, mademoiselle?"

"No, Madeleine, I'm only discouraged. I can't find a job."

Madeleine placed the tray in front of Jeanette. "Please forgive me for being so bold," she said, "but I've liked you from the day you arrived. Not because you've been generous with your tips, but because you're so courteous to me. I think you need a friend, a person to talk with . . . yes?"

"You're right, Madeleine. I do need a friend, and I need a job."

"Where have you looked?" said Madeleine.

Jeanette told her. "At this point I'm willing to take anything. I'd be grateful . . . I don't care what it is or how hard to do. . . ."

"All right," said Madeleine. "If you really mean you'll take anything . . . I'll see what I can do. Now drink your coffee and eat your rolls. Tomorrow could always be worse, remember that. Also remember better to worry on a full stomach than an empty one." They smiled at each other, and each knew she had found a new friend.

Madeleine had a relative, Uncle Jacques, who owned a laundry, where most of the family worked except for herself. She made more money, she told them, in service, although there was another reason for her preference, which she now used on her new friend's behalf. At first he refused to hire Jeanette, but when Madeleine pinched his cheek and sat in his lap . . . knowing his feelings about her that he'd more than once tried to indulge . . . he finally relented. Jeanette went to work for him from seven in the morning to seven in the evening—and sometimes to eight. She started with the hand laundry, stirring the cauldrons of boiling water. One day when one of the relatives became ill, she was asked to do the ironing. To Uncle Jacques' surprise, she did it with finesse. She remained in that job, but for all the praise she received, she earned barely enough to pay her rent.

Each morning at five-thirty Jeanette dragged herself out of bed. She dressed as though she was going to a position of distinction. She took the metro across town, and got to work a little before seven. Then she changed into a white uniform and stood on her feet all day. By closing time she was ready to drop, and had to force herself to wash her face, comb her hair, and get back into her street clothes before she went home, where only Madeleine knew the demeaning work that she did during the day.

One evening when she returned home there was a message from Monsieur Dryfus asking her to call him the next morning.

"Oh, Jeanette," he said when she got through to him, "if you're free this afternoon, I believe I might have a situation for you. Can you meet me at three o'clock?"

She was almost hysterical with relief as she assured him she would. She quickly told Jacques she was ill, went home, changed and arrived at Monsieur Dryfus' office promptly at three o'clock.

"I believe, Jeanette, there may be a position for you with the Dupré family. Poor Madame Dupré has recently suffered a very great loss. Her only daughter and son-in-law were killed in an automobile crash on their way to Cannes. They left three small children, who are now in the custody of their maternal grandmother."

He sighed deeply, remembering all too well the loss of his own first wife. . . . "Does the name Dupré mean anything to you?"

Jeanette shook her head.

"No? Then let me tell you something about the family." And he told her that both Madame and Marshal Dupré's ancestors had come from the aristocracy of the Bourbon dynasty, and that if it hadn't been for a diminutive Corsican who helped spread a revolution, well, very possibly Madame Dupré might now be at court in the service of France. At any rate, after the revolution many in the aristocracy were permitted to retain their estates as well as their titles. Among them were the Dupré and Duval families. When the two great families were joined by marriage, it was a symbol to the Parisiens that the aristocracy still lived and would be perpetuated. But for Antoinette Duval and Henri Dupré, their marriage was more than an alliance of two illustrious houses; it was a bond of love and devotion that would last over twenty years. They were passionately in love. Antoinette was considered one of the great beauties of her day. Raven-haired, with dark, liquid eyes and the skin of a cameo, her waist was eighteen inches when cinched in. Henri would never need to think of taking a mistress. Antoinette would become both his wife and his mistress.

The announcement of their marriage had Paris in a whirl. The parties honoring the engaged couple, and the planning and shopping for the wedding were so extensive the lovers had little time to be alone. By the time the marriage day arrived, both of them could hardly wait to slip away. . . . They spent their honeymoon at Henri's château in Provence. For three months they stayed there absorbed in their love. Exactly nine months from the day of their wedding, Denise was born in Paris. Two years later, they had a son, Jean-Paul, named for Henri's father. It was Antoinette's hope to present her husband with many sons. But when the third child came—another son— the birth was so difficult and prolonged she could never have another. The second boy was named Etiènne, after Antoinette's father.

Jeanette was entranced with the story. Her mind had traveled back in time. . . . She had almost forgotten why she was here, but Monsieur Dryfus brought her back sharply.

"Dear Madame Dupré lost her beloved husband four years ago, and I'm afraid she's never recovered from his death. She continues to be in mourning. But it is Denise's children who especially need you. They're now with their grandmother in Paris, and the present governess, who's elderly and quite rheumatic, wants to go back to Provence, where Denise and her husband lived. A new governess is needed, and of course I thought of you."

"My heart goes out to the children," Jeanette said, tears in her eyes.

"I was sure it would. Well . . . are you interested in the position?"

"Yes. But do you think I'm qualified?"

"Yes, I do. In fact, I took the liberty of speaking to Etienne about you and have arranged an interview. Would tomorrow morning at ten be convenient?"

"Oh, *yes* . . . that will be fine."

"In that case, I'll tell Etienne that you're coming."

Jeanette hesitated in front of the mansion on the Boulevard Victor Hugo. The blinds were drawn. For a moment she felt chilled and unsure of herself, but she walked slowly up the brick path and ascended the steps. The front door was hung with the black of mourning, relieved somewhat by a wreath. Jeanette placed her finger on the bell and rang. The door was opened by an elderly butler, who led her to the library and asked her to be seated. Monsieur Dupré would be down presently. She sat in a high-backed winged easy chair. The room was breathtakingly beautiful. There was a marquetry desk, with heavy ormolu. The walls were lined with walnut bookshelves. An Aubusson rug covered the center of the marquetry floor. Above the mantel was a portrait of Marshal Dupré, dressed in his fine uniform, which was covered with the medals he'd won. It was apparent why Madame Dupré had fallen in love with him. He was probably the handsomest man Jeanette had ever seen. . . .

She looked at the coat of arms on the opposite wall, and then the door was being opened and her heart began to beat faster . . . she sat erect and folded her hands in her lap. She wasn't facing the door and so couldn't yet see Monsieur Dupré.

As he slowly approached, she heard a peculiar thumping sound. When he stood in front of her she prayed that the expression on her face didn't reveal her shock: Monsieur Dupré, walking with a cane, apparently had a club foot. His left shoulder was tilted and he was slightly humpbacked. On his right sleeve he wore a black armband.

Although he was only twenty-five his hair was beginning to gray at the temples. Jeanette noted a strong resemblance between him and his father, especially through the eyes. Dark brown, deep-set and soft, there was compassion and kindness in them which seemed to go with people who suffered. Still, he wasn't handsome.

Jeanette tried with all her reserve to pretend that she hadn't noticed his deformity or the four-inch platform on his shoe.

He seated himself behind the desk. Jeanette was startled when he finally spoke. His voice was magnificent. There was a resonance, a depth, in the words he spoke that made her forget his deformity. So swift and sudden was the transition, he became almost beautiful when he was talking. A simple word like "mademoiselle" seemed to have magical connotations.

"As you know," he began, "Monsieur Dryfus was kind enough to recommend you to us. Most highly, I might add. However, the responsibility for three young children is not a small one. More than anything else, perhaps, it demands a great deal of dedication. In all candor, young as you are, might you not be doing yourself a disservice by taking on such a position?"

She had known her youth would be a disadvantage, but she answered softly, "No, monsieur, I don't feel that way. I think above all one needs a love of children, and that I have."

Etienne Dupré seemed pleased. Watching her carefully, he proceeded to tell her a little about the children, and how it might be especially difficult to reach them now since they were suffering the loss of a governess and both their parents.

Jeanette assured him that she was no stranger to loss.

He was impressed. The other applicants were experienced, but they seemed to lack the warmth of this girl. In any case, what guarantees were there in this life when his own sister and her husband lay side by side in their grave, and just two weeks ago they were loving parents who never dreamed they wouldn't live to see their children raised to adulthood. What better was there to trust than one's instincts . . . ?

He came to a decision. "When could you begin?"

"As soon as I'm needed," she said, delighted.

"Would tomorrow be all right?"

"Yes, I have no other commitments."

"Good. I'll make all the necessary arrangements. We'll expect you at nine."

They discussed the salary, and the interview was over. Jeanette could hardly believe her good fortune.

Etienne knocked on the door of his mother's room.

"Is that you, Etienne? Please come in." She lay on a chaise longue, a damp cloth over her swollen eyes.

"I'm happy to see you out of bed," he said. "Are you feeling better today?"

How could she answer such a question without telling a lie? The pain would never go away.

"Yes," she said. "I'm better today. Now, tell me about the girl. Did you hire her?"

"Yes."

"You don't think she's too young?" They had discussed Jeanette's age the night before.

"She is certainly young," he said, "but rather than being a handicap, I believe her youth may be an advantage."

"I'm shocked at your judgment, Etienne."

"I knew you would be. So am I. I was quite surprised when I hired her."

"Then why did you do it, especially when there are so many women who come recommended with portfolios?"

"I think it was partly the character, the strength and forthrightness I sensed in her, but also her . . . well, her warmth . . . in some ways she seems old beyond her years. . . . When I considered the children and what they need at this time, I decided in favor of her youth and eagerness—"

"Strange recommendations for a governess, Etienne."

"Perhaps she won't be a governess in the conventional sense, but she's really very intelligent and poised, she's been educated at one of the best schools in London, speaks French fluently, and, as I said, is mature beyond her years—"

His mother looked at him in amazement. "And all of this you discovered in a ten-minute interview?"

"Yes."

"Was your judgment altogether objective?"

Etienne observed his shoe. He hobbled to the window and stood before the drawn blind which kept the room in semi-darkness, grateful that his mother couldn't see the expression on his face.

Madame Dupré was so accustomed to Etienne's infirmity that sometimes she forgot he was not a whole man. She knew she had offended him. "Come, Etienne, sit beside me."

He took his place beside her once again.

"Please forgive what I said," she continued. "I'm sure that what you did was in the best interest of the children. . . . But why didn't you hire a French girl?"

"Oh, Mother, how provincial you are. I didn't hire her because she's French or English. I hired her for what she is, a lovely and I suspect most capable young woman named Jeanette Hack."

"Jeanette Hack? That isn't an English name—"

"No, I suppose not . . . I don't really know its origin—"

"What is her religion?"

"Monsieur Dryfus tells me that she's a Jewess—"

"A Jewess?"

"Yes . . . does it matter?"

"No, Etienne, but what about the children's religious training?"

"I'm sure she won't try to convert them—"

"That is not what I mean, Etienne. But will she, for example, take them to mass?"

"Let's not look for ghosts, Mother. I'm sure all that can be seen to without any problem. So the matter is settled. Please rest now. I'll bring the children to you later."

He kissed her briefly on the cheek and left.

Madeleine sat on Jeanette's bed as she packed. She was astounded by what Jeanette had been telling her. "You mean you actually spoke up to Monsieur Dupré?"

"No, Madeleine, I'd hardly call it that."

"Well, I assure you no French girl would have had the courage."

"He thought I was too young. But I showed him that inside I am not so simple, so naïve."

Madeleine was flabbergasted. "Where did you learn so much?" she said. "Where did you find your courage?"

Jeanette laughed. At last she had a job. "I don't know, somehow I just managed to summon it up. I'm not sure I'll ever know what really decided him to hire me, but he did and that's the important thing. . . . You know, Madeleine, in a way I need those children as much as they need me."

"Ah, my dear, you are marvelous. May I tell you something? When you first came, I thought you were just a young small kitten, but you're really a tigress that will not be beaten down."

Jeanette laughed: "Oh, my dearest Madeleine, I'm far from being a tigress. I'm many things. I'm frightened, I'm lonely, I'm sometimes very blue, but when I reach the bottom, I just try to pick myself up and start all over again.

There's a great deal you don't know about my life. I was born part peasant. And in spite of all my education, I think it's the peasant who pulls me back up."

Jeanette sat down beside Madeleine and took her hand. "I'll never forget how you were there when I needed you most, and what a friend you've been to me."

Madeleine began to cry. "You make it sound as though I'll never see you again."

"No . . . no, Madeleine. We're friends forever. We'll see each other often, I promise you. . . ."

Sixteen

Monsieur Dupré led Jeanette down the second-floor hall to the children's wing, the same quarters he, Denise and Jean-Paul had shared as children. A large square playroom formed the center. Off to the right were three small bedrooms, just large enough to accommodate a single bed, a night stand, a chair and a dresser. To the left was the governess' room and bath, somewhat larger and quite attractive.

Mademoiselle Valeriese, the old governess, her bonnet already on, was waiting to leave.

"Mademoiselle Valeriese, may I present Mademoiselle Hack?"

The old governess scrutinized the young woman and thought, My God, their grief must have driven them mad. This new one is only a child herself. Is she to attend to the needs of these children? Unbelievable! She cursed her bones and her age for compelling her to relinquish her charges to a mere slip of a girl. Oh, the toll that time exacted. She had been with her babies since the birth of young Lucien, now seven years old. Nicole was five and Desirée only three.

"Here are their schedules and some suggestions," she said. "I know you will love the little ones." She hoped so, at least. Then she looked at the three to whom she'd given so much of herself and said, choking back the tears, "And now, my little darlings, it's time for me to leave you. You are the oldest, Lucien. Be kind and watch over your sisters."

She bent down to kiss them, the tears rolling down her cheeks. Then, amidst the cries and protests of the children, she took her leave.

"Now," said Etienne to the children, "I have a wonderful surprise for you. Can you guess what it is?"

"No," said Desirée, who had cried the hardest, "I can't."

"The surprise is Mademoiselle Hack. Say good morning to mademoiselle."

Desirée looked at Jeanette and snuggled closer to Etienne. Nicole ran to her room and plopped down on the bed. Lucien glowered.

"Good morning, Desirée," said Jeanette. "Do you like dolls?"

Desirée nodded her head.

Jeanette went to her room and came back with a colorfully wrapped box. She handed it to Desirée, who tried to undo the wrapping, but her tiny fingers couldn't manage it. Jeanette bent down and took Desirée's fingers in her own, guiding them. When the wrapping was off, Desirée lifted the top of the box. Inside was a doll, the perfect size for a three-year-old to cuddle.

"Thank you, mademoiselle." Desirée examined the hair and the eyes, then held the doll close, smiling back at Jeanette.

Jeanette breathed a sigh of relief. Thank God she had thought of buying a gift for each child, knowing how difficult the transition would be.

"Lucien, please come here," said Etienne. Lucien had gone to the window. He turned around slowly and walked to his uncle. "Lucien, greet Mademoiselle Hack and make her feel welcome."

Lucien's eyes were lowered. He wouldn't look at this terrible person who was trying to replace Mademoiselle Valeriese.

"Lucien, look at me. Mademoiselle has kindly consented to come and live with us."

Lucien didn't reply, obviously wishing she had kindly consented to go somewhere else. He despised this intruder, he always would. . . . His mother was gone, his father was gone, and now Mademoiselle Valeriese was gone. Everyone was going away and leaving him. He looked at Jeanette and said very carefully, "Go away. I hate you. Go away." He ran into his room, slamming the door behind him. Jeanette understood his feelings all too well. . . .

Etienne was badly shaken. He knew that of the three, Lucien had suffered the most. His intelligence was well above average, and he was so very sensitive. Seeing Desirée dozing off in Etienne's arms, Jeanette took the child, who still clutched the doll in her arms, and gently carried her to her room. She laid her down, covered her with a blanket, and returned to the playroom.

Etienne still sat with his hands over his eyes. Finally he sighed, looked up and saw Jeanette. "Please, I'm sorry, won't you sit down?" he said.

Jeanette lowered herself into the chair nearest her, which was one of the children's.

"I want to apologize for Lucien's rudeness," Etienne said.

"Oh, Monsieur Dupré, there's no need for that, I assure you. I understand how they feel. It's been a very difficult time for all of you, and especially for the children."

"Yes, but foolishly I had hoped it would be less difficult."

"Of course, monsieur. But it's only natural that they should be frightened and resentful of me. It will take time. But with love and patience I believe the children will become accustomed to me . . . at least I shall work hard for that. It's a pity, though, that Mademoiselle Valeriese was obliged to leave just when they needed her so much. . . ." Where, he wondered, had he found the wisdom to hire her? She was even comforting him . . . "But life seems to have a way of healing wounds. Please trust me, monsieur. I'll do my very best to serve the children well."

He nodded his head. "I do believe you."

"I'm very grateful for that, and now, may I make a suggestion?"

"Of course."

"I'd like to wear ordinary clothes, if I may, instead of a uniform. I think that would be best. I think the children will be less apprehensive if I appear less formidable, as though I were one of them."

"I believe you're absolutely right."

"Good, and may I ask your indulgence in one other matter?"

"Yes . . . of course."

"Might we have a small piano?"

"Do you think that would help?"

"Yes, I do. Music is a wonderful way to divert the mind, especially with children. I think it might help a great deal."

"All right, I'll attend to it immediately."

"Thank you. And now I'd like to try again to introduce myself to Nicole . . . this time alone."

He rose at once. Before leaving, he said, "Thank you, mademoiselle, for all your understanding."

Jeanette had a doll for Nicole, too, which she proceeded to give to the child, and which Nicole immediately threw against the wall. Jeanette picked it up and placed it gently on the bed alongside Nicole, who turned immediately toward the wall.

"I know you may find it hard to believe, Nicole, but I bet we're going to be very good friends—"

"You're *not* my friend. Mademoiselle Valeriese left because of *you*. Lucien said so. Go away, I hate you."

"That's too bad because I like you very much. And Lucien is mistaken. . . ."

Turning her head, Nicole looked at Jeanette appraisingly. Jeanette got up to leave. "You'll see. We're going to become friends. . . . And now, my dear, go and wash. It will soon be time to visit your grandma."

As Jeanette left, she knew the war hadn't been won, but at least the campaign had begun and she thought the opening battle had ended a little in her favor. She saw Nicole walk to the bathroom to wash. But when the time came to go, Lucien refused, saying he would visit his grandmother with Uncle Etienne only, and, of course, Nicole promptly followed suit.

Time to go to work, Jeanette decided. "Lucien," she said, "get out of bed at once." She spoke with authority, but without anger. "I must take you to see your grandmother. That will be my job from now on. The sooner we understand each other, the better it will be for all of us. Now make yourself presentable. Immediately."

He glared at her, but Jeanette turned and left the room. The moment she turned, he stuck out his tongue. He knew he would have to obey her . . . after all, she was bigger

. . . but he still hated her. She was his enemy. He would ask Uncle Etienne to send her away.

When they entered her room together, Madame Dupré was still on her chaise longue.

"Good morning, Madame Dupré," Jeanette said. "I am Mademoiselle Hack."

Madame's eyes were good and she scrutinized the girl closely. Etienne must have taken leave of his senses, hiring her. She was much too pretty, much too thin and much too young. For the life of her, she couldn't understand what had taken possession of Etienne. How dare a governess be dressed in a simple silk frock like some English schoolgirl. She would certainly speak to Etienne. . . . "You may leave us now," she said. "Come back in fifteen minutes."

When Jeanette had closed the door behind her, Lucien began to recite his list of complaints. Mademoiselle Hack was loathsome, and he would never obey her. She was mean, hateful. Nicole joined in. "We despise her, don't we, Lucien?"

"Yes, and we always will."

Desirée sat on the chaise, snuggling up to her grandmother. "Isn't she beautiful, Grandmother?" she said, showing her the doll.

"What . . . ? Oh, yes, quite beautiful," Madame Dupré said, absorbed in the others, and scarcely noticing the doll.

"That woman gave it to her," Lucien said angrily.

"She gave me one, too," added Nicole, "but I threw it against the wall. Lucien told me not to take anything from her."

Her grandmother was shocked. How unorthodox! The very idea, to present the children with gifts on her very first day! The girl had to be devious. She would speak to Etienne and have her sent away.

When Jeanette came to pick up her charges, Desirée got down from the chaise and ran to meet her, taking her hand. The other two children didn't acknowledge her presence until Madame Dupré finally said, "Go, children. I will see you again before bedtime."

On the way out, Jeanette nearly collided with Etienne coming in. She decided the second skirmish had gone to the opposition, and silently laughed to herself, reminding herself this was a job, not a field of battle. . . .

"Did you have a nice visit with the children, Mother?" Etienne asked when they were alone.

"With the children, yes. With that . . . person, emphatically *no*. I do not approve of her, Etienne."

"But why—"

"First of all, she had the audacity to present herself before me improperly dressed. And, furthermore, the children clearly dislike her, especially Lucien. Of course, at her age, Desirée is like a small puppy who can be enticed by anything, especially a doll, which I resent that girl's giving her, and I understand she made the same overture to Nicole. . . . It's really most irregular and . . . improper. Altogether, she's thoroughly unsatisfactory."

Etienne sighed. How very French his mother was in her rigid sense of propriety. "And all of this you discovered in fifteen minutes?" he said wryly. "I think you've been prejudiced by Lucien."

"Prejudiced by Lucien, a mere child? Please don't patronize me, Etienne. My powers of observation are better than that."

"Mother, I believe that I've had a better opportunity to observe Mademoiselle Hack's behavior with the children than you have."

"Then perhaps you can explain to me why she isn't wearing a uniform."

"Because we decided that everyday clothes would be better. The children will feel less strain—"

"*We* decided?"

"Yes . . . replacing Mademoiselle Valeriese will not be easy on any of us—"

"Ah . . . and that satisfies you, does it, her appearance?"

"Yes."

"Well, it doesn't satisfy me. A governess is a governess, and a guest is a guest, and she is neither. I believe she will be a bad influence on the children, and I wish her to leave as quickly as possible, the moment she can be replaced."

Etienne was beginning to get angry. "I have no wish to defy you, but I don't think you realize how important this young woman can be to the children. I do. And until such time as I find her unfit, she will remain. We really should be grateful that she came to us when she did. I'm convinced that she understands the children's upset, and can help them to overcome it."

Madame Dupré's shoulders sank back into the chaise. "You've never spoken to me in that tone of voice in your life, Etienne. I'm surprised at you . . . why are you being so protective of *her?* What can she possibly mean to you . . . ? I do believe she has bewitched you." Her voice was quivering.

Etienne dug his fingers into the edge of the desk. His patience was almost gone. He looked his mother in the eye. "Never . . . *never* say anything like that to me again. Twice you've suggested that my intentions might be personal. They are not. Now, the subject is closed. . . ."

Etienne left the room. Madame Dupré began to cry. She loved Etienne more than all the others. True, she loved them all, but he was special. It was she who had brought him into the world deformed, something for which she could never forgive herself. From the moment of his birth she had questioned herself: had she committed some terrible sin to call for this punishment from God? And now Etienne was angry with her, something she could not bear. . . .

The four of them sat at the round table in the center of the playroom having dinner. All afternoon Lucien and Nicole had ignored Jeanette, and it was no different now. They just sat there, toying with their food, although they were very hungry, hoping Mademoiselle would press them to eat, at which time they'd begin their refusals. But Mademoiselle had no such intention. She and Desirée enjoyed their meal enormously.

"Isn't this delicious?" Jeanette said, smiling at Desirée.

And Desirée, her mouth full, answered, "Yes, mademoiselle."

"That's a good girl, you've almost finished your dinner." Desirée smiled back. "Thank you, mademoiselle."

Jeanette removed Desirée's plate, went to the serving cart and came back with two small crystal bowls of fresh strawberries. "Look," she said, placing the bowls before them. Lucien and Nicole, who loved strawberries, pretended not to notice. Lucien, incensed by mademoiselle's indifference, elbowed his plate off the table, at the same time trying to pretend it was an accident. He waited for her reaction.

Jeanette picked up the broken plate along with the food and merely said, "Accidents will happen." This was not what Lucien wanted her reaction to be. If only she had spoken harshly or had spanked him, he could have gone to Uncle Etienne.

Jeanette couldn't help laughing. She picked up Desirée in her arms and whirled her around the room. It was at that exact moment that the door opened, and Jean-Paul Dupré entered. Quickly, Jeanette put Desirée down and composed herself. Desirée ran to her uncle.

He picked her up, kissing her on both cheeks. "My little darling, you look as delicious as the strawberry stain on your chin." He wiped it away with his handkerchief.

"Uncle Jean-Paul!" Nicole screamed out.

"Nicole, my little one," he said, picking her up in his other arm and kissing her. She placed her arm around his neck, burying her head in his shoulder.

"I'm so happy to see you," she said.

"You're still happy to see me, although you saw me only last night?"

"Yes."

"Ah, my two beauties, you shall see me often. Now, come. Let us have a nice chat."

Jeanette was spellbound. Jean-Paul's presence had taken command of the room. She couldn't move. It was as though the portrait downstairs of Marshal Dupré had come to life. The resemblance was almost frightening. She was awed, overcome . . . he was so handsome, so urbane. . . . She had no words to describe what she was feeling . . . as though she'd been struck by a bolt of lightning. Her heart raced. She felt things inside herself she hadn't known she could feel. Her feelings embarrassed her . . . gave her a sense of guilt as, all of a sudden, thoughts of her mother, of what they'd said about her, came into her mind, and were banished immediately.

Jean-Paul was now looking at her, and saying, "Forgive me, mademoiselle, I am Jean-Paul Dupré. You must be the new governess."

"Yes, sir. I am Jeanette Hack." She stammered slightly.

He nodded, clearly approving what he saw. Well, this

time at least Etienne had brought a little spring into the house, not some old crow. The closer he observed Jeanette, the better he liked her. In the proper setting, she could be beautiful. In fact, she was already. He couldn't understand why his mother had objected earlier, although her perspective was hardly his own. . . . "I hope you'll be happy here," he said, and after Jeanette managed to get out that she was sure she would be, she backed out of the room, leaving him to have his "chat" with the children.

In her room she went immediately to her bathroom and turned on the cold water, splashing her face, hoping, praying, that her extraordinary reaction to Monsieur Jean-Paul had not been as obvious as she feared it had been.

With mademoiselle gone, Jean-Paul summoned Lucien, who was overjoyed at seeing his uncle, and quickly launched into the list of complaints he had given his grandmother. Jean-Paul listened patiently. When Lucien had finished, he said, "Lucien, sit down. Let's discuss this man-to-man. It's no one's fault that Mademoiselle Valeriese left, least of all Mademoiselle Hack's."

Lucien seated himself near his uncle's chair as Jean-Paul continued. "Now, Lucien, I understand your feelings. In my own work, in the diplomatic service, I find a lot of things I don't agree with, and many that I dislike. Being a diplomat, though, teaches a man that it's easier to catch flies with honey. Do you understand what I mean?"

Lucien tried to think it over, not really understanding how all this really applied to him and the new intruder. "But Uncle, she's been so mean to Nicole and me. How can I be nice to her? She just likes Desirée."

"Well, I understand why you would take a belligerent attitude—"

"Bel-liger-ent . . . ?"

"Yes . . . angry. However, let's consider something else. When she's inconsiderate, what would happen if you were nice . . . and treated her with the greatest respect? Perhaps she would feel guilty, and treat you like Desirée. Usually when you're nice and kind to someone, they treat you the same way."

"No, Uncle, I know she won't."

"Maybe not, but I would suggest you try. If she continues to be mean, then we can talk again and discuss a different strategy. Doesn't that make good sense?"

Reluctantly . . . "All right, I'll try . . . but if she doesn't change, will you send her away then?"

"We'll see, but first you do your share. Is that agreed?"

"I'll try."

"Very good. That's the most any man can do."

When his visit was over, Jean-Paul knocked gently on Jeanette's door. She took a deep breath, straightened her shoulders, lifted her chin and tried to compose herself. It was no use. She opened the door, not daring to look up into his face.

He smiled. "We've had a lovely visit," he said, "and now I'm leaving. But I want to welcome you and tell you I hope you'll enjoy the children as much as I know they'll enjoy you."

"Thank you, sir," she answered, in a voice that sounded almost aloof, and far from what she felt. She was also grateful to him, knowing he had told a lie, knowing all too well what Lucien must have said about her. He smiled, bowed his head slightly and left.

It was difficult to keep her mind on the children, but when her attention returned to them, she did notice a slight change in Lucien's attitude, not quite so defiant as it had been. And if Jean-Paul had straightened out a few things with Lucien, could Nicole be far behind? Thank you, Monsieur Jean-Paul.

When they were told to get ready for bed, the two older children obeyed. Then Jeanette attended to Desirée. She listened to her prayers (which had been underscored in black ink on Mademoiselle Valeriese's list). She kissed and held the child for a few moments, then gathered up the blankets and tucked her in. "Sleep well, my little one."

She next went to Nicole, who was already kneeling, her elbows on the edge of the bed, her hands poised under her chin, looking up toward heaven. When she had finished her prayers, Jeanette tucked her in. Someday she'd be able to kiss her good night, but not this evening. It was too soon. "Sleep well, Nicole. I'll see you in the morning."

"Thank you, mademoiselle." It was brief, but she too was not hostile as before. Like brother, like sister . . .

Lucien was already in bed. "Lucien, have you said your prayers?"

He remembered the lecture Uncle Jean-Paul had given him about winning the flies with honey. "Yes," he said. "I can say them by myself, thank you."

"Oh . . . I see. Well, in that case, I hope you sleep well. Good night." Jeanette left the room without another word, almost smiling to herself.

Lucien lay staring up at the ceiling, and suddenly the tears began to pour. . . . He turned over and buried his head in the pillow. He had been so wicked to Mademoiselle Hack, he had treated her cruelly. Uncle Jean-Paul had said it wasn't her fault that Mademoiselle Valeriese had to leave. No one was to blame, least of all Mademoiselle Hack. In a way he'd known that, but he longed for his old governess, he'd loved her so. And now he was without his mother and father. He cried for a long time before he finally fell asleep.

As Jeanette was about to undress in her room, there was a soft knock on the door. She wondered who it could be. Etienne? Jean-Paul? A shiver went through her. She composed herself, smoothing her hair, adjusting the collar on her dress, took a deep breath and slowly opened the door. It was Etienne. First she was disappointed, then delighted. She was comfortable with Etienne, and safe from her inner self, not like some bumbling, fumbling schoolgirl, tongue-tied with her first crush. "Good evening, Monsieur Dupré," she said, holding the door open.

"Good evening." He came in, hobbled across the room and sat down.

"The children have already been put to bed. . . ."

"Yes, I thought they would be. I came to ask you how the day went."

"All things considered, I think quite well."

"Truly?"

"Yes, especially after your brother left. I felt an immediate lessening of tension on Lucien's part. I think your brother was very helpful."

"No doubt." He might have known it. Jean-Paul, always the arbiter, always the winner. . . .

Jeanette noticed the touch of resentment on his face and a slight bitterness in his voice. Apparently she had said something that disturbed him, but she couldn't know what. She changed the subject. "Mr. Dupré, may I take my day off on Saturdays? I usually attend memorial services for my father then. Saturday is the Sabbath for us."

He was brought back from his thoughts of Jean-Paul. "Of course. That can be arranged without any problem."

"Oh, thank you. Mademoiselle Valeriese's list says that the children attend early mass on Sunday. That too will be no problem."

Etienne returned her smile, but it was edged with sadness. Monsieur Dryfus had told him that Jeanette, too, had recently suffered a great loss. "I've known of your father's death from the beginning. . . ." He stood up abruptly to leave and on his way out told her that the piano would be delivered the next day. "Good night, mademoiselle," he said.

"Good night, monsieur."

A lovely man, she thought, as she went to her bathroom and let the bath water flow into the tub. She undressed and stood nude in front of the long mirror attached to the door and looked at her body. As thoughts of Jean-Paul, not Etienne, came rushing into her mind, it was like discovering herself for the first time. She was really too thin; her breasts were too small and flat, not at all like the voluptuous Madeleine's. She lifted them, trying to imagine how they would look fuller, concluding that she simply was not sensuous . . . but suddenly, that was very much what she wanted to be . . . full-breasted and voluptuous. Starting tomorrow she would eat more, much more. . . . She toyed with her hair, piling it on top of her head. If she tried a little harder, she decided, she could be quite pretty. Well, she would try. . . .

The bath water had almost reached the brim of the tub. She turned off the taps just in time to avoid a disaster. She drained some of it, got in and lay back, dreaming of how it would feel to be loved by a man like Jean-Paul. It would, she decided, be heaven. But before her fantasies could take her very far, they were replaced by logic. He undoubtedly had his pick of the most beautiful women in Paris, and here she lay, hopelessly flat-chested and pale by comparison with those women. . . . She was a nobody, a governess. Thank God one's thoughts belonged only to oneself, and she would never need risk the amusement he would surely feel if he even suspected hers. . . .

She got out of the tub and wiped herself dry. Then put on a fresh cotton nightgown and got into bed, trying to think of something, *anything*, to divert her mind . . . she thought about Aunt Deborah and Uncle Leon . . . about Madeleine. . . . But Jean-Paul came back, again and again, and for the first time in her life she knew, she acknowledged, the stirrings of desire. She wanted him beyond belief.

She was brought up sharply by an outburst of cries from Desirée. Jumping out of bed, she ran to the child, picked her up, and held her close. "It's all right, my little one, it's all right. Jeanette is here and nothing can hurt you." She carried the child to her bed . . . comforting and soothing her. And there Desirée slept, close in Jeanette's arms all night.

Lucien's attitude began to show signs of a definite change, and Uncle Jean-Paul continued to talk to him. By the end of the month he had capitulated. Jeanette responded in kind, knowing that what he needed most in the world was just to be loved. Sometimes she gave him even more attention than the others, when she felt the situation called for it.

One evening after she'd listened to his prayers and gathered the blankets around him, Lucien looked up at her, his large brown eyes soft and no longer guarded. Sensing the moment, how difficult it was for him to make the first overture, respecting his pride, Jeanette sat down on the edge of the bed, and slowly, tentatively, took his hand in hers. In a moment, he reached out and hugged her. She kissed him on the forehead as he clung to her, tears in his eyes. It had been a long time since he'd been embraced by someone soft who smelled of sweet-scented soap . . . by someone like his mother. In that moment all the pent-up feelings came tumbling out, and from that time on their friendship truly began.

On Saturdays the children now missed her terribly. Lucien would remain silent, somewhat sullen, staying for the most part in his room. When she returned in the early evening they ran to her joyfully, as though she'd been away for a week. Each time she brought them a gift, not expensive, but a reminder of how much she loved them.

One Saturday she returned with toy instruments. A drum for Lucien, a piccolo for Nicole, and a horn for Desirée. She had begun to give them piano lessons, and now they could have an orchestra as well.

Jeanette played the piano, Lucien beat the drum in time to the simple French song she played while Nicole hummed into the piccolo and Desirée blew the horn. They loved it and begged for more. It was more fun than they'd ever had with Mademoiselle Valeriese. The concert came to an end abruptly when Jean-Paul walked in. He began to laugh at the sight. Jeanette had been embarrassed. After shakily greeting him, she was forced to go to her room in order to stop trembling. No matter when she saw him, he brought out the same incredible feeling. . . . It was sheer misery.

When the children had been put to bed she felt very restless. Wanting to talk to someone, she went downstairs to the kitchen. Clothilde, the cook, had just finished her chores. When she saw Jeanette she was surprised, especially since it was Saturday. Jeanette had never come to the kitchen at this time of night. She had liked Jeanette from the very beginning. She wasn't like that so superior Mademoiselle Valeriese, always trying to put on airs as though she were born to the purple, the very idea. This one was modest, along with a spirit Clothilde admired. Clothilde knew how she had conquered the children and how Monsieur Etienne had been her champion when she was hired. Yes, she liked this one more than just a little.

Jeanette returned the older woman's affection. True, Clothilde tended to rule the other servants, her word was law and few disputed her. She not only had seniority, but in her mind this house was her birthright. She was a woman of violent likes and dislikes; there were no in-betweens. She loved Madame, was completely devoted to her. Although they were about the same age, for all her hard labors Clothilde didn't look her fifty-five years, whereas Madame, for all her luxurious living, looked much older. Of course, Clothilde had noticed the abrupt change in her mistress almost from the day her husband, Marshal Dupré, had died. . . .

"Sit down and have a cup of coffee," she told Jeanette now. And for a while, they drank in silence, Clothilde peering over the rim of her cup, observing Jeanette. Finally, without any preamble, she said, "You're lonely tonight, yes?"

"I suppose, a little."

"Well, that's natural, a young girl on a Saturday night with no boyfriend. Why do you come back so early on your day off?"

"I like it here . . . besides, I have nothing else to do—"

"You have no friends?"

"Well, one, a dear friend—"

"Ah, a young man, and you come home so early? What kind of a romance is that?"

"No, my friend is a girl, her name is Madeleine. I spent the afternoon with her."

"Ah ha. I see. But I think you come home for more than one reason."

Jeanette's heart jumped. Had Clothilde discovered her need to see Jean-Paul, not to miss the possibility of seeing him for a moment in the evening, which was when he usually came. . . . But then she reasoned, how could she? She'd said nothing.

"You miss the children, no?"

That was true. In fact, when she left for the day, it was almost with a feeling of guilt, as though she was abandoning them. "Yes, I miss them. . . . "

"I knew it. You see, dear, our jobs become our lives. Whether good or bad, that's how it is. Whatever her age, Mademoiselle Valeriese was still a virgin when she left. I'd bet money on it. Why do you think I'm alone in the world today? Because I paid more attention to the Duprés than I did to my husband, Marcel. I gave him too much freedom to stray, and so one day he went off, without a word. . . . Ah, well, that's life. . . . "

"Are you trying to tell me, Clothilde, that I shouldn't have taken this job?"

"I'm not trying to tell you anything. I'm just an old party philosophizing. When one decides to go into service, it is like going into a nunnery." She laughed.

"Why didn't you ever remarry?"

"Who had time? Besides, this is my home and the Duprés are my family."

"You've been here a long time, haven't you?"

"I was practically born here. My mother was here when Marshal Dupré's mother and father were the masters. I saw the children born." For a moment she was quiet, then continued. "To think of Denise, that beauty, in her grave

. . . it's unbelievable. . . . But of all the children, Etienne is the best. I love him the most. And, I might say, Jean-Paul the least. He's a scoundrel, that one, although I must admit a most charming one."

"But how can you say that . . . ? I'm shocked," Jeanette said, and blushed, in spite of herself.

Clothilde's eye noted it. "I see he's gotten to you already, yes?"

Jeanette didn't answer, certain that her voice would confirm Clothilde's suspicions.

"No need to answer," said Clothilde. "I can see that he's charmed you." She pursed her lips, then said, "Now listen to me, my dear. I'm going to tell you something I've told very few—"

Jeanette came to Jean-Paul's defense automatically . . . if it was derogatory she didn't want to hear it. "Please don't, Clothilde. I have the highest regard for Monsieur Dupré."

"Of that I have no doubt. In fact, I suspect you're already in love with him."

Jeanette was stunned. How transparent her feelings for Jean-Paul must be. Suddenly, she had to confide in someone. "Yes, yes, I am, Clothilde. I know it's ridiculous but I can't help it. But he must never know . . . *please* . . ."

Clothidle sighed. "You asked me not to tell you, but I'm going to, all the same. I'm going to tell you because you're very young, and vulnerable and . . . well, I am a mother, with a daughter, of course older than you. But when she was young, your age, she met and fell in love with and went off with a sailor from Marseille. I thought I would die . . . and today I don't even know where they are. . . . I guess my own experience, my daughter's, makes me feel as I do toward you. So listen to what I have to tell you. . . ."

She began with the birth of Etienne, when Jean-Paul was four. Until Etienne's arrival, Jean-Paul had been not only the baby, but also the idol of his mother, who showered him with love. He was, too, the first boy, the great gift Antoinette had given her husband to carry on the name of Dupré. And, in return, Jean-Paul not only loved his mother, he possessed her. He wanted her to love no one else but him. Even at that age his jealousy had been obsessive. Then, suddenly, a stranger had come into his life, a deformed stranger, and had taken his mother away from him. From the moment of Etienne's birth, Jean-Paul had despised him, not only because the new one had replaced him in his mother's affection, but because she left him for long periods of time, taking the deformed monster away, seeking, searching, for a cure. They went from one European specialist to another—to Germany, to Vienna, to Switzerland. Wherever she heard there was a new specialist, they went. . . . None of the doctors had a cure. Finally she became resigned to the fate of her youngest child.

Once, when the family was at the seashore, the children were playing in the surf. Jean-Paul swam out a little farther, and insisted that Etienne swim out to meet him. Etienne, only five, tried to walk out to meet his brother. Although the water was shallow, Etienne lost his footing and the undertow began to drag him away. He panicked, calling out to Jean-Paul and filling his lungs with water. Jean-Paul did nothing. He *wanted* this wicked monster who'd deprived him of his mother to drown. If it hadn't been for Denise, who saw what was happening, Etienne would have drowned. Denise had awakened the governess, who had fallen asleep on the beach. The governess had managed to swim out to Etienne and tow him in. She laid him face-down on the beach and pumped the water from his lungs. When the grandmother, Madame Dupré, learned what had happened, she blamed the governess entirely and dismissed her at once.

Clothilde continued, "Now you see, my dear, why Madame was so concerned when you came to take charge of the children, feeling that only an older woman was qualified?"

"Yes, I can understand that. But how can you accuse Monsieur Dupré of wanting something so dreadful to happen to his brother? A brother's jealousy, perhaps, but—"

"Believe it, my dear. I know what I speak about. Once when the boys were older, in the heat of an argument, Jean-Paul became so angry he shouted at Etienne, 'She should have let you drown.' "

Jeanette shook her head. She couldn't, wouldn't believe this was true.

"All right, maybe it's good to have illusions," the older woman said.

"Clothilde, the Jean-Paul Dupré I have met is not an illusion. He's kind, and understanding. He's helped me tremendously with the children. I could never have won Lucien over so quickly if it weren't for him."

"I've no doubt of it . . . but don't you see? He must always *look* good."

Jeanette hesitated before speaking. Finally she said, "Clothilde, forgive me for asking this . . . but why do you hate Monsieur Jean-Paul so much? Isn't it, perhaps, because Monsieur Jean-Paul is everything his brother isn't?"

"No. It's because he isn't honorable."

"He isn't *honorable* . . . ? How can you say that? Among other things, I understand he has a very responsible job with the government, very unusual for so young a man—"

Clothilde laughed until tears came to her eyes, and she wiped them away with her apron. "Oh, my dear, did you ever hear of a government, especially ours, that was honorable?" And then she became serious again. "I also dislike him for this . . . he tries to appeal to poor Madame to give him the inheritance that should have been Denise's, instead of sharing it equally between himself and Etienne. If he could he'd deprive Etienne of this house—"

"How do you know all this?"

"Why, you silly little duck, you think that because I stay in the kitchen I don't know what goes on in this house? I know everything. Jean-Paul is avaricious, and vicious . . . money hungry. He'll go to any lengths to get what he wants. He probably won't be content until he becomes Mr. President himself."

"But he already has so much. Why should that be so important to him?"

"Because he wants everything, to be the most important one. . . . And even that wouldn't satisfy him. He even married a woman he despises because she could help him to win his goals. It wasn't a marriage at all, it was a merger. But he's been punished . . . the one thing he wanted was a son. His wife has had four miscarriages—and he doesn't give a tinker's damn for her, only her money. Jean-Paul has three loves—himself, money and his mother. Probably in that order."

Jeanette was stunned and angry. "Why have you told me all this—"

"Because I don't want you to be taken in. Jean-Paul is irresistible to women. He has a mistress now. The first, you think? No, dear. I've stopped counting. He can't resist the temptation of a female, and I don't want you to be the next one hurt. Everything Jean-Paul puts his hands on he maims and destroys. I don't like him, I don't approve of him, and I never shall. I warn you, I ask you, to take care. Don't let your feelings run away with you. At best you would only be a conquest."

"Clothilde, you're just wrong . . . he's never intimated, nor made a gesture that was not gentlemanly—"

"For your sake, I hope he continues to act that way, but I doubt it. . . . Well, I've at least shown the charming Monsieur Jean-Paul Dupré to you for what he is. He's not worth the little finger of Monsieur Etienne. And now, dear, we're both tired. Tomorrow is another day. . . . Please don't dismiss what I've told you."

As she lay in her bed in the dark, the night seemed foreboding, frightening . . . Jeanette thought of things she'd never wanted to recall again. . . . But the past couldn't be ignored. Who knew better than she what brothers could do to one another? Maurice had cheated her father. The circumstances were different from those Clothilde had spoken of, but still, it couldn't be forgiven. Rubin had been denied his inheritance because he'd violated convention, supposedly brought shame to his name by marrying her mother. But the situations must be different. They *must* be. Maurice was a cheat, a thief. How could anybody compare him and Monsieur Jean-Paul. . . .

Jeanette told herself that Clothilde had spoken sincerely but totally out of prejudice, as though in some way she could transform her favorite, Etienne, into Jean-Paul by degrading Jean-Paul. It was just impossible for her to believe otherwise. . . . Oh, God, she wished that Clothilde hadn't told her such things. But it didn't matter, Jean-Paul *was* all the things she felt about him. He had to be. . . . She blocked out what she didn't want to believe, couldn't believe.

She hadn't known, though, until tonight that Jean-Paul

was married. It had been a startling surprise. His wife had never come to visit the children even once. All she'd known was that he didn't live in his mother's home. Since he was twenty-nine, and away so much of the time on official business, Jeanette had concluded that it was simply a better arrangement for him, but now that she knew he was married, she suddenly felt threatened. Of course, he could never have been hers. But still, she had at least been able to fantasize that one day she'd become a great beauty, maybe even the toast of Paris. And that suddenly he'd discover her and fall hopelessly in love with her. As she was with him. Of course, she knew it could never happen, but still . . .

And as for Jean-Paul's wife . . . well, she no doubt was petulant and arrogant, and independent . . . like her father's wife . . . no wonder he didn't care for her. . . . She didn't even have the decency to visit the children, or their grandmother. If Jean-Paul despised his wife, as Clothilde had said, then surely he was justified.

As the weeks passed Jeanette felt a peace and contentment she'd not known before. What she'd felt from the very first for Jean-Paul didn't diminish, but she was satisfied merely to be in his presence when he came to visit.

The children adored her. She thought she understood now something of what Clothilde had meant when she told her that going into service was a way of life. They seemed to be her children; she felt they had transferred their love for their mother to her. In fact, they felt so close to her that they now called her Jeanette. Their memories of Mademoiselle Valeriese were distant and no longer a threat.

Only Madame was appalled that the children called her by her first name, but Etienne quickly overruled his mother's objections, a task made easier since she, too, had seen the enormous change in the children since Jeanette's arrival. They were, undeniably, happy, contented children, when just a short time ago they'd been bewildered and confused.

So Jeanette's life was full. She had her children, and her love . . . though the latter had to be secret. And each day Etienne made a contribution with his understanding, gentleness and concern, always supporting her. He came to visit at least twice a day, which pleased her. He complimented her on how well the children were doing and listened patiently to the simple piano recitals the children were only too eager to perform, a considerable accomplishment in itself, she thought wryly.

Today when Etienne came to visit, Jeanette was helping Lucien and Nicole with their reading as Desirée sat on her lap and listened. Jeanette looked up and smiled, ready to stop the lesson, but Etienne gestured for her to continue. Quietly he sat down in the large wing-back chair and observed the group, thinking it was a sight worthy of a painting by Renoir. Etienne felt a warm contentment in this place, as though no harsh world existed outside this room.

When the lessons were over, the children greeted Uncle Etienne with kisses, and then Lucien played on the floor with his soldiers, while Nicole and Desirée played house, pouring make-believe tea and serving make-believe pastries.

"Good morning, sir." Jeanette smiled at Etienne. "I'm sorry we were in the midst of our lessons when you came in."

"I'm happy you were. The children seem to me to be reading remarkably well, or is that just a doting uncle's pride?"

"No, you're quite right. They're really exceptional in their comprehension. They learn so quickly that I'm giving them more advanced lessons. Monsieur Dupré, I've hesitated until now, but there are some things I'd like to ask your permission to do with the children. . . . May I?"

"Of course."

"Well, they've never been to the carousel or the park. I thought it would be great fun if we visited the zoo. And I know they'd enjoy an excursion to the Bois de Boulogne."

"I see no objection to that. Whenever you're ready to go I'll have André drive you."

"Monsieur, another thing . . . in their own best interests, I think they should have more exposure to people. Instead of being driven, I'd like to go by metro . . . and have lunch at a sidewalk café. And, also, I suspect they'd enjoy a boat ride down the Seine."

"I hope you don't intend to complete this safari in one day."

She laughed. "No, sir . . . we'll do it gradually. I want the children to learn that life can be full of adventure."

"You make it sound so exciting I almost wish I were seeing Paris for the first time with such a governess. . . ."

Etienne understood very well why the children loved her. What a remarkable young woman she was. He was more grateful than ever to Monsieur Dryfus for recommending her, and shuddered to remember that he had almost sent her away. . . .

Seventeen

Traditionally, by the twenty-fifth of June the Dupré household was in preparation for the exodus to the château in Provence, where they would spend the summer. They usually left Paris on the first of July, returning September first. This year was no exception. This year it would be an especially welcome respite after the sorrow the family had suffered. It would be good to feel the serenity of the countryside, to walk in the Dupré vineyards, to feel the good earth of Provence under their feet . . . the summer should help to restore their spirits.

Following their departure, the furniture was draped in white linen, giving the enormous rooms a ghostlike atmosphere. The Baccarat crystal chandeliers were covered, and also the Sèvres and the paintings, since only a caretaker and his elderly wife would remain in the house during their absence.

At eight o'clock on July first, Madame, dressed entirely in black, was escorted by Jean-Paul to the waiting limousine. Marie Jacqueline Eugenie Mallette, Jean-Paul's wife, was already seated when Madame got in. Jean-Paul sat between them, and Etienne took the seat attached to the partition that divided the family from the driver, in front of his mother.

In all, there were four vehicles. The second limousine was reserved for the children and Jeanette, who brought toys and books along to hold the children's attention on the long drive. A large touring car carried Clothilde and her staff, and a lorry took the remaining household servants and all the provisions for the journey, which took almost two days.

The trip was broken with a stop at the Auberge de la Fontaine aux Muses, where the Duprés had a standing reservation each year. Several times during the journey Phillipe, the driver of Jeanette's car, tooted his horn, which was the signal to stop. All four conveyances then came to a halt and the potty chambers were brought from the lorry. Once relieved, the children climbed back into the limousine and the entourage continued. By eleven o'clock they were halfway to Lyon, and the lead car turned off the road into a green meadow with shade trees. Soon there was a flurry of excitement. The household staff seemed to know exactly what to do. Within minutes a small striped-canvas cabana was erected. Inside were potty chambers both large and small, towels, soap, pitchers of water and wash basins for the family to refresh themselves. Collapsible canvas chairs were arranged for the adults around a big white linen cloth, spread out on the grass. The wicker hampers were unpacked. The wine, which had been chilled on a block of ice inside a large metal tub, was brought out. Clothilde was, of course, in charge of all these arrangements.

The family then settled down to a marvelous luncheon of cold meats, salads, bread, cheese and fruits. Although Clothilde had outdone herself again, none of the family seemed impressed, but to Jeanette it was like a fairy tale, or something out of *Uncle Vanya*. Madame was sitting there like a *grand dame*, which, indeed, she was. Alongside her sat her daughter-in-law. It was the first time Jeanette had seen her. She was shocked. Marie Jacqueline was not at all what she'd expected. She was almost ugly. Her nose ran, and her eyes watered. She was constantly using her handkerchief. She apparently suffered from dreadful allergies, complaining continually about the weather. One minute it was too hot, and the next it was too cold. The insects were almost intolerable to her, although no one else complained. No *wonder* Jean-Paul had mistresses, Jeanette thought. She also realized, with small credit to herself, that Marie Jacqueline's discomfort was giving her a guilty sense of pleasure.

Desirée was full of mischief, since she had slept a great part of the way. Now she wanted to play tag with Lucien, who refused. Then she begged Nicole, but Nicole refused, too. Finally she said, "Jeanette, please chase me . . . ?"

As Jeanette got up, Etienne said, "No, Desirée. Let mademoiselle rest. She's tired like the rest of us."

Madame shot an imperious glance at Etienne. How dare he include Jeanette with the rest of them . . . the very idea!

Desirée persisted. "Please, Jeanette?"

Etienne was about to speak again when Madame said, "Oh, very well, go along, my child, with mademoiselle. But be *careful.* . . ."

By two o'clock the entourage was again on the dirt road to Lyon. At seven they arrived at the Auberge de la Fontaine aux Muses, and with considerable pomp, the management staff came forward to greet the Duprés. A bouquet of flowers was presented to Madame. How privileged, as always, they were to see her and her family. The Duprés were taken to their suites, where bottles of chilled champagne awaited them, while the servants retreated to quarters reserved for them in another building. The Duprés occupied the entire second floor, along with Jeanette. Madame's suite consisted of a large bedroom, a smaller room for her personal maid, Renée, an oversized sitting room and a bath. Jean-Paul and his wife had the suite next door. This suite, however, had two bedrooms, since Jean-Paul and his wife hadn't shared the same bedroom since just after their marriage. The suite also had a sitting room and two separate baths. Etienne's suite was less imposing, with one large bed-sitting room and a bath. Jeanette and the children were given the fourth suite down the hall—a spacious room with three single beds placed close to one another, two large wing chairs, a small, round dining table and four matching chairs. Jeanette's room connected, and there was one bath to accommodate the four of them.

Because of the long trip the children were attended to immediately. Dinner was brought to them, and they ate with great relish. Soon after they became restless and cranky and were bathed and put to bed. They fell asleep, uncharacteristically, almost immediately. Jeanette went to her bedroom and wrote to Deborah and Leon, and to Madeleine. Then she bathed, and finally fell asleep, with sweet thoughts of Jean-Paul. . . .

Madame, too exhausted to dress and go downstairs, had decided to have dinner sent to her room, and Jean-Paul, not wanting to eat alone with his wife, suggested that they all join their mother.

Shortly after dinner they all said good night and kissed Mother on the cheek, told her they hoped she'd feel more rested in the morning and went to their separate rooms.

Jean-Paul was restless. He sat on the edge of his bed, overcome with boredom. Marie Jacqueline had been especially tiresome today. He had loved Provence since childhood, but having to spend the long summer there with her was like drinking hemlock. At least in Paris he could escape . . . service in the diplomatic corps took him, thank God, to faraway places, such as the one he'd only recently returned from, Algiers, where he was attached to the foreign office. And he'd still be there if it weren't for Denise's death. The only time he was really happy was when he was away from Marie Jacqueline. Out of town, he did miss his mother, but he missed neither Paris nor his mistresses, whom he could always replace wherever he went. And he could always visualize his dear wife hanging the large crucifix over her bed, religious fanatic that she was. He wondered how she would survive the summer without the divine help of Father Verdous. He had to laugh. She couldn't possibly sleep, not even one night, without the protection of the image of Christ above her bed. When she went to confession, what the hell did she have to confess? She led a completely celibate life, and had in recent years become a recluse, taking care of her cats, numbering six at his last count. Those damned cats, of course, were the reason for her allergies. She'd been to one specialist after another. They all gave her the same diagnosis: her condition was caused by the animals. When she refused to give them up, saying she'd rather be ill than be deprived of what she considered were her children, the doctors all suggested she see a psychiatrist. Perhaps, they said, it was anxiety that initiated the attacks she had, which brought with them not only the wheezing, but the runny nose, the watery eyes and the headaches. The awful headaches.

Damn it, he thought, maybe he had been just a bit too ambitious at twenty-four in marrying her. Was all the money worth it? He asked himself the question often, and the answer was always the same. Yes, it was. Maybe the cats would kill her; in that case, there'd be no question about it. What bothered him the most was that Marie Jacqueline, unproductive bitch that she was, hadn't even been able to provide him with a son. She'd become pregnant all right, but she had always miscarried after three or four months.

These trips to Provence were always difficult. The mere fact that she was with him made them so. He avoided her as much as possible but he couldn't leave her in Paris, if not for the sake of propriety, at least out of respect for his mother. As far as his mother was concerned, where a husband went, so went his wife. Talk about crosses!

It was late, but he decided to go down to the dining room. The last guests were leaving as he came in. He sat at a small table and a young girl approached him.

"Good evening, monsieur. What is your pleasure?"

His eyes strayed to the full bosom that overlapped the peasant blouse, then to the flaxen hair. He wanted to say, "You," but instead he smiled his famous disarming smile. "Brandy, mademoiselle."

When she placed the snifter in front of him, Jean-Paul reached for it and tipped it over. The young girl blushed and became flustered as the liquid dripped on his clean white trousers.

"Forgive me, monsieur, I've ruined your trousers. Please pardon my clumsiness." On the edge of tears, she tried to repair the damage by wiping the spill on his pants leg. When she bent down, he was pleased to look inside her blouse.

He took her hand and gently guided it. "My dear, you're making too much of this. Accidents happen. . . ."

"I know, monsieur, but this is unforgivable—"

"Anyone as pretty as you is easily forgiven."

"You're too kind, monsieur."

"Not at all. Trousers can be cleaned, but feelings are not so easily repaired. It could happen to anyone," he said, still holding her hand.

"Thank you, monsieur. May I get you another brandy?"

"Only if you'll join me."

"But I can't do that—"

"Why?"

"It's against the rules to become friendly with the guests—"

"But there's no one here now."

"I know. But still, if anybody should see me sitting with you, I'd lose my job . . . you do understand? Although of course I'd be most honored. . . ."

"Of course. I shouldn't even have suggested such a thing"—he smiled—"and now I will have the brandy, if you don't mind."

When she brought him another drink, he took the glass between his hands and twisted it back and forth. His eyes had not left her for a moment.

"Can I get you anything else, monsieur, before I leave?"

"Oh, I'm sorry. I didn't realize you were through."

"That's quite all right."

"Are you on your way to meet your husband?"

"Oh, no, monsieur. I'm not married. I live with my mother."

"But I bet there's a young man waiting for you."

"No, monsieur. . . ."

"But you do have a young man? Maybe more than one?"

"No," she said, "just one."

"Just one . . . then it must be serious."

"No . . . I haven't decided whether to marry him or not."

"Why is that?"

"Because he's a farmer and I want to see Paris before I get married."

"Paris?"

"Yes, monsieur. I've never been far from Lyon. And if I don't go to Paris before I marry, perhaps I never will. . . . Please forgive me, monsieur, but I really have to go now. Good night, sir."

She walked back through the kitchen to get her coat, then went out through the back entrance and walked down the gravel path.

Standing at the end of it was Jean-Paul. She was startled, and breathing a little too hard. "Good night, monsieur," she said again, and walked past him.

Jean-Paul followed her. "Please allow me to walk you home, mademoiselle."

"No, thank you, monsieur. It's strictly forbidden—"

"But who would know? As a matter of fact, I was going for a walk myself. It would be my pleasure to have your company . . . walking alone is too lonely, especially on such a lovely night."

"Yes . . . that would be nice . . . but if I were found out, then what?"

"Oh, my dear mademoiselle, you worry too much for someone so young and charming. Besides, who will know? If you don't tell, I promise I won't."

She looked at him, directly this time. "All right, monsieur. But let's hurry. . . ."

As they walked, she talked constantly, although he scarcely heard what she was saying. Her mother was a laundress, her father a member of the merchant marine and was away most of the time. She told him about her farmer boyfriend. . . . Jean-Paul answered by saying "Yes," "No," "How delightful"—or whatever.

When they reached the front door of her house, the lights were out. As they stood in the moonlight, she thanked him for walking her home. "I enjoyed it. . . ." She put her hand on the doorknob.

He took her other hand in his and kissed it. "This has been one of the nicest evenings I've had. Just meeting you." He bent and kissed her. Then, slowly and calmly, he closed his arms around her body, feeling the firm bosom move beneath his embrace. She didn't resist. The kiss started slowly, then gathered force until she clung to him, one hand fondling his face, her fingers running through his hair. He placed his own hand on the doorknob as he freed it from her grasp and turned it. Then he pushed the door open with his foot.

He picked her up. She pointed out her room to him. Once there, he stood her on her feet, continuing to kiss her. He undid her blouse, unbuttoned the bodice, released the skirt, then took off the petticoat. He kissed the exposed nipples. His mouth ventured downward. She stepped out of her panties, then her shoes. She removed the round garters, pulled off the black silk stockings and stood before him, nude. She then quickly undressed him, taking off his jacket, his tie, unbuttoning his shirt. She kissed his body as her fingers unbuttoned his trousers and shed his underclothes. He lifted her off the floor, her legs wound around him, and by the time he lay down with her in his arms, he had already entered her. She was not naïve, as he had first thought, but clearly a bitch in heat.

Obviously he wasn't the first to have her. . . . She made love passionately, keeping pace with each of his twists and turns. Her responsiveness was remarkable . . . she knew when to go slowly, when to push harder, to squeeze, to entice, and when to glide and guide hands to the right places. When the climax finally came, they both lay quietly, in complete satisfied exhaustion.

The last thing he heard before dropping off into deep sleep was her voice whispering in his ear, "You are magnificent, monsieur."

Slowly, he opened his eyes. He yawned, then sat up abruptly. My God, it was morning! He shook the sleeping body next to his. The girl awakened languidly, stretched and reached her arms out to him.

"What time is it?" he said.

She looked at the bedside clock; it was five o'clock.

Thank God! They were scheduled to leave at eight to reach Provence by dark. He hurried into his clothes as the girl watched him.

"Must you go, monsieur?"

"Yes, to my great regret. It's best this way, before your mother wakes up. No one must know about this—just as you said last night."

"Will I see you again?"

"Nothing could keep me away, I'll be back in September—"

"But that's such a long time from now."

"Three months, what is that?"

"A very long time, after last night."

"We'll take up where we left off. And someday you'll come to Paris and be my guest—"

"Do you really *mean* that?" she said, getting out of bed, not bothering to cover her naked body.

"Do you think I could ever forget you? After this?" He slipped into his jacket, kissed her on the forehead. She reached for his mouth, but he was already on his way out, saying, smiling, "Now, I must go, really. Until the next time . . ."

He walked rapidly, running when he could, across the pasture. Once back at the Auberge de la Fontaine aux Muses he took the stairs two steps at a time, and reached his room. He shaved, then took a bath, lying back in the tub, laughing quietly at the evening's success. Suddenly he realized he didn't even know her name. Well, it didn't matter. Any port in a storm . . .

At eight o'clock the Dupré entourage moved out, amid good-byes and much waving from the management. They drove at a more moderate speed, twenty-five miles an hour, because the roads were bumpy and had begun to narrow. There were new delays. . . . From time to time a herd of sheep crossed over the road going from one field to another. Marie Jacqueline had a coughing and sneezing attack from the pollen and had to be administered to from the ever-present medicine kit, from which she took a pill, then inserted the atomizer into her nostrils, inhaling deeply.

Looking at his wife, Jean-Paul said, "Perhaps these trips are too strenuous for you. Perhaps you should have stayed in Paris. . . ."

She glared at him. "You speak as though these spells are my fault."

"Well, aren't they?"

"How dare you say that to me! You *know* I'm allergic to pollen—"

"That's my point. If you'd get rid of those damned cats, or stay away from the pollen, perhaps you wouldn't have so many allergies."

"Everything I enjoy you criticize," she said. "And in case you haven't noticed, I don't *have* the cats now, so how can that—"

Madame Dupré could stand no more. "Jean-Paul, I won't allow you to speak that way to your wife. I think you owe Marie Jacqueline an apology."

He bit his lip, and without looking at her finally said, "I'm sorry I spoke to you that way." His famous smile was missing. Then he picked up the mouthpiece and instructed André to stop the car. André signalled the other vehicles and stopped. Jean-Paul got out of the back seat and into the front, where he sat with André until they reached the Moulin le Cols, where they would lunch.

It was just twelve o'clock, and the party was greeted profusely by the owner, the chef and the staff. By twelve-thirty the family and Jeanette were seated at the large round table. The wine was poured and a country luncheon served. But for all the bucolic atmosphere of the deep, lush countryside—which could be seen through an entire wall of glass doors—lunch was a silent, depressing affair. The adult Duprés ate almost mechanically, neither enjoying nor savoring the good food which had been so carefully prepared for them. Each kept his, or her, own thoughts.

Madame sighed with impatience. What, she wondered, has become of my family, my life? Jean-Paul was unhappily married. He was completely incompatible with his wife, which pained and grieved her. They were childless, which also grieved her. Jean-Paul was unkind and contemptuous toward Marie Jacqueline, which further grieved her . . . although in the beginning, when he had announced his intention to marry, she had not approved of the union. (That, at least, was a comfort.) Not because Marie Jacqueline was unsuited to become a Dupré. She was. In fact, the Mallettes were fully as distinguished as the Duprés. Their name evoked equal respect. But, really, she had never cared for Marie Jacqueline. The girl was neither warm nor pretty nor appealing in grace. From the beginning, she had known that it was not a marriage of love. She knew that Jean-Paul was not sufficiently mature at twenty-four to be a faithful and devoted husband, such as she had had. He still had too many wild oats to sow. But she had not opposed the marriage, wrong as she knew it was. And now her only daughter was gone, and her dear Etienne would remain a celibate all of his life, wifeless and childless, with no one to care for him. What *would* ultimately become of her dearest son . . . ? Oh, dear God, she thought, I thank you, heavenly Father, for sparing my beloved Henri the sight I now see before my eyes. She took out a white handkerchief, edged with black lace, from her sleeve and pretended to wipe her brow, but the handkerchief went to her eyes as she wiped the two glistening tears that were ready to fall down her cheeks. She blinked back the rest and continued to attempt to eat.

Jean-Paul looked across at his mother. She was the only person in the world who could stir in him a feeling of true, honest love, and guilt . . . even remorse. And at this moment, as he saw the handkerchief reach her eyes, he felt all three. He never wanted to make her unhappy, as he'd done today, but he simply couldn't stand Marie Jacqueline and her eternal wheezing. He hated having his mother see the worst in him, which he always tried to prevent, wanting her to see only the little boy of four, whom she'd loved, the love he still remembered and wanted. . . . With all the compassion he was capable of, his heart went out to her, knowing how she suffered when his father had died, when not even *he* could console her, as he was unable to comfort her now on the death of his sister and brother-in-law. Nothing and no one could replace them, or diminish their memories for her. If only he, Jean-Paul, had been enough for her, but of course he never was, which he could never accept, or understand. . . .

Sipping his wine, Etienne observed Marie Jacqueline. He knew it wasn't the cats or the pollen. It wasn't the allergies that caused her illness, it was the lack of love, of compassion, that was killing her. There were many ways to die . . . not only the way his sister had perished. Yes, he felt more than sorry for Marie Jacqueline. He couldn't even express his pity in words. Let her have her cats. What else did she have? No husband, no children to love and be loved by. At least she might have given them what she'd been deprived of. What's going to become of us, he thought. Just a decaying family, that's all we are. After our generation, the Dupré name will be finished. The children were only half-Dupré. The house of Balevre, the name of the children's father, would at least be perpetuated by Lucien, but . . .

The coughing started again, and Marie Jacqueline tried desperately to suppress it by taking a sip of wine. She knew Jean-Paul would say nothing this time, with his mother present, but she felt his irritation anyway. Stronger than irritation, his anger. Dear God, why had she married him? How different he was from the young man who had courted her, showering her with gifts and flowers and candy. She'd been the envy of every debutante in Paris. She'd plucked the most eligible plum, especially considering she was three years older than he was. He'd been so handsome, with such perfect manners. He was such a *complete* gentleman, and so clever at turning a phrase. Like day into night was the change in Jean-Paul, almost from the very moment he had taken her to their marriage bed. He wasn't kind. He wasn't gentle, as he should have been, since she'd saved herself for him. He was brutal when he entered her on their wedding night, as though she were an enemy, not his bride. She would never forget that . . . or forgive him for it.

After that, on the dutiful occasions when she performed her wifely and religious obligations, she did so with revulsion, hoping . . . praying to the Virgin Mary that at least she would be blessed with one child. If at least one son could be born, it would put an end to any further sexual responsibilities toward her husband. But Mother Mary apparently had reason not to bless her with a son, and, finally, after four miscarriages, Jean-Paul never again stepped over the threshold to her bedroom. There was no need; he had mistresses who relieved him. She wondered, as she had many times before, how two brothers could be so different, coming from the same womb. She felt drawn to Etienne, almost as though they shared an affinity. If only Jean-Paul had Etienne's nature, and his own magnificent body, how different her life might have been. . . .

The only one who had no such gloomy, regretful thoughts was Jeanette. For the first time, she was sitting in an intimate circle with the whole Dupré clan. From time to time her eyes wandered to the scenery beyond—but not without first glancing at Jean-Paul, feeling her excitement at just being with him in a situation as familiar and intimate as this. It no longer mattered to her that she had to keep secret her love for him inside herself. It was enough that in her fantasies he belonged to her . . . when she grew warm from wanting him all through the night. It was a desire she knew would never become reality, but her life seemed fulfilled just the same . . . just knowing she loved, was able to love, this way. . . . She laughed to herself, watching the red-eyed, drippy-nosed Marie Jacqueline. Silly goose that she'd been, thinking herself too thin and not pretty enough. If indeed Jean-Paul had married Marie Jacqueline for the reasons Clothilde had said—which she doubted—then he surely deserved the money. It should have been enough for *her* just being Madame Jean-Paul Dupré.

After lunch was over, Madame retired. So did Marie Jacqueline, to rest before resuming the journey. Jean-Paul went off for a stroll through the meadow and lay down under a tree, feeling the marvelous earth beneath him. He was thinking of the girl who was waiting for him in Provence. He'd had a liaison with her for several summers now, the buxom wife of a farmer, much the same sort as the little tart he'd taken last night. He enjoyed these women of Provence; they were worth a dozen Paris courtesans. Their instincts guided them. There was nothing studied in their advances. There were no games, no tricks, just pure animal hunger. . . . With such delicious thoughts, he fell asleep.

By two o'clock the entourage was progressing again. In the second car, the children were restless. Lucien fussed at Nicole, who complained, "Lucien won't let me have the red crayon."

"Why, Lucien?" Jeanette said.

"Because I need it for my picture, and she's using yellow and green."

"But I want to make red flowers now," said Nicole.

"Let Lucien finish and then you can have the red."

"I want it now."

"No," Jeanette said firmly. "When Lucien has finished, he'll let you have it. He had it first, so that's only fair."

"He didn't. I did," said Nicole.

"That will be enough," Jeanette said. "Come trade places with me, Nicole. I'll sit between you."

"You love him more than you love me," Nicole said.

"I love you all the same. I have no favorites. Now, how would you all like to sing?"

"I would," said Desirée, the unconscious peacemaker, who was sitting on Jeanette's lap.

"All right, let's begin."

And as they did, Desirée suddenly pointed and called out excitedly, "Look at the cow." Only to be told promptly by the man of the crowd that it wasn't a cow but a horse, to which Desirée responded, "It's a cow," and then, looking up at Jeanette with her large brown eyes, she said, "I think it looks like a cow." Jeanette hugged her, laughing. "If you think it looks like a cow, darling, then that's what it is," she said. "Now, for heaven's sake, let's all *sing*."

Finally, miracle of miracles, they managed to arrive at the château. It was dusk. The château and grounds were surrounded for miles by a low field-stone wall. The iron gate had been opened and the four vehicles twisted and turned around the gentle curves of the tree-lined road. It was fifteen minutes after they passed through the gate before . . . standing regally, there was the main house of the château.

The door of the first car was held open as Madame was helped down from the limousine by Etienne. The rest followed.

Three servants were waiting on the steps. They had been at the château in the service of the Duprés for more years than anyone could remember. Louis, the caretaker, and his wife, Brigette, stood alongside Gabrielle, the housekeeper. They greeted each member of the family with properly restrained but obvious delight. Madame was presented with a bouquet of flowers. After thanking them all, she walked into the foyer. The interior was magnificent. The provincial furniture had been carved by the best craftsmen in France. Many of the pieces were over two hundred years old, as was the château, which was kept in constant repair. Unlike those in the Paris house, the paintings here were serene and pastoral. Many were still lifes. The one Jean-Paul had always loved the most pictured a brace of wild ducks strung up by their pink-mauve legs, their plumage so real he wanted to touch the softness.

The floors were polished brick, and the house smelled of mellow-scented furniture wax. Wildflowers were placed everywhere. Gabrielle had worked feverishly all day putting them into vases in every room. There was a total of twenty-two bedrooms, and, at the height of the Dupré dynasty, all of them had been used. Now only the suites on the second floor were needed, and they were reached by a wooden staircase. The banister railings had been carved by a master artisan from Burgundy, who had also carved the long refectory table and sixteen matching high-backed chairs in the dining room, now glowing with the patina of age.

Jeanette was enthralled by it all, but she wasn't to know the pleasure of living in the large house. Close by was a large cottage where all the Dupré adults had stayed in their childhood. But her disappointment was short lived. The cottage turned out to be a diminutive replica of the château, built with the same perfection of detail, and furnished in the same provincial simplicity and elegance.

Her room was charming, the wallpaper was rouge toile

and the curtains matched it. The bed and the small chandelier were brass. The light bulbs were covered by tiny silk shades. She adored it.

The children's rooms were much the same in size, and they, too, were colorfully decorated with wallpaper and matching fabrics. Each had a great four-poster canopied bed, which needed a footstool for the children to climb into.

After they had been bathed and dressed in fresh clothes, they were summoned to the big house for supper. As they walked through the grounds, the landscape was silky with moonlight.

The adult Duprés were already assembled, refreshed, at the long dining table. They were enjoying aperitifs—which were usually served before dinner in the sitting room across the wide brick entry. But tonight such formalities weren't observed. The Duprés were all too tired; they wanted just to get supper out of the way so they could retreat to the privacy of their separate quarters.

Unlike the protocol in Paris, here in Provence the children and Jeanette would take their meals with the family. Jeanette was shown to her chair and the children were seated alongside her.

Etienne said grace. Everyone lowered their eyes except Jeanette, who looked at the bowed heads and thought of how much reason the Duprés had to praise the Lord. He had certainly bestowed His blessings in abundance on them. . . . If the Duprés had their tragedies, they certainly weren't alone. No one escaped. Jeanette couldn't feel altogether sorry for the Duprés, surrounded by such splendor as they were.

The first night's supper was never a hot meal. Tonight's menu was vichyssoise, stuffed fluted eggs, cold sliced capon, and fresh bread with country butter. The wine bore the vintage on the label of the Dupré vineyards. Dessert was a basket of walnuts and a plate of cheeses.

During the meal, there was little conversation. Jeanette was neither included nor excluded, except for an occasional glance from Etienne. She didn't speak at all until after supper, when she asked Madame's permission to leave in order to put the children to bed. Madame nodded her approval. The children kissed her first, then Uncle Etienne, then Uncle Jean-Paul, and then, reluctantly, Aunt

Marie Jacqueline. They disliked kissing her because she always smelled of medicine and looked so pained. . . .

The next day the children woke up at dawn, hardly able to contain themselves. At six-thirty, Lucien decided that Jeanette had slept enough. Nicole agreed. With Desirée tagging along, they knocked on Jeanette's door. There was no response. Lucien opened the door. Jeanette was still asleep. As the leader of the pack, he tiptoed to the bed, looked at her face and listened to her even breathing. He was determined that she should share the morning delights. He shook Jeanette gently. "Are you awake?" he whispered.

Half awake, half asleep, she blinked her eyes, then opened them and turned to see three beautiful, eager faces. "I am now," she said, smiling.

Desirée tried to climb onto the bed. Jeanette lifted her up, then kissed her, as Desirée snuggled close. "You look like peaches and cream, my little doll."

Desirée giggled and kissed Jeanette, touching her face with tiny fingers.

"You, Nicole, come to the other side." Jeanette helped Nicole climb in. "You look like the morning sun. And you, Lucien, look like you're ready for mischief, as usual."

Lucien smiled and sat at the foot of the bed, folding his legs beneath him. "Jeanette, you should *see* it," he said.

"See what?"

"Everything. The ducks and the chickens and the pigs and lambs and the pasture and . . ." On and on he went, listing the wonders of the country that he'd secretly explored earlier that morning.

How marvelous to see the world through the eyes of a seven-year-old, Jeanette thought. What an age, when the whole world seems so young, without a wrinkle of age on her old worn-out face. She wouldn't for a moment deprive Lucien of his first day there. She herself had so few such childhood memories. . . .

"All right, let's all dress and have breakfast. Then off we go."

Nicole and Desirée were dressed in cotton peasant dresses and Lucien wore short beige pants, knee-length stockings and ankle-high buckskin shoes. Jeanette wore a peasant skirt and blouse from Brittany which she'd bought in Paris. The children told her how pretty she looked, and she considered it a high compliment.

They walked to the château for breakfast.

Except for Etienne, the family was still asleep. He was already up to greet them, dressed in country clothes—brown corduroy trousers, held up by a wide black leather belt with a silver buckle. His red-and-white-checked shirt was open at his neck, around which he wore a white handkerchief. The sleeves of his shirt were rolled up, exposing his hairy arms.

"Good morning, Uncle Etienne," the children said. They kissed him and seated themselves, hurrying to get breakfast out of the way.

"Good morning, youngsters, and you, mademoiselle. Why are you up so early? I should think you'd be exhausted." As always, his voice was deep and rich, making Jeanette feel warm and comfortable. There was something so gentle about him, so compassionate . . . like Papa. . . .

She smiled. "Not these three. They've been up since the crack of dawn. I think Lucien already has our itinerary planned. But what about you? Why are you up so early?"

"Well, one of my great pleasures is working in the vineyards with the men. I really look forward to it each year. In fact"—he hesitated—"I tend to find Provence very seductive, like a beautiful country maiden, you might say,"—and noticing her blush, and rather surprised at his own language with her, he hurried on with—"and now I suspect you'll want to see about getting some breakfast for the children, but may I warn you in advance that Clothilde isn't in a very good mood this morning—"

"Why not?"

"It happens every year. She and Gabrielle, the housekeeper, have a feud. Each feels that the other is encroaching on her domain. But in a day or two Clothilde will win out. She always does."

Jeaneatte laughed as she went to the kitchen. Copper pots hung from the wall above a wooden drainboard and a butcher's table. The floor was red tile. There was an enormous wood-and-coal stove and, in the center of the room, there were a table and chairs to accommodate the household staff.

"Good morning, Clothilde."

"Good morning." Clothilde's reply was automatic. She couldn't have cared less who had a good morning. "Now you've come for breakfast, I suppose. . . . Why are you up so early?"

"Because the children are restless."

"You're too easy with them, Jeanette. You'll see. You should be more strict. They need discipline, do you hear me? A firm hand on their buttocks won't hurt." She boiled the water for coffee and the eggs, and stirred the porridge.

Jeanette, knowing the answer in advance, put her arms around Clothilde's more than ample body and said, "Why are you so angry, and on such a nice morning?"

"Ha . . . some nice morning. In a few minutes Madame Gabrielle, the general, will come in here and try to order me around. But today I'm ready for her. This kitchen is mine, and mine it will remain. When I leave, then she can do as she pleases. But while I'm here, she'll listen to me."

Jeanette took the pudgy face between her hands and said, "I love you, Clothilde. Please don't be upset."

"Love!" Clothilde said, somewhat less caustically. "For you to love is not too difficult. You love me, you love . . . I won't mention who, you love the children, you love the day, you love the country. Soon, however, you'll run out of things to love."

"Yes, I can't deny how many things I love, Provence included."

"By the end of the summer you won't love Provence quite so much. You'll see. It gets boring and hot and you'll die from impatience to get back to Paris and the cool breezes of autumn. . . . Now go inside and leave me to my kitchen. Breakfast will be brought to you."

When Jeanette got back to the dining room, Etienne was talking with the children, but he at once turned his attention to Jeanette. "What did I tell you?" he said.

"You were right. But when I left, she was fighting back a smile. As you said, Clothilde is bound to win."

Etienne laughed, nodded and got up, picked up his straw hat from the seat of the chair beside him and walked out through the large double doors leading to the portico. Jeanette watched him limp down the path toward the vineyards, until he disappeared from sight. A wonderful man, no question.

Jeanette now reviewed the timetable given her by Etienne. Disciplines and schedules were somewhat relaxed at Provence. Mealtimes, however, were exact. Lunch was served at twelve-thirty, out in the garden under the large linden trees. At two o'clock the Duprés retired to take their afternoon naps. Dinner was served by candlelight in the dining room at seven-thirty because of the children, to the displeasure of the adults, who preferred the later dining hour of Paris. . . .

Their life in Provence settled into a familiar pattern. Etienne, an early riser, always seemed to be on hand when Jeanette and the children got there in the morning for breakfast. Of course, Madame and Marie Jacqueline slept later and had their breakfast in bed. Jean-Paul was always impeccably turned out, even here in the country. Some mornings he came to the breakfast table dressed for hunting, sometimes in riding breeches. Horses and bagging a covey of quail were his great country pleasures. At least among those safe to talk about.

Somehow there never seemed to be enough time for Jeanette and the children to do all the things they planned the night before. One day they'd pick wild strawberries, the *fraises de bois* that were so delicious. Jeanette taught the children the difference between mushrooms and toadstools. Sometimes they gathered wildflowers and from the book she'd brought along she would identify them for the children, and herself. . . . And there was the day Etienne took them through the vineyards and they strolled among the arbors, Etienne explaining which grapes made which wines, and then he took them to the pungent-smelling winery where the grapes would be made into wine in the fall. And another day, riding their ponies in the ring, the children challenged Jeanette to mount up and ride with them. At first she refused—she was terrified of horses, she'd never ridden before—but finally she got up on one, and although she was only five feet, two and a half inches tall, she felt ridiculous with her legs almost touching the ground, and the children laughing and screaming as they watched her bump up and down in the saddle. Suddenly the pony reared and before any of them realized what was happening she'd slipped off the saddle, and onto her derrière. . . .

The only morning all the Duprés assembled at the same time was Sunday. After breakfast Madame, holding a black silk parasol above her head, her family clustered around her, set off for church, the servants following as the procession made its way to the small chapel nestled among the trees. Their confessions were heard and their absolutions given by Father Durond, the parish priest, who'd been their friend and father confessor for more years than he could remember, and he was always asked to join the family for lunch. In the afternoons, with the proper amount of time allowed for digesting, Uncle Etienne, the children and Jeanette changed into bathing suits and walked to the lake that had been man-made many years ago by some Dupré ancestor. Jeanette always attached lifebelts to Desirée and Nicole, but Lucien could swim without such aids, which made him feel very proud and grown up. Often Etienne sat on a canvas stool and painted. He was more than a Sunday painter. Since childhood, painting had been his great love, his only gratification. His mother had often urged him to show his work, but he felt that what he painted belonged to him, was for him, alone. He had neither the desire nor the need to show his work. It was his private world, his mistress, his love. . . . Watching him, Jeanette felt once again how much Etienne was like her father. . . .

Suddenly, one morning it was the twelfth of July, 1935. . . . Today she was twenty . . . hard to believe . . . and today there would be a lovely picnic in the meadow.

"Please come with us today, Uncle Etienne," Lucien pleaded at breakfast.

"No . . ." Etienne said. "I'm sure you and Mademoiselle will have a better time alone without your old uncle tagging after—"

"Please do come, we'd all enjoy it," Jeanette broke in, convinced that he really wanted to come along.

"Well, thank you, Mademoiselle . . . in that case I think I will."

It was settled. The children clapped their hands. The wicker pony cart was harnessed, the picnic hampers were placed in the storage box and everyone climbed aboard. Jeanette and the two little girls sat in the back of the cart and Etienne took the reins, Lucien sitting beside him. Away they went, going briskly along the bridle path until they reached the grove of olive trees at the far end of the estate.

When the unloading chores were finished, Jeanette and the children set off with butterfly nets and jars. Etienne leaned against a tree and watched. He knew he'd remember this day forever. Later, when he'd picture the scene in his mind, in order to paint it, every detail would be fresh and vivid.

They romped through the fields, their nets billowing out, and after an hour returned with their catch, the brilliant butterfly wings fluttering in the jars. Etienne thought they were too beautiful to be captured, and surprised himself by saying so. Looking at him, Jeanette thought how right he was. "Shall we let them go?" she said. "Your uncle is quite right. After all, the fun was in the catching." And after a few objections from the children, they did let the gorgeous creatures out of their jars, and seeing them fly off, even Lucien, who'd protested at first, was glad they'd done it.

Jeanette now spread the white linen cloth on the ground and arranged the food on it—the salads, thick slices of country ham, stuffed hard-boiled eggs flavored with herbs, bread and butter, wine, milk, cheese and fruit.

After lunch, Nicole said, mysteriously, "Close your eyes, please, Jeanette."

To make sure she wouldn't peek, Desirée put her hands over Jeanette's eyes. When she was allowed to open them, the children clapped and sang "Happy Birthday." Astonished, and delighted, Jeanette watched as Lucien put down in front of her a birthday cake covered with white frosting trimmed with rosebuds and green-tinted leaves, bearing the inscription, in pink icing, "From All of Us Who Love You." There was one candle in the center. Jeanette took the cake in her hands and looked at it, then at the children, and then at Etienne. In spite of herself tears came into her eyes as she put it down and gathered her charges together, hugging them.

Nicole said proudly, "We knew about it for a week, but Uncle Etienne made us promise we wouldn't say, and we kept our promise." To which Desirée added a "Me too," and Jeanette felt the tears coming again.

When they'd finished the cake Lucien went to the cart and came back with several small packages, which he handed to Jeanette.

"Please open them," Etienne said. "The children have waited a long time for this." And Desirée confirmed with "Open mine first. . . ."

Inside Desirée's package was a handkerchief embroidered with blue bowknots.

"My favorite color, blue," Jeanette said. "It's so beautiful, I'll only use it on special occasions. . . ." Nicole's gift was a blue satin handkerchief case. "Nicole, my beauty, I adore it, and I adore you even more," Jeanette said, embracing the little girl. . . . And now Lucien's moment had come. Jeanette gasped when she opened his gift—a small heart-shaped gold locket inscribed with the date. "Lucien, it's beautiful. I'll treasure it forever." He smiled and said in manly fashion, "I'm glad you like it."

Finally Etienne handed her his gift . . . a gold and blue-enamel music box decorated with hand-painted scenes of France. Slowly she lifted the lid, and as she did so the music box played Debussy's *Clair de Lune*. Jeanette, deeply moved, did her best to thank Etienne, who in turn was clearly delighted by her reaction.

Afterward the children lay down on the blanket to nap and Etienne went off for a walk, saying he would return soon. As she watched him hobble away she thought what a pity for such a fine and decent man to be deprived of the pleasures other men took for granted. And that she too had taken for granted until she'd met him. . . . And she thought of how happy he had made her today, planning everything, and wished there were some way she could adequately repay him.

Shaking her head, she gathered up the remains of the picnic and put them in the cart, poured fresh water for the pony to drink and then lay down beside Desirée, her mind filled with thoughts, not of Etienne, but of Jean-Paul. . . .

Jean-Paul, who at the moment lay in a hayloft with his Provençal mistress, their bodies merging, as her diligent husband attended his fields in the heat of the summer's day. . . .

How long she'd been asleep, or how long Etienne had been observing the four of them, she'd no idea . . . but she did know he was now gently tapping her on the shoulder, saying it was time to go back. She gathered up the sleepy children, wiped their faces with cold water, and they were on their way. . . . each with his own private thoughts about a very special day. . . .

When the pony cart came into view, as it approached the courtyard, Madame looked up, stunned. She was tending her rose garden, a task she performed daily, dressed in black cotton, a soft, large-brimmed straw hat tied under her chin with black ribbon. She stood with her mouth open, the spade in her hand. Etienne had not only spent the day with Mademoiselle and the children, he had driven the cart, which one of the grooms should have done. She flinched as she saw him help Jeanette down. What was the modern world coming to! That she should live to see a Dupré son pay such attention to a governess. She'd never seen Etienne behave in such fashion. True, Jeanette's position was above that of a housemaid or a nursemaid, but still, as everybody but she seemed to forget, she *was* only a governess! Madame didn't like it. Furthermore, she didn't like Mademoiselle. She felt that in some way the girl was . . . calculating. . . .

Suddenly, a new thought entered her head. Was it possible . . . did Jeanette have *designs* on Etienne? Was she taking advantage of his . . . condition . . . to better herself? After all, who was she? A nobody whom Etienne had selected. Oh, dear God, I'm getting too old for all this . . . and she put her spade down, went through the French doors, through the sitting room, up the stairs to her rooms and asked Renée to draw her bath. Next she took a headache powder. She simply had to lie down and rest her mind before dinner.

Jeanette opened the double doors of the armoire and cast her eyes over her Provence wardrobe. In addition to the peasant clothes she wore during the day, she had brought with her mostly simple, conservative dresses, since she knew Madame's distaste for anything but a uniform. She had selected her wardrobe with a careful eye to color and style, again so as not to antagonize Madame. There was, however, one exception, and today *was* her birthday. After all, she would never be twenty again. Tonight she couldn't resist. Longingly, her eyes rested on the pastel blue silk dress, her favorite. Should she be bold and wear it? Did she dare risk it? Was she taking too many liberties? She hesitated, then made up her mind, feeling a new kind of exhilaration as she did so. . . . After her bath she splashed herself with cologne, then took out a blue silk slip trimmed with ecru lace and held it up to her body. How she loved the feeling of the silk against her skin. . . . She put on silk stockings, attaching them to a garter belt, then high-heeled white shoes. She combed her hair, which was now slightly longer than shoulder length, since she had not cut it during the summer. Looking into the mirror, she put the comb down and twisted the thick brown mane into a coiffure on top of her head. After pinning it in place, she pulled back the sides . . . which made her neck look swanlike. Her skin had tanned just enough to give it a healthy glow, which further enhanced her deep blue eyes and dark lashes. She tinted her lips and cheeks a delicate pink, ever so lightly, embellishing the fine-textured skin. Completely groomed, she looked at her reflected image as though discovering herself for the first time. She was pretty; yes, she was. In fact, tonight she felt beautiful. Her eyes wandered to her breasts, which had developed and filled out, thanks to the good food and air of Provence. She was still slender, but her body had become fuller. Her pelvic bones no longer protruded quite so much, but her abdomen was still tight and taut. She was, indeed, on her way to becoming a woman, with the kind of potential she dreamed of, and yearned for. . . . When she finally stepped into the blue dress, she looked at her reflection full-face, then sideways. The dress was now slightly tighter around the bust, which pleased her . . . the heart-shaped locket Lucien had given her fit perfectly in the V-shaped neckline.

She pirouetted round the room like a ballerina, then gathered up the children and together they walked to the big house, where the Duprés were having their aperitifs in the sitting room . . . and where all eyes were now suddenly on her. Conversation stopped. Her heart was pounding as she said, "Good evening." She went directly to the chair she usually sat in, crossed her feet at the ankles, held her hands in her lap, and sat with all the poise and dignity she felt unaccustomed to.

Madame swallowed her aperitif quickly and asked for another. Jean-Paul poured the rich liquid from the decanter and handed it to her . . . while Etienne thought he'd never seen anyone quite as lovely as Jeanette was tonight . . . and Jean-Paul for the first time felt a distinct male reaction to her. She was, no question, bewitching. Somehow he'd never noticed, and he promptly found himself wondering what she would be like in the same hayloft where he'd spent his pleasurable afternoon. But then he felt obliged to push aside his erotic fantasy, remembering his father's anger at discovering him making precocious love to the upstairs maid, and telling him *never* to get involved with a servant, that it could only lead to all kinds of distasteful complications. . . . Better, his father advised, now that his son was, so to speak, of age, was a visit which he'd arrange. And Marshal Dupré was as good as his word, sending Jean-Paul to the address of a woman with a distinguished reputation in her profession. The upstairs maid, of course, was dismissed.

No . . . much as he desired this unpicked fruit, he would dismiss the notion.

Marie Jacqueline had noted the not unfamiliar expression on her husband's face, and reflected that if only Jean-Paul wanted her own body as he obviously did this brazen nobody's, she would gladly have given up her eternal reward in heaven.

The conversation was picked up by Etienne, who wanted to do all he could to put Jeanette at her ease. When dinner was finally announced, Madame gave her unbounded thanks to heaven. The salad was marvelous, crisp and cold, with Clothilde's secret thyme dressing. The wine, selected by Jean-Paul, was poured into the pewter goblets. Dinner had been prepared to perfection by Clothilde (who had earlier cursed Jean-Paul for putting so much buckshot in the pheasants he had bagged the day before, but after she'd baked them in herbs and wine sauce and seen how good they looked, her antagonism was forgotten).

With a flourish of pride the butler walked completely

around the table, showing off the game on a large pewter platter surrounded by an assortment of garden vegetables. As an added bit of color, Clothilde had arranged some pheasant feathers among the birds. It was a sight to behold. Madame definitely approved.

"Did you kill them all, Uncle Jean-Paul?" Lucien asked.

"Yes, indeed. You should have been there, Lucien."

"Will you take me with you some day, please?" said Lucien.

"Of course."

"*Not* until you're older," said Madame.

"Why, grandma?"

"Because first you have to be taught how to handle a gun—"

"Uncle Jean-Paul will teach me, and Uncle Etienne can come too—"

"No, Lucien," said Etienne. "I'm afraid I don't hunt."

"Why not?"

"Well . . . I just don't believe in killing."

Jean-Paul directed an angry glance at his brother, his dear so pious, so long-suffering crippled bastard of a brother who couldn't shoot worth a damn even if he wanted to. Half a man was all he was . . . good for nothing but helping in vineyards, picking grapes and keeping accounts . . . a crippled damn bookkeeper. . . .

The friction in the air didn't go unobserved by Madame, who changed the subject abruptly with "And how did you spend your day, children?" (As though she didn't know.)

"We had a birthday party for Jeanette," said Nicole.

Madame forced herself to smile. "Where, darling?"

"In the meadow. Uncle Etienne planned it for us."

"How *nice* of you, Etienne."

"Yes. . . . Well, it was most delightful," he said, not missing her tone.

Jeanette was becoming increasingly uncomfortable as she found herself the focus of the conversation. She wet her lips but remained silent.

"I gave Jeanette a handkerchief," Desirée said.

"And I gave her a handkerchief case," Nicole said.

Lucien bragged, "But *I* gave her a locket that Jeanette said she'd wear forever—"

"Indeed," Madame said, narrowing her eyes. "And you, Etienne? What was your gift?"

Etienne was embarrassed by his mother's rudeness in pursuing the subject. "My gift was an effort to thank Mademoiselle for what she's given to the children."

Jean-Paul was amused. It always diverted him when Etienne fell from their mother's favor, however briefly. Etienne would be forgiven tomorrow; he always was. . . .

"How delightful for Mademoiselle to be so well appreciated." What exactly, Madame wondered, had Etienne given her? She would have to find out later from the children. . . . "Well, in any case, happy birthday . . . Mademoiselle. I'm most pleased that your day was so pleasantly, and fruitfully, spent."

To the best of Jeanette's recollection, this was the first time Madame had ever addressed her personally, even in obvious sarcasm. "How very kind of you, Madame," was the best response she could manage.

"May I offer my best wishes for a long life," said Jean-Paul, "filled with many happy returns of this day."

Jeanette could hardly get out her polite if heartfelt—in his case—thanks.

Marie Jacqueline, for once, said nothing, and thereafter everyone ate in silence. After the chocolate soufflé had been served and scarcely touched, the family retired to the sitting room for demitasse and brandy. Jeanette took up her post in the corner.

"Grandmother," said Lucien, "Nicole and I would like to play a duet that Jeanette taught us."

Taking up her tapestry, Madame answered, "Not tonight, my dear. We've all had a long day, especially all of you."

"I'd like to hear them," said Etienne, "and I think you'll be pleased by their progress. . . ."

Madame didn't look up from her handiwork. This . . . this girl, she thought, has obviously bewitched him, he'd never been so defiant about her wishes. She no longer seemed able to control him at all, but to disagree now would only widen the breach that had developed between them since *she* had come into their home.

"Go ahead, then, my children," she finally said, drawing up a battle plan.

They played the little French song Jeanette had taught them with almost no mistakes, and Lucien crossed his left hand over his right in the proper place, which he loved to do. It made him feel like a real virtuoso. When they had finished, Uncle Jean-Paul shouted, "Bravo!" and applauded, as did Etienne. Marie Jacqueline remained mute.

"Now you play something, Jeanette," said Lucien.

"Another time, Lucien."

But Jean-Paul insisted. "Please, Mademoiselle, will you do us the honor? I'm sure Mother would enjoy it."

In her fury, Madame stuck the needle into her finger as she attempted to push the yarn through the tiny hole.

Jeanette sat down on the bench as though she were awaiting the guillotine, her mouth dry, her palms sweaty. She began to play the only piece that she could think of, *Clair de Lune*, the same tune played by the music box Etienne had given her. As she slowly began the poignant, haunting melody, the atmosphere in the room seemed to change. Her touch was soft . . . near-poetic. . . . Every note, every phrase did its job in conjuring up the appropriate images of moonlight and unfulfilled love. When she finished, there were tears in her eyes. She dropped her hands on the bench, stood up and turned to face the room.

Madame's tapestry now lay in her lap. She, too, had tears in her eyes. She was not a woman to give compliments easily, but without even thinking she said, "Thank you, Mademoiselle. You play very well."

Jeanette met her eyes. "You're very kind, and now may I ask to be excused? It's past the children's bedtime. . . ."

And she finally escaped.

After that evening, although Madame spoke little to her in a personal way, Jeanette knew that she had gained new stature and respect in her eyes. . . . When they met in the garden, or at mealtimes, there was a reserved cordiality in their greetings. For Jeanette, this was enough. She was, after all, well aware of her position. She hadn't been hired to become an intimate member of the Dupré family . . . except with the children. Still, she expected to be treated with dignity. She had certainly earned that much.

Eighteen

Unbelievably, it was August. How quickly the summer days were dwindling, Jeanette thought. Still, there were a few more weeks to savor, a few more weeks to see Jean-Paul. When they returned to Paris he would go back to Algeria . . . the thought made her ache. . . .

One Sunday afternoon, as Madame relaxed on the sofa in the sitting room, her needlework in hand, Etienne stood at the open door leading outside, watching Jeanette and the children play cricket on the lawn. He could not take his eyes away from her, or stop marveling at how beautiful she'd become, and how great his longing for her was . . . except, he reminded himself grimly, that was a pointless dream . . . one day she'd meet some healthy young man who would take away the person he wanted most in life. . . .

His mother observed him, reading the feelings written on his face. And quietly grieved for him. She knew he was suffering. From the beginning she'd suspected how he felt about this girl. She remembered how she had fought him . . . wanting to send Jeanette away. It grieved her, but the situation had to be faced. . . . She knew she had been stubborn, and perhaps selfish. She owed her son so much . . . after all, it was from her womb he had come deformed. He hadn't asked to be born. It was time to atone, and to pay something on the debt she owed him.

"Etienne," she said without preamble, "you love this girl, don't you?"

Without turning, his eyes still on Jeanette, he answered without hesitation. "Yes."

"You have from the very beginning . . . ?"

"Yes."

"Come sit beside me, Etienne, please. I want to talk to you."

He walked over and sat down beside her.

"Etienne . . . why have you never thought of marrying?"

He got up abruptly, went to the cabinet and poured himself a brandy. "Why do you even ask me that, Mother?"

"Because you're a fine man who needs a wife."

He looked at his mother as though she'd lost her senses. "*Look* at me, Mother. Perhaps you're so accustomed to this foot that you don't really see it. Well, believe me, other people do, including young women, who don't marry men because they're 'fine,' but because they're somebody to fall in love with. And who would fall in love with me? Why should any woman want a cripple? I don't want to marry a woman who's only interested in our wealth. So what's left? Somebody with a generous capacity for pity. Could I live all my life on pity? I'd say not."

"Oh, Etienne . . . but what will happen to you? When my times comes you'll be alone with no one to care about you—" She began to cry.

He went to her side. "Please, Mother, there've been enough tears in your life. Please, no more over me. Besides, I've accepted my situation. It even has its rewards. I've been blessed with many gifts . . . I paint and do a fair job of it, at least it pleases me. I've been given a kind of perspective beyond most, who don't need it, I grant you—"

"But you're so *lonely*. I can never take the place of a wife or a mistress."

He got up and poured another brandy and this time sipped it slowly. "Well . . . you see, Mother, being crippled doesn't deprive one of his manhood, and not to be indelicate . . . but from time to time I have a few ladies who are quite willing to bestow their gifts on me. I grant you, it's not exactly an until death do us part situation, but at least for a consideration, in pleasant surroundings, I might add, they do me the favor of not being aware of what I am. . . ."

And now she was crying uncontrollably, and although he begged her not to cry she couldn't stop. Through her tears she said, ". . . what a husband and father you would be. . . ."

"Well, Mother dear, perhaps providence has other plans for me. Who knows? Maybe there are worlds beyond. Now, please, enough of this. Please go to your room and rest, and promise me not to concern yourself so about me. Many people have crosses to bear much heavier than mine."

He helped her up from the sofa, and, almost dutifully, she went to her room. She was reclining on her chaise longue when Jean-Paul, just back from riding, stopped in to see her and, of course, saw that she had been in tears. Pulling up a chair beside her, he said, "Mother, you seem so troubled."

"I'm afraid I am—" and started to cry again.

"Please don't cry. I can't bear to see tears in those lovely eyes. . . . I know how you feel, but you must concentrate on how happy Denise was—"

"It's not for her that I'm crying . . . not this time. It is poor Etienne. . . ."

His jaw muscles tightened. "Why Etienne? Has something happened to him?"

"Something *happened* when he was born . . . he'll be a cripple all of his life—"

"But why are you carrying on so now? He's well adjusted to his life. I doubt that he ever thinks of it—"

"Oh, Jean-Paul, how *wrong* you are. Etienne is in love, don't you understand? And he can't even ask this girl to be his wife."

Jean-Paul was shocked. "Etienne in *love*? Mother, do you realize what you're saying?"

"Yes, I realize fully. Do you think because he doesn't walk the way other men do that he doesn't have the same feelings . . . or desires?"

"Well . . . I'm sure he does . . . but who is the girl? And how do you know?"

"The girl is . . . Jeanette. . . ."

Well, he thought, the world was full of surprises. So

Etienne, the righteous cripple, was in love. . . . Unbelievable. But he was pleased . . . for at least Etienne would be deprived of the girl, just as he, Jean-Paul, had been deprived of his mother by a snivelling Etienne. . . . Yes, indeed. Jean-Paul was very, very pleased.

"Mother, please don't cry. Things have a way of working themselves out, you know. Etienne is a smart man. Maybe he'll propose, after all, and maybe she'll accept him. After all, being a governess isn't quite the same as being a Dupré."

"Jean-Paul, don't play games with me. . . . You know as well as I do that he'll never let her know. Dear God, I wanted so much for all of you. Now Denise is gone, you're unhappily married and without children, and Etienne is . . . Etienne. Dear God, what have I done to deserve this?" She clenched her hands until the knuckles were white.

Jean-Paul leaned over and took her in his arms. "No, dearest mother, you mustn't talk that way. . . ." And he stayed with her until Renée arrived to help her with her toilette.

After she'd bathed and dressed, Madame left her room quietly and walked down the stairs, through the front door and along the path to the cottage. At the door she paused, then knocked.

Jeanette, dressed in a peignoir, was resting while the children slept. She got out of bed and went to the door. When she opened it, she stepped back in shock.

"May I come in?" Antoinette Dupré asked quietly.

"Please do."

The older woman entered.

"Please forgive my appearance," Jeanette said. "I was just resting. . . ."

"You look more than presentable, mademoiselle."

"Please have a seat, Madame."

She sat down in a chair she'd used so many times when her own children were young. "Mademoiselle, I've come to speak to you about a very delicate matter."

Jeanette was dumbfounded. She could think of only one thing . . . something terrible had happened and she was about to be dismissed. She braced herself to accept it.

"Please sit down. . . . I hardly know where to begin . . . you see, I've come on my son's behalf. . . ."

Jeanette's heart was a hammer. Did Madame know about her feelings for Jean-Paul? Had Clothilde betrayed her? Trying to keep her voice under control, she said, "Your son?"

"Yes, my son . . . Etienne has, quite simply, fallen in love with you."

Jeanette was stunned. She was unable to speak.

"He'd be furious with me if he knew I was here. Please understand, mademoiselle, that you're the first woman he's ever loved, and probably will be the last. With his . . . infirmity, he won't come to you. He doesn't feel it proper."

Jeanette got up and stood behind her chair. "Madame, I don't know what to say. . . . What you tell me is so sudden and surprising that I'm, well, I've no idea what to say. . . ."

"Mademoiselle, do you think you might find it possible to care just a little for Etienne? He's a fine man. . . ."

"I *do* care a great deal for Monsieur Dupré. My affection for him is deep, but I'm not . . . I'm not in love with him—"

"My dear, may I speak to you not only as a mother, but as a woman?"

Jeanette nodded, still not fully believing what was happening.

"All marriages don't begin with love. . . . I mean, of course, romantic love. But as people grow to know each other and mutual respect develops, love can grow out of that. Being crippled is only a surface handicap. It's the whole person that counts. Etienne would offer you a love so deep and lasting. . . . I do know my son. I know his generous spirit, the talent he possesses. . . ." There were tears showing in her eyes which she tried to hold back.

Jeanette's heart went out to this woman who until now had seemed to despise her. This was a mother humbling, by her lights humiliating, herself for her son, pleading for his life. . . . And to whom? A governess. She couldn't just say, "No, Madame, I'm afraid I could never enter into a marriage without love. . . ." Instead she said, "Madame, I wish there was a better way to tell you, but marrying Monsieur Dupré is, I'm afraid, out of the question for me."

"Will you be honest?"

"I'm trying to be."

"Do you find him grotesque, repulsive?"

"Oh, *no*. He's a remarkable man. I'm only sad that my own feelings just don't make it possible, and I assure you it has nothing whatever to do with his . . . infirmity. In fact, quite the contrary. I admire him enormously for all he's done and is in spite of it."

"Yes. . . . Well, may I ask you a very personal question?"

"Please . . ."

"Is there . . . are you in love with someone else, whom you do wish to marry?"

Jeanette paused for a long moment. . . . "Yes, I'm in love with someone else . . . but wanting to marry and being able to do so are different things."

"By that you mean . . . ?"

"The gentleman in question already has a wife."

"I see. . . . Are you committed to him in any way . . . ? Please forgive my being so personal and inquisitive—"

"There is nothing to forgive. What you are asking is understandable, but the answer is no. He isn't even aware that I'm in love with him."

"Then would you think carefully about Etienne, about the life he could offer you . . . ? As you got to know him better, keep in mind, please, that you might discover in him things that would bring about a change in your feelings. . . ."

Until this moment Jeanette had no idea how extraordinary this woman was. She wanted to show her all possible respect. "Madame, this has happened so quickly I must have time to think. You see, in my religion, as in yours, marriage is a sacred vow, not to be entered into lightly. It is forever—"

"But you will at least consider it?"

"Yes, Madame . . . I'll do that."

"Thank you, my dear. I won't press you for an answer. But by trying you'll have my undying gratitude. And whatever your eventual decision, *please* don't let Etienne know that I came to you and *begged*." She said the last word so softly it was almost inaudible.

"You have my sacred word, Madame."

"Thank you. . . . And now I must go before the others

find I am missing, and soon you will have to get the children ready."

The two women looked at each other for a long moment. Then, without another word, Madame turned and went out of the room. Jeanette shut the door. She stood, leaning against it. . . . Oh, Papa, I need you so. . . .

That night, when the children had been put to bed and were sleeping, Jeanette sat under the weeping willow on the round bench beneath it. What in God's name should she do? She needed to talk to somebody, but who . . . ? And suddenly, Jean-Paul was standing in front of her, silhouetted against the star-studded night.

"Why in the world are you sitting alone out here?" he said, sitting down beside her.

She thought her heart would stop . . . it was the first time they'd ever been alone together . . . and finally she was able to get out a rather feeble, "Thinking, just thinking . . ."

"About what? Would you like to share some of your weighty thoughts with me . . . ?"

"As a matter of fact, I would, but I believe some things are best left unsaid. . . ."

"Well, then, much to my regret, I expect I will have to leave—"

But before he could even turn to go, her defenses came down, the pressure simply overwhelmed her, and she blurted out to him what she'd been thinking over and over to herself—"I love them, I love them so much and now to have to leave them, the most precious things in my life. I feel as though they're my own and I'd hoped I could stay with them for years, be part of their life and they be part of mine. . . . Oh, I know it's terribly selfish of me but some things you just can't accept and be so calm and lady-like. . . ."

He looked at her closely, surprised by this outburst from the normally restrained Jeanette, so proper and polite. Of course, at first he hadn't a clue what she meant, but then it became clear she was talking about herself and the children, but why she should be talking about leaving them he couldn't imagine.

Very carefully, gently, he put her head on his shoulder,

and she didn't resist. She was beyond resisting, welcoming the relief and the support she so desperately needed.

"My dear girl," he said, "I've not the slightest idea why you think you must leave, but I can assure you—"

"No, you can't assure me, monsieur, and I can't explain, not to you, not to anyone, but I assure you, I must leave—"

"My dear, I assure you that you can tell me anything . . . and it will be as though it were never said."

She took her head from his shoulder and looked at him. His expression was entirely serious, and she gave in to what she had been wanting to do right along. "Do you truly promise . . . ? Because I don't want to hurt anyone, I don't want—"

"I promise. You can trust me, I've never gone back on my word. I hope you'll believe that. Now, what is it that's so terrible?"

"I believe whatever you tell me. . . . Well—Your mother came to the cottage today, and . . . and told me that Etienne is in love with me . . . but I can't marry him, even though I truly admire and respect him. I don't love him, and to stay here now that I know would be impossible . . . too awkward . . . too risky for him, and for me too if he should ever discover that I knew his feelings. I don't think I'm strong enough to play such a game. *Before* I knew his feelings it was different, but now that I do, well . . . I can't stay." And when she began to cry again, Jean-Paul, gentleman that he was, decided there was nothing to do but take her in his arms and kiss her. And confused and frightened of her own feelings for him, she finally broke away, shook her head and ran to her room, where she sprawled across her bed and cried as she hadn't cried since her father died.

After several moments, without looking up, she felt his presence, and then realized he had followed her and was bending over her, here, in her bedroom.

"My darling, you're not alone . . . I'm here and I'll help you." He lifted her face.

"But, monsieur, how can you possibly help me?"

"The first step," he told her, his face all seriousness, "is to prevail on you to call me Jean-Paul."

She couldn't . . . if she did, he'd know immediately how she felt about him. . . .

"Please," he persisted, "at least try . . . 'Jean-Paul,' it's really not so difficult if you put your mind to it. . . ."

She looked at him, and slowly said what she'd wanted a million times before to say, though not with the feeling, which she still held back, "Jean-Paul . . ."

"You see, it hardly hurt at all, I trust . . . and now we need to work out a plan, the first and most important part of which is to make it possible for you to stay here—"

"But I told you, I can't possibly do that."

"Yes, of course you can, and you will. And do you know why? Because you love your charges and are devoted to their well-being. And because you love being in this fine house . . . and because, my dear Mademoiselle Jeanette, it is not only the children who need and want you, it is also me, surprising as this may be to you . . . and I wonder if it can be a total surprise. You are a very much needed part of my life as well . . . my life that I have no doubt you've noticed is not exactly filled with marital bliss. My life, dear Jeanette, that I hope you'll have the generosity to agree is entitled to a little happiness too. . . ."

Stunned, despite his suspicions to the contrary, she could only manage, "You want *me* . . . ? But I had no idea, truly. . . ."

"Then I have been either too discreet or not artful enough in conveying my feelings. In any case, I meant every word I said. You must stay, this is your home, and I . . . I am a man who loves you, Jeanette, and that, believe it or not, is the first time I have ever said those words to a woman and meant them."

In her confused state of pleasure and guilt, she didn't examine what this said for his undoubtedly similar protestations to his wife before marriage, or for his credibility for the future. Who was she to examine with detached or even minimal logic the unexpected realization of a dream she hardly had dared entertain in privacy. And now, here it was in reality, this incredible man telling her that he loved her, meaning it. . . . "But what about Etienne," she said. "How can I stay, knowing how he feels, and now you . . ."

"Etienne isn't important—".

She winced. "Please, don't say that. Etienne is very important—"

"No, not now . . . now it is you and I who are of over-

riding importance. I wonder if you understand what I've
been saying to you. . . . Jeanette, I love you. . . ."

Which, if something short of the truth, was not entirely
a lie. He was and had been for some time more than a
little attracted to this exquisite young creature. The notion
of taking her to bed had powerfully aroused him. . . .
After all, this was no country girl from Lyon. This one he
wanted now, and for many nights to come. The opportunity had been deliciously handed to him, by the one who
would be most hurt by it and whom he wanted most to
hurt. It was too perfect to miss, and he had no intention of
doing so. . . . "Jeanette, did you hear what I said? Did
you believe me, because I meant—"

She had heard, and now she said his name with the
feelings she'd up to now struggled to hold back. "Oh,
Jean-Paul, please, I do believe you . . . and I can tell
you now, ashamed as I was for so long to even admit it to
myself, that I love you too . . . from the moment, I
think, that you first came to see the children. . . ."

He took her in his arms, kissing her passionately, and
without resistance unbuttoned her blouse and slowly removed her skirt and underclothing, and then he was beside
her, holding her, caressing her, fondling and exploring her
body unhurriedly, and then, slowly, as gently as possible,
he entered her. . . . And lying beneath him, feeling him,
knowing him inside her, the pain became a joy, the reality
of the dream making it all worthwhile. She was in a place
she'd never been before, and she never wanted to come back
from. . . . And for him, it was a moment of surprising
sweetness, different from any other he'd known. . . .

Afterward, when they were lying in each other's arms,
he said, "Now do you see, my dearest, why I couldn't possibly let you leave?"

"Yes," she answered sleepily, "yes, Jean-Paul," and saying his name seemed as natural now as breathing.

"And there will be no more talk about leaving, or talk
about us to anyone, which would make things too difficult
until I can figure out the rest of our plan. . . ." They fell
asleep then.

When he woke up it was dawn. As he slipped out of
bed he saw the blood-stained sheet, which doubly excited
him . . . not only because he'd been her first, but also,

the delicious bonus that now Etienne never could be. And she would stay, because he wanted her to be there, living in Etienne's house, a constant reminder of his impossible love for her. Jean-Paul wondered how long Etienne would be able to stand it. He was, after all, still a man . . . as his mother had pointed out . . . a man with feelings to satisfy, or be destroyed by.

What a perfect situation. Small wonder that in the pleasure of it Jean-Paul was not inclined to remember the injunction of his father against precisely what he was doing.

A week passed. When Jeanette's time of the month came round and she showed no sign, she became alarmed and frightened. . . . She couldn't eat or sleep . . . she'd never missed, not even by a day. In desperation, she told Jean-Paul.

This was something he hadn't bargained on, but strangely he was excited. *If* she was pregnant, then what should the next step be? He asked her to wait another few days, which he needed to think on it.

Four more days passed and still there was no sign. When he met her in the garden that night she was beside herself with fear. . . . She knew she'd be disgraced by bearing an illegitimate child. Her cousin Julian had been right: she'd end up in the gutter. . . . Like mother, like daughter . . .

"What can we do, Jean-Paul? I'll *have* to leave now—"

He took her hand in his. "Are you sure . . . ? Can you be sure you're pregnant?"

"Yes. I know I am."

"All right, then . . . listen carefully. There's only one way I can completely protect you and the child."

"How?"

"By having you marry Etienne—"

"*No*, I can't do that, not ever, feeling the way I do about you—"

"Yes, you can. Because now so much more is involved. There's going to be a child, my child and yours. Everyone will believe it's Etienne's, but we'll know it's ours. And the child will be a Dupré. That's very important to me. Nothing need change between us. Do you think that just because you're married to Etienne I would give you up?

Never! You'll be Madame Etienne Dupré. Our child will be born in the same bed I was born in. Etienne will be only a convenience."

It seemed a wicked deception to perpetrate on Etienne, and yet, if she failed to agree she would surely lose Jean-Paul—the mere thought of which terrified her.

". . . You'll go to my mother and tell her you've thought it over carefully, that if Etienne will come to you and propose, you'll devote the rest of your life to making him happy—"

"No, Jean-Paul, *please.*"

He held her very close. "Yes, my dearest, you *must* do it."

"I'm not even good at pretending—"

"Then learn, darling. Diplomacy can open many doors. . . ."

He had thought it over carefully and knew exactly what the strategy should be. This marriage had to take place for two compelling reasons. First, Jeanette was expecting his child . . . the fulfillment for him of a long-standing obsession. He'd see to it that the child would love him more by alienating its affection from Etienne. It would be so simple. He could do so much more with a son than Etienne could. He'd take the child on excursions . . . skiing, hunting, riding, boating. He'd be the completely devoted uncle . . . *and* godfather, to his one and only son. From now on his behavior with Etienne would be carefully adjusted to be more brotherly.

Secondly, he wanted to ensure that his brother's new wife would be his mistress. That would be a joy he could almost taste, had already tasted. By the very act of marriage Etienne would become a cuckold. Perfect. Damned ingenious, in fact. No wonder that someday he'd be Premier. . . .

His thoughts were interrupted by Jeanette, saying, "Jean-Paul, I still feel it's so wrong. There must be some other way—"

"My darling, if there were, would I even think of subjecting you to this? But what else is there . . . ? I am, after all, married, and we both know my wife would never allow me a divorce . . . not to mention that it would destroy my mother. . . . So how else can I protect both you and our child? This *is* the only way. . . ."

He took her in his arms, held her, kissed her, and carefully explained what she was to say to his mother. Later, he would suggest to his mother how she should approach Etienne.

Still protesting, but knowing she could not resist him, she finally said, "When do you want me to speak to Madame?"

"Tomorrow, I think, when everyone is resting. You'll go to Mother's room and I'll stay at the cottage while the children are asleep. . . ."

Jeanette knocked softly at Madame's door. Renée opened it. When Madame saw Jeanette, she sat up in bed and promptly asked Jeanette to sit beside her, wondering what the decision would be and steeling herself for an expected turn-down.

Jeanette's hands were trembling. There was no choice, as Jean-Paul had said. And beside her love for him and wanting to please him, she owed him so much. . . . After all, he could have abandoned her, agreed that she leave— pregnant, unmarried, disgraced. . . . It was his love that fortified her, and, hopefully, her undeniable respect and affection for Etienne that would make it . . . somehow . . . tolerable, she told herself. Now she squared her shoulders and, forcing herself not to turn back, said, "Madame, as we agreed, I've thought seriously about marriage to your son."

"And . . . ?"

"I've searched deeply within myself, and find that I care very much for Monsieur Etienne. . . ."

Madame's face relaxed somewhat, then tightened again. Jeanette still hadn't said she would marry him. "And what conclusion have you come to?"

". . . I've come to realize that . . . love can happen in many ways, that through respect, a bond of love can grow . . . as you said. I respect Monsieur Etienne more than any other man I've ever known, except my father. When I came into your home, it was he who was my friend and champion from the first. We have a great deal in common. And in my heart I believe from all this a deep understanding of each other can grow . . . and perhaps that is the best kind of love. . . ."

Madame sank back into the pillows as Jeanette finally said what she'd been waiting to hear.

"So I've made my decision. If Monsieur Etienne wishes to marry me, my answer is yes."

Tears came to Madame's eyes. She had been genuinely touched—as well as relieved—by what Jeanette had said and the eloquence with which she said it. She reached out her arms to embrace Jeanette. "Oh, my dear, you can't know what this means to me, how happy you've made me. I only regret that I didn't appreciate you as quickly as Etienne. The loss is mine. But at least now I can understand why he loves you so much."

And as she talked, Jeanette thought of what else she was withholding besides her relationship with Jean-Paul . . . that inside her womb lay his unborn child. Until this moment she hadn't really considered the responsibilities of motherhood. But now the reality of it became frightening . . . and she wondered if she would be capable of Madame Dupré's kind of fierce, self-sacrificing protectiveness of *her* child, and avoid the selfish behavior of her own mother. . . .

That night Jean-Paul went to his mother's room to act out his self-appointed role.

"Mother," he said, "I need to talk to you."

"About what, Jean-Paul?"

"Well, although I realize you don't consider it overworked, my conscience bothers me. About Etienne."

Madame looked carefully at Jean-Paul. "I confess such sentiments do surprise me somewhat. You've never been, to my memory, especially concerned with Etienne—"

"That's true, but I can grow too, Mother, and I too can be wrong. Etienne deserves some happiness in his life, as you have so often told me, and, frankly, while I probably will never truly like him—to pretend so would, after all, be hypocrisy—I realize the pain I have caused you by my attitude, not to mention him."

"Truly, Jean-Paul?"

"Yes, Mother. It's very sad to see a grown man so lonely. Etienne deserves better. . . . Now, I've thought a great deal about what you told me, I mean about Etienne's feelings for this girl, which I must admit I didn't take seriously at first, and I honestly think you should urge him to court her. After all, Mother, many men with physical handicaps marry and live happy, fulfilled lives. Why not Etienne?"

Delighted and grateful for his support despite her nagging skepticism, she said, "I've told him exactly the same thing but he refuses to listen."

"Then you must make him listen, and stop feeling that his life is over. At twenty-five, it should just be beginning. . . . Of course, we don't know how the girl will feel about him—"

"But we do," said Madame. "She is devoted to him."

"How do you know this?"

"She told me, Jean-Paul. I had a talk with her. . . ."

Jean-Paul pretended appropriate surprise. "Ah . . . well, then, that should make things easier. . . . All you need do is to tell Etienne that the girl can't stay here any longer. . . ."

"For what reason?"

"Your reason is her confession to you when you questioned her about *her* reason for saying she wanted to leave . . . her confession that she loved him, that it had begun with his defense of her when she first came, and now after a summer had grown to such proportions that it simply wasn't fitting that she continue to live under the same roof with him . . . and so, unfortunately, she would simply have to go. . . ."

"And you believe Etienne would be convinced, especially so soon after telling me his own feelings for her, which he felt could hardly be returned—just as he has felt about other women?"

"Mother, I believe it, regardless of the perhaps seeming coincidence. And the reason is, Etienne so badly needs and wants to believe it."

"Oh, Jean-Paul, if only it could be . . ."

"Trust me, Mother, and trust yourself. I know it will be."

"Dearest Jean-Paul, it seems I have been blessed by both my sons. . . . Now come here and let me kiss you."

Jean-Paul, smiling, did so.

The next morning Madame asked Etienne to come to her room. She hadn't slept well, worrying, despite Jean-

Paul's assurances, over Etienne's reaction to what she would say to him. She reminded herself, though, that what she had to say was, after all, the truth, regardless of how startling it might be to Etienne, and this, together with, as Jean-Paul had wisely said, Etienne's desire to believe, would work in her favor. Still . . .

When Etienne was seated in front of her, she told him simply and directly everything that Jean-Paul had said, adding—also the truth—that while at first she hadn't liked Mademoiselle, she had learned to admire her for her way with the children, and that she herself had had intimations of Mademoiselle's feelings toward him on more than one occasion . . . seeing her on returning from the birthday picnic with him was one in particular that she recalled . . . and only his own long-standing misguided conviction that no woman could love him because of his infirmity had kept his eyes shut to what was developing right in front of them. Rushing along, not allowing him to interrupt despite the look of growing amazement on his face, she said that it truly was a pity that Jeanette could never reveal her true feelings toward him. . . . she'd only confessed them to her after she'd pressed her about her statement that she was leaving despite her well-known devotion to the children. . . .

When Etienne finally found his voice, and his mother allowed him to respond, he shook his head, still incredulous. "Mother, you are telling me that Jeanette actually said she felt toward me in a way . . . that she could find it at all possible to love me—"

"That, Etienne, is exactly what I am saying, and it is the truth. All I can pray, for the sake of your happiness, is that you are able to accept it."

"Oh, Mother, you know how much I want to accept it. And, of course, she *must* stay, especially now. . . . Forgive me, Mother, I still can't quite believe it, but if it is true, if it *can* be true, then all I can say is that I thank God . . ."

Deeply moved, and relieved, Madame embraced him as he thought about the impossible that seemed to have happened, and told himself that if it was really true . . . and he was increasingly willing to believe it . . . then this evening, after dinner, he would ask Jeanette to become his wife. . . .

During the day he watched her with a new intensity, hoping at the same time it wasn't as obvious to her and others as it seemed to him, feeling weak with hope, and fear, at the same time. She did talk to him often, and, yes, she did indeed seem unusually warm . . . and responsive . . . to him. All through dinner he could hardly restrain himself as she met his glances . . . no question of it, why hadn't he noticed more earlier . . . ? and even smiled diffidently. If anyone had asked him what he was eating, or even who was there besides Jeanette, he'd have been hard put to answer.

Nonetheless, the meal was especially festive, since Madame had instructed Clothilde to spare no effort or attention. It had been a very long time, indeed, since Madame had felt such true happiness. And with this happiness, she had another surprise in store for Etienne. She had thought all day about which ring he should present to his beloved. She had looked over carefully the gems in her jewel box, her eyes wandering back and forth. At last she made her decision. The large emerald surrounded by diamonds would be perfect. This would make the engagement binding. She had already begun to make arrangements for the wedding . . . at least in her mind. . . . She wanted the nuptials to take place as quickly as possible in case Mademoiselle should have second thoughts, which she quickly dismissed as unthinkable. Still, she would see that it took place soon after their arrival in Paris.

After dinner the family went as usual to the sitting room for coffee and brandy. Soon Jeanette, with the children, took her leave on cue from Jean-Paul. Then Madame invited Etienne to her room, where she gave him the ring.

"Mother," he said, "I still can't believe this is happening to me."

"Believe it, my son. God has a way of rewarding those who deserve it, and He has singled you out. He hasn't forgotten you. Now, my dear, stop wasting your time with me . . . there is somebody far more important waiting, I would guess, to hear a very important proposal. . . ." And saying it, she hugged him, and then watched him leave, tears clouding her eyes.

* * *

Etienne waited outside until the lights in the children's bedrooms were turned off, then impossibly nervous, knocked at Jeanette's door.

Her face lighted up when she saw him. "Good evening, monsieur, won't you come in?"

"Thank you . . . but would you mind if we went outside for a bit . . . ?" And offered his hand, which she took with some hesitation, not wanting him to feel that she was being too forward.

The leafy patterns of the willow tree danced around them on the lawn. The evening was balmy and cool. When they reached the willow, Jeanette sat down.

Etienne was determined not to wait any longer. "Jeanette," he said, "as is hardly a secret, I don't have Jean-Paul's gift with words so I'll say this the only way I know how. . . . Until today I had no idea that you . . . that you cared for me. God knows, I still find it difficult to believe. . . ."

Her heart was pounding as she began the charade. . . . "Your mother has told you . . . ? But she promised—"

He reached for her hand, remembering the special quality of *Clair de Lune* the night she'd played it. "Dearest Jeanette, she didn't really betray your . . . confidence. I'd never have known, you've never stepped out of your role of governess . . . but she felt she had to tell me when you said you were going away . . . and why. After all, she knew how I felt about you too and—"

"Monsieur Etienne, what can I say—?"

"Only what you said to my mother . . . that you do care for me—"

"Oh, but I do, I truly do," and she started to cry, not, as he assumed, out of relief, but because she really did care for him—even if not as he thought . . . and as she wished. Yes, if only she *did* love him, if only this deception she despised weren't necessary. . . .

"Jeanette, I love you. If you can accept me for what I am, and am not"—he half-smiled—"I give you my word . . . no, I give you my love, and my life—"

"I'm not really worthy of—"

"Don't say that, please . . . not when I've finally gotten up the nerve to ask you to . . . to marry me. Will you . . . ?"

She buried her face in his shoulder, but he could hear a muffled "Oh yes, Etienne, yes . . ."

Gently he lifted her head and tilted her face so that their eyes met . . . eyes that were even lovelier, if possible, he thought, glistening as they now did with tears. He wiped them away, then slowly, hesitantly at first and then with a boldness that surprised himself, took her in his arms, felt the loveliness of her, and kissed her for the first time. When he finally released her, he took out his mother's ring and slipped it carefully on her finger, looking at her intently as he did so.

"This is my life, my life with you, and the circle means it will never end. I promise you that, darling. And even though I will never be able to give you enough—"

"Please, Etienne, you have already given me more than enough, more than . . . everything."

They sat there for a while, his arms around her, around the world. And then it was time to go back, and before leaving her at the cottage he embraced and kissed her again, and, nearly beaming, said he doubted he'd sleep a minute that night, but didn't care, didn't, in fact, want to. It would be too awful to wake up and find this had been a concoction of his imagination. No, he wouldn't risk that. . . .

Later, when they'd finally parted and she'd gone to her room, she lay down on her bed and let her feelings flood out, at the same time telling herself that at least she did care for him, and that she'd do her best to make him happy, but along with it came the thought that had been there before . . . that she might, indeed, be her mother's daughter . . . a thought interrupted by the emergence from the shadows of the man who had arranged this strange new turn in her life.

"You seem to have done very well," Jean-Paul said, "judging from the ecstatic expression on the face of my dear smitten brother. Can you doubt that you have done him a favor, not to mention, of course, ourselves . . . ?"

"Please, Jean-Paul, please go away. Not tonight. I can't see you tonight after—"

"Oh come now, Jeanette." He went to her and gently lifted her shoulders, his voice quiet and calm. "There's hardly reason for remorse, although I wonder if perhaps you didn't overplay your role just a bit. Please remember, my darling, who the real man in your life is. . . ."

She looked at him, shook her head. "Oh, God, Jean-Paul, what we're doing is wrong, it's sinful. How can we live with such deception? How can I hurt Etienne, the finest man I've ever—"

"Please, darling"—and his face tightened momentarily—"I think you will find it easier than you think . . . that is to say, you've already made him the happiest man in the world. You didn't, I'm sure, actually say you loved him, you're too careful and honest for that."

"No, but I didn't say that I didn't love him either. He *believes* I do, and that is the deception."

"Yes, and it is what we agreed to. Now, my dearest, when we return to Paris I won't be going to Algiers. I'll stay close to you, and after you and Etienne marry, things will work out and all the difficulties you imagine will adjust themselves. Trust my judgment. I tell you again you have no reason to feel remorse or guilt . . . you have made Etienne a happier man than he ever dared hope to be, given him what no other woman would." He took her in his arms, stroked her hair and lifted her face so that their lips met. "What matters most, let's not forget, is the child, *our* child . . . never forget that. Or me." And then he quickly, skillfully proceeded to make certain that she did not.

Nineteen

On the third of September the house on the Boulevard Victor Hugo became once again the address of the Paris Duprés. Provence seemed very far away as a frenzy of preparation for the wedding began. There were fittings to be arranged, lists to be made up, menus to be planned, all under the supervision of Madame. New arrangements had to be made for the children since Jeanette was no longer their governess. She was now living in one of the bedrooms on the second floor, down the hall from Madame.

Instead of interviewing a new governess immediately for the post, Jeanette spoke to both Madame and Etienne of a dear and trusted friend who could take charge of the children until after the wedding, when Jeanette could hire someone permanently. Madeleine was asked to come temporarily, and accepted only too gratefully.

With the help of Jeanette, who instructed her, Madeleine was moved into the children's quarters. Because she and Jeanette were friends, the children took to her immediately, especially since Jeanette was still their mentor.

One day, in spite of her busy schedule, she went to see Clothilde. She and Jean-Paul had decided that she must, since Clothilde was the only other person who knew about her love for Jean-Paul.

When she entered the kitchen Clothilde turned around abruptly, somewhat startled. Coldly she said, "Oh, it's you."

Jeanette hadn't expected hostility from Clothilde, but

she smiled, though her stomach was doing somersaults.
"Yes, it's me. I wanted very much to see you."

"Why?" Clothilde said, shrugging her shoulders.

"Because we've been friends. More than friends . . .
confidants."

"Ah, I see. Would you like a cup of coffee?"

"Yes, thank you."

As they sat at the kitchen table, Clothilde looked at Jeanette without speaking. Trying to keep her voice even
and cheerful, Jeanette said, "Clothilde, I'm very happy,
and very much in love."

"With whom?" Clothilde asked bitingly.

"With Monsieur Etienne, of course."

"Really? When you last sat down in my kitchen, weeping away, you were oh so in love with Jean-Paul. What
happened so suddenly to change your feelings?"

Jeanette's throat became dry as she took a sip of the
coffee. "Clothilde . . . have you forgotten what it was
like to be nineteen years old and head over heels in love
. . . ? What I felt then was only the infatuation of a
schoolgirl, attracted to an older man for the first time. You
yourself admitted that although Monsieur Jean-Paul was a
scoundrel, he was irresistible . . . didn't you?"

"Yes, I did. I said it then and I say it now. So what
happened to your infatuation?"

"The more I saw of Etienne's gentleness and understanding, the more we were thrown together, the more I
realized it was Etienne I truly felt for. It didn't happen
suddenly, like a comet shooting across the sky, it happened slowly, during the days we spent together in the
country. The more I learned about him . . . the stronger
my feeling grew. . . ."

Clothilde looked directly into the eyes of Jeanette, and
what she saw there was truth and honesty (and she was
not entirely wrong). "Now I am happy, my dear. Etienne
so deserves your love. And his . . . infirmity . . . doesn't
bother you?"

"It brings him closer to me . . . I'm not exactly perfect
myself, Clothilde."

Clothilde embraced the young girl. "Dear, I had many
doubts, I must admit. All I can say is I pray your life
together will be filled with joy, and many children. . . ."

Jeanette thought she would faint, but managed to

steady herself, then kissed the old woman and went to her room. The mis-truths, half-truths (she resisted calling them half-lies) didn't come easily . . . but she turned her thoughts to Jean-Paul, fortified herself with her overwhelming feelings for him. . . .

Ten days after the return to Paris, Jeanette was presented to Paris society at a reception given in her honor at the Dupré mansion.

Before going down to greet the guests, Madame sat at her dressing table as Renée coiffed her hair. Looking at her reflection in the mirror, she thought of the role she had played, and what her obligations were to Etienne.

Although she was still officially in mourning over the death of Denise, she felt she owed this to Etienne. Should she . . . could she deprive him of his supreme moment? This was the first time he'd ever known such joy. Who did this moment belong to, the living or the dead? Strongwilled woman that she was, Madame decided it belonged to the living. She would always have time to weep, but that could come later. Tonight she would smile. She would wear black, but it would not be too somber. There had been enough grief in this house, and for such a long time.

When Renée finished, she selected a flowing black Chantilly lace gown that showed off the white skin of her neck, around which she fastened a heavy strand of long pearls attached with a diamond clip. Now she walked down the stairs, taking her place beside her son and future daughter-in-law. She felt enormously proud as she looked at Jeanette, dressed in a printed flowered chiffon gown from the House of Dior. She wore the locket Lucien had given her, and on her left hand sparkled the emerald and diamond ring.

Madame held her head high as she introduced Jeanette, the receiving line proceeding on into the salon. She knew all too well the whispers, the gossip, the phone calls that would be exchanged tomorrow. All of Paris would be talking. Not only was Antoinette Dupré allowing a governess to join the bloodline of the august house of Dupré, the girl was also a Jewess! This bothered Madame not at all. These people didn't know the circumstances of her life, and she would make no excuses.

As Jeanette saw Jean-Paul come through the door and

approach them, her nerve almost failed her. To strengthen herself, she held on tightly to Etienne's arm. Etienne smiled down at her adoringly.

Jean-Paul kissed his mother's cheek, then Jeanette's hand as she diverted her eyes. And then to Etienne . . . "I want to extend my heartfelt congratulations. I hope this will be the prelude to a long and happy life."

The brothers shook hands as their mother looked on, blessing Jeanette for being the one who had brought her two sons together in some understanding for the first time in their lives. "And where is Marie Jacqueline?" she asked Jean-Paul.

He shrugged. "Unfortunately, Mother, she wasn't up to coming. She has a terrible migraine headache."

"What a pity," Madame replied.

Etienne, especially generous in his own state of euphoria, felt especially sad for Jean-Paul this evening . . . how different Jeanette was from the pitiful Marie Jacqueline, and how grateful he was. . . .

When she went to bed that night, Jeanette lay awake staring at the ceiling, wondering if she could endure the strain of the next few weeks. She was weary, frightened and apprehensive that something might still happen to prevent this marriage. Suddenly she felt her abdomen. Oh God, please don't let anything happen to . . . don't punish my child for what I am doing. . . .

She got out of bed, turned on the desk lamp, took out the ledger and began to write:

> *Forgive me, Papa . . . I haven't been able to confide this part of my life to you. . . . That's why I haven't written. Your shame would be too much for me to live with. It's almost too much for me to bear, but I love Jean-Paul, the feeling I have for him simply overwhelms me, terrifies me . . . I can't live without him. It's shameful . . . I confess my weakness. . . . Even now I want to feel him close to me . . . though we've agreed not to until after the wedding. Please forgive me, Papa . . . I promise to try to atone for the wrong I'm doing to Etienne. . . . Some way, I will do that . . . I must. . . .*

Finally she fell into an exhausted sleep.

* * *

The religious terms had been agreed upon: Jeanette would not convert to the Catholic faith, but she had agreed without reservation that any issue of Etienne's and hers would be raised according to his religion, and the document was signed.

The wedding would take place in the large salon. Two hundred and fifty guests would attend. . . . And the reception would be held in the white and gold ballroom. The furniture was moved out of the salon and the gilt chairs were placed in rows on either side of the aisle. The altar was set up. Now all that remained was for the florist to decorate.

Two days before the wedding, Uncle Leon was due to arrive. But Aunt Deborah couldn't attend. In the last few months, she'd become completely bedridden. Jeanette was brokenhearted . . . they were, after all, the only family she had.

As Etienne and Jeanette waited for his train at the station, Jeanette thought how long it had been since she'd seen her uncle. Seven months? It seemed a century since that day she'd kissed him good-bye at Dover. . . .

But now, incredibly, wonderfully, there he was, getting off the train, and she ran to meet him, then hugging him and clinging to him as though she would never let go. She felt so safe in his arms. Both of them were crying. There was so much to remember, and so much to try to forget. Finally, taking Leon's arm in hers, she brought him over to meet Etienne, her husband-to-be, and as the two men shook hands, there were more tears in her eyes, and she looked away, stealing a moment to try to recover. . . .

After dinner that evening Madame chatted with Uncle Leon in the small formal salon where they took demitasse and brandy while Jeanette played the piano softly for Etienne's ears only. She played all the things he loved. Chopin, Mozart, Poulenc . . . she closed with their music, the melody that had brought them together, *Clair de Lune*. . . .

Early the next morning, the Sabbath, Jeanette and her uncle attended synagogue. When memorial services were over, they walked to the Tuileries gardens and sat quietly for a time. Finally Jeanette said, "Uncle, we've had so little time alone, let me take you to a place I love very much."

And she took him to the little café on the Avenue de l'Opéra. Leon was charmed.

As their orders were taken, Jeanette couldn't take her eyes from her uncle, scarcely believing that he was actually with her again. He had changed so little, and she had changed so much.

As though reading her thoughts, he said, "You've certainly grown up in such a short time. I can hardly believe you're the same girl—"

"I'm not, Uncle . . ." And indeed she wasn't. . . . "It was difficult to write you, I mean about the joy and happiness I've found here in Paris. . . ."

Leon looked admiringly at his niece. "You are happy, Jeanette. I can see it in your eyes. And if anyone deserves such happiness, God knows, it is you."

In spite of herself, she blushed. If he knew what secrets she held inside her, she wondered how happy he would be for her then. . . . She thanked God he could not read her thoughts. . . .

Looking at her, he asked tentatively, "Jeanette, is there anything . . . anything at all you would like to tell me?"

She nodded, feeling that she had to tell him. "Uncle Leon," she said, "Etienne knows about my father's death, but . . . not how it happened . . . I've kept that from him. . . . But even more important, I told him that Mama died when I was five years old. . . ."

Leon looked down, idly rearranging the crumbs on the table. . . . If only that were true, Rubin would be here today, seeing his daughter being married. . . .

"Uncle, I don't want to, but I think about her sometimes, more than I ever thought I would . . . and I'm almost positive that I've seen her picture in the papers here, with Count Alexis Maximov. It must be him, I remember him, and I remember—"

"Well, that's possible, of course," Leon said, "but you were so young when she left and—"

"I was young, but I'm afraid in some ways I was older than you knew, Uncle, and I remember, oh yes, I remember what she looked like, I remember so many things, too many, and I know I recognize the lady I have seen in the papers. . . . Whatever else she was, she was a beautiful

woman, my mother, you always said so, Father did, and I
had eyes to see as well. She's changed so little over the
years, and the Count Alexis Maximov can only be the man
I thought of as . . . well, do you know, Uncle, when
Papa was away in the war, I used to think that Alexis was
my father . . . in fact, I wanted him to be. Up till then
he was the only father I knew. But, of course, I hardly
feel that way toward him now, nor have I for years . . .
not since he took my mother away. . . ."

Leon knew she was right, that it was indeed Magda,
although she'd made an almost childish—well, wasn't
Magda in so many ways childish, for all her worldliness?—
an almost childish effort to disguise herself by changing
her first name. His friend Dryfus had reported to him the
presence of Magda some time ago, but he hadn't, of
course, mentioned it to Jeanette in his letters, hoping that
perhaps she'd not be aware of it, be spared the knowing.
Well, there had been no realistic chance of that, he now
realized, but at least she might never have to meet her
mother again. . . .

And as though a part of his thoughts, Jeanette was saying, "I'm terrified, Uncle, that I may have to meet her one
day, see her face to face. I don't know what I would do, I
don't know if I could stand it. . . ."

"I doubt it will happen, my dear. After all, you are
hardly of the same age group, you and your fine husband-
to-be hardly move in her circles or are likely to. But even
if you do, even in that unlikely event, I have confidence
in you, my darling. You will be what you are, a fine young
woman, and you will behave with the dignity and courage
that are you. Your mother cannot be more than she is. You
cannot be less. And now enough of this. . . . My favorite
niece is about to have a wedding. I suggest we order ourselves a wicked French drink of cognac and celebrate."

She nodded, smiled, and was infinitely grateful.

The Countess Alexis Maximov, lying in bed, had just
seen the newspaper announcement of the impending marriage of . . . her daughter! Impossible . . . impossible
to take in, to absorb. But there could be no denying it . . .
Mademoiselle Jeanette Hack, English, former governess
to the distinguished family Dupré, engaged to marry

Etienne Dupré, brother of Jean-Paul Dupré, member of the diplomatic corps. . . .

My God, she thought, she'd heard nothing, known nothing, of the girl's whereabouts or fortunes since Solange's death. . . . Camail had been able to tell her nothing . . . and now suddenly, after all these years, less than a mile away her daughter was preparing her marriage and she could be no part of it, not even able to see her . . . tomorrow *her* child would become a bride and she, the mother, was excluded . . . still the pariah for all her social credentials as Countess Maximov. Dear Alexis, he could give her only so much . . . he could not erase the past. . . . And now that past came rushing back and it seemed only yesterday that she had romped on the bed with her little doll . . . and heard the echo of carousel music . . . and saw a little girl with balloons in one hand, clutching the hand of Alexis with the other. . . .

Her daughter, a governess, and now marrying into the fine family of Dupré. . . . Dupré . . . she held the name in her mind, not for its familiarity, because it was known as one of the finest in all Paris. . . . But there was something more about it, something personally familiar to her . . . and then suddenly she remembered actually meeting a Dupré, a Jean-Paul Dupré, yes, she was sure of it now. . . . She had met him at the reception Alexis had taken her to, and she remembered thinking him so young to be in the diplomatic service. Well, we have something in common now, monsieur, she thought. You are the brother of my soon-to-be, brand new son-in-law. . . .

Oh, God, how strangely lives were interwoven. . . . Tomorrow would be a very bad day for her . . . very bad. . . . Shaking her head in disbelief, she got out of bed and took down the small portrait off the wall, the one painted by Camail, and held it tightly against her, as though trying to bring to life the little girl that was its subject, and thinking . . . Alexis, dear Alexis, not even you can comfort me now. This time, as she was before, Magda Charascu is all alone. . . .

Twenty

October 1, 1936

The day of days arrived, and both Jeanette and Madame were thankful, though their reasons were in no way the same.

As Jeanette stood in her room, wearing the white satin wedding gown covered with seed pearls and lace, Madame drank in the sight of her. Jeanette was radiant. "I wanted to see you before you became my daughter. And that is how I feel. No one can replace my child, but I feel as though God had sent you to us to help soften her loss. You've brought me untold joy by giving yourself to my beloved son. Now you will be one of us, ours. From now on, I want you to call me Mother, and you will be my daughter."

Jeanette embraced the woman. "It's been so long since I've been able to say, or even think the word 'Mother.' I promise, I promise you . . . to make Etienne happy. . . ."

"I know you will, my dear, and I promise to love you as my own," and she took the heavy strand of pearls from the purple velvet jewel box and slipped them over Jeanette's head. "These were given to me by my mother-in-law on my wedding day. I pass them on to you with the same love. Wear them well. . . ."

And Jeanette, watching her leave, tears in her eyes, swore to herself that she would. . . .

In another part of the house, Etienne, fortified with

more brandy than he'd ever had before, struggled with the pearl studs. He wasn't intoxicated, he was nervous, too nervous even to let himself be helped by his dresser. He had to do something with his hands. Keep busy, his mind kept telling him. He struggled with the white bowtie, which wouldn't hang straight.

"Here, let me help you with that," said Jean-Paul, who had just come in. Within moments the tie lay perfectly even. "I know how you feel, Etienne. I've been through it myself. All you have to do is relax."

"Relax?" Etienne said. "How can I? I'm scared to death."

"May I offer you my best wishes," Jean-Paul said, "for a long and happy life? I congratulate you. You're a very fortunate man to have the love of such a very charming young woman. And she is no less fortunate."

Etienne looked at his brother. Jean-Paul really seemed to mean it, and for the first time he felt a bond between his brother and himself. "Thank you, Jean-Paul, from you that means a great deal—"

"Well, I should think the time has come for you and me to be brothers, to put aside all those old rather childish matters . . . after all, we are grown men now. Let's act as though we were. I give you my hand on it." A masterful piece of diplomacy, he thought, considering Etienne's willingness to believe it.

The two brothers shook hands and embraced.

"All right, then," Jean-Paul said, "it's time for the best man to lead his little brother to the altar. . . ."

The music had begun.

Jeanette walked, almost regally, down the marble staircase, her long Valenciennes lace train guided from behind by Renée. The candlelight satin gown and juliet cap that demurely framed her face made her look majestic. She carried a bouquet of lilies of the valley.

At the entrance to the salon she was met by her uncle. Renée adjusted the veil and then retreated. Jeanette took her uncle's arm. Lucien was waiting at the altar, dressed in short black velvet pants, a white silk blouse-shirt and a short velvet jacket. He was very nervous as he held the white satin pillow on which rested the two gold marriage bands.

Preceding Jeanette were Nicole and Desirée, dressed in

long white organza dresses, gathered at the waist and encircled with pink velvet ribbons tied at the back with bows. The girls carried golden baskets filled with rose petals, which they dropped on the white-carpeted aisle.

Finally, to the strains from *Lohengrin*, Jeanette and her uncle walked slowly down the aisle between the two rows of flower-filled standards toward the altar. A hush descended. All eyes were on Jeanette, and there were admiring whispers on her beauty, her bearing, her grace. Tomorrow would be time enough for less flattering speculation . . . such as that she had married Etienne for his money and position, and why someone of her apparent breeding had become a governess in the first place, with such a distinguished uncle from London. . . . But for this moment such thoughts were put aside as Jeanette reached the altar and her uncle kissed her lightly on the cheek, handed her over to her husband-to-be and took his place beside Madame.

Jeanette knelt before the altar, side by side with Etienne. And in the solemn and sacred ceremony they were united, as each said the vows. . . .

When Etienne lifted the short veil that covered her eyes, he looked at her as though trying to memorize her, wanting to remember her face at this moment all his life. Then, gently, he kissed her, and she returned the kiss.

Well, thought Jean-Paul, it had been done. . . .

Madame did not cry during the ceremony, although she wept tears of joy inside. Jeanette also held back tears, afraid that if she relaxed control she would become hysterical when she saw Jean-Paul standing to one side. Tears were openly shed by Madeleine, who sat in the very last row, outfitted for the first time in her life in a fashionable dress, a gift from Jeanette as well.

The receiving line was long but the Duprés graciously accepted the congratulations of all. Monsieur Dryfus whispered to Jeanette his pleasure at playing a role—however inadvertently—in bringing her together with Etienne.

After the ceremonial protocol, Jean-Paul came up to his brother, who was sitting beside Jeanette. "And does a brother have the right to kiss the bride?"

Etienne laughed. "Yes . . . but only once, mind you. From now on they all belong to me."

Gravely, Jean-Paul kissed Jeanette . . . then said,

"And now may I have the honor of dancing with Madame Etienne Dupré?" He whirled Jeanette away without waiting for an answer.

Jeanette found herself in Jean-Paul's arms, the last place she wanted to be, this evening. . . . In only a few hours she would be taken to her marriage bed by another man, and thinking of the man she couldn't marry. . . . As they danced he held her tight, his arm around her thin waist, feeling the firm breasts under the wedding gown. . . . He even imagined he could feel the new life growing within her womb. . . .

"You're holding me too close—"

"Don't worry . . . with all these people no one will notice a little brotherly affection."

"You're upsetting me, Jean-Paul . . . how do you expect me to survive tonight—"

He smiled for the benefit of anyone who might be watching. "You've survived all right up to now. . . . In just a short while, the worst will be over. Take heart, my love. While you're making Etienne the happiest of men, I'll be the one who's suffering the most . . . that you're not in my arms."

"I don't want to dance any more, Jean-Paul. Take me back."

He did, saying, "And now, dear brother, I give you back your wife," kissing Jeanette's hand and placing it in Etienne's.

And now the moment had arrived for the newlyweds to leave. As they went up the stairs the unmarried girls waited below for Jeanette to throw her bouquet. She aimed it at Madeleine, then turned around and disappeared with her . . . husband. . . .

Madame had been moved out of her quarters three days before and into a suite down the hall, feeling it only right, after all, that the bride of a Dupré should have that particular suite. . . . It had been given to her when she had married Henri. Etienne opened the door for her, and she walked into the room with the famous four-poster bed. On either side the rouge-colored damask draperies, tied back with silken cords, cascaded to the floor. A fire glowed in the low marble fireplace, and the room was filled with the fragrance of white roses. Chilled champagne was waiting in a silver wine bucket. Earlier, the bedspread had been removed, revealing the white satin comforter and the white satin sheets trimmed with lace. Inside matching satin pillow slips lay enormous down pillows. The lights had been dimmed.

Jeanette gazed at all the luxury . . . Madame Etienne Dupré . . . all hers . . . all for her . . . and she was weeping inside. Oh God, why couldn't she have fallen in love with Etienne? How beautiful it would have been, the way it should be . . . instead of this agony. . . .

Her thoughts were interrupted when she heard the champagne cork pop and the champagne bubble over.

"I'm not very good at this, I'm afraid," Etienne said, pouring the champagne into the silver toasting goblets, engraved with the date, and the names Etienne and Jeanette. Madame had taken care of everything.

"To you, my dearest . . . may our lives together be as joyous as tonight is for me. . . ."

They raised the goblets and clinked them.

"That's my wish, too, Etienne," she answered, her words almost the echo of a stranger to them both.

They sipped the wine in front of the fire, without speaking. When they finished, Etienne went wordlessly into the dressing room that had been his father's.

Jeanette undressed in Madame's dressing room, quickly putting on her nightgown. She got into bed, hoping Etienne would come back soon and not delay what had to be accomplished. He seemed to take forever.

Finally he came to the bed and looked at his bride. He took off the long dressing robe and got into bed beside her. The lights had been turned off, and only the glow of the fire illuminated her. He reached out, drew her to him, and gently kissed her lips. Wanting to consummate their marriage as quickly as possible, she took his face in her hands and kissed him with less restraint. Overcome, delighted, by her response, he unbuttoned his pajama top underneath the comforter, slipped out of his bottoms, then gently picked up her gown. She helped him take it off . . . and soon all restraints were submerged as the two of them became one. . . .

Much to Jeanette's surprise, Etienne was not only a sensitive but an ardent lover. Jean-Paul had aroused her to a kind of terrifying excitement. Etienne's gentle passion created different stirrings in her that she tried to resist, wishing he hadn't awakened them. . . .

After his passion had been satisfied, she lay in Etienne's arms, feeling guilty about her thoughts of Jean-Paul. She was terribly confused. She hadn't expected to succumb to the gentle lover in her husband.

She was a very confused young lady, loving Jean-Paul as she did, and still deeply enjoying Etienne as she just had. Somehow she had thought his . . . his problem would disqualify him from such skillful lovemaking, which was of course ridiculous, but still . . .

For a moment she'd forgotten what had brought her to this marriage bed, had almost wanted to . . . but now reality came back to her sharply. Jean-Paul was owed her gratitude and love . . . it was he who had made sure her child, their child, would be born in wedlock . . . right here in this bed, this night . . . so far as the world would ever know. . . .

Etienne awoke early and lay in the enormous bed watching his bride sleep. If possible, she was more beautiful asleep than awake. He listened to her even breathing. What other man had ever been so blessed . . . to have a wife such as this. . . . He still couldn't quite believe it, that she actually was his . . . and then thought of how easily . . . eagerly even . . . she had accepted his love on their wedding night, and was able to believe it more. . . .

Her eyes still closed, Jeanette stretched languidly, arousing herself from sleep. When she opened them, and saw Etienne, she smiled.

"Did you sleep well?" he asked. Moving closer, he took her in his arms.

"Oh, yes, I did—" And despite her upset and confusion over her role, after a while she indeed had slept well, and this surprised her.

Tightening his arms around her, he kissed her urgently, and as she responded, her body melding into his, they consummated their marriage for the second time.

Afterward, kissing her gently, stroking her, he said, "You've brought the world to me, Jeanette. . . . Nothing exists for me outside of this room except you."

And at that moment she could have answered in honesty that it was the same for her—though she held back, realizing that her profound affection for this man almost made her forget she was not in love with him . . . much as she might have wished otherwise.

Her thoughts, and their idyllic moment, was shattered by the chimes of the Sevres clock on the mantel. "Etienne, it's eleven o'clock. There's so much to be done before we leave."

Then he showered, shaved and slipped into his trousers. As he pulled on his socks, he looked at his shoes. The four-inch platform that had been his nemesis since birth no longer seemed important to him. . . . He reached in the closet for his red brocade dressing robe trimmed with a red satin shawl collar. He tied the satin sash around his middle and went back to the bedroom. Jeanette was waiting, refreshed from her bath, wearing a light blue satin gown and matching sheer peignoir that tied at the neck with a blue satin ribbon. Her hair had been carefully combed and hung loosely below her shoulders.

"Let me look at you," he said, taking her hands and holding her at a distance. She seemed so tiny, so petite. Drawing her close to him, he whispered, "I love you . . . and what's more I can hardly contain myself when I see you."

Smiling, she said, "I'm afraid you'll have to use some restraint, since I believe breakfast has just arrived. To paraphrase, man lives not by love alone . . ." and was amazed at her ease with him.

A breakfast fit for the bride of a Dupré—ordered by Madame—was wheeled in. "I don't remember eating a thing last night," she said, "and the children were so precious and excited."

"I know . . . poor Lucien's hands were shaking when he held the ring, he was as nervous as I was. Matter of fact, the only one who seemed calm was Jean-Paul, for which I thank him. He helped calm me down before the ceremony with, not incidentally, the help of a brandy. It's a wonder I didn't stagger going to the altar."

The smile left her face momentarily . . . for at least this one day she wished there could be no mention of him, of her and him. . . . She changed the subject. "Your mother came to see me before the wedding, and I deeply appreciate it. Do you remember the first time I met her, Etienne . . . when I took the children to see her? You know, she frightened me so, I thought I would faint. . . ."

He reached across the table and took her hand. "I know . . . Mother can be very stubborn at times, but she is also fiercely logical. Once she sees the wisdom of something she can even capitulate gracefully. And once one wins her friendship, it's theirs forever. . . ."

And Jeanette nodded agreement, remembering the day at the cottage when Madame had humbled herself . . . and thinking of her she also thought of her mother . . . and thrust the thought aside. "You know, Etienne, in some ways you're very much like her, in the very best ways. . . . And I'll never forget your kindness to me from the very first—"

"It was easy, I assure you. After all, I fell in love with you from the first . . . like Mother said, you bewitched me on sight, and she was right."

She took a final sip of coffee. "Yes, well, I really think we should get ready, dear, it's getting late and there's so much to do before we leave. . . ."

The family was waiting when the newlyweds emerged downstairs. Jeanette was wearing a sheer wool mauve dress with matching suede shoes, bag and gray gloves. The sable coat that she carried draped over her arm had been a present from Uncle Leon. The sable hat sat back on her head, revealing the chignon, carefully twisted at the nape of her neck by Renée's able hands. Etienne wore a gray tweed tailored suit and fedora. He no longer wore the black armband . . . his mother had insisted he not, and he was grateful to her for it.

When the children spotted them coming down the stairs they ran to them and Jeanette embraced them as they all told her—and using her first name—how much they would miss her, and hurry back . . . and they were promptly corrected by Madame, who told them, "Aunt Jeanette . . . Aunt Jeanette, from now on, children." Jeanette assured them she would write every day and that a month was, after all, only four weeks, and Nicole pressed her with, "You won't forget to write?"

You won't forget to write, will you, mama . . . of course, all the time . . . Jeanette blinked back the tears, wanting to forget, remembering. Time wouldn't behave, the past never really went away. . . . But this was now and the future. . . . "Of course," she said, "I'll write and

I'll be thinking of you every minute, just as your uncle will." . . . Next she was greeted by Madame, who kissed her and whom she thanked for the lovely wedding. And as Madame held her, she thought how strange it was that she had begun despising this girl, and now had genuinely come to love her, and to be able to see her poise and warmth for the precious realities that they were. If only Jean-Paul had been so blessed in his marriage . . . what a difference between her sons' two women. . . . And just as quickly she dismissed the depressing thought of Jean-Paul's chronic sniffler.

"And you, Uncle Leon," Jeanette was saying, "what a joy it has been for me to have you here to share this with me. Thank you, dearest uncle."

And finally the moment she'd dreaded. Standing in front of her, smiling, Jean-Paul held and kissed her hand, saying how *well* she looked this morning, and she rather abruptly withdrew it, trembling, which helped but didn't entirely reassure him that she was still merely playing her appropriate role.

Finally Jeanette embraced Madeleine. "I don't need to ask you to take good care of the children, my dear friend. I know you will." And they stood for a moment looking at each other, remembering the not so distant past.

Twenty-one

The trip lasted well over two days, and took them through the Swiss and Italian Alps. They changed trains once in Milan, then the train sped on across the Apennine Mountains. When the Milan-to-Rome express finally came to a halt in Rome, the Duprés were driven to the Excelsior Hotel, which would be their address for the next two weeks.

That night, amid the splendors of Rome, Etienne said, "Jeanette . . . do you have any idea what it means to me . . . that you love me?"

Somewhere in his voice, she thought, there seemed to be almost a plea, and she quickly said, "And do you know how much you mean to me . . . ?" And meant it, at the same time knowing she would be . . . had been unfaithful to him. . . . Somehow she would, she had to, learn to live in two emotional worlds. She *would* be a good wife to Etienne . . . while still being the mistress of Jean-Paul . . . the father of her child. . . . And she would not only have Jean-Paul's child, she'd also repay Etienne for his kindness and love and have children by him as well.

She fell in love with Rome. It seemed to have been there forever. She loved its cathedrals and museums, its fountains and its restaurants. All the glory of the Renaissance was reflected in its art. The only difficult moment came one day at the Spanish Steps. They were an agony for Etienne to walk down, but he was determined to do it. He attracted a great deal of attention, stepping down side-

ways in his slow, patient way. Jeanette, hating herself for
it, nonetheless felt some embarrassment . . . and, again
in spite of herself, felt herself becoming irritable their last
night in Rome as they sat at a table in the magnificent
dining room of the Excelsior Hotel, the champagne chilled
to perfection, the dinner superb, and watched the other
couples dancing, wishing that—

She pushed the dangerous thought from her mind, but
it lingered—try as she might to eliminate it—just as it did
during the next weeks in Florence and Venice, before, finally, returning home to Paris.

To Paris, and to . . .

On the second night of their return to Paris, the newlyweds were honored at dinner. Madame had invited only
an intimate group of relatives and friends. Jean-Paul, naturally, was among them.

When they adjourned to the small salon for coffee and
brandy, Etienne wanted to join the bridge players. Since
Jeanette hadn't yet learned to play, she walked across the
hall to the large salon, sat down at the piano and started
to play a Chopin waltz. Jean-Paul soon joined her.

"Did you miss me?" he said.

"Yes," and did not look up from her playing.

"Very much?"

"Yes . . . please, not tonight, we can't talk now . . ."

"I've taken an apartment, I know you'll like it . . ."
and he wrote down the address, tucking the slip of paper
into the cleavage between her breasts (the owner assert-
ing ownership). He described the balcony that looked out
on the Eiffel Tower, and the magic of the lights that enhanced their city by night. . . . They would share it together. . . . There, in their hideaway, all of Paris would
belong to them.

The next afternoon Jeanette took special pains with her
appearance. Her hands trembled as she adjusted the thin
straps on her satin slip. When she had finished, she put
the sable coat over her slender shoulders and picked up a
box containing a dress she wished to have altered.

She went to the library, where Etienne was hard at
work on the estate accounts. He looked up from the desk.

"You look especially delicious, and where are you off to?"

"Only a few errands, darling . . . but this is Paris, after all, and one should try one's best to match her beauty." A too pretty speech, she thought, and hurried on with, "I'll be back long before dinner." She kissed him and left.

Getting into the limousine, she told André to drive her to Dior's, and he needn't wait, she'd either call to be picked up later or take a taxi home, she wasn't yet certain which. Once inside the salon, she waited until André drove off, then immediately she walked out to the street and hailed a taxi that drove her to Jean-Paul.

He was waiting. She had hardly knocked when he opened the door, took her in his arms, kissed her and lifted her off the ground, kicking the door shut with his foot. It was the same for her . . . the nearly mindless, helpless frenzy she felt with him almost from the first . . . as he carried her to the bedroom, her coat falling from her shoulders to the floor in a heap. Their lips still together, he unbuttoned the back of her dress, released the shoulder straps of the slip and slid it from her body. He unbuttoned the fastening of the tiny lace bra as she hastily untied the sash of his dressing gown, under which he was naked. As they clung together, she felt his hardness touch her. He kissed her distended nipples, her abdomen, and beyond. Finally he spread his legs out and she lay beneath him. She wanted him as never before. As he entered her she moaned.

"Jean-Paul . . . oh God . . ." And then he was entering her, thrusting, turning, and in the final moment before the culmination, he whispered, his voice rasping, "Too long, away too long . . . belong here . . . with me . . . don't forget it . . ."

Spent and exhilarated at the same time, she lay back now in his arms, content not to talk, only to luxuriate.

Not so Jean-Paul, whose "curiosity" about her time with Etienne was still very much alive. "Last night you didn't want to talk. . . . Now tell me."

She hesitated. "Jean-Paul, you know what I feel for you, but please, I ask you to also make it possible for me to have this life with you. And for that . . . well, I ask you not to question me about my life with Etienne. . . ."

He looked at her, trying to camouflage the anger he felt. . . . However, he had to concede, unreasonable though it might be. "It's merely that I am concerned about your feelings, how you are managing in a difficult situation—"

"I realize that, darling, but when we're together like this, here in this lovely place, I don't want to talk about anything but us, to think about anybody but us. This is a special world that belongs to us, and when we're here, there isn't any world outside. . . ."

All his diplomatic training did little to modify his feeling of distinct unease. It seemed, he suspected, that the lady wanted to share his body but her life belonged to his precious little brother . . . except wasn't that precisely the arrangement he'd wanted . . . ? He wasn't being too consistent, he told himself, for a gentleman whose career was one of opportunistic reason. And, telling himself that, it did no good at all.

"Please understand," she was saying, "I do have to leave you and go back to . . . him. At least while we're together let's please pretend that only you and I exist," (not adding that otherwise they might not be able to exist at all).

He smiled. I surrender, as a good diplomat should when in a cul-de-sac. "But I surely am permitted to ask how you are feeling . . . the morning sickness, have you had any?"

"Yes, but thank God I've been able to get to the bathroom before it became too bad—"

"And when will you tell Etienne?"

"Tomorrow, I think. After I see the doctor. . . ."

He felt immensely pleased, concentrating once again on the original guiding purpose behind this whole arrangement that he had so skillfully arranged. And, almost to himself, he said, "A son, soon I will have a son and—"

She laughed. "And how are you so certain it will be a son? Maybe it will be a lovely baby girl—"

"No. My first child will be a son."

"Very well, sir, if you say so, and now I really must . . ."

"You really must stop talking," he said, drawing her close to him, "and only think of how you are going to be my son's mother, and always are going to belong to me. . . ." And he made love to her once more, as though to prove his argument.

Afterward, when it was nearly past the time to go, she felt a slight dizziness as she dressed to return to Etienne, looking as well groomed as when she had left him. And later, at dinner, she could honestly say—indeed she welcomed it as an escape—that she did not feel well and would she be forgiven if she went to bed early? Madame expressed concern and hoped she would feel better. Etienne took her upstairs, leaving Jean-Paul alone in the salon with his mother.

"How is Marie Jacqueline?" Madame said. "It's a pity she can't be with us—"

"I know, Mother, but as you realize, she really isn't well at all. . . . I'm afraid her allergies are even worse. Mother, I've done everything I can think of . . . doctors, everything . . ."

"Jean-Paul, I don't want to pry into your personal life, but can't you somehow persuade her to get out of the house? She's become so withdrawn. I noticed it in Provence this summer. She scarcely left her room. Can't something be done?"

"No, Mother, I'm afraid not . . ."

Madame sighed. "Such a pity . . ."

The next morning Jeanette knocked on her mother-in-law's door.

"Come in, my dear. How are you this morning?"

"I'm not sure, Mother. I didn't feel or sleep well last night, and I feel slightly ill this morning."

Madame's face lit up. "What do you mean by ill? Please give me the symptoms."

"Well . . . I feel a slight nausea—"

"Oh, my dear . . . I do think we must make an appointment for you to see our doctor."

"But why—"

"To see if you are pregnant, of course. You are, after all, a bride, a married woman . . . and married women eventually become mothers."

Jeanette, feeling almost like another person, outside of herself, watching herself perform, looked properly surprised. "But we've been married so short a time."

Madame laughed happily at her new daughter's charming naïveté. "It can happen, I assure you, very quickly, my dear." She immediately reached for the telephone and called Dr. Bernier's number, which she knew well from memory. She had called him often enough through the years. An appointment was made for two o'clock that afternoon. "I'll go with you," she added.

Jeanette very much preferred to go alone, but quickly, eagerly, answered, "Would you? That would be a great comfort. But, Mother, let's not say anything to Etienne until we're completely sure. He might be so disappointed if—"

"You're absolutely right. We won't say a thing. But imagine his joy if it's true."

"Oh yes. I pray he will be . . ."

Madame waited in the reception room, hoping against hope that her Etienne would now have what she had always most wanted for him . . . and for herself. . . .

After the examination Jeanette sat across from Dr. Bernier.

"Well, my dear," he said, "I believe you are going to be a mother."

"Are you sure?"

"Almost certain. Of course we will run tests to be on the safe side, but you seem to be at least two months along—"

Jeanette clenched the arms of the chair. "That's impossible. We were married less than a month ago."

He looked at her, frowned slightly and said, "Oh . . . well, your uterus appears to be somewhat large for so short a time—"

"I don't see how it can be that far along." The color had drained from her face.

He sat back, took off his glasses and wiped them with his handkerchief. He knew very well that she was more than a month into her pregnancy. He'd been practicing too long not to realize what the situation was. Either the child had not been conceived by Etienne, or the couple had had premarital relations. In any case, he'd been a trusted friend and doctor to the Duprés for a very long time. What he wrote in his records would be discreetly worded.

He put on his glasses again and smiled at the young woman sitting across from him, knowing how she must feel at being discovered. "Perhaps I'm mistaken about the time . . . this soon, it's difficult to make a categorical statement about that. But I must tell you there's little question that you are pregnant."

She looked away, on the edge of tears. What if Dr. Bernier confided in the family? Oh please, God, I beg you, even though I'm not deserving, please . . . help me . . .

God, or his equivalent at the moment, answered sooner than expected, as Dr. Bernier said, "In any event, you need not worry, Madame Dupré. Premature, seven-month babies do very well."

She looked up at him gratefully, even though she knew he was protecting her to protect the sensibilities of the Duprés. Whatever, he had her undying thanks. Next he discussed the necessity of prenatal care, and set up appointments for monthly visits. Then, his arm around her shoulders, he walked her back to the reception room, where he greeted Madame. "Well, my dear Madame Dupré, it seems you're going to be blessed with another grandchild. My congratulations to you and to Etienne. I'm sure our young mother will come through splendidly. . . ."

Madame was delighted . . . Etienne would be a father, and nothing would be spared in Jeanette's behalf. . . .

Madame left it for Jeanette, of course, to break the news to Etienne, and Jeanette waited until they retired to their bedroom for the night. "Etienne . . . ? I have some news . . . good news to tell you."

"Yes?"

She swallowed hard, moistened her lips and began, "Maman and I paid a visit to Dr. Bernier today."

"The obstetrician?"

"Yes, Etienne . . ."

He seemed unable—or unwilling?—to grasp the logical inference. Her heart was pounding. Did he suspect? But how could he? No, she chastised herself, she was allowing her mind to play games, born out of her own guilt. More likely it was the suddenness of the reality of impending fatherhood so soon after their marriage. . . .

"Etienne, we're going to have a child."

He stared at her uncomprehendingly. Then he frowned

and shook his head, as though he couldn't possibly have heard right. Then he looked at her again. "A child?" he said.

"Yes. A child. We're going to have a child."

He was incredulous. A deep blush colored his face at the same time his eyes brightened with joy. He grinned. Jeanette believed that she'd never before seen him look so happy. He knelt down in front of her and put his head in her lap. "You've brought us so much happiness, and now this . . ."

She cried softly from the release of her own anxiety. "I hope I can always make you happy."

"Have no fears on that, my dearest. You have already given me more than any man has the right to dare hope for."

And when they retired that evening, he held her in his arms with a special mixture of tenderness and strength . . . lover and proud possessor.

Life, by its own invention, tended to settle into a pattern of schedules and routines. Both Etienne and Jeanette were early risers. Most mornings she put on a casual dressing gown and the two of them had breakfast alone, leisurely, since it was Madame's habit to sleep late and have breakfast served to her. They took that meal in the morning room. Jeanette loved this room best of all. It was filled with plants and ferns of all sizes. The double doors opened onto a garden that even in winter was enchanting. She adored the green dining table and the chairbacks on which had been carved baskets of flowers, painted in colors. Here, it always seemed like spring. The pictures on the walls were of flowers, most of them painted by Etienne. The floors were parquet squares, high polished, in the center of which lay an oval Brussels rug. The border was wide, and the design an exact replica of the chairbacks.

When they finished eating, Etienne usually went to the library and read the morning paper. Jeanette went to the children's room, making sure to see Lucien before he went off to school. Then Madeleine attended to her chores, as Jeanette sat with Nicole, going over her lessons, while Desirée played house with her dolls.

Many mornings Etienne would come in later, sitting quietly and with pride as Jeanette bent over the table, intent on the girls' instruction. Desirée was beginning to read simple books with pictures. She was very bright and so keen that after reading a story once or twice she could recite it by heart. It was all Jeanette could do to restrain from squeezing Desirée affectionately as the cadence of her gentle, sweet voice rose and fell. And for a half hour each day the little girls had their piano lessons. Both children showed promise of becoming accomplished, but of the two, Desirée displayed the more exceptional talent, her pudgy fingers playing back and forth over the gleaming, responsive keys.

At noon, Jeanette would go to her room and dress for the day, then lunch with Etienne and Madame. She ate very sparingly now. In fact, she dieted strenuously. Of course, she took her vitamins and calcium tablets, plus milk, which the doctor had stressed to her, but she wanted to gain very little weight during the pregnancy, making sure the unborn child would not be too large for a babe supposedly born in the seventh month.

Madame objected heartily, insisting that Jeanette was not eating enough for two. Madame believed that expectant mothers should indulge, it was their duty. But Jeanette was ready with the excuse that since her pregnancy, food tended rather easily to upset her. It was sheer torture, though . . . always being famished, and at bedtime she reluctantly indulged herself with a glass of hot milk and crackers in order to sleep.

On the appointed afternoon she dressed as usual, eliminating the satin slip under the wool dress . . . . Jean-Paul was always so anxious at their rendezvous, she accommodated him—and, to be honest, herself—by wearing as little as possible. Putting the key in the lock, she felt the by now too familiar rush of undeniable excitement, anticipating his taking her in his arms, making her feel what she both craved and hated . . . except this time it was tinged with a sense of fear as she stepped across the threshold. Usually Jean-Paul met her at the door. Something was wrong today, she knew it. After pouring herself a brandy, she looked out at the bleak winter day, at the Eiffel

Tower just beyond, shivering as she pulled her coat more snugly around her. After waiting a half hour, she went to the telephone and called his home.

The butler answered. "The Dupré residence."

"May I speak with Monsieur Dupré?"

"He's not in, may I take a message?"

The butler seemed somewhat harassed. "He had an earlier appointment with Monsieur Dryfus on a legal matter. . . ."

"Oh, I'm . . . his secretary and am calling to check . . ."

"Ah, well, Monsieur left about fifteen minutes ago, although I can't say where he's gone."

"I see. Then he must be on his way." She sighed in relief. Something must have delayed him, but why hadn't he called? She told herself not to think about it. He would explain later. The important thing was, he was now on his way. She took another brandy to warm herself, then went to the bedroom and undressed, although Jean-Paul always loved doing this for her. Well, today he would have to forego that pleasure . . . their time together would be shorter than usual. . . .

As she lay in bed, nude, her desires began to increase, and with them, her anxieties as the minutes turned to hours. By four o'clock she was frantic, certain that something dreadful had happened, but she could not possibly wait any longer. . . .

By the time she got home her pulse was racing and her head throbbed with pain. She did not go straight to Etienne as she usually did. (Actually, after spending the afternoon with Jean-Paul, her affection for Etienne was even greater.) She went directly to her room, took two aspirins, and lay down. . . .

"My God, I've been so worried . . . it's five-thirty. I didn't know you were home." It was Etienne. She had fallen asleep.

"I'm sorry . . . forgive me . . . I came straight to the room. I was feeling so ill . . . just before I came home I felt terribly nauseous—" She forced a smile. "You understand—"

"Yes, of course . . . the baby . . . but your hands are so cold. How do you feel now?"

"I'll be fine. Truly . . ." At least I will if nothing is wrong with Jean-Paul . . . please God, let nothing be wrong. . . . She finally managed to persuade Etienne that there was no more cause for concern but agreed to be more careful about going out in taxis.

At eight o'clock she and Etienne dressed for the evening and went downstairs as usual to join Madame for their aperitif, and Madame remarked on how pale she looked, remembering but not mentioning Jacqueline's miscarriage during the early months of her pregnancy, and urged Jeanette to eat more . . . she really *must* . . . and rest too during the day, and Jeanette promised. . . . And then Madame's thoughts, as did Jeanette's, turned elsewhere.

"I'm surprised Jean-Paul is so late this evening," Madame said. "He's usually here by now."

"He probably had to stay late at the office," said Etienne. "I'm sure he'll be along soon."

But eight-thirty turned to nine o'clock and there was still no sign of Jean-Paul. "I can't imagine why he hasn't called," Madame said anxiously. "He never fails to call if he's going to be late."

"I'll call his home," said Etienne, realizing that Madame's concern was heightened by her memory of what had happened to Denise.

He had just left the room and picked up the receiver to call Jean-Paul when Jean-Paul himself walked in. Etienne, intercepting him at the doorway, was stunned. "My God, what happened to your face?"

Jean-Paul shook his head, not able to speak yet. The right side of his face had deep lacerations, as though it had been clawed, leaving the crevices swollen and red. "I had to come here, I had to be here," he finally managed to get out.

"Of course you did," Etienne said, putting his arm around his brother's shoulder, "but for God's sake, what *happened*?"

"Let me have a brandy. I'll tell you but I must sit down. . . ."

"Sit here while I prepare Maman for this."

He helped Jean-Paul to the gold-leafed chair in the vast hall, then went to his mother. "Maman . . . Jean-Paul is here . . . in the entry." As she promptly got up, Etienne said, "Wait, Maman, something has happened, now please don't become alarmed . . . he's all right but his face is bruised. . . ."

Jeanette slumped down into the chair without a word. Madame braced herself. "Please bring him in immediately."

Etienne did, and she saw his lacerated face. She took a compulsively deep breath. "Dear God . . . Jean-Paul, what has happened . . . ?"

Etienne handed him the brandy. He gulped it down, then another, which he sipped slowly. Jeanette watched in horror, but, she told herself, at least he was safe.

"I hardly know where to begin," Jean-Paul said, collapsing in a chair. "When I got back from dinner last night Pierre was waiting in the hall. He was white. Obviously, something was very wrong. I asked what the problem was, and he asked me to go straight to Marie Jacqueline's room. When I got there, it was a shambles. The sheets and pillow cases were torn to shreds. The furniture was turned every which way and her cats were pawing at the drapes. They had been ripped away from the window, and lay in a heap on the floor. And in the middle of the bed lay one of her cats . . . dead. God, the sight of that cat. . . . Marie Jacqueline was all disheveled, her hair unkempt and falling loose. Her eyes were glazed and wild. As soon as I came in, she ran to the door and locked it and threw the key into the fire. She was cursing and screaming obscenities. Pointing to the dead cat, she accused me of killing her child . . . her baby." Jean-Paul shuddered and shut his eyes. "She had strangled it. . . ." He could still hear her accusing voice, which he would not repeat to them . . . "I know that you and Jeanette . . . your own brother's precious bitch of a wife . . . are lovers. . . ." He'd been certain that she couldn't possibly *know*, which didn't at all diminish the shock of hearing her speak out her wild suspicions . . . which, of course, were the truth.

He continued, "She screamed it out, over and over again, 'You've killed my child and you've killed me too.' Finally she ran to the bed, picked up the dead cat and used its claws to claw my face. I suppose I was in shock. I kept trying to control her, to quiet her down. . . . Finally she dropped the animal and went at me herself. Her strength was incredible. When I tried to take hold of her, she lashed out at my face and kicked with her feet. Finally I was able to tie her hands with a piece of cord and put her on the bed. But she kept on screaming. I think she'd simply gone mad. I thought I was going mad. I managed to tie her feet together and secure a piece of sheet around her mouth, it helped quiet the screams some . . . and then I got outside the room by climbing down the ivy at the window. I called the psychiatrist who'd been taking care of her. When he came, I opened the bedroom door with the master key. The doctor gave her an injection that put her to sleep, then we talked about what the next move should be. He told me he'd noticed a decided decline in her behavior in the last few weeks, which I must admit he'd spoken to me about before . . . I should have paid more attention but Marie Jacqueline was always such a private person; in fact she had become a recluse, as you, Maman, noticed . . . but *this* outburst I had not anticipated, nor had the doctor."

He paused, taking a deep breath, and sipped the brandy. They all sat waiting. "Well, the doctor said I had no other choice. I had to commit her—"

Madame gasped. "Where did you take her?"

"To a private sanitarium. I signed her in under an assumed name."

"Oh, Jean-Paul . . . how will she be treated?"

"She'll have the best of care. The psychiatrist assured me of that. . . . It's taken forever and I should have called you, but I didn't know what to say. Please let me apologize. There were times when I thought I'd never feel sane again myself. . . ."

"But how long will she have to stay?"

"I don't know, they don't know . . . there were a million papers to sign and they kept asking me questions. . . . Three psychiatrists had to be consulted. . . . When I finally got back to Paris I went home and changed my clothes. . . . I'd told Pierre to say nothing to anyone. I came straight here from my home. . . ."

Jeanette was trying to remain outwardly calm. Inside, she was weak with shock, and relief, and fear. . . . At least now she understood why the butler earlier had been so vague in his hesitation when she'd called impersonating Monsieur Dryfus' secretary. . . .

"You'll stay tonight, of course," Etienne said. Jean-Paul agreed, and Madame sent him to bed at once. She'd have Clothilde send a tray to his room. . . .

* * *

Jean-Paul lay exhausted in his old bed, in the same room he'd slept in as a boy and young man, up to the time of his marriage to Marie Jacqueline. His mother was watching him now much as she'd done, he thought, when he was a child, and memories of her then came back to him . . . her strength and comforting, the way she'd come to his room dressed for the opera, her dress always rustling and billowing out, a cerise velvet gown, it was . . . and the smell of her perfume that somehow always made his nose itch. It was still there now, this evening, and it comforted him. . . .

After she'd said goodnight he lay in the dark, watching the fire die down in the grate. She had even thought of the fire, although the room hadn't been used in five years. She should have been Marshal Dupré. How quickly she got things done. She had aroused the servants immediately, and fresh bed linen had been placed over the mattress. The comforter had been brought out of storage, a supper prepared, and all of this within minutes . . . clean towels, pajamas, slippers, a robe. . . .

He had imagined that Marie Jacqueline's life would be short, especially the last couple of years, but *this* he had not bargained for. Put away as she was, she could live for a very long time. People without responsibilities could retreat into themselves, their very madness less of a strain than coping with the stress of normal day-to-day life. Well . . . there it was . . . he was shackled in marriage, which he could do nothing about. She was still alive . . . and so was Etienne . . . but at least he had his dear brother's wife as his mistress. Except, ironically, she was the only woman he'd ever really wanted as his wife. And although soon he would have a son, he would not be able to acknowledge him as his own. . . .

At least he did have control now over Marie Jacqueline's estate. She had neither father nor mother, sister nor brother to contest his power over it. When he went back home, he'd have the bedroom cleaned and the door to it sealed, so he could block out the fact that she'd ever lived. He would also, he assured himself as he lay in the dark staring at the ceiling, do away with those damn cats. . . .

Down the hall, Jeanette lay in Etienne's arms, but her body was tense and unresponsive. When Etienne finally had fallen into his characteristically deep sleep, she slipped carefully out of bed, put on her peignoir and left the room. She walked down the hall to Jean-Paul's room and quietly opened the door, locking it behind her. Quickly then she was in his arms, holding him, caressing him . . . pouring out her need for him, and her relief that he was here, safe . . . and exhausted and battered as he was, he responded. . . .

Afterward, relaxed, feeling calmer than he had in twenty-four hours, he said, "I know this will sound harsh, darling, but I wish she had died, it would have been better for her . . . for everybody. . . ."

"*Don't*, oh please don't have such thoughts . . . We do have each other—"

"That's not true. I don't have you . . . I only share a small part of your life—"

"No, Jean-Paul, it's Etienne who shares only a part. . . . Please, let's accept what we have. . . . Nothing in life can be perfect, I know something about that . . . but you and I have so much together, let's be satisfied with that. . . ."

But he wasn't satisfied . . . and, masking his anger, took hold of her and, without preliminaries, made love to her again. And for her it was, as always with him, the impossible, irresistible mixture of wild excitement and guilt.

She lay beside him for a while, until she realized he'd fallen asleep. Then, carefully, quietly so as not to disturb him, she removed her arm from across his chest, got off the bed, unlocked, opened and closed the door, and went back to her husband's room, and bed.

Twenty-two

In the months that followed, Jeanette showed very little. In reality she was seventh months pregnant, but thanks at least in part to her regimen she looked no more than five. After today, they had decided, she and Jean-Paul would abstain from love-making, fearing that it would be too strenuous . . . and dangerous . . . at this stage. But it seemed to Jean-Paul, as he lay beside her, that he could feel the child inside her kick, a thrill he had thought he would never experience. . . .

And then, excitedly, another thought occurred to him. "Darling," he said, "I've decided there can't be too much of a good thing, not, at any rate, with a natural-born mother like you. . . ." He smiled and stroked her hair. "I absolutely have decided, no arguments now, that we should have more children, more lovely children that are only yours and mine. . . ."

And looking at him, she realized her answer would have to be the beginning of the first serious deception between them, because much as she owed him, much as she was overwhelmed and a part of him, this she would never do. . . . Any more children would be Etienne's—she owed *him* that—and . . . admit it . . . she wanted them to be . . . but Jean-Paul would never know, could assume what he wished. . . . And she heard herself answering him, "Oh yes, Jean-Paul . . ." But in her lie she turned away so as not to face him.

* * *

Of course they saw each other each night at dinner, and often during the day, when Jean-Paul would come to chat with maman, and stay for lunch. Madame was knitting furiously.

After dinner, the four Duprés played bridge. Etienne had taught Jeanette how to play, and she found that she enjoyed it very much. The only time she left the house now was in the company of Etienne or Madame.

The nursery was being refurbished. The brass directoire bassinet had been padded once again with tufted white satin trimmed with tiny blue bows. Once Etienne had asked, "What if it's a girl?"

Maman had answered, "I think it will be a son, but if it isn't . . . and I only say if . . . we'll change the ribbons to pink."

Sheer white netting had been gathered and hung around the bassinet, held by a brass rod that curved at the top, where an enormous blue bow was sewn. All the Dupré children had spent their first month in this enclosure. It could be swung gently back and forth. The rocker in which Madame had held her children to her breast was placed beside the bassinet. Then the brass crib, still as bright as on the day Denise, her first-born, had slept in it, was brought to the nursery and placed in the corner. The layette had been hand-sewn by the best seamstress in Paris.

Madame spent hours telling Jeanette about the mysteries and glories of motherhood.

When she approached her (actual) eighth month, Jeanette began interviewing governesses for the older children. After seeing a dozen less than ideal applicants in the course of one day, Jeanette told Etienne that she was almost ready to settle for anybody, she was so weary of the task. She finally hired the woman with the best recommendations, a widow in her middle forties. Madeleine would serve as a nursemaid for the new baby when the trained nurse left after her confinement.

One morning, at the beginning of her ninth month, Jeanette tripped on the last step, going down to breakfast. She'd managed to hold onto the banister as she fell, and seemed more frightened than hurt, but Dr. Bernier was nonetheless called, and all felt relieved when the doctor agreed that she was, and understandably, more frightened than anything else. But at one o'clock in the morning, her water broke in bed, drenching not only herself, but Etienne. Having not the slightest idea of what to do, he called his mother, who came rushing into the room. It was her greatest concern that this child not be imperfect as Etienne had been. She called Dr. Bernier immediately and asked him to come at once. The bedding was replaced, and Madeleine helped Jeanette bathe and get back into bed. Madame alerted the entire staff to be prepared for any eventuality.

Clothilde boiled large pots of water, and even Jean-Paul was summoned. Dr. Bernier arrived an hour later, knowing full well that it would probably be a long time before he was actually needed, but to please Madame he had brought with him his obstetrical nurse, who immediately took charge.

"Are you in pain?" Etienne asked her nervously.

"No . . . at least not much. The pains are still too far apart to be severe."

But soon they became more frequent, and she gripped his hand tightly, wincing and moaning as the pains became more sharp.

"Just relax between the contractions," said the nurse, "and try to breathe naturally. You're too tense, madame."

Jeanette tried, but the next pain was so sharp she bit her lip and cried out. Etienne felt the pain as keenly as though it was his. She held onto his hands, digging her nails into his flesh, until it subsided. It was now six o'clock.

"I think you should leave now, Etienne," said the doctor. "I want to examine madame again. You may come back later."

Etienne kissed Jeanette.

"You will come back?" she said.

"Yes, as soon as the doctor says, but I'll be just outside your door."

Throughout the night and into the dawn her screams became louder and more frequent. Etienne came and went from Jeanette's room, and although her suffering was unbearable for him to watch, still stayed beside her until once again he was asked to leave. Dr. Bernier vowed that this would be the last Dupré child born in this bed. It was a thoroughly archaic practice. What he needed now was his hospital staff, equipped with modern facilities, including a little gas anesthesia from time to time. He no longer believed in complete natural childbirth. She needed an episiotomy. By two o'clock in the afternoon he was convinced that, Jeanette being as small as she was, a delivery at home would be next to impossible.

Dr. Bernier knew he should perform a Caesarean. He watched Jeanette writhe in pain. Finally he told her, "You simply can't go on this way. I'm going to make arrangements to have you taken to the hospital—"

"No, no . . . my child . . . must be born in this house . . . in the same bed his father was born in—"

"Madame, you're in no condition to make that decision."

She hung on weakly to his hands. "Please, doctor . . . let my child be born here. . . . It *must* be. . . ."

"Believe me, madame, I think I know what's best—"

She bit her hand so hard the teeth marks left deep indentations, the perspiration pouring down her face. "I won't go . . . I refuse to go. . . . No one can make me. . . ."

When he saw the look of determination in her eyes, he said, against his better judgment, "All right. We'll wait a little longer."

In the small sanctuary downstairs adjacent to the library, Madame kept to herself. She knelt with her rosary, praying to Mother Mary that she beg her Divine Son to look down on this new child about to come into the world and make him healthy and whole. And allow his mother to survive the ordeal. . . .

As the hours passed, the screams became more frequent. Jeanette lay in a pool of sweat, almost too tired to cry out. But somehow, with each pain, the screams came. Etienne was frantic and sat with his head in his hands. Jean-Paul, who'd come upstairs now, talked as though to comfort him, although, of course, it was himself that he was trying to reassure. He hadn't been able to see Jeanette, but hoped she knew that he was just outside.

At this point, she was aware of none of them, of nothing except the pain and the hope that God would forgive her. . . .

The hours kept ticking away, though they seemed to pass more and more slowly. At eight o'clock in the evening Dr. Bernier examined her once again. The baby had dropped somewhat, but not enough. A Caesarean was too dangerous to perform, and the doctor chastised himself for allowing Jeanette to override his better judgment.

The minutes ticked away. Suddenly Jeanette let out an ear-shattering scream. Etienne began to groan . . . this simply could not go on. Dr. Bernier examined her again, and glory be to heaven, he began to see the beginning of life.

After twenty hours of excruciating labor, Jeanette's child was delivered in a breach birth. Breathing hard, she relaxed at last, drenched in perspiration, as the child, still in its placenta, was placed on her abdomen. She looked down at the tiny figure, and from that moment, she was never to know a love as great, as all-encompassing, as this. She had fought, and she had won. And, for now at least, it seemed God had forgiven her. . . .

This was the flesh of her flesh. She did not think of Jean-Paul, or of Etienne, but only of this small pink ball that lay on her belly. . . .

Once the cord had been severed, the nurse prepared the child and brought it to its mother. Dr. Bernier, in his shirt sleeves and mopping his forehead, went into the hall where Etienne and Jean-Paul were waiting. He took off his glasses and wiped them. "Well, Etienne," he said, "you have a son."

Etienne was almost transfixed. Jean-Paul couldn't restrain a little jump for joy, repeating, "A son . . . a son!" He took Etienne by the shoulders and shook him. "You lucky man, you have a son. A son, a new Dupré."

"Yes, by God, I have a son." Then, turning to Dr. Bernier, Etienne asked, "How is she?"

"Fine. The labor was very hard, and unnecessary. How she came through it, I don't know. I wasn't sure there for a while. But congratulations, she's going to be fine."

"Thank God," Etienne said. "When can I see her?"

"Soon," and the doctor went back in to see his patient.

Jean-Paul ran down to give his mother the good news. She came back upstairs with him and went to Etienne at once.

"Oh, Etienne, my son. Now you yourself have a boy. How blessed we all are."

They embraced. Jean-Paul watched his crippled brother

secure in the arms of his mother, when it should have been him in her arms being congratulated. . . .

When Jeanette had been freshly gowned and groomed, with Madeleine's help, and had the infant in her arms, Etienne came to her side and kissed her. "Thank you, my love, for this gift."

The child weighed less than six pounds. Tiny and wrinkled as he was, Jeanette thought, he did seem to look like Jean-Paul, though only a little more than any Dupré. The sign of the family was unmistakable and strong.

Madame stood at the other side and kissed Jeanette, then looked at the child and thought with satisfaction . . . this was a new beginning for the Dupré line, a glorious one to perpetuate it. Jean-Paul, who had just come in, kissed Jeanette on the cheek. "Congratulations . . . you and Etienne are surely the most fortunate people in the world, and since I have been asked to be godfather, may I offer all of my thanks for giving us all a Dupré to carry on our name." And then, like a true diplomat, he kissed her hand. During his speech, she kept her eyes steadily on a point on the wall behind him. . . .

"Now, I think you should all leave. I believe madame is very tired and should rest," Dr. Bernier said as he put on his coat. "And I'll see you in the morning," he said to Jeanette.

Antoinette Dupré detained the doctor as he was leaving. "Thank you, thank you, doctor, but please tell me one thing. . . . Will the baby have to be put in an incubator?"

"No. Why do you ask?"

"It's always been my understanding that a premature baby required one."

"Not in this case," he said quickly. "The baby's weight is quite normal."

"Really . . . ? My babies, of course, weighed much more—"

"But you, Madame, were able to carry nine months."

"That's true. . . ." And then she forced herself to ask, "And is the child perfect in every other way?"

"Absolutely perfect. . . ."

The nurse arrived soon after the doctor left. She would remain with Jeanette and care for the newborn child. She was a large and jovial woman in her mid-fifties, and most efficient. She took charge immediately.

Although Jeanette was exhausted from the long ordeal, she asked to hold the child for just a little longer. She couldn't get over the miracle of him. The nurse assured Madame that the child would be returned to her at seven o'clock in the morning. That would be his nursing time.

Jeanette reluctantly relinquished her son into the capable hands of Mademoiselle Loire, who took him down the hall to the nursery. Madeleine was waiting there to see the baby, all wrapped up in blankets. Looking at his tiny face, she could hardly believe that her friend Jeanette was both a Dupré *and* a mother. . . . Madeleine laughed to herself. Life was more unpredictable than anything. . . . Jeanette, who had stood on her feet twelve hours a day, working for Uncle Jacques, was now on her way to being the lady of the house. . . . God had singled out Jeanette for something special, no question, Madeleine decided. Clearly, she had been destined for more important things than Uncle Jacques' laundry. . . .

Madeleine was brought out of her daydream as Mademoiselle Loire began to instruct her on how to take care of the infant. After all, Madeleine would take over the duties when Mademoiselle Loire left in a month. But Madeleine was too filled with awe even to contemplate that eventuality . . . the baby was so tiny, almost lost in the folds of the blanket. How could she, simple ordinary Madeleine, take charge of a child born a Dupré?

Promptly at seven o'clock in the morning the whimpering, hungry child was brought to his sleeping mother and laid at her breast. He sucked greedily, but without satisfaction, since Jeanette's breasts had become dry. The nurse attached a small breast pump, trying to begin the flow of milk, but little came.

This is not a nursing mother, thought Mademoiselle Loire, but she had been at her profession too long not to be prepared for such an emergency. As the child began to cry, Mademoiselle went immediately to the nursery and produced a small sterile bottle from her bag, together with a can of powdered formula which she mixed with boiled water. Later in the morning Dr. Bernier would, of course, prescribe, but this would have to suffice for now.

When she returned, Jeanette was in tears and extremely

upset, secretly knowing that because of her strenuous dieting she'd be unable to nurse her child. She hated herself, but what else could she have done? The child had to appear premature. This didn't appease her, however, as Mademoiselle took the child from her and sat in the chair, putting the rubber nipple into the infant's mouth. Almost at once, the crying subsided as the baby sucked contentedly.

When he'd had his fill, Mademoiselle handed Jeanette her child. "I believe we're going to have to bottle feed the baby."

Jeanette bit her lip. "Maybe if I take a lot of nourishment I could do it?"

"Dr. Bernier will know what to do. . . ." The nurse tried to reassure Madame, but Madame was not reassured. A baby should lie at its mother's breast, feeling the warmth of her love instead of sucking on a rubber and glass contraption. She, and no one else, was responsible for this.

But Dr. Bernier prescribed a bottle. "Many children do as well, or even better, that way," he said.

"I don't believe that."

"But it's true. Besides, we have no other choice."

"What would happen if I took more nourishment?"

"It's too late for that, I'm afraid. A mother's milk is built up during months of pregnancy. You're even thinner now than you were when you first came to see me."

She knew all too well he was not unaware of the reasons for her excessive dieting. "Well," she sighed, "if it must be, then at least I want to do the feeding."

"During the day, but the night feedings will be given by Mademoiselle Loire."

"No," Jeanette demanded. "I want my baby brought to me for all his feedings, day and night."

"Very well, if that's what you want. . . . Now, please, let me examine you."

He wasn't at all pleased when he saw the tear, vowing that this would be the last child born in this bed. All of it could have been avoided if only Madame had consented to have the delivery in the hospital. He should have been more insistent, but after ten days of confinement he would take her to surgery and repair the damage. He discussed this with her now.

"How long will I have to be there?" Jeanette asked.

"A day or two at the most. But it must be done. And now I have some instructions which must be carried out to the letter. You, my dear, are a very stubborn young woman." He smiled, shaking his head. "I insist on it. During the next week, you're to do very little visiting. I want you to get back your strength and gain some weight."

"I promise," she said, and smiled back.

"All right. Now get some rest. I'll see you tomorrow."

As he opened the door, Jeanette said, "Dr. Bernier, I can't thank you enough for . . . well, for everything you've done for me. . . ."

He turned to look at her . . . this lovely young woman. He saw the gratitude in her eyes as she met his. He nodded his head in reassurance. Her secret was safe with him. . . .

Etienne came in soon after and kissed her softly on the lips. She drew him closer. "Motherhood hasn't transformed me into a saint, Etienne. You can do better than that."

"I can do much better than that," and he kissed her with more vigor, than drew up a chair and sat at her bedside. "How are you feeling this morning?"

"Happy. And how are you feeling?" she asked, knowing he hadn't slept well.

"The father will survive. . . ."

She smiled. "Etienne . . . isn't he beautiful?"

"Like his mother . . ."

"Well, thank you, sir . . . you mean I look like a little red lobster?"

Etienne laughed. "I mean he's a Dupré, through and through. . . . In fact, he looks exactly like Lucien did when he was first born."

She lay back against the pillows. . . . If only the child *was* Etienne's.

"I'm tiring you, dearest, and Dr. Bernier left strict instructions about visiting. I'll leave you to rest now."

She reached out her hand, which he took. "Thank you, thank you for your gift to me . . . your gift of love—"

"No, darling, it's the other way around. You have given me a son, *our* son. . . . Now rest."

"Will you be back soon? Please?"

"If you promise to eat and to rest and not to talk much. Otherwise, solitary for you, madame," and he kissed her on the forehead and left.

During the day Madame paid her a visit, telling her how much happiness she had brought into this house (not mentioning that a year had passed since Denise's demise and so the year of mourning was over; for her it was especially significant that a new life should come at just this time). She left then, saying she was on her way to see her newest grandchild.

Late in the afternoon, Jean-Paul came to see her. They were alone. He embraced and kissed her much too strongly, and when she said, "Please, Jean-Paul, I know how pleased you are, but this is not the time. . . ." He was annoyed and took a seat near the fireplace. She understood his feelings. The baby was his child, but Etienne was the one being congratulated. . . . "Have you seen the child?" she asked, softening her tone.

"The child? Don't you mean *our* child?"

"Yes, of course . . . our child."

"Then why don't you say so?"

"Jean-Paul, you're angry, and I understand, but only you and I know the child is ours."

"We're alone now, why offend me by saying 'the child'?"

"Come here, Jean-Paul." When he'd come back to her bedside she said, "Jean-Paul, I *do* know how you feel, not being able to acknowledge your own fatherhood, and I realize how much easier it is for me, lying here and having everyone make a fuss over me while you stand in the shadows . . . but please remember we knew this would happen. So . . . please, Jean-Paul, be kind to yourself as well as to me and try to accept the beauty of what we have brought into this world, the two of us . . . don't punish yourself because other people don't know. It's enough that we know, and I'll do my best to try to make it up to you . . . we'll spend time together . . . you and I and the . . . our baby."

As he stood looking down at this fragile girl in the enormous bed, his tension and anger did begin to subside. Of course, what she said was true . . . what other possible way was there for him? A smile broke through. "You're getting to be a better diplomat than I am," he said. "Well, may I now at least kiss the mother?" And he did, this time more carefully.

"Now, go in and see *your* beautiful son," she said quietly, "who looks just like you. . . ."

He nodded happily, kissed her on the cheek and left. Appointment to the Diplomatic Corps or the Croix de Guerre, he thought. For an orphaned ex-governess, this little lady was managing, no question about it. . . .

The days of confinement dwindled. Each day the children went to see their new cousin, watching wide-eyed as Jeanette fed him. When the feeding was over, Jeanette gently rubbed the baby's tiny back, waiting for the burp. With this accomplished, the two girls climbed onto her bed, Nicole on one side and Desirée on the other, and Jeanette let the little girls hold the infant on their laps. They couldn't get over how tiny he was. Like a doll, Desirée said, and Nicole agreed. Even Lucien was impressed.

Etienne sat in an easy chair and watched. What a sight they were to paint. . . .

Finally the time came for Jeanette to go to the hospital to have the surgical repair the doctor had prescribed. Afterward Dr. Bernier told her that she shouldn't have personal relations with her husband for another six weeks. Etienne was still occupying separate quarters.

She went home and began to gorge herself, and in a few days was putting on weight, which Etienne was delighted to see. She was plied with tempting cream soups, pâtés and desserts filled with whipped cream that Clothilde made sure would excite her appetite. . . . But Jeanette, self-deprived for so long, needed very little coaxing, and by the time of the christening she was her old self again.

For his baptism the infant was dressed in the same silk and lace robes that Jean-Paul and Etienne had worn. The same tiny lace bonnet was placed on his head and tied under the chin by his doting grandmother, who for the first time in many years had changed from black. Instead she wore a light-gray silk dress with matching shoes and bag and white kid gloves. She had carefully selected the jewels which such an occasion called for. Her hat was a small cloche covered with violets, and around her neck she wore a sable scarf. This, she felt, was the way a Dupré grandmother should look when she witnessed a new heir being anointed into the faith.

The excitement grew with every moment as Jeanette dressed with the help of Madeleine, who, of course, would also be present as a guest.

Etienne walked into Jeanette's dressing room and saw her standing there in a hyacinth-blue silk suit with matching pumps and bag. Her tiny hat, adorned with spring flowers, sat on the back of her head, revealing the chignon. Around her neck she wore the pearls that Madame had given her on her wedding day, and the diamond clasp shone brightly whenever the sunshine caught it, embellishing its many facets. With delicately rouged lips and cheeks, her fair unblemished skin, she was indeed something lovely to look at, and he could not get enough of her.

She returned the compliment as she observed him in his gray striped trousers, deep gray waistcoat, gray silk cravat, in the middle of which was a pearl stickpin—the whole topped off with a shiny black top hat that he now carried. Just as she was about to slip on her short soft leather gloves he took her hand and fastened a diamond bracelet around her delicate wrist.

"Oh, please, Etienne, you've already given me so much, you're too good to me, and so good for me," and meant every word in ways she could never tell him.

He held her for a long moment and then went into the nursery, where Madame already held the child in her arms, and the three of them walked down the stairs to join the rest of the family . . . including, of course, Jean-Paul, who stood there with Uncle Leon. Leon had arrived only yesterday and would be returning immediately after the ceremony (which, for him, was something of an alien affair and one he would never have attended if it were not for his beloved niece and her child . . . this, he had decided, he owed the memory of her father as much as herself). The adults rode in the same limousine, with Madame holding her grandchild, while the older children and Madeleine followed behind in the second on their way to Nôtre Dame Cathedral.

The baptism was solemn and touching. For a brief moment, though, Jeanette wished it might have been different, remembering when she and her father had gone to synagogue on Saturdays. Stealing a look at Uncle Leon, she suspected he would understand and share her thought, but his face revealed nothing. . . . Jean-Paul was handed the child for the blessing, and to take the oath of godfather. And for more than a brief moment he too wished things were different. Merely anticipating the birth of his child that he wouldn't be able to claim for his own was one thing, but holding *his son* in his arms—his own flesh and blood—that was quite another, and he wanted to call out to all of them, to somebody, that this boy was his, they couldn't take it away from him. . . . He remained silent, stone-faced, as the new name was given—Henri Etienne Dupré.

A reception followed at the house on the Boulevard Victor Hugo, during which the guests appropriately fussed over and admired the new baby, some saying he looked like Etienne, some like the late Marshal Dupré and even a little like Antoinette. All agreed Henri was a beautiful, healthy baby, and toasted the proud parents. No one, Jean-Paul noted as he stood by drinking his champagne too quickly, mentioned any resemblance of the new baby to himself.

CHAPTER

Twenty-three

In July Jeanette turned twenty-one, and this year the
birthday party was held in the ballroom. It was an evening
that Jeanette adored. In one year she had gone from the
depths to the heights, and while she had her own inner
reservations, this night she was determined to let herself
go and savor the full measure of all of it. She did regret
that it would be the first summer that the Dupré family
would not go to Provence . . . because of the new baby
. . . but for the month of August they would take a house
in Deauville, which was only two hours by train from
Paris. . . .

And then suddenly, whirling from one dance partner to
the other, her face flushed with excitement, Jeanette
found herself in the arms of Jean-Paul, and as he twirled
her away, his arm tightened around her waist, and his
voice equally tight was saying, "When?" and she, taking a
deep breath, answered, "Soon. . . ."

The doctor's six-week period of abstention had passed
and Etienne had moved back once again to their suite,
where, for the first time in months, he made full and passionate love to his wife (the depths of this man, the
strength and gentleness of him were something that few
would have guessed, as Jeanette had not really known until their first time together).

The next day Jeanette went to a Doctor Samuel Blum in

a building on the Champs Elysées, not far from the offices of Monsieur Dryfus, where she was fitted for a diaphragm, which she would never be without when she was with Jean-Paul. She had made up her mind when Henri was born, from now on any children she might have would be Etienne's . . . and soon the time would be on hand for her first meeting with Jean-Paul. . . .

And then it was at hand, and she drove to it in the roadster she'd been given on her birthday and that Etienne had taught her to drive on the back roads to Versailles. Now she could come and go as she pleased. . . .

When she nervously put the key in the door, Jean-Paul was there to open it wide and immediately take her in his arms, kissing her and carrying her into the bedroom. And when they finally lay together, it was as though a dam of longing had burst, especially for him, though she did not deny or attempt to deny to herself that some of the old feeling was still there for her as well. Their love-making was a kind of frenzy . . . as though they could not get enough of each other, their bodies independent of their senses, taking over and demanding a satisfaction that was beyond them to furnish. For Jean-Paul it had been a special misery, this waiting, since for the first time in his life he'd given up his other mistresses, almost masochistically holding himself out for the one woman he knew—but couldn't accept it—that he could never really have.

Finally noting the time, she abruptly sat up in bed. It was six-thirty, she'd lost all sense of time. She reached for the telephone as Jean-Paul tried to take it from her and pull her back down on top of him. "André, please let me speak to Monsieur Dupré," and Jean-Paul buried his head in the pillow to muffle her words explaining to Etienne that she would be a little late, yes, Antoine her hairdresser had kept her waiting longer than usual, she would be home shortly. . . .

When she came back from the bathroom, dressed and ready to leave, it was a question in Jean-Paul's mind which he wanted to do more—rip off her clothes and make her impossibly, compromisingly late for her precious Etienne, or kill his beloved brother, who had been and seemingly always would be in his way. . . .

* * *

Except for the not so extraordinary colic and the painful cutting of the first center tooth, baby Henri was growing altogether normally into a chunky, handsome and happy child. His sounds of contentment were delicious and satisfying to his parents and relatives.

His favorite, it seemed, was Etienne, who was completely devoted to him and was perhaps something more of a treat, not being with him as much as his mother. On Sunday mornings Etienne would bring him to their bed, imitate his wonderfully ridiculous sounds, which he and the baby seemed to share a special knowledge of, hold him in the air with outstretched arms as the child kicked and giggled. . . . And it was on such mornings as these that Jeanette felt her affection for Etienne grow even stronger as she watched the two of them, sensing, knowing that they were becoming a family . . . something she had never really known herself . . . and feeling this she felt even closer, and safer, with him, and wanted to shut out all that might intrude or threaten. . . .

During the next six months Jeanette found herself on a dizzying dazzling carousel, her hand firmly attached to the brass ring. She had, after all, the best of all possible worlds . . . her lover, her child and her loving, devoted husband who deliciously and shamefully indulged her with a new ring, a new necklace, earrings, whatever he thought might please her . . . and for any occasion, however minor. It was a heady time, with the blessing of endless diversions to turn one's nagging doubts and uneasiness away. And in addition to everything else, the other children were, of course, growing and changing . . . Lucien turned eight, Nicole became six and Desirée four. Madame, too, had a birthday. Etienne's hair turned strikingly and prematurely gray at the temples, which made him, she felt, look even more distinguished. A proper note for his birthday, in honor of which, and without the help of Madame, who was only too happy to relinquish her place to her daughter-in-law, Jeanette arranged a gala birthday party. Etienne was now twenty-six . . . Jean-Paul would shortly be thirty. . . .

It was a very special year. Jeanette's life took on a momentum of such delights that from time to time she had to pinch herself to make sure it was all real. The Etienne Duprés, along with Jean-Paul, who often was in their party, were surrounded by a coterie of friends at the ballet . . . the opera . . . the new art shows . . . Jeanette was chosen one of the best-dressed women in Paris. Her clothes—Etienne insisted, and she couldn't pretend she didn't delight in them—were from Dior.

On a particular afternoon, after she and Blanche Canard had lunched at Maxim's, they went on to Dior's fall showing. Waiting for the parade of models to begin, Blanche was asking Jeanette what she thought about the new hemlines, and Jeanette was about to answer when it became clear that something had struck her that would make small talk, indeed any talk, altogether impossible. She had turned suddenly pale, and when Blanche asked what was the matter, was she ill, Jeanette did not answer.

How could she, when she had just received the shock of her life. . . . She had seen her past across the room . . . she had seen—impossible and yet undeniable—the smartly turned out figure of her *mother*. And not only had she seen her, but she had looked directly into her eyes, because at that moment Magda had happened to glance up, and the two of them . . . mother and daughter . . . stared across the room, across the years, directly and shockingly at each other.

Magda, always impulsive, had all she could do to restrain herself from going at once to her daughter, but the possibility of it was quickly eliminated when Jeanette, her whole body stiff, got up and, without saying a word, walked out of the salon, leaving a completely bewildered Blanche Canard.

Sitting in the back of the limousine on her way home, Jeanette would have liked to believe that she had been mistaken, it had been such a long time, but of course she knew that was nonsense. . . . She'd seen her mother's picture several times before, as she'd told Uncle Leon. There was no mistake, no mistaking her, or the rush of painful memories that now came back to her, and most especially the memory of her father's death. . . .

This evening was to have been the culmination of a particularly pleasant day, an attendance of the opening of the opera, and for some time Jeanette thought of canceling, pleading illness, but realized it would have been unfair to

Etienne, and indeed, to herself. Her mother had done enough . . . why should she be allowed to cause her further loss, even something so frivolous as the opera . . . ? No, she would force herself to go, and to celebrate her defiance and liberation, she chose an exquisite gown—a jade green, iridescent taffeta with matching bouffant cape, and slipping on her diamond and emerald jewelry, she even managed to hum an aria from *Carmen*, the opera of the evening.

When Etienne saw her, and took her in, he could only shake his head and mutter, "Magnificent, absolutely magnificent, my dear, but we must hurry or˜ we'll miss the overture . . . and Jean-Paul, as usual, is getting very impatient. . . ."

During intermission the Duprés went down the grand stairway to the lower level for refreshments. As they stood there, champagne glasses in hand, friends stopped by to chat with Etienne and Jeanette. Jean-Paul, feeling bored, wandered off, not in the least interested in how Marcel Larousse had enjoyed his trip to the United States with his overstuffed wife, or how much they had loved New Orleans because, you understand, it is, after all, French. He was about to give up his search for relief when he felt a tap on his shoulder and, turning, saw a familiar and most welcome face.

"Alexis," he said, "how pleasant to see you . . . and you, Countess, radiant as ever, if I may say so."

"And thank you, sir," Magda—now Margot Maximov—said, remembering him from the first time they'd met and she'd thought him so young . . . so attractively young . . . to be in the diplomatic service. "I don't believe we've seen you for some time. . . ."

"The loss is mine, Countess, and now, if you'll give me a moment, I'd very much like to introduce you to my brother and his wife," and before Jeanette could say a proper good-bye to the Larousses, Jean-Paul had taken her by the arm and led her over to meet "my good friends Count Alexis Maximov and the Countess Margot. . . ."

Jeanette stood frozen, not hearing, only seeing and not believing it possible that twice in the same day she could be seeing . . . her. She was unable to acknowledge the introduction. She thought she might faint. No, she was sure of it. Etienne, and Jean-Paul, couldn't help noticing that something was obviously wrong with her, though they had no idea what. Could she be that much in awe of the countess?

"Jeanette . . ." Jean-Paul said quietly.

"Yes . . ." His voice might have been a distant echo.

"I'd like to introduce the Count and Countess Alexis Maximov. . . ."

Finally managing some measure of composure, she answered coolly, "How do you do, I'm . . . pleased to meet you."

Smiling, "The pleasure is ours," Magda answered her daughter.

Memories again, an avalanche of them, came down on Jeanette . . . I love you, Uncle Alexis . . . oh, ma petite poupée, Mama loves you so much. . . . She had to leave . . . to get out of there. . . . "Etienne, I'm sorry but I must go. I'm afraid I'm not feeling well, you'll remember I said I wasn't earlier. . . ."

"Of course, my dear," and made his hurried apologies and good-byes to the count and countess and told Jean-Paul to please stay and enjoy the opera and they would take a cab home.

Later, in the cab, Etienne decided that Jeanette had simply been overdoing it with all her activities and what they needed was a holiday, preferably the fresh air of Switzerland, which would surely restore her. In fact, the trip would celebrate their first anniversary. She would, he assured her, love Lucerne with its mountains, its magnificent view from the terrace of the hotel . . . she'd learn to ski . . . yes, definitely, a holiday was exactly what she needed. . . .

Etienne drove with the aid of special pedals, but in spite of herself, and especially when she was as now away from Paris and in difficult terrain, she felt less than secure with him at the wheel, though of course she would say nothing. More important, though, was her being away from Henri, which made her feel as though a part of her had been left behind. There were times when the pretending seemed more than she could endure, and at night she often stayed awake well into the early morning staring up at the ceiling while Etienne slept peacefully, unaware of her feelings. She tried to tell herself that she was being unreasonably pettish, that she had everything a woman could want, but there was no denying that she felt completely hemmed in at Lucerne. She hated the mountains, they gave her claustrophobia. She found the hotel too quaint, almost cute, and the people pretty much the same. Skis and snow and hearty talk of special waxes and slopes and exotic skiing terms left her literally and figuratively cold. Finally she could do nothing else but ask Etienne to cut their holiday short, pleading a bad case of homesickness.

It was one o'clock in the morning when they arrived home, but Jeanette couldn't wait and went at once to Henri, picked him up and held him close to her. Half asleep, he yawned and stretched, then opened his eyes and smiled with the delightful grin that she'd especially missed, and she told him that he was "just like your father, irresistible when you smile . . ." and the six-month-old infant smiled back even more.

The next morning, although she'd had very little sleep, she arose earlier than usual, feeling exhilarated at the prospect of seeing Henri. She relieved Madeleine of her duties and took over bathing Henri, who splashed about excitedly, kicking and wading in the tub at the same time that Jeanette held him encircled and guided him. When he was dried and powdered she brushed his hair with a soft baby brush, parting it on one side. He looked and smelled delicious as she dressed him and took him down to breakfast with his papa, after which she would take him to see his cousins, and after that . . .

After that would be what she had been both looking forward to and dreading. Jean-Paul . . .

It was immediately clear that something was decidedly amiss. There was none of his usual open-armed welcome, which, in a sense, she was grateful for, but it made her uneasy, nonetheless. When she asked him if something was bothering him, he casually answered nothing at all, what could possibly be bothering him, now that she was here? He formally poured her a glass of champagne, assuring her it was "quite delicious, you know this vintage, it's the one from the Dupré vineyards in Provence."

The inference about Provence, where the liaison had begun, was too pointed. But now her own anger was building. "If you don't mind, Jean-Paul, I would prefer we dispense with these games—"

"Games? I'm not aware of any games. I'm only aware of the beautiful wife of my brother who, if I may be so bold, seems to be taking her wifely duties just a touch too seriously—"

"What in the world are you talking about? What would you have me do, ignore my husband—"

"To hell with your husband. I can't stand your devoted attention, your—"

"My God, Jean-Paul, this is really too much. Like it or not, Etienne *is* my husband, and you know when *you* first suggested this, yes, let's not forget whose idea it was . . . that it would not be easy to—"

"I didn't assume that you would . . . well"—and his voice was abruptly subdued—"become so fond of him that you—"

"Yes," she said, her voice rising, "I am fond of him, *very* fond. . . ."

"Are you so certain you're not in love? Going off on a second honeymoon, sending me a postcard of the Alps. My God, I could almost smell the edelweiss and hear the yodeling. . . ." His voice had risen again as his control slipped away.

"And what should I have said to my husband? 'No, I'm so sorry, darling, I can't get away for a holiday with you because I have a lover, a lover crazy with jealousy who happens also to be your brother'—Oh, my God, Jean-Paul, don't you realize how torn I am between my feeling for you and my life with Etienne? I'm a wife to two men, leading a double life. . . . It's not, I assure you, the simplest role in the world—"

"No, I suppose it isn't, though it might be if you hadn't allowed yourself to become so . . . attached to him, to my poor dear brother that everybody all his life has been so damn concerned about. . . . Hasn't it ever occurred to you that I'm excluded from everything about my own son . . . everything important I have to hear second or third hand . . . even when I want to hold him he reaches for Etienne . . ."

His upset only reinforced hers, and putting her hands

over her ears she ran to the door, down the stairs and, tears streaming down her face and blinding her, rushed to her car. She sat inside with her head on the steering wheel, feeling wretched, for what seemed hours. When the tears, and the hurt, had subsided some, she was able to think more about what Jean-Paul had said, how it was true that he *had* been left out, living, really, on the periphery of her and Etienne's life, not being able to share the life of his only child, a son, and how ungenerous she had been to remind him of the past, which really had little to do with the hurt of the present. And now her heart went out to him. She dried her tears, got out of the car and went back up the stairs. As she opened the door she saw Jean-Paul sitting with his head in his arms, the champagne bottle smashed against the fireplace, the wine staining the carpet. She went to him and put her arms around his neck and kissed him. . . . "Jean-Paul, I do understand . . . I know it is difficult for you."

He held her close. There was no pretense. "I need you. Very much. When you're not here I feel that my life stops. I can't help it . . . I want you to belong to me, even though I know it's not possible. . . ."

She ran her fingers through his hair and whispered, "But I do belong to you, you know that. Your son is my son. Whatever happens, wherever you are or I am, there is nothing and nobody that can change that. You must not forget that. Not ever . . ."

He sighed. "Yes, I know, but it doesn't seem enough. Damn it, you've become an obsession—"

"Hush, I beg you. When I see you like this . . . hurting yourself . . . I can't stand it—"

"All I know is that if I ever lost you my life would be over. I would have nothing—"

"But you'll never lose me. . . ." And at the moment, she meant it.

Afterward they made love, almost as though it were to be for the last time.

Twenty-four

Magda was not a woman to be easily discouraged, nor would she allow her feelings, wounded though they were after two rejections, to hinder her determination. Not after, to her astonishment, she had found her daughter again. She would continue to try to win at least her friendship, if not her love. That, she knew, would be asking too much. . . . She was willing to settle for less than love, for any token of acceptance.

She was planning a dinner and sent invitations to the Etienne Duprés, as well as Jean-Paul. . . . He should be the agent to bring them together.

But Magda didn't take into account that her grown daughter's nature, not surprisingly, was as determined as her own. . . .

When Jeanette got the invitation, she angrily tore it up. A few days later while the family was having luncheon with *maman*, Jean-Paul said, "I talked to Countess Maximov yesterday. She told me that you and Etienne had been invited to her party too. . . . We can all go together—"

"We won't be going," said Jeanette, her lips tightly drawn.

"But I thought you'd be pleased to be included—"

"Why?"

"Her parties are famous."

"I know . . . I've read about them often enough." Jeanette was trying to keep her voice under control. "I declined the lady's invitation, I wrote a note of regret."

Jean-Paul was genuinely confused, even mystified. Was Jeanette jealous? The Countess was also on the best-dressed list, but that seemed rather petty, and Jeanette was not petty . . . and then he recalled how strangely she had acted at the opera. . . . Well, whatever, she was obviously annoyed and, frankly, he was not reluctant to provoke Madame some. . . . "Still . . . it seems a pity to deprive yourself, and Etienne, of such an occasion. I take it you're not especially impressed with the Maximovs?"

"That's ridiculous . . . I don't even know them."

"Then perhaps you should reconsider. . . ."

"I don't *want* to reconsider—"

"May I ask why?"

. Her look was decidedly one to kill. . . . "Because, Jean-Paul, we are already too busy. . . . Etienne and I discussed it. Besides, they are much too old for us, and I dislike accepting invitations which I don't wish to reciprocate. . . . Now, if you will excuse me . . ." and she abruptly left for her room.

Jean-Paul was not the only one impressed by Jeanette's reaction to Countess Maximov's invitation, but when Etienne attempted to question her about it she made it as clear to him as she had to Jean-Paul that she really didn't want to discuss it, that it was just another party and surely they had more interesting things to talk about. Whereupon he decided that the discretion of silence was the better part of curiosity.

A week later, Jeanette received another invitation, which she also tore up. Then, two weeks later, another. This was getting to be impossible. She made up her mind to make the *Countess* leave her alone once and for all.

She called for André and had him drive her to the Isle of Saint Louis.

Jeanette waited in the hall as the butler went to announce her to the Countess. When the two finally stood facing each other, Magda's face was radiant. At last, her daughter was here . . . with her. . . .

"I'm so . . . so very happy to see you."

Jeanette's face was a mask. She merely nodded.

"Shall we go into the salon?" Magda said, now uneasy as she noted Jeanette's reaction. After they'd seated themselves, she said tentatively, "May I offer you a sherry or—"

"Nothing, thank you. This isn't a social visit."

Magda was on the verge of tears as she reached for a cigarette. Her hands were shaking. "Then may I ask why you have come?"

Jeanette took a deep breath, trying to control herself, feeling an internal shaking as she fought to push down her own natural hunger to reach out to this woman who was her mother at the same time that she despised her. . . . "I don't know how to say this . . . I didn't expect or imagine this meeting, but I suppose I knew that some day it would have to happen. . . . I don't want to be unkind, but I've come here to tell you that . . . well, I suppose I came here to tell you that I hated you and never wanted to hear from you or speak to you, but that really isn't the truth. . . . The truth is that I want to tell you something that can never have the same meaning to you that it should have . . . because we are no longer mother and daughter, but I will try to tell you anyway. Do you know what it's like to be a child and feel that you don't have a mother? Even though you know who that mother is? A child, for all they say about the wisdom of children, *doesn't* understand. Well, now *I* have a child, and while I am less than a perfect mother—in fact in some ways I am too much my mother's daughter—I know that at least I could never walk away from my child . . . he's my life, he comes from me. . . . No, at least I could never walk away from him, not even for a man . . . another man. . . . I said I was no saint and I'm not . . . after all, I'm your daughter . . . but I could have a dozen lovers and nobody could come between me and my child. . . . You didn't even keep your promise to write. I waited, day by day, just hoping, until finally I had to accept that you had forgotten I ever existed. . . . By the way, did you know that after you left my father deteriorated to the point where his mind was no longer right, that he was in a sanatorium? . . . And did you know that he died two years ago? That he committed suicide . . . ?"

Magda had visibly flinched at that last, and then her face had gone slack. How to register the awful feeling of guilt, and of, yes, hate too? Because how do you love the instrument of your own condemnation, even if she is your own daughter? But that last passed quickly, and what was left was the guilt and the shock. Oh yes, she had heard from Camail—a rather brief and cool note—that Rubin had died, and she had thought of writing for details but decided it would be hypocritical, and besides, what could she really do about it? But *this* . . . taking his own life . . . God was indeed punishing her, and at the moment she was quite willing to believe she thoroughly deserved it, having forgotten long since her own reasoning at the time for leaving him, and their daughter. Now was not the time for self-justification. In fact, she almost welcomed the wave of guilt and remorse. And feeling this way, what could she say to her daughter, her beautiful, outraged, well-married daughter, about her love and gratitude that she had finally found her? Her daughter clearly thought her unworthy of life, let alone a daughter's love, and she tended to agree. . . .

"So please, if you don't mind . . . no more invitations," Jeanette was saying. "I have long since told my husband and his family that I had no mother, that she died when I was five . . . and that's the way I feel. . . . If we should meet again, accidentally, please make it as painless as possible for both of us . . . we are after all both adults now and I want to tell you that"—she was getting breathless now—"saying all this gives me no pleasure, I don't feel any sense of revenge . . . only, to tell you the truth, the loss of a mother I never had. . . . Well, I trust you and Uncle . . . your husband will continue to have a pleasant life. . . ." And then she had turned and run to the front door and was out before Magda could say a word.

Somehow—she barely remembered it later—Magda was able to climb the stairs to her room . . . and then she went completely to pieces, crying deep sobs that would not stop. Alexis, hearing her, came in and held her, like a broken child, in his arms. Barely coherent, she tried to tell him what had happened, what Jeanette had said, about Rubin. "Oh, God, Alexis, I know what she meant . . . that I killed him . . . and in a way I did. . . . And it seems I killed my daughter too. . . ."

And try as he might to console her, to tell her that Jeanette was understandably an overemotional young lady who had got some of her facts out of perspective, she would not be consoled, and there seemed no relief from her torment. . . .

* * *

Time and the seasons did pass, though, following the events of that terrible day. Christmas came, and many of the Duprés attended midnight mass at Nôtre Dame, after which they went home to enjoy the traditional supper, sleeping late on Christmas morning—at least as late as the children would allow them.

Then, astonishingly, blessedly, it was spring once again. The chestnut trees were green once more and the sidewalk cafés were filled with the lovers of Paris. . . . May, and Henri became one year old. He took his first toddling steps into the outstretched arms of his father. There was a party for him in the garden, and Henri sat in his high-chair, pounding on the attached tray with a spoon. The icing of the cake all over his face was wiped away by his doting grandmother, who held him, but he struggled and reached out for Etienne as Jeanette and Jean-Paul looked on. . . .

Etienne in fact now spent most of his time with Henri, taking him each afternoon after his nap to his studio, where he sketched and painted. He tried to paint Henri, but his son was a less than cooperative model, never still for a moment, getting into the paints, smearing his hands and face, which made Etienne give up in helpless laughter, and he would pick up the little boy and hold him above his head, which delighted Henri, who matched his father's laughter, and then Etienne would give him a mock-frown and say "We will try again tomorrow."

The first word Henri said was "Papa."

In July, the family again went to Deauville. Jean-Paul had found a secret place for their rendezvous—which at first Jeanette resisted, then could not. At least neither of them was missed from the house, since Madame napped in the afternoon and Etienne painted prodigiously here, there and everywhere during the afternoons. Although their time together was hurried and shorter than it was in Paris, both, in their fashion, were satisfied. Jean-Paul loved to spend time with Henri, taking him out by himself, which not only benefitted the status of an uncle, but a godfather too. For Jeanette, less was better. . . .

Jeanette did everything she could to become pregnant by her husband, wanting very much to give Etienne a child. But all her efforts were unsuccessful, and she decided to have a talk with Dr. Bernier. When she got back to Paris she went to see him her second day in town.

"How are you getting along?" he asked.

She half-smiled. "I'm afraid your question is more pregnant than I am. I've been trying but . . ." She shrugged.

He nodded, then examined her thoroughly. "I find no reason why you can't conceive. I see nothing wrong."

"Then what should I do?" She tried not to sound anxious.

He smiled. "The same thing you're doing now."

Her cheeks began to burn. Imagine, and she with a lover as well as a husband, but with the doctor she did feel uncomfortable and ashamed . . . he knew Henri was not Etienne's . . .

"Sometimes," he said, "you can try too hard. Anxiety itself can be a deterrent. Perhaps you're just too tense when you have relations with your husband."

"Yes, I think you may be right. I want so badly to give Etienne a child. . . . You must be right. I watch my period dates, hoping they won't appear, and when they do I become upset and sometimes very depressed."

"Then my advice to you, young lady, is one word—relax."

She nodded. "Thank you, Dr. Bernier, I'll try to take your advice."

And she tried, but still nothing happened.

That winter she and Jean-Paul began a more serious and frequent round of arguments. The last confrontation had been the worst. He had wanted her to visit her uncle in London, where he would meet her for three weeks in January. This, of course, was doubly impossible and she refused, which infuriated him. In a rage, he went away for two weeks, ostensibly on government business. He would telephone the house and talk to his mother, then speak to Etienne, but never ask for her.

When he returned he apologized for his behavior. He asked her to forgive him and she did, but somehow, for her, it now seemed to matter less.

And the baby was still a source of conflict. At least once a month Jean-Paul had a fit of jealousy—sometimes mild, sometimes worse—during which he accused her of alienating the baby from him. This was nonsense, and she told him as much. But in spite of her efforts to reason with him—perhaps even because of them—Jean-Paul seemed to become more and more resentful about the role he was playing. . . . She tried to explain that his jealousy was destroying what they had together. But Jean-Paul didn't see it that way. He badgered her; his demands were becoming unbearable. When she got home after one of those scenes she often felt ill, too weary to go down for dinner. Nothing ever seemed to be settled. It was as though they were on a seesaw—up, down, no balance or equilibrium.

Jeanette observed the new year of 1938 by coming down with a cold. It started innocently enough with a runny nose and a slight fever. But two days later she had a very sore throat, making it painful to swallow. Etienne summoned the family doctor. When Dr. Roget examined Jeanette he suggested that an ear, nose and throat specialist be called in for consultation, since he was only a general practitioner. However, he did diagnose a strep throat. This diagnosis was corroborated by the finest specialist in Paris, Dr. Oubert, who prescribed a complete rest. Jeanette should be placed in isolation. She was fed intravenously because swallowing was so difficult. Nurses were brought in around the clock, and she was carefully watched. But her temperature rose and her condition grew worse. At times she was delirious, calling out for Etienne, who now—to hell with the doctor's instructions—slept in a bed by her side. She cried for Papa, for Henri, for her mother. . . . Her temperature finally was reduced some by alcohol rubs and ice packs, but the whole family kept vigil. Jean-Paul moved temporarily to his mother's house in order to be near her. His inner moods were black. He blamed himself for causing her so much grief with his jealousy, vowing to make it up to her and never again question her or make demands on her. If only she lived.

Finally, on the eleventh day, Dr. Oubert said, "I think we have reason for some hope. I find her condition slightly better this morning. Her temperature has stayed down within reason during the last twenty-four hours, and if this continues I feel reasonably sure we can expect to see a day-to-day improvement."

"Thank God," Etienne said. If prayer did any good, then God must have heard his.

· With the major infection gone, Jeanette was brought a little nourishment and was spoon-fed by Etienne. Now that she was on her way to becoming herself again, the entire household relaxed from the gloom of the past week and a half. . . .

Three days had passed since her recovery, and Etienne had fallen asleep that night at ten o'clock, exhausted from the many days of anxiety. Suddenly he was aroused out of his heavy sleep by moans threatening to become screams.

"My God, what's wrong?"

"My back . . . Etienne, I can't stand the pain—"

"When . . . I mean, how long have you—"

"Around midnight, I think. . . ."

"Why didn't you call me?"

"I hoped it would go away. . . ."

He immediately called Dr. Oubert, and within half an hour the doctor was examining Jeanette as she now screamed out in pain. He took a syringe from his bag, filled it with morphine and injected it into her vein. Soon after she relaxed and her breathing became more even.

When she had fallen asleep, Dr. Oubert asked Etienne and Jean-Paul to join him in the hall. "Her condition is serious. The complications from the streptococcal infection have affected her kidneys. I'd like to call in Dr. Villon. He's the best urologist I know."

"Of course, Doctor," Etienne said, thoroughly shaken and ash-white.

"I'll have a nurse called at once . . . injections will be necessary from time to time."

At four-thirty A.M. Dr. Villon was shown in to Jeanette's room. He discussed her condition with Dr. Oubert while Etienne and Jean-Paul waited in the hall. Then Dr. Villon spoke to Etienne.

"Monsieur Dupré, Madame should be hospitalized at once for tests and x-rays."

Stunned, Etienne nodded and asked, "How serious is it?"

"Let's wait for the tests."

At the hospital, Jeanette was wheeled in to X-ray immediately. Tests were taken but the results would not be known for several hours. She was wheeled in a bed to a large corner room where the two brothers waited.

At eight o'clock, Jean-Paul left to inform his mother, who nearly collapsed with fear and thoughts of Denise and Marie Jacqueline, then somehow managed outwardly to compose herself and accompany him to the hospital.

The news was not good as the doctor spoke to Etienne privately. "The former infection has indeed affected her left kidney. It's so badly damaged, I'm afraid the other one will also become involved." Dr. Villon's expression was very serious.

Etienne slumped down in his chair, barely able to speak. "What can be done? . . ."

"Monsieur Dupré, the truth is there is very little hope if both kidneys are involved. The left one is almost completely atrophied, and if the other one becomes worse . . ."

Etienne went white as the doctor hurried on with . . . "I have considered one possibility—"

"Yes, *anything* . . . Good God . . ."

"There's a physician, a professor, Erlichstein, who was at the University of Heidelberg until 1936 when he was forced to leave Germany because of Hitler. He was offered a fellowship in London to . . . experiment with kidney transplants."

"Well, for God's sake, what are we waiting for? Get him—"

"One moment, please. So far, Professor Erlichstein has only performed these transplants on animals. There is no clinical data on humans. His success with animals, however, has been impressive. If we can persuade him to operate on your wife—which I certainly can't guarantee—would you be willing to take the risk?"

"Take the risk, you ask! What other choice do we have?"

"All right. Such an unorthodox procedure requires some eyes to be shut and some mouths to be stilled—"

"Don't worry about that, my brother has some influence and I—"

"Provided I can convince the professor, we still need a donor—"

"*That* is no problem. I happen to have two very healthy kidneys."

Dr. Villon looked carefully at Etienne. "Monsieur, are you certain you want to do this? It's very dangerous. . . ."

"My wife is dying. How can you ask such questions? Now, let's not waste any more time."

The doctor nodded. "None, I assure you, will be wasted."

Etienne gave the bad news to his mother and Jean-Paul. Then he told them of the new kind of surgery. Madame began to pray silently. She knew it would take a miracle. . . .

Late that afternoon Dr. Villon spoke to Etienne again. "I've just gotten off the phone with Professor Erlichstein. . . ."

"Yes? . . ."

"At first, he was reluctant. But when I told him that you yourself—the husband of the patient—had volunteered to provide the kidney, he changed his mind. He's agreed to perform the operation. . . ."

When she heard the latest news, Madame went directly to the small sanctuary, closed the door, then knelt down and prayed. She remained there until Jean-Paul came down to insist that she go home. She did so, but only under protest.

At nine o'clock the next morning Doctor Erlichstein was in conference with Dr. Villon, who would assist him. The results of Jeanette's blood tests were examined, as well as her urine. Etienne was x-rayed, and tests were run. The two doctors prepared for surgery. Wife and husband would be operated on simultaneously. The professor would explain the procedure, step by step, to Dr. Villon in the operating room.

The surgery took hours, during which the doctors found Jeanette's left kidney badly damaged, but the right one should function normally, they felt, with the help of the transplant.

Following the surgery, Jeanette and Etienne were taken to separate rooms to recover. The operations had been a success, but certain aspects of her case would have to be falsified. The miracle couldn't yet be announced to the world. But each doctor felt that he had been true to the oath he had taken. Hopefully, a life had been saved. Both men would sleep better that night.

* * *

Etienne recovered quickly and without complications. Within two weeks he was on his feet and dismissed from the hospital. This was not the case with Jeanette. Her previous streptococcal infection had sapped her strength before the operation, so her recovery was slow, much slower than the doctors had hoped. She ran high temperatures, she was in constant pain.

At one point within the first forty-eight hours, the doctors feared that perhaps the transplant had been unsuccessful, that Jeanette's body might reject the new kidney. Tubes were inserted into the urethra in order for her to void.

Studies by laboratory technicians were analyzed and the results suggested that the source of infection was in the bladder. A relatively new "miracle" drug was administered. The drug was a risk, since it also affected the kidneys, but the doctors felt that they had no choice.

The days turned to weeks, the weeks to months, and, thanks to the doctors, the miracle drug, and a miracle from a higher source, as *maman* pointed out, Jeanette was able to be discharged from the hospital after three long, tortuous months. Her weight had gone down drastically, and she felt unbelievably weak.

Her convalescence at home was slow, but gradually, finally, she began to rally. Little by little her appetite returned. She was allowed to leave her bed and sit in a chair for a short period each day. Then she was told she could walk, although just back and forth in her room, which she did with the help of Etienne's arm.

Each day Madame and Jean-Paul paid her visits. And finally she was allowed to see Henri, whom she longed for. He had grown so much during her illness she could hardly believe her eyes. He was two and walked and talked, saying the most delightful things, making her laugh and cry at the same time. She tried to hold him close to her, but not for long. He would leave her bed and play, getting into everything, and Etienne would be forced to take him back to the nursery. The other children came, too, along with Madeleine and Clothilde. Etienne had been not only her comfort, he had, in fact, saved her life. What more could a man do for a woman . . . a husband for a wife? . . . And what else could she feel for him except the profoundest love?

By June she had recovered to the point that Etienne could take her for short drives in the country. With the coaxing of Madame and Clothilde, her appetite began to return. Gradually she gained a little weight, which pleased Dr. Villon, who continued to see her each day.

After it appeared that Jeanette's recovery was complete, Etienne asked Dr. Villon if it was safe to take her on a three-month Mediterranean cruise. The doctor was enthusiastic. There was nothing like an ocean voyage to restore the spirits, he assured him.

They planned to leave after Bastille Day, the fourteenth of July. Jeanette wanted to be with the children, to see their excited faces as the fireworks burst in the air. They planned a special celebration, which would be a birthday party as well; she would be twenty-three.

Dinner started earlier than usual. Henri sat high on a stack of pillows between his mother and father. Jeanette could *feel* the look on Jean-Paul's face—his fine resolutions to himself during her illness had been beyond him to keep. She refused, though, to let it bother her. Tonight was much too special.

After dinner, Etienne gave her his gift—a ruby and diamond necklace and earrings to match. She decided that they were the most beautiful jewels she had ever seen. And the most unnecessary.

"Etienne, darling, thank you, but you have already given me . . . everything." There were tears in her eyes as she kissed him.

All eyes were on them as Jean-Paul got up and poured himself a large brandy and gulped it down, then poured himself another.

Finally Henri became sleepy and, going to Etienne, he climbed on his lap, sucked his thumb and put his head against Etienne's chest. Madeleine was called to take the child to bed. He kissed Etienne first, then his mother, his grandmother, the other children.

Then: "Kiss Uncle Jean-Paul," Madame said.

For a moment he hesitated, then quickly obeyed, planting a small kiss on Jean-Paul's cheek as he took Madeleine's hand and said good-night.

As a finale, each of the children played a short piece on the piano. How grown up they were, Jeanette thought, remembering the day she had arrived.

When, on Etienne's arm, she walked up the stairs to their room, she thought the day had been the most satisfying she had ever had in her life. Her life . . . yes, this was a true birthday. She had *really* been born. Reborn. At twenty-three.

On the fifteenth of July Jeanette and Etienne waved good-bye to the family from the window of their compartment on the train that would take them to Le Havre. There they would board the boat. The only moment she felt sad was when she saw Henri waving good-bye, and wished he were old enough to go with them. She already missed him.

She looked at Jean-Paul. How lonely he seemed. They hadn't been together since shortly before her illness, and she wondered briefly how he had been managing. But only briefly.

When they reached Le Havre and boarded the ship, the excitement of boat whistles blaring, clouds of flying confetti, waving of handkerchiefs by friends and family that stood below was contagious and they joined the milling crowd at the rail, waving to no one in particular, calling out to anyone at all their delight. It was a marvelous, magic moment.

Their suite on the boat was a sitting room, bedroom and bath, all spacious and well furnished. Jeanette went to the porthole and looked out at the soft blue sea, watching the white ripples of the water.

"Etienne, I'm so happy we came. It was a wonderful idea, and you are a wonderful man whom I happen to adore—"

He encircled her with his arms, her back to him as she still looked out the porthole. "Between the devil and the deep blue sea," he said, and she turned, smiled and kissed him.

"Some devil," she said, kissing him again . . . "and now, sir, what about that lovely champagne?"

Etienne bowed low, then uncorked the champagne, which had been chilled to perfection in a silver bucket. "Here's to both of us," he said, touching his glass to hers. "To you and me, together . . . one . . ." He kissed her and quickly changed the mood with, "Now I want you to rest while I go up on deck and see the purser and make arrangements for the late dinner sitting."

"All right, darling, but don't be too long?"

"Wild horses and so forth . . . Now into bed with you, young lady." He kissed her and left.

The first night out Jeanette, dressed in flowing white chiffon, wore her rubies for the first time, as well as the diamond bracelet and wedding band. Her shoes were ruby red, and she carried a tiny beaded bag of the same color. Etienne wore a tuxedo, and they complimented each other extravagantly; beaming at each other shamelessly as they waited for the elevator to take them to the main salon, where they sat at a table for two, not needing or wanting any other company. Etienne was immediately aware of how often other men turned their heads to admire her. Women looked, too, though their reasons for doing so were different. . . .

For Jeanette, there was only one man in the room. He was no longer lame. He was easily the handsomest man there. He was her husband, and she wanted to shout it out to everyone in that dining room, everyone in the whole world. . . .

Later that evening, lying in bed waiting for him to join her, she said tentatively, "Etienne? . . ."

"Yes?"

"Can I talk to you about something?"

"What kind of a question is that?"

"Well . . . please come closer, over here . . . yes, that's better. . . . I'm afraid I have a confession to make—"

He smiled. "Well, that does sound pretty serious . . . please proceed, Madame, and I'll try to be generous—"

"Etienne, be serious . . . this isn't so easy. . . ."

"Sorry, darling, go ahead."

She took hold of his hand. "When we were first married, I loved you as a kind and wonderful person. You reminded me very much of my father . . . but I thought . . . I thought I wasn't *in* love with you."

"I knew that."

She looked startled, and then there were tears in her eyes. "And you still married me . . . knowing that?"

"Yes . . . and I would again."

"Why . . . how could you want me as your wife if you knew I wasn't in love with you?"

"Because . . . I loved you so much, it just didn't matter. I would have been happy if you had never changed, but you have, and—"

"Yes, I've changed, but not as much as you think, or as I would have thought. . . . I'm trying to say that I loved you more than I understood . . . even then . . . but I had to grow up, and with it grow into that love. . . . Do I make any sense, darling? . . ."

"The very best, from my point of view."

"And, Etienne, it was *you* who helped me grow into that love for you . . . your kindness from the very first, and understanding. I knew I *liked* you so much, and that was the beginning. . . . And, please, Etienne, don't *ever* think that I came to love you out of gratitude"—and when he started to protest, she shook her head and said, "no, please, let me say it so I'll never have to say it again, or you ever have to think it. It happened long before that, just how or exactly when I'm not sure. I'm only sure that I love you more than I have ever loved anyone in my life, or ever will."

"Jeanette, darling, what can I say except—"

"I should have told you all this before, a thousand times. . . . Etienne, I want another child so badly, we've tried so hard—"

"No—not after what you've been through, darling. It just isn't necessary. You've already given me something I never believed I'd have, a son. I certainly don't need other children. All I need or ever want in my life is you and Henri."

Taking her in his arms, he kissed her, and she whispered, "Etienne, make love to me."

"I want to, but are you well enough?"

"For you, I am strong. Please, darling, *please* . . ."

He did not keep her waiting.

The cruise was marvelous. At each port they bought presents for everyone. Whenever the ship docked, they ate at exotic restaurants, Spanish, Moroccan, Turkish, Greek, Italian, tasting dishes they'd never had before. It was a whole new adventure . . . and part of it was discovering themselves. . . .

The warm balmy nights aboard ship were as close to paradise as they ever expected to get. . . . Their days were filled with activities, but Jeanette especially enjoyed sitting on deck as Etienne read poetry aloud to her. She would close her eyes and listen to the resonance of his voice and relax in the pure pleasure of it. Of him.

"Etienne, I love your voice . . . aha, I have it, *that's* when I must have fallen in love with you, the moment I heard your devastating voice that first day in the library. Do you remember? . . ."

"I'll never forget . . . and I also think you're crazy. Did you, by the way, hear me sing? Better be careful."

She laughed and reached over and hugged him.

And then, as though it were only yesterday that they'd come aboard at Le Havre, the trip was over and they were debarking at Le Havre.

When the Paris Express came haltingly to a stop, they were met by the entire family. And dinner that night was very festive indeed. On top of their joy at returning home, they were celebrating their anniversary.

As Jeanette was dressing for the party, Madame came in to see her.

"I can hardly believe you're the same Jeanette that you were three months ago. . . ."

"Oh, *maman*, I never had such a good time. A *good* time. Do you understand what I mean? Etienne was such a joy."

"I think that Etienne is walking on the clouds. He looks like a man who's just come back from his first honeymoon."

Jeanette took her mother-in-law's hand. "You are a very wise woman, *maman*."

"And what makes me so wise?"

"Remember what you told me that day in Provence?"

"You mean the day I proposed to you?" She laughed.

"You told me that out of respect love can grow."

"Oh, did I say that? Well, I agree, I am indeed a wise old woman, especially if my brilliant, lovely daughter-in-law says so."

"Joke if you like, *maman*, but the fact is I have fallen madly in love with your son. My husband."

The older woman put her arms around Jeanette. "Thank you, thank you for talking to me this way, and I no longer joke. I also remember something you said."

"What?"

"That you would make Etienne a good and devoted wife. And this you've done before everything else. But knowing that you're in love with him as well makes my life complete. . . . Now finish dressing or I shall cry, which would be silly since this is a party," and she hurried out of the room.

Jeanette stood quietly for a moment, allowing herself to savor the special feeling of pleasure and contentment left with her after her talk with *maman*. Her look was drawn to the four-poster bed. From now on, it and she would belong only to Etienne. Jean-Paul would never invade their privacy again.

Deciding that was easier than facing the prospect of telling him in person, but she'd made up her mind she had to do it. When the roadster stopped in front of the apartment building which had been their place of rendezvous for three years, Jeanette hesitated before getting out. She straightened her shoulders, got out of the car and walked up the stairs.

Jean-Paul knew at once that he was meeting a different Jeanette. The expression on her face seemed to confirm his worst fears. He felt it, he knew it. He had, finally, lost her.

"Come in," he said. "After all, we're not exactly strangers."

His tone surprised her. She wasn't certain what it meant.

"Sit down. Take off your coat . . . it's warm. . . . I don't want you to catch cold. . . . Especially since you look so healthy and radiant after your cruise. I'm sure it must have been marvelous, a fine tonic, just the thing to recuperate by. . . ."

"Yes, it was, Jean-Paul."

"Of *course* it was. I've never seen you look more glowing. In fact, you've filled out so, one would think perhaps you might even be just slightly pregnant. Now, wouldn't that be jolly? Etienne a father for the second time, and this time no problems. No guilt. No Jean-Paul. *Are* you pregnant?"

His voice terrified her. She tried to relax, to compose herself. This was not the way she had rehearsed it.

"I take it silence means no. Very diplomatic. . . . Well, whatever, I must say you certainly look different. And now, my love, suppose you tell me just what this new you *is* all about."

Jeanette was trembling. She didn't know how or where to begin. How did she tell the man she'd once thought she loved, without question the man she'd been obsessed with, that the obsession was over? The man whose child she had borne?

She took a deep breath. "Jean-Paul, I would like to discuss this like two civilized people—"

He began to laugh. But there was no humor in the laughter. He had heard those words before, but they had been spoken by him to the several ladies he'd been obliged to deprive of his attentions. He didn't at all care for the situation being reversed.

"Jean-Paul," she began again, "during my illness I had a good deal of time to think. I found myself taking a hard look at my life—"

"And what, my love, were your findings?"

"I didn't like what I saw. I suppose I never did, but I was careful not to look too closely, for my own selfish reasons that I could somehow usually justify to myself. . . ."

"And now . . . why are you looking so closely now?"

"I was a schoolgirl when I met you, Jean-Paul. I was also a very bitter young person. I was entitled, I felt, to anything, everything."

"And now?"

She didn't want to cry if she could help it. She also wouldn't discuss Etienne if she could possibly help it.

"I discovered I couldn't go on living the way I had been. How can I explain it, Jean-Paul? You intrigued me, fascinated me. I was innocent, but in a way I wasn't. My feelings were close to the surface. You knew what to do with them. . . . Please, Jean-Paul, I'm not blaming you . . . much more myself. . . . But I do know that what I felt wasn't love. I think you know it, too—"

"We had a child," he shouted. "We had a child. You've conveniently forgotten, it seems, who the father is." He was deep into his third glass of brandy.

"No, I haven't, and it was seeing what I thought was your genuine pain at not being able to claim your son, to have his love, that made me understand I'm not the only one who has been hurt, but, Jean-Paul, you must accept it, his father is Etienne, and cruel as that is for you—"

"That crippled little bastard couldn't be the father of anything—"

"You're wrong, Jean-Paul. Etienne may walk with a limp, but I assure you he's less crippled than you . . . or I."

"Why, you pitiful little slut, how dare you? I picked you up from nowhere, a damned nobody. I made you respectable, a *lady* . . ." He shook his head and finished the brandy. "You could hardly wait to take what I gave you every time you came here. . . . But I gave you much more—I gave you a home and a child with a name. My God, you should be in the gutter where you belong." He wanted to choke her, kill her. . . .

"You really gave me nothing. You only had me believing that. You used me, *and* your mother, by conniving to hurt Etienne, whom you've always despised. Clothilde told me how you tried to drown him. I didn't believe it then, but I believe it now. She told me that sooner or later you destroy everything you touch. Your wife is in an institution because of you—"

And now all his restraint was gone. "Suppose your crippled husband knew that Henri isn't his. What do you suppose he would do? I'll tell you. He'd throw you out, which is exactly what you deserve. God knows you don't deserve to have the name Duprél"

She'd been expecting it. "He might, Jean-Paul, and he would certainly be justified. . . . But I don't think you'll tell him, because if you did I would have no reason not to also tell him how you manipulated us all, including your mother, into the marriage. I don't think I'm what you've called me, Jean-Paul, but you may be right, perhaps I'm not a lady . . . at least not if that means fighting for my child and my husband."

His body seemed to slump. He had lost out to his lousy crippled brother, a man he despised with a passion, just as he now despised this outrageous girl. He had *given* them a child, a son, a boy he loved. And now he was helpless to do anything about it. She was right . . . if his mother ever learned the truth, she would never forgive him. . . . He might even lose his inheritance. . . .

But he promised himself one thing . . . if it took the

rest of his life, he would even the score with both of them. Somehow, some way, he would do it. "All right, get out of here, you miserable little whore. Go back to your precious crippled husband. . . . I only hope that some day your body is as repulsive to him as it is to me. . . ."

How she ever got home, she would never know. She got into bed and put her hands over her ears, trying to shut out the memory of Jean-Paul's words. Over and over again, they reverberated in her head. She felt such hatred for herself, she wanted to die. . . . Jean-Paul had done a far better job than he could ever guess. . . . Oh, Papa, am I, after all, my mother's daughter . . . ?

For weeks she couldn't face herself. Sometimes she fell into deep depressions. She found herself asking her husband time and time again, "Do you love me?"

He was bewildered by the question. Did she really need reassurance? Surely she already knew? That was a question she had never had to ask before.

And for the first time in their marriage, she even made excuses when he wanted to make love to her, excuses he couldn't quite accept but he didn't press the issue. She had almost died . . . the doctors had warned that they couldn't predict all her reactions, that even months after the operation there could be unforeseen complications. . . . When she was ready she would let him know.

She knew Etienne was confused—though she was glad the doctors had provided a built-in excuse—but how could she make love to Etienne when she felt so unworthy . . . unclean, even . . . ? She didn't leave the house for weeks, remaining shut up in her room most of the day . . . my God, like Jacqueline. . . . She scarcely saw Henri, feeling she wasn't fit to be his mother. Her mind lived now in the torment of the past. She was, she decided, the most sinful woman alive, and there could be no atonement. . . .

One day, unable to see her as she was any longer, Etienne came to their room and sat in the dim shadows that came between dusk and evening. "What's wrong, my dearest? Don't you feel well? Please tell me."

She lay motionless on the bed, her hand over her eyes. "It's nothing, Etienne. Really nothing—"

"I'm going to call Dr. Villon, there's something wrong that you're not—"

"*No*, please don't. I'm a little tired, that's all."

"But you seemed so well and happy when we came back from our holiday."

"I'm *tired*, that's all. I'll be all right in a few days."

"Will you do something for me?"

"Anything . . ."

"Tomorrow, I want you and Henri to take a long drive with me into the country and we will have lunch. . . ."

She opened her eyes and turned to look at him. "Do you love me?"

"Of course I do. You *know* that."

Tears were running down her cheeks and she reached out to him. "Oh, God, Etienne, I'm sorry, I'm so *miserable. . . .*"

That evening, thoroughly alarmed now, he went to see his mother. "Maman, I'm very worried, there's something terribly wrong and I've no idea what it is. She doesn't want me to but I think I really must call the doctor—"

"Listen to me, Etienne . . . I'm not certain, but I strongly suspect that Jeanette wants another child, and through no fault of hers . . . or yours . . . hasn't been able to become pregnant. I know how I felt after your birth, when I wanted another baby so much . . . your father did too . . . and wasn't able to . . . well, Jeanette is probably going through the same disappointment, and depression. Just have patience, Etienne. That's what a woman needs most of all. Believe me. . . ."

Of course, she was right, and he remembered their talk about another child and how he'd turned aside the idea. No wonder she kept asking, "Do you love me?" Oh, God, why had he been so stupid?

The next day he insisted they drive to the country. The weather was cold and crisp and fall was in the air as the leaves drifted slowly to the ground. He saw to it that she was bundled up in a fur coat, and her lap covered with a car robe. Henri wore a navy blue overcoat, a beret, a red knitted muffler and mittens. He sat between them, and clearly enjoyed the ride and magnificent countryside.

By noon they found a quiet inn where they stopped for lunch and sampled the new Beaujolais. The proprietor poured it himself, with a flourish.

"Delicious," said Etienne, after letting it rest on his palate. He hoped his own grapes had produced as fine a vintage. As he looked at Jeanette picking at her food and forcing a smile, he decided he was going to have to be not only patient, but more reassuring to her about his love.

And as she looked at him, she made up her mind to make a special effort—which, of course, was the beginning out of her long funk—to be more pleasant and responsive to him. He'd been so incredibly kind and patient. . . .

When they returned home Jeanette did seem in somewhat better spirits. That night Etienne thought he read a change in her and proceeded to make passionate, almost desperate love to her, and she did her best to respond in kind. She owed him this, at least, and so much more. . . .

In the weeks that followed she seemed gradually to restore herself until suddenly, one day, she realized that she hadn't awakened with the too familiar, ugly, haunting thoughts of Jean-Paul.

As for Jean-Paul, it seemed he had been sent off to Tunisia by the Foreign Office. That, in any case, was what he had told his mother. It at least helped to explain his continued absence from the house. . . .

But in December he returned, and one day he called his mother on the telephone to ask if he might come to dinner that evening and bring a friend. Madame was overjoyed. Excitedly, she went over the menu with Clothilde, making certain it included every special dish that Jean-Paul loved. She personally selected the red, white and gold Limoges service, and the Bacarat wine goblets. She decorated the table with red roses in a crystal-and-bronze bowl with five-branched candelabra at either end, welcoming in the Christmas season, and her son too long away from her table.

Jeanette fought to keep her new-formed composure when she heard Jean-Paul would be there, but inwardly she was far from certain she could get through the evening. But she *had* to. He was out of her life . . . well then, prove it. . . .

She dressed with special care in a long, delicate pink gown. Her hair was fussed over until it was exactly the way she wanted it. She would not give him the satisfaction of knowing the agony he had put her through. Her cheeks were rouged slightly more than usual . . . to show her off well in the candlelit room.

But when the doorbell rang, her heart began to beat loudly in her ears. For a moment she thought she might faint. Then he was there, coming into the room, with a dazzling woman on his arm.

"Maman," he said, kissing her on the cheek. "I've missed you very much."

"And I you, Jean-Paul," she answered, at the same time appraising her new guest. She knew perfectly well that Jean-Paul had mistresses, but still . . . a son did not bring a mistress to his mother's home.

Jean-Paul recognized the look on Maman's face. Laughing to himself he said, "Maman, may I present Madame Lazare, the wife of our distinguished ambassador to Tunisia?"

"How do you do?" Madame said coolly.

Jean-Paul understood the tone of Maman's voice, both when she was pleased and when she was not. He realized that she was wondering where and with whom the distinguished ambassador himself was dining tonight. . . .

Madame Lazare said, "May I thank you for having me this evening. I'm truly pleased, Madame, to meet you and your family."

"The pleasure is ours," Madame answered with reserve.

After making the introductions, Jean-Paul turned his attention completely to Etienne. After fifteen minutes of seemingly innocuous small talk he said, "Tell me, how is my godson?"

"Getting bigger every day, and into more mischief than you can imagine."

Jean-Paul laughed. "I can't imagine where he would get such habits . . . certainly not from you, or his mother. . . ."

Jeanette, furious, could only pray the evening would end soon. Obviously Madame Lazare had been brought here for her special benefit. Even at the risk of offending his supposedly beloved Maman. Well, she would play his game and beat him. . . . "You must miss Paris, Madame Lazare, when your husband's work takes you away?"

"Not at all. I'm here more often than I am in Tunisia. After all, I must do all my shopping in Paris."

"Then that must take you away from your husband a great deal?"

"My husband is so busy with his duties, I'm afraid he hardly has time to miss me before I am back. Tunisia is a most delightful place. You must come and visit us."

"How kind of you. . . ."

Jean-Paul stood watching, pleased. He had slapped Jeanette in the face, and she knew it, although he had to admit she was handling herself far better than he'd imagined she was capable of.

At dinner Françoise Lazare sat across from Jean-Paul. Unfortunately, Jeanette found herself seated next to him. Etienne sat at the head of the table, Madame sat at the other end. Jean-Paul talked a great deal, telling amusing little stories that made even Madame laugh a little. Jeanette could hardly stand to listen to the sound of his voice, and it was all she could do to remain through dinner, but she would stay if it killed her. . . . She smiled now at Madame Lazare.

"Do you have any children?" she said, which was rather obviously out of context in the conversation.

"Yes. Two—a son and a daughter."

"How nice for you. And where do they attend school? Here in Paris?"

"Oh, no, in Switzerland."

"How nice." Jeanette's voice was somewhat slurred. She had been drinking more than usual. "We hope our next child will be a daughter and the next a son, although it doesn't really matter. We'll be grateful for whatever comes along. Won't we, darling?"

"Yes, indeed," said Etienne, beginning to feel increasingly edgy and concerned for her.

"But we will never send them away to school, will we, darling? Children grow up so quickly. Parents deprive themselves of the joys of their childhood by not having them close at hand. . . . Why, our own Henri will soon be three, and we've *definitely* decided he will go to school here in Paris . . . so his father and I can see him every day. Of course, the schools in Tunisia are probably unsuitable."

Françoise Lazare was definitely offended. Jeanette knew it, Etienne knew it. Madame knew it, and thought, bravo, Jeanette! Jean-Paul, looking at Jeanette, wanted to kill her.

Dinner finally came to an end. Although Jeanette had a

headache, she was determined not to go to her room before Jean-Paul and his friend left . . . not even if it killed her.

They returned to the salon. Without being asked, Jeanette said, "In honor of Madame Lazare, the wife of our distinguished ambassador to Tunisia, I'd like to play my husband's favorite piecé, *Clair de Lune.*" She was by now also feeling decidedly tipsy.

Adjusting her gown, she sat down and began to play. One or two bars were slightly ragged, but she continued to the end. Staggering, ever so slightly, she got up and curtsied as though before royalty, smiled brilliantly at Jean-Paul, then seated herself next to Etienne, and took his arm.

"That was . . . delightful," Madame Lazare said coldly. "And now, thank you, Madame, for a . . . for your hospitality. But I have an extremely early appointment in the morning. . . ."

And she walked to Jean-Paul's side and took his arm, the arm of a very frustrated diplomat. . . . The little bitch, Jean-Paul thought, she'd learned the master's technique too well. Never mind, his turn would come, he hadn't forgotten what she'd done to him. He'd find a way, have no fear about *that*. . . .

He kissed Maman good night, thanked her for dinner, saying he would be here *every* evening from now on since he was back in Paris to stay. He put his hand on Etienne's shoulder, barely touched Jeanette's hand, which she extended regally, if unsteadily, and with Madame Lazare clinging to his arm as though it were a life raft, made his departure.

The morning after, Jeanette reviewed her behavior and realized she'd no doubt been drunk for the first time in her life. Had she, she wondered, made a complete ass of herself? She said it out loud at luncheon to Madame, adding, "I hope I didn't embarrass you, Maman."

"Not in the least . . . I was *proud* of you. I don't understand at all, Jean-Paul bringing that woman here, unaccompanied by her husband. The very idea! He knows I am no fool, that I know about such things. Why would he offend me, and in my own home . . . ?"

Jeanette wished she had never brought up the subject, and was grateful when Etienne joined them, and the conversation turned to the latest news. "What do you think, Etienne? Will there be a war?"

"I'm afraid so," he said, "but I'm sure that we French can handle Herr Hitler. . . ."

Jeanette was relieved to hear it, and unable not to be grateful as well for a likely side effect . . . Jean-Paul, in his government role, would surely be too busy to fulfill his threat of the previous evening to be with the family every night for dinner.

Twenty-five

Hitler was an excrescence flowing across Europe. It was feared that before long, France and England would have to become involved. With the threat of war in the air, as Jeanette had suspected, Jean-Paul no longer joined the family at dinner. That, at least, saved some embarrassment. He often was detained at the Foreign Office well into the night. He threw himself into his work with all his vigor. The stronger Hitler became, the more territory he acquired, the more Jean-Paul became convinced that one day Adolf Hitler would, as he had boasted in *Mein Kampf*, rule the world. And Jean-Paul was determined to be on the winning side. Secretly, he became purposefully pro-Nazi, joining with those who felt the same way.

At the first meeting he attended, he was more than a little surprised to see some of the leading French statesmen and diplomats also present. Naturally their sympathies were a guarded secret, and Jean-Paul was appropriately cautious. When he discussed the force and magnetism of *Der Fuhrer*, he was careful to make sure that the people he talked to were of the same opinion. . . . His diplomatic training, as he'd always known it would be, became increasingly valuable.

It was a crisp, cold January morning when Jean-Paul Dupré arrived at Templehoff Airport in Berlin. A limousine dispatched by the French Embassy was waiting. The car, tri-colored flags attached to the front fenders, sped along the wide boulevards, which were lined with banners of bold red swastikas on backgrounds of white. Golden eagles hung above the entries of all the state buildings, presumably to make Berlin look like Rome at the height of its might and glory. Black- and brown-shirted S.S. men were everywhere. Many people all over the world feared that Europe was on the verge of war, that if the little house painter from Munich occupied Poland the conflict could become incendiary. But here, in Berlin, all appeared to be calm and serene. Well-fed, well-dressed Berliners went about their normal routines—shopping, working, eating their wiener schnitzel and guzzling their schnapps.

That evening at a diplomatic reception Jean-Paul actually had the opportunity to observe Hitler at close range. After waiting in line to shake hands with *Der Fuhrer*, Jean-Paul stood near him, a glass of champagne in his hand, observing every detail of his features. He concluded that Hitler was neither the caricature he was made to appear in the cartoons nor the madman seen in the movie newsreels. Instead, he seemed rather shy and retiring. Even when he laughed there was, Jean-Paul thought, an inner reserve about the man. His deep-set eyes seemed to take in everything at a glance, as though he were making mental notes to be made use of later. To Jean-Paul there was also a magnetic strength and fascination about his presence that was undeniable. He was commanding, he was intense. He had taken a broken, degraded nation left to die after the Treaty of Versailles and transformed it into a world power, ready to respond to his will. The German people worshipped him, and why shouldn't they? He had given them back their dignity . . . even his enemies admitted that. Germans could once again hold up their heads. He was their leader, their savior, but beyond that, he apparently had the ability to outmaneuver every nation he set his sights on. Why had his troops been allowed to take Czechoslovakia when they could have been stopped in their tracks? Adolf Hitler was a force to be reckoned with. Some people said that if Mussolini had been stopped in Ethiopia, then Hitler might never have realized how easy it was to grab. But Hitler was smarter than Mussolini. He didn't have to fight, he merely took what he wanted, then waited for the outcries of indignation that were not backed up by force.

The next night Jean-Paul witnessed a special open-air celebration. Corps of young men and women paraded for their leader. When Hitler himself appeared, they became hysterical—and chanted, "Heil Hitler!" with their arms shooting up like spears. Jean-Paul was convinced of his power. Perhaps Hitler would rule the world for the foreseeable future. The old order of things was dying, that was indisputable. And the new order of Nazism led by Hitler was dawning. At the time of *Mein Kampf* few people had taken the little man in the baggy trousers seriously. Many did now. More would later. . . .

When Jean-Paul returned to Paris, he submitted his findings. Hitler, he reported, wanted only peace. The threat of war was slight.

By 1939 Germany was at war with France. The French Maginot Line had been considered impenetrable. Hitler destroyed it like a row of wooden blocks. France surrendered soon after and the house painter danced a jig on France's soul. Paris was declared an open city, not to be destroyed. It was to be the Nazis' pleasure dome. A showpiece of their Teutonic benevolence. Barbarians, indeed.

By 1940 France was completely occupied. Jean-Paul's private judgment had been vindicated. He was on the winning side, his allegiance was to Pétain and the Vichy government, of which he was now a high-ranking official.

The Jews of Paris were in the process of being systematically rounded up. Etienne, frantic with fear that something would happen to Jeanette, worked feverishly, and paid lavishly, to have all her official records changed. Birth certificate, marriage license, passport—anything and everything pertaining to Jeanette Hack Dupré was adjusted to hide the fact of her Jewish heritage. Etienne paid a visit to the priest and exacted a promise from him that Jeanette would be certified Catholic. The monsignor crossed himself and vowed that if questioned he would say nothing about falsified records.

Etienne breathed a little easier . . . and prayed that he had indeed protected Jeanette. . . .

Etienne was not the only one concerned with Jeanette's future safety.

Tonight, in a mansion on the Isle of Saint Louis, the Countess Alexis Maximov shared his same concern as she was entertaining at a lavish dinner the most important officials of the Nazi Party in Paris, together with those who controlled the Vichy government, among whom was Jean-Paul Dupré. Looking around at the assemblage of butchers, dressed so elegantly in their bemedalled uniforms, she was pleased. They all looked, she decided, extremely *useful* for her purposes.

After the party was over Magda sat at her dressing table, looking at her own image in the mirror, and laughing sardonically. Alexis hadn't been there tonight, but he might have been whispering in her ear from the distant past, telling her now as he had then that she couldn't stop being an actress, she owed it to the world to share her talent that God had given her. . . . And she remembered that she'd told him she didn't want to be an actress, she wanted to have a fine salon to help her child do well in society. . . . Well, her ambitions for Jeanette hadn't worked out quite as she'd hoped they would, but Magda couldn't complain. It's strange, Alexis, she thought, I'm both an actress and a lady with a grand salon. The trick, of course, is to be convincing, whatever one is at, whatever role one is playing. Do that and one can manage anything. Well, almost anything. . . . Some things, dear Alexis, are beyond our powers, out of our hands. . . .

One day a year and a half ago, Magda thought her life had come to an end. She had gone into the library and had discovered Alexis unconscious on the floor. She watched helplessly as servants took him upstairs and laid him on the bed. She summoned the doctor, and waiting for him had almost driven her out of her mind. When the doctor finally arrived, she was asked to wait outside the bedroom while Alexis was examined. Afterward he'd told her her husband was gravely ill, that he had suffered a massive stroke and was almost completely paralyzed.

"Almost . . . ?"

"Yes. Except for a slight mobility in the right hand, I'm very much afraid he is totally para—"

"His mind, what about his mind?"

"That doesn't appear to be impaired. He'll have his

memory . . . he'll be able to hear, to comprehend, to see. Eventually his speech should improve, but at first it may be difficult to understand him. . . ."

No . . . she would *not* go to pieces . . . she would be calm, ask sensible questions. "And what would you suggest?"

"He must have constant care. I will arrange for a capable staff of nurses to—"

"No, you won't . . . so long as I'm alive, my husband will be in my care . . . Alexis will be taken care of by people who love him. . . . Now please tell me what he'll need."

"He will need someone with him twenty-four hours a day." The doctor taught her to use a syringe. "Small amounts, to relax his mind. . . . That's usually the problem with stroke patients who can still use their minds . . . their apprehensions sometimes cause insomnia. . . . Also, he'll need an anti-coagulant to thin his blood. . . . I will let you know when he can be moved to a wheel chair, but that won't be for some weeks. Meantime, he must be turned and massaged, and this should be done about every four hours, so he won't develop bed sores. . . . Now, do you still insist on this?"

"Doctor, I know what you're trying to do, and I appreciate it, but I repeat, I will take care of my husband."

He left then, shaking his head, and Magda immediately went to Alexis' room, a room they had happily shared for so many years. The bed in which Alexis now lay so still, in which he had known so much love and tenderness. . . . She still couldn't absorb it—Alexis paralyzed? She moved a chair next to him, and sat down, taking his hand in hers. . . . "Dearest Alexis, why *you?* It was *your* strength that kept me going while Rubin was away in the war . . . your strength that kept me sane, wouldn't let me give up when my daughter told me I was not her mother, that I was dead, as she'd told her husband. . . . Well, my love, now I will be *your* strength. . . . You've been my life, now I will try to be yours. . . ."

For months letters of sympathy arrived, along with flowers, gifts, telephone calls, all of which were acknowledged by letter, but she herself would neither see nor speak to anyone.

It was a quiet afternoon some three months after his

stroke. "Alexis, my dearest," Magda was saying to him, "the library could be turned into a lovely bed-sitting room. . . . It's so pleasant, with the woods outside and the fireplace . . . you always enjoyed the terrace, the way it looks out on the Seine. . . . Dr. Roget says that you soon will be able to be helped into a wheel chair. The coming and going would be so simple. . . . Would you enjoy that? Blink your eyes if you would. . . ."

Patiently she asked the question three times. She was about to repeat it when he blinked his eyes. . . .

"Oh, Alexis, I'm so glad . . . I want you to enjoy the sunshine and fresh air and I'll sleep on a very comfortable couch, both of us will move downstairs. . . ."

He stared at her . . . by now she knew every look.

"You think I'm giving up this room as a sacrifice? Don't be so conceited, my dearest. I'm selfish, I *want* to be with and near you."

He blinked . . . the blink was angry. The decision was no.

Alexis was moved downstairs, and on those days when he could be wheeled outside, he basked in the warmth of the sun. He seemed to be happier, at least life had become tolerable. The haunting, pathetic look was no longer written in his eyes. Magda had someone to care for . . . to love and to comfort. . . .

When rumors of war reached her ears, they came as a shock. She hadn't read a newspaper, or listened to the radio in months. Suddenly, once again, she seemed to be a prisoner of her memories, locked into a world of déjà vu. "England will not allow a small nation to be invaded . . . Germany is destined for war. . . ."

One day Pierre, her old friend from those earliest days in Paris before Rubin, and now officially the butler and really her friend, confessed to belonging to the underground. Her people . . . Jews, he told her, were being slaughtered like cattle, by the thousands. . . . "We have an underground in Germany," he said, "and all over Europe. . . . Will you help us?"

Two friends of Pierre's were in the small salon waiting to meet her. Without another word, Magda went in to meet them.

They looked like ordinary men, not in the least menac-

372 • *Cynthia Freeman*

ing. After the introductions, they came straight to the point.

"You have an underground tunnel that leads to the Seine. Under your house, you also have an enormous labyrinth, and a maze of tunnels. They're exactly what we need as an escape route—"

"You really think it will come to that?"

"It already has. . . . Tomorrow Germany will declare war on France. Believe me. . . . May we count on your cooperation?"

Magda agreed and told Pierre to take the men down to the maze, and they thanked her for her help—

"My *help?* Pierre tells me that thousands of Jews are being killed. . . ."

"That's true . . . although the Germans deny it. The American government and ours have spoken out against it, but the reprimands are not strong enough. . . . What are the Jews to Hitler, he is after the world. 'Tomorrow the world' . . . that's what he says. . . ."

Magda shuddered. Everything was changing. Her whole world was falling to pieces. . . . "Is there anything else I can do . . . money . . . ? Do you need money?"

They, of course, did, and Magda wrote a check.

"Please don't concern yourself . . . we won't be seen coming or going . . . there are two hidden doors which don't appear to have been used in years. I doubt if anyone knows they exist . . . even you. Well, again, our thanks . . . good-bye."

That had been almost a year ago, but to this day every time she thought about a small band of men carrying on the dangerous task of espionage just beneath the floors she walked on, she found herself breathing a little harder. Alexis knew nothing of this. He often sat on the terrace, as he had today, and watched the German patrol boats going up and down the Seine. But what he thought, after having it explained to him that a war was raging in Europe, Magda could only guess. . . .

Alexis had now been given his medication and had fallen asleep when Pierre came to ask if, once again, she would see his friend, and she went with him at once.

"Anjou wants to talk to you alone," Pierre said. "I'll go back to the Count."

She found Anjou standing before the fireplace.

"*Bon soir*, Countess."

"*Bon soir* . . ."

"The last time we sat in this room, you made it clear we could count on your help—"

"Yes, anything. Please don't hesitate."

He looked at her searchingly. "Well, this time we are asking a great deal . . . it involves a very great personal sacrifice."

"You make it sound ominous. And what does it involve?"

He paused, then: "A liaison with the top . . . with the head of the Gestapo here in Paris . . ."

She sat motionless, then, shaking her head and smiling mirthlessly, she said, "That, monsieur, is indeed a personal sacrifice. . . . But really you must have . . . others working with you who could do this. . . . Why me?"

"No one else, I'm afraid, quite fits the part as well as—"

"The part?" In spite of herself and knowing the seriousness of the situation to bring him to make such a request, she realized she was feeling a certain defensiveness . . . perhaps even indignation?

"Yes. Exactly."

"I must say, you make it sound like some sort of farfetched play in which, I presume, I am to play the *femme fatale*—"

"That's just about it, Countess . . . and you are perfect for the part . . . you have the beauty . . . the prestige . . . the elegance. . . . But most important of all, you have the intelligence and dedication. Pierre has made that clear, but it was fairly obvious even on first meeting you."

"This is, I suppose, all very flattering, but did it also occur to you that I also have a . . . husband to whom I'm completely devoted . . . who needs me . . . who would certainly not approve of such conduct. . . . And did it occur to you how much, how deeply, I *despise* these Nazi bastards?"

"Yes . . . we know that. . . ."

"And yet you want me to have a liaison with one of them? Really, Anjou, I'm afraid this time you're asking too much—"

"Are we . . . ? Do you know how many Jews we've saved because we had access to your tunnel? With the Germans at our heels, it wasn't always easy, but we saved the lives of hundreds of children who would otherwise have been slaughtered."

Magda was pacing back and forth. . . . Her mind kept whispering to her . . . children . . . children . . . Jeanette, my daughter . . . Henri, my grandchild. . . . I *am* a mother, and a grandmother even if it isn't acknowledged . . . my children . . . children must be saved. . . . She sat down, lit a cigarette. *"If* I agree, do you have a plan?"

"Yes."

"Tell me about it."

"The man you would make contact with is Christian Reichart." Apparently Anjou was too caught up to see the absurd, indeed, disgusting, irony in the name for a Gestapo chief, but she couldn't overlook it, and winced when she heard it. . . . But Anjou was going on: "He's chief of the Gestapo in Paris. He's handsome, blond, very Aryan, of course. Also calculating and ruthless. . . . His fondness for extraordinarily attractive women is almost a joke, but I assure you he is not a joke. He is not easily fooled or taken in. One would need to be very clever."

"And you think that I—"

"Yes. I believe, Madame, that you have all the credentials, including that of being a good listener." (She had to smile briefly at that. A good listener, yes, she'd learned that as the mistress of a fine salon, but she also was a good talker. She'd surely have to work on that if . . .)

"And what if they discovered that I am a Jew?"

"I don't think that's at all, even remotely, likely—"

"But I've lived in Paris many years, you know."

"Yes, we know. Your old friend Pierre has known you from your earliest days, and at that time you had no friends except Pierre. And your husband—for reasons that we understand and you needn't worry will ever be revealed by us . . . they are, frankly, of no interest to us—has done a brilliant job in creating a new identity for you and demolishing the old. Your papers show that you come from a Polish family of royal connections. I think you know the rest. . . . I'm sorry"—and it was clear he meant this personally—"but it does seem that you're the most likely of all people to undertake this." (She took it he was also being delicate in not mentioning Alexis' condition, which, practically at least gave her a "freedom" she would not otherwise have.) "You are an actress, and as I understand it, what is known as a 'natural.' Perhaps you can think of this—although I offended you when I first mentioned it as such—as a role in a play, a very important role in a not very pleasant, but nonetheless, as I'm sure you'd agree, very important play."

She sat looking at him for several moments. Well, Magda Charascu, welcome back . . . not that you really ever left . . . but now the countess needs you, and so do your children. . . . What the hell are you waiting for . . . ?

"How . . . how would I meet this Reichart?"

Anjou nodded emphatically, as though to seal the deal. "Next Thursday at the German Embassy, at a gala there. You will be invited, we will see to it. After that . . . the rest is up to you. May I assume we have your commitment?"

". . . You already know that the answer is yes."

He nodded again. "Pierre will be your contact. We will communicate only through him."

No thank yous, no good-byes. No time.

There was also no sleep for her that night. Alexis stood in the shadows of her memory, along with her promise of fidelity to him. There had been no conditions set then. It had been unqualified.

Grateful for the morning, finally, she dressed and went downstairs to him. "Good morning, my love. . . . I see you've already been shaved, you look very handsome, I must say." His eyes followed as she straightened the covers. As usual, coffee and croissants were served. She talked of unimportant things, and gave answers to her own questions as though they were his. By now she understood the nuance of every look. . . . "You want to see out, of course, darling," and she cranked the handle at the foot of the bed so that his back was in a slight sitting position. Later she would need help from Pierre to put him in the chair.

By now he had recovered to the extent of being able to make sounds that only vaguely resembled articulate speech but which she had learned to translate with considerable accuracy and intuition. And when they made no sense at all, she answered casually, vaguely, as though they did and as though she understood completely. She was very good at it. Just now he was mumbling something. She listened carefully. . . . "Oh, so you think I look tired?" Immensely frustrated by his attempts to communicate with his garbled speech, Alexis fell back, as he usually did, on answering "Yes" with his blinking signal. . . . "Well I'm not really tired, darling . . . it's more than that. Alexis, something extraordinary has happened. I want to do something. I mean, I don't want to but I feel I have to. . . . Oh dear, I don't seem to be getting to the point, forgive me. Alexis, this may sound like something out of a bad melodrama, and indeed it would be at any other time, except as you know this is not any other time, this is wartime and the damned Nazis are all over Paris and I have a daughter who is Jewish and I have a grandson who's Jewish too. He has Jewish blood, never mind how they raise him as a good little Catholic. He is a Jew, one drop is all the Nazis need, you know that. . . ." She looked at him, shook her head and smiled. "I really do go on, don't I, darling? Well, the *point* is, Magda Charascu, alias Margot Maximov, has come back for her premiere performance, to be a . . . a spy for the underground. I know, I know, I'll have to learn to keep my mouth shut, which won't be easy, but I do have big ears and they have usually been wide open, so I've had good training there. . . ." She rushed on, wanting to get it all out at once and not sure she could in a way that wouldn't be ruinous to both of them. . . . "Pierre—he's one of them—brought his friends here and we talked and they seem to feel I can be of help . . . going to parties, giving parties, which I already do, of course, being friendly with some of the right people . . . that sort of thing. . . ."

She couldn't bring herself to be more specific, to actually mention Reichart and her assigned "role." All the time she'd been speaking he hadn't taken his eyes from her, but now they looked out to the river, the Seine. The Nazi patrol boats plied up and down the water . . . in place of the once pleasure-filled *bâteaux mouches* . . . their swastika-adorned flags, obscene pennants, flapping in the gentle breeze. He had understood every word that Magda had said, as well as those that she had not said . . . the words behind the words "the right people, that sort of thing." He knew very well what they meant, and they chilled and terrified him. . . .

He turned back to look at her, and as he did so he saw in her face the face of a very little girl, a little five-year-old girl named Jeanette . . . damn his mind, so clear in a helpless body, and with its clarity memories now came flooding back, memories too precise, too well remembered. . . . "Oh, Uncle Alexis, I love you so much. . . ." The voice of Magda's daughter, now finally found by her mother. Years ago he had told Magda he would kill her if she ever deceived him, but she never had, she'd been a marvelous wife and woman to him, and now he was a cadaver that she'd dedicated herself to keeping alive. . . . Well, she would need no terrible sickness to kill her if he denied her this chance to live for her daughter, because that was what it was to her. He would simply be signing *her* death warrant, as the Nazis had signed them for so many other Jews, if he were to discourage her now and anything should happen to her child, and grandchild. . . . He would play the game with her, pretend with her that he knew less than he did. It was, after all, the least—and the most—that he could do. . . .

She was watching him very closely, hardly daring to breathe. He had been looking at her but not seeing her. Now his attention had clearly come back. And slowly, emphatically, he blinked, giving the signal. Giving his assent. . . .

Just the anticipation of Thursday, and meeting Christian Reichart, made her ill. But Thursday arrived, and she forced herself to be calm as she prepared for the evening, for her most important role. The stage had been set, the play was about to begin, curtain going up.

She went down the stairs, looking, she hoped, positively radiant, feeling ready to throw up. She was dressed in layers upon layers of delicate pink chiffon. The top was bare, except for thin shoulder straps, exposing her porcelain skin. Silver pumps showed slightly below the dress as she walked. Her diamond necklace was dazzling. She found herself repeating Solange's words to Rubin so long ago . . . "She will do, Rubin . . . indeed, she will do." God, she hoped so. . . .

It was in a gold and blue baroque ballroom of the German Embassy. A Viennese waltz—naturally—was playing. Appraising the guests, she was shocked to see so many acquaintances present. Tonight they were not only fraternizing with the enemy, they were paying court to their oppressors . . . and, of course, imagining that she was here doing the same. . . .

Above the din of voices she heard someone calling her name. Jean-Paul Dupré. Taking her hand in his, he kissed it. This man, her daughter's brother-in-law, was also the enemy. . . . And now, suddenly, he seemed dangerous, menacing. She must push the thought aside . . . he was Etienne Dupré's brother, after all. Perhaps he was doing the same thing she had been asked to do . . . and, hardly professional yet in her new role, she found herself hoping that Jean-Paul's assumptions about her being here would be the same.

"Countess, I'm delighted to see you."

"Thank you, Jean-Paul."

"You've been missed about town. How is Alexis?"

"Much improved . . ."

"That's good news. But you're alone this evening?" She must have joined our side, he thought. How sensible . . . after all, she's a sensual woman, with a dying husband on her hands . . . and a lover . . . ? There must be . . . and probably more than one. . . .

"May I introduce a friend?" He led her over to his latest mistress . . . a tall slender blonde in a black satin gown, bejeweled with pearls and emeralds. She was a German model turned actress. . . . Paris, she said, was not Berlin, but it had its compensations . . . Jean-Paul among them, she thought—he was so generous, the jewels and furs were fabulous, sometimes she almost forgot he was a Frenchman, supposedly a sympathizer but still a Frenchman and so had to be watched . . . that was the word from Christian Reichart, and one paid attention to Christian. . . .

She stood laughing, with a glass of champagne in one hand and a cigarette in the other, as Jean-Paul waited for the joke being told by a baldheaded General to conclude, then made the introductions.

"How long have you and Jean-Paul been . . . friends?" she said.

Smiling at Jean-Paul, Magda said, "I believe he was just

beginning to shave the fuzz from his chin. . . . What were you, Jean-Paul, seventeen?"

"Eighteen." He gave her back his irresistible smile.

"Eighteen?" Her name was Fredericke Von Brenner. "Were you really ever eighteen, Jean-Paul?"

"I believe so," he said with mannered roguishness, "though, as I recall, fairly precocious—oh, Colonel Reichart, how very good to see you again. May I present Countess Maximov. . . ."

He kissed her hand, and as he did Magda felt, along with her revulsion, that now the play had, indeed, begun. No question, he was quite a specimen. He gave off charm on charm. He knew how to make a woman believe that she was the only person in the room. . . . Well, he was the only man in the room for her. This was the enemy, and now that they were face to face she was almost relieved. She understood her job. He was a man, she could handle it. This would be one conquest he would regret making.

"May I have the pleasure of this dance, Countess?" he was saying.

"If you like," she said, her voice faintly arch and not especially impressed. Well, that didn't offend him. In fact, he found it refreshing . . . besides, along with her title, this one also was a *woman* . . . that was clear. He wondered how it was that he hadn't met her before. . . .

After the dance he summoned a circulating waiter for champagne. "To your health, Countess."

"And to victory . . ."

He looked at her closely. "You find the German occupation acceptable? For a French woman . . . by the way, you are French?"

"No . . . my husband was born in Russia, but we've lived in many places. His allegiance is to whatever government serves us well."

"And yours . . . Countess?"

"My allegiance is more specific; my mother and grandmother were German—"

"You were born in Germany?"

"No, in Poland . . . where my father was born."

"I see . . . I take it they met on a holiday, fell in love and got married?"

"You must be clairvoyant. . . . That's almost precisely

the way it happened. My mother, though, was never anything but German, as were our servants, and my governess. Yes, I'm quite German."

"Even having spent your childhood in Poland?"

"Geography has nothing to do with feeling. You are in France at the moment."

He smiled slightly. "Countess . . . you seem to be a rare combination of beauty and intelligence. Why haven't we met before?"

"My husband suffered a very serious stroke and I've been . . . out of things for some time. But now the doctors say he no longer needs my constant attention, so I felt I should do what I can for my people. . . ."

After three more dances she decided the time had come for a strategic withdrawal, and when he asked to see her home, she kept a careful balance between being coy and eager—managing a faintly interested coolness.

By the time they arrived, Magda knew perhaps more about Christian Reichart than he about her. He was married, his wife had brought a large dowry to the marriage, his three children were his favorites. He was fond of small children, dogs, horses. His wife owned a bank, which he controlled. He had ambitions for the top intelligence job in Germany . . . Heinrich Himmler's, no less. He was young, he had patience, he would wait and it would come. Paris was his showcase. . . . The Fuhrer would notice.

Magda offered him a glass of kümmel, and as he sipped it in the spacious salon . . . a good distance from the bedrooms, and Alexis, he admired the antiques and paintings, which, if it weren't that he was so taken with Magda, he would have had no qualms about requisitioning along with the entire place. But not for now. Later, of course, he'd have both.

Magda watched the wheels of his mind turning. Suave he might be, but hardly subtle. He sat down beside her on the sofa. "Tell me about your husband."

Matter-of-factly she repeated the details of Alexis' stroke, as though it were something long since adjusted to.

"But how could you cut yourself off from the world? You strike me as a very normal woman. . . ."

"As I told you, I felt I had an obligation, that is the way I was raised . . . the German way. . . . Surely you understand that"—(just as surely, she thought, as she understood what his questions were leading up to. . .). "Now, with the war, I feel I must involve myself . . . as I said, I'd like to be useful in some way."

"Is that why you came to the Embassy this evening?"

"Yes, I suppose so. . . ."

So far he was very pleased, and even a little flattered— not common for him. This was a woman of obvious means, titled, and a genuine German sympathizer . . . not the sort he'd been meeting lately whose politics and bed partners were strictly a matter of who was on top . . . he smiled to himself at his private little joke. No, this one had, so far as he could make out, nothing at all to gain, and if he should later discover otherwise, he would know how to act . . . but for now, she was for the taking, and he was an experienced taker.

"Tell me," he said, "do you still love your husband? Truthfully, now."

She shrugged her shoulders. "I married rather young, without experience. The marriage was quite appropriate . . . I was attracted to Alexis . . . I respected him enormously . . . he was an older man . . . I still respect him. . . ."

"But now he is a sick older man. And you are . . . as you are . . ." (Time to get to it) . . . "Don't you ever want other men?"

Right on schedule, she thought. Just like a good German, damn his rottenness. . . . "Are you asking for confessions, Colonel? Those are for priests or very old friends. . . ."

"I am hardly the former, but would very much like to be the latter. . . . I repeat, no other men?"

"None. Never."

"Difficult to believe."

She looked at him. "Not at all. More than anything else, I've never met another man I found equal to Alexis, that I could admire, look up to as I have him."

He immediately went up to her, pulled her close to him. "Are you so certain of that?"

"Not quite so certain as I was."

It was, of course, all that was needed. And afterward, on the bed, feeling numb so as not to be sick, she reminded herself again that it was a role, that she was playing a character that was not herself, and that more and better lives than her own were dependent on the success of her performance. . . .

Three months passed. Her relationship with Reichart had fallen into a pattern. Thank God he worked all day, leaving her free to care for Alexis. . . . But at night . . . She had unquestionably become his mistress, and more than one of the colonel's associates envied his extraordinary good fortune . . . she entertained beautifully, the perfect hostess, and what a pleasure she must be in bed. . . .

By now, in fact, Magda had learned how to handle not only her own emotions but his as well. She was his confidante, and without realizing it he gave her much valuable information in the context of their easy, familiar conversation. Familiarity, she thought, not only bred contempt (hers) but also confidence (his).

She knew how to calm him, massaging his neck and shoulders when he came to her, raging about what would happen. "If we don't find out how those damn Jews are escaping . . . I'll send the whole office to Berlin to be shot . . . I swear it."

"The Jews are escaping? How?"

"If I knew the answer to that I could—"

"Listen to me, Christian . . . perhaps the French are buying off your men?"

He looked at her shrewdly. "I wouldn't say this to everyone, but I think that's precisely what's happened . . . and I swear I'll find out—"

"If anyone can, I'm sure you will. . . ."

He was tired. He wanted to take a bath. She led him into the bathroom and turned on the water taps. While the bath was filling, she undressed him. He especially liked that.

While he lay back in the tub, closing his eyes, and began loudly humming his favorite Wagnerian—naturally—aria . . . God, how she detested it . . . she went out to the bedroom, quickly took the briefcase off the desk, opened it and went through the contents. She'd done it a hundred times, and her memory had become so keen that she could remember dates, times, places and names without writing them down. Quickly her eyes read through the pages, making mental notes. Suddenly her heart almost stopped beating. There it was, in black and white.

The dossier read: Jeanette Hack Dupré. Jew. One son, Henri. Time of arrest, 7:00 A.M. Date, November 2. Destination, Dachau.

Meticulously she put the contents back into the briefcase, replaced it on the desk. She began to tremble, and couldn't stop. November 2 . . . my God, *tomorrow* . . . She wanted to kill him at once. But if she killed him, would that save Jeanette and her son? No. Then what should she do? Whatever she decided, she must *not* panic. Now was the time for matching wits. . . . She ordered herself to remain calm . . . to play out her role. She had a feeling that, for better or worse, it would soon be over.

It was no problem for her to dissolve a sleeping pill in his coffee during dinner . . . he was already drowsy. . . . Afterward he got into bed and, sitting next to him, she said, "You know, my dear, you really need to relax more." And he'd sleepily agreed, smiling and holding her hand, and then his grip relaxed and he had fallen asleep . . . soundly, she hoped, at least for a few hours. She personally saw to it that his cup was carefully rinsed out . . . not a trace could be left in the cup to arouse suspicion . . . then went straight to Pierre and told him the awful news. "I'll stay with Alexis until you get back. . . . Go to Anjou . . . tell him what's happened . . . he'll know what to do. Oh, God, *hurry* . . ."

Late that night the doorbell rang at the Dupré mansion on the Boulevard Victor Hugo. A small man wearing wire-rimmed glasses was admitted. Impeccably dressed, he took off his hat, revealing the sparse hair on his shining scalp. Nervously, he waited for Etienne to come to the library.

When he joined him Etienne was dressed in his robe and slippers. "Charles, my dear friend, what brings you here so late? Sit down. You look sick. Let me get you a brandy."

Charles sat down in a chair facing the painting of Marshal Dupré. His forehead broke out in perspiration. He gratefully accepted a glass of brandy.

"Now, Charles, tell me what's wrong?"

"Etienne—I don't know how to tell you this—"

"Relax, calm yourself. After all, we've been friends for a

very long time, since our days in school together. Now please tell me . . ."

Charles hesitated, cleared his throat. "Etienne, you know that for me to exist, I have to pretend to support the present regime. I have no other choice, I've been in the government all my life . . ."

"I understand, you know that . . . but what is so pressing tonight?"

"Etienne, I am a *Frenchman*. I may seem to work with the Germans but I am also in the underground, and it would mean my life and the lives of my children if that were known. You understand that . . . ?"

"Of course, Charles, and I admire you for it. I wish I . . . but never mind . . . does your coming here tonight have anything to do with me?" he suddenly asked.

Charles hesitated, then answered very quietly, "Yes, I'm afraid it does . . . Etienne, the Gestapo is scheduled to pick up your wife and son—"

Etienne looked at him as though he hadn't heard, and then as though what he'd heard was the outpouring of a crazy man. . . . "Charles, I know you mean well, but this is impossible, surely you're mistaken . . ."

"I wish I were, Etienne, God knows I do. But you must believe it, there's not much time—"

"What do you mean, not much time? What time? When . . . ?"

"Seven, tomorrow morning—"

"My God, you're certain?"

"Yes, Etienne, I'm certain—"

"How did you find out?"

"Don't ask me that, Etienne."

"But I want to know, I must know . . . how could the Gestapo possibly find out? All the records were changed . . . a priest . . . Who could have told them? Damn you, Charles, *tell me* . . . "

The man slumped down in his chair. He couldn't find his voice. Etienne went to him where he sat and shook him. "*Tell me.*"

Silence. Then . . . "Jean-Paul . . ."

Etienne stared at him again as though he were a mad man. Surely he was wrong. Jean-Paul had less than a brotherly love for him, he knew, and there had been times when it was clear that some tensions existed between him-

self and Jeanette. . . . But to think that . . . no, it was
monstrous, impossible . . . "Charles, I ask you again, are
you sure . . . my brother . . . ?"

"Yes, absolutely sure. We have our people working all
over Paris. I was informed, and told to come to you at
once. . . . Etienne, you must believe it. I swear it . . .
on my children, I swear it. . . . Etienne, you aren't the
first, I'm afraid you won't be the last. . . . And now
you've got to put aside your disbelief and listen carefully
to what I tell you. You must go to Switzerland. Take the
route to Basel . . . that's *very* important, because that
road has no strategical importance to the Germans, there
are only a few border guards at that check point. For
God's sake, Etienne, go now and give your family a
chance. In a few hours it will be too late. . . ."

Etienne nodded, finally accepting. "Charles, dear
friend, I've no idea how I can thank you, I know the risk
you've taken coming here to say this to me . . . you must
go now."

As Etienne entered the room, Jeanette sat up in bed,
startled. "What's wrong?" she said. "You look so pale."

He sat on the bed and held her close to him. "I've something to tell you . . ."

From the sound of his voice, she knew it was urgent.
"What's wrong, Etienne?"

"Darling, I want you to listen to me. . . . I want you to
pack a bag with only the basic necessities. Then go to
Henri's room and do the same. When you've finished,
bring him back here, put him to bed and let him sleep.
Get dressed in your warmest clothing. Take only the coat
you will wear. Just before we leave we'll dress Henri—"

"*Leave?* Oh, my God, I understand, it's because of me.
No, Etienne. You and Henri stay. There are places I can
go but you and Henri can't leave—"

He took her face in his hands. "Sshh, we've no time for
such nonsense. We're a family. We're driving to Switzerland together. I've had the passports for a long time, we'll
have no problems—"

"No, Etienne, I can't let you do this for me—"

"I'm doing it for you *and* me, and our son. . . . Now,
please, darling, do as I ask. . . . I've something to do be-

fore we leave, so dry your tears, there's no need for them. Just thank God we still have time." He kissed her quickly and went to dress. She followed him.

"Where are you going, Etienne?"

"I'll be back shortly. Just do as I ask. Tell *no one* we're leaving."

"Not even Madeleine?"

"No one. Not even *maman* . . . I'll tell her just before we leave."

Somehow, Jeanette managed to pull herself together, but as she did what Etienne had asked, she knew that it was she and she alone who had brought this terror down on their home. She felt an overwhelming sense of foreboding as she packed, then went down the hall to get her son. Quietly, so as not to awaken Madeleine asleep in the adjacent bedroom, she picked up her sleeping child. . . .

It was two A.M. when the door of Jean-Paul's house was opened by his butler. "*Bonsoir*, monsieur. Your brother is asleep. Shall I—"

Etienne pushed him aside with his cane and made his way loudly up the stairs to Jean-Paul's room.

Switching on the bedside lamp, Jean-Paul saw Etienne coming toward him, his breathing labored, his eyes clearly showing his rage and hatred. He knew immediately why Etienne was here. He felt sick to his stomach. How . . . how had he found out? Who . . . ?

Etienne stood over the bed now. He lifted his cane and struck his brother across the chest.

"You're crazy . . . you damn cripple, get out of my house."

Etienne's answer was to drag him out of the bed. Jean-Paul broke away and staggered against the wall, Etienne following.

"You unbelievable, depraved bastard . . . I knew how you felt about me, but why Jeanette? My wife, the mother of your child—"

"*My* child? You *are* insane."

"I'm not insane, or blind—"

"What the hell do you mean?"

"I mean, I know. I've known from the beginning, as soon as Jeanette told me she was pregnant—"

"And you've put up with that? You've lived with her knowing *that?*"

"Yes. You wouldn't understand it, but I lived with that. Do you really think I don't know about you, how you've behaved with women, what you've done to your own wife? Do you imagine I don't know that you married her for her inheritance, would have refused to divorce her for Jeanette? No, my Casanova brother, you did me a favor. You swept her off her feet, a young girl, a young and innocent girl. I could never have done that, but I could recognize a gift, and that is what she gave me, and I was grateful for the opportunity to take it."

"Were you also grateful that she was my mistress . . . ? You didn't know *that*, did you? All those years, she was coming to me—"

Etienne went even paler, and for a moment felt a stabbing sensation . . . and then there was no more time for such indulgence, only for getting out the last of his fury against the cringing—yes, by God, cringing—figure in front of him. . . . Except now, of course, he understood Jean-Paul's special hatred for Jeanette. She had left him, humiliated him, and for his cripple of a brother. And now he was taking his revenge, but what kind of man would . . . ?

"My God, Jean-Paul, I finally understand you, and it sickens me so much I can't even bring myself to break this cane over your miserable head—which, God knows, you deserve. But Henri, *your own son* . . . Henri is a Jew too as far as your friends are concerned. *What kind of man are you, a man who'd destroy his own son?* That, I can't understand—"

"Never mind about my son, I've taken care of him. I always will—"

"You've 'taken care of him'? You're crazy. Do you really think those people are going to be *loyal* to you? Do you think they are about to make exceptions for a traitor, a collaborator, when they have gassed millions of their own people?"

The sweat was pouring from Jean-Paul now.

"You didn't plan this as carefully as you thought. This time you have the Nazis, not a young girl and your mother, to deceive and use . . . oh, God, I should kill you . . ." But instead he pushed him against the wall, and with all his strength hit him with the back of his hand so hard that Jean-Paul reeled and the blood came from his mouth as he slumped to the floor. If he went on, Etienne knew, he would kill him, and would have been pleased to pay for the pleasure of it, but he suspected there were others more practiced than himself in such matters who would take care of Jean-Paul. . . . And meanwhile there were Jeanette and Henri . . . and there was *maman* . . . poor *maman*. . . . He'd tell her as little as possible, but he had to prepare her.

He took one last look at his brother slumped in a heap on the floor, then turned and left.

At first when he told her that the three of them had to go to Switzerland immediately—leaving out the identity of the informer against Jeanette—she simply refused to take it in. And then, all the wonderful regal reserve and strength that she'd maintained through so much loss and tragedy in her life simply gave way, and she was what she was . . . a terrified and stricken old lady, crying her heart out for what she could neither comprehend nor accept.

Etienne held her until she'd quieted some, then took her face in his hands as she'd done to him when he was upset as a child, and, speaking slowly and with emphasis, told her, "No one, *maman*, no one, it's important you remember that, must be told about our leaving or where we are going. I feel guilty for even telling you, but I wanted to spare you at least the worry of not knowing, of imagining God knows what. But I repeat, if anyone asks you, you must say you weren't told, that we wanted to protect you. Our lives depend on it, *maman*. . . ."

She looked at him now, more composed but still shaking. "I'll do my best, Etienne, but, please, let's see what Jean-Paul can do. He does have influence, after all. He is in the government. He is so clever . . ."

"No, *maman*. Jean-Paul is as helpless in this as any of us. Believe me. You mustn't involve him, it could be very dangerous for him. . . . Now, remember what I have told you. . . ."

Of course he hadn't told everything. What would it serve to destroy in her eyes, to take away from her the last of her family? Let her go on believing in him as long as she could, it would hurt no one. To do otherwise would surely kill her—her firstborn a traitor and murderer . . . surely that knowledge would be the end of her. . . .

As they took their good-byes, she said very little and, watching them get into the car, then drive off, she felt numb, a brief defense against the grief that soon began to intrude as she stood there in the dark . . . Denise; Etienne, her favorite; Jeanette, whom she loved as a daughter; poor Marie Jacqueline; her precious Henri; her beloved husband . . . all gone now, all except Jean-Paul. Thank God, at least, for that, for Jean-Paul. . . .

Jean-Paul, trying to soak out in the tub the throbbing pain in his chest, was even more bothered by the fact that Etienne had been forewarned and that Jean-Paul had no idea by whom. . . . And he wondered what Etienne had told *maman* . . . in a way, that was most terrifying of all to him, having to face her if she knew. . . . His thoughts went from that unpleasant prospect to a mounting anger at whoever on his staff—it had to be one of them, with access to privileged information—had given him away. Well, he would find out. . . . He lay back, gingerly touching his jaw, wondering if it were broken, trying to block out the image of Etienne and his astonishing turn-about performance. Finally, long after he'd closed his eyes, he achieved the temporary escape of deep, obliterating sleep . . .

. . . out of which he was awakened by the jangling of the telephone. He glanced at the clock, still half-asleep. 5:30. He picked up the receiver, said "Hello," and listened to his mother's voice at the other end, demanding, importuning that he come at once. . . .

It was the same voice that he had heard the night Denise had died, the same sound of anger and despair and bereavement. . . . My God, had that little bitch actually told her, no she wouldn't disgrace herself to *maman*, not even now. . . . He must get hold of himself. . . .

By the time he reached the house on the Boulevard Victor Hugo he was wet with perspiration although the morning was chilly. He put his thoughts together slowly, piece by piece, testing the effects. . . . If necessary he would say he'd been *forced* to reveal Jeanette's real identity by the Gestapo, that they'd used their very persuasive methods on him, and, even more, he might still have been able to protect her but they already had information from other sources, other informants, and to hold out further would only have jeopardized *maman*, led them to her and the rest of the family. . . . She needn't worry about Henri, or Etienne, he would somehow manage to protect them . . . it was Jeanette, he was very sorry, but that was the truth of it . . . it was Jeanette they wanted. . . . Well, perhaps it would work, perhaps.

When he saw her face, whatever courage he'd contrived before arriving quickly deserted him. She wasn't the same woman he'd seen only a few days ago. She had aged ten years. Her face was gaunt, the bones standing out under the parchmentlike skin. She shuddered inwardly.

She turned slowly to look at him, aware that she was about to disobey Etienne's strict instructions, but surely, Jean-Paul, his own brother . . . her first-born son . . . "Jean-Paul, I can't believe it's happened, this awful thing, this—"

"What has happened, *maman?*"

She hesitated for a moment, then remembered Etienne had said he hadn't wanted to involve his brother, who was, after all, in the government . . . so of course Jean-Paul didn't know. . . .

"*Maman*," he said, breaking into her thoughts, "I asked you, what's happened? Why are you so upset?"

"Jean-Paul, they've found out about Jeanette . . . the Gestapo—"

"*What?* . . . impossible . . . how? . . ." His tone was appropriately dismayed, disbelieving (and privately he felt enormous relief . . . she didn't know about him, after all), and became more so as she went on with the details about when Jeanette was to have been picked up and the man who had come the previous night to warn Etienne.

"What man, *maman?*" he asked, trying to sound far more casual than he felt.

"I've no idea. Etienne said it would be dangerous for the man, and for me too, perhaps, if he told me his name."

"Of course, Etienne was right. . . ."

"But I did ask him to talk to you, that perhaps you could help. . . . Jean-Paul, I've made my feelings clear to you more than once. I hate the Germans and I don't like it that you even work with them, even though I'm sure no son of mine could be a real Nazi, and I know your duties are important, but above all I know you're a Frenchman and in your own way I realize you feel you're doing the best for your country that you can do now. . . ." She looked almost pleadingly at him. "Tell me, Jean-Paul, tell me that I am right."

"Of course, *maman*, you are completely right . . . we all do what we can, in the way we can do it best."

"I knew it . . . and if only Etienne had asked you for help—"

Jean-Paul was cautious. "And why didn't he, *maman*?"

"He said it would do no good, and that you would only be endangered yourself if he involved you. . . . And now it's too late."

Jean-Paul put aside his curiosity about his brother's remarkable forbearance. "I'm afraid I don't understand, *maman*. You put things in the past. You say 'too late' . . . ?"

It was out of her mouth before she could . . . or would . . . think about it further. She had to tell somebody, her own son. . . . "Etienne has left with Jeanette and Henri—"

" 'Left' . . . ? and . . . where has he taken them, *maman*?"

". . . Switzerland."

"When, *maman*?"

"Oh, Jean-Paul, I'm not sure, I think about two o'clock, perhaps a bit earlier . . ."

"And you waited this long to tell me?"

"I gave Etienne my word not to tell anyone and—"

" 'Anyone' . . . ? I'm your son, don't I have a right to be told?"

"But he made it clear it might be dangerous for you to be involved, because of your position. . . . It was for your sake, he was thinking of you, and now I've put you in danger too, Jean-Paul, but I couldn't help it . . . I couldn't be alone with this any longer." She looked at him, without pretense, without her old brave air, regardless of the personal sorrow. "I suppose, Jean-Paul, I am, after all, just a very old, very frightened woman. I only hope I haven't lost you too by my weakness. . . ."

He nodded, trying to hide his impatience, and to seem to reassure her, and then, finally, asked what was primar-

ily on his mind. "And Henri . . . couldn't you persuade
him at least to leave Henri with you, with us? He'd surely
be safer here."

"It happened so quickly, Jean-Paul. I'm sorry, but I
don't think I could have persuaded them. They'd never
have left their child behind."

He nodded, told her he was sure she was right, and
then she was saying, "Couldn't something be done, Jean-
Paul? Couldn't we bring them back? Don't you have
enough influence . . . perhaps someone could even be
bribed? Never mind the cost, please try, Jean-Paul. . . ."

He sighed, for his reasons, not hers. "We'll see, *maman*. . . ."

Riding back to his home, Jean-Paul found himself with
more conflicting thoughts and feelings than he was accustomed to, or comfortable with. Seeing his mother as she
was—broken, pleading, asking him to reassure her of his
loyalty, that he wasn't a Nazi . . . his deceptions now
and over the years left him feeling something that at least
touched on shame, which all his life he'd considered cow-
ardice and the refuge of weak and stupid people. And the
thought of *his* son, caught up in his own calculated revenge against his brother and Jeanette—*them*, he had no
regrets about—well, it was a horrifying accident, but
Etienne was right, he hadn't taken everything into account, and that thought once again made him wild to lay
his hands on whoever it was that had alerted . . .

And he thought of the Gestapo's reaction about that as
well. . . . Wouldn't they first and naturally suspect *him*
. . . the brother of the man, and a damn Frenchman, none
of them trustworthy, of course. . . . Wouldn't they decide that he had weakened at the last moment and when
he realized he couldn't stop what he'd started had alerted
his brother and advised him to leave. . . . He'd made a
mess of it, face it, he told himself, and there was a flash of
honest revulsion for himself as well, but he quickly reminded himself that there was nothing to do now except
to protect himself as best he could . . . nothing would be
served by sacrificing himself, and he still might save
Henri, he *had* to save his son. . . .

Once home, he went to the telephone and put through

a call to the residence of Herr Heinrich Kessler. He warned himself to be calm, and *convincing* . . . his son's life depended on it.

The connection was made.

"Kessler." The voice was like a knife.

"Jean-Paul Dupré speaking."

"You are calling in regard to the matter discussed?"

"Yes, but there have been some changes, which is the reason for my disturbing you. . . ."

"What changes?"

"The individual discussed has, it seems, been informed and is attempting to leave the country—"

Kessler's voice was ice. "Informed? Interesting. And where exactly has she gone?"

". . . Switzerland, I suspect, perhaps Basel . . . my brother knows the country well and it would be the logical—"

"Very logical," Kessler interrupted, and quickly asked for, and received, the make of the car, description of the passengers. "That will do for now. We will attend to the matter—"

"One more thing, please, Herr Kessler . . ."

"Yes?" The voice was impatient.

"You agreed from the beginning that in this case you would overlook that the boy is half-Jewish. I was very honest with you about the special circumstances . . . that I am the boy's father—"

Silence.

"I am asking that care be taken to see to it that he is returned safely to Paris. . . ."

"We shall do all we can."

"I have your word on that, sir?"

"You have impertinence to ask such a question."

"I'm sorry, sir, but you can understand my concern. . . . I'd also like to be present when the boy is brought back, returned to me . . ."

"Out of the question, Dupré. Now I'm afraid you must excuse me."

And the line was dead.

Kessler called Reichart at once. Magda answered the phone. "Colonel Reichart, please, Herr Kessler calling."

No amenities, or uncertainty about who was answering the telephone. Kessler and most of the German command knew Magda's relationship with Reichart.

Magda shook Christian awake. "Who is it?"

"Herr Kessler."

Irritated at being awakened so early in the morning, Christian grabbed the receiver from Magda's hand. When he heard the news, that the Dupré woman had escaped, he was considerably more than irritated. "Damn you, Kessler, I warn you, she had better be found—"

"I assure you she will be, sir. We have already taken steps—"

"To hell with your steps. Find her and stop her. . . . You've been making too many reports like this to me lately. Too many of them are getting out, it's got to stop. . . . Do you follow me, Kessler?" And hung up before he could hear the "Yes, *sir*," in reply from the other end of the line.

While he'd been talking, Magda had been casually brushing her hair in front of the mirror, doing all she could to hold in the joy and relief she felt. The call had to be about Jeanette, that word had gotten to her husband and that she had managed to escape.

"Damn it," he was now saying, as much to himself as to her, "this is getting to be an epidemic. Where the hell are the leaks coming from? . . . We have tight security, we . . ."

And as he talked his eye casually took in the beauty of Magda and the sensuous line of her arm and back as she combed her hair, and then strayed to his briefcase, lying open on the desk next to her dresser . . . his briefcase that held the papers with schedules of just such arrests as this one involving Jeanette Hack Dupré. Kessler had said they suspected the brother-in-law . . . none of those damn collaborators were reliable . . . but Reichart was beginning to have a different notion, a different and shocking and altogether humiliating one for him. . . . His solicitous noble-born ladyfriend with the conveniently sick husband, *she* had access to that briefcase at will . . . careful as he was, he'd allowed himself to come to trust her. She'd been with him nearly every night, had never given him a moment's trouble or the slightest grounds for suspicion, had in fact often given him useful—if not especially important now that he thought about it—pieces of information that she had overheard at her various parties. . . . But come to think of it, the momentum of escapees had increased rather markedly since shortly after he'd taken up with her. . . .

And then last night, the solicitous business with the bath . . . of course, it wasn't so unusual, she'd been that way on more than one night, but last night she seemed especially attentive, and then the deep sleep he'd fallen into almost immediately after dinner, most unusual for him no matter how tired he was, he always took a long time to relax from the day's tension and to fall asleep. . . . Of course, he'd been drugged, and by none other than his precious Countess. . . .

Feeling his eyes on her, Magda slowly turned around, aware that he'd become suddenly very quiet. "I know you're upset, Christian, and I'm sorry that—"

"I'm sorry that I can't kill you right now—"

"What? . . . That's a rather remarkable and not very funny thing to say and—"

"Oh, give it up. I've been stupid and I've paid for it, but at least now I know who's been responsible. My darling, beloved countess . . . Well, aren't you going to deny it? I believe that's customary for all spies. Or are the rules different for whores?"

Magda said nothing, merely looked steadily at him, but she felt a profound relief—the pretending, the play-acting was over. Somehow word had gotten to Jeanette and she'd escaped . . . and that made everything she'd gone through worthwhile. . . . And now, Magda Charascu, curtain coming down . . .

She barely paid attention to the rest of his threats and rantings . . . he would kill her on the spot, would dearly love to, but that would be too easy for her. . . . He was on the phone, making arrangements to have guards sent at once before he left, and then telling her if she tried to escape she would be shot. . . .

After he'd gone, she went immediately to Alexis, and knelt by his bedside. "It's over, my darling," she whispered softly, careful not to wake him. She called in Pierre and told him what had happened. "Tell Anjou," she instructed him. "Tell him to contact his people. . . .

Jeanette has left, but now they'll be alerting guards to stop her. . . . Please, hurry, Pierre. She'll need their help . . . and don't worry about Alexis, I'll see that they don't harm him. . . ." They embraced without a word, two very old and very good friends.

After Pierre had left, Magda picked up the syringe and this time filled it with a massive dose of morphine. She rolled up the sleeve of Alexis' pajamas, as she'd done so many times before, and injected the drug into his vein. She sat down on the bed beside him, took him in her arms, kissed him and held him until she felt his body slowly becoming cold. "Good-bye, my love, rest well." And then she lay him back down and placed the sheet over his head.

Turning, she went to her desk, sat down and wrote two notes.

The first was to Pierre, asking him, if he returned before the Germans, to see to it if possible that Alexis had a proper burial. He was, after all, a Count. . . . And, she added to herself, the only man in the world, except for her father, that she had ever really loved.

The second was to Colonel Christian (the irony of his name seemed greater than ever at this moment) Reichart:

> *Dear Colonel:*
>
> *I am grateful to you for the opportunity, at last, to make my life have some meaning. Jeanette Hack Dupré is my daughter. The informant we used to pass on my information to her husband was your friend Jean-Paul Dupré, who, you may remember, first introduced you to me. He has turned out to be a patriot after all.*
>
> Signed *Magda Hack Charascu, of Bucharest. Jew.*

She carefully folded the two notes into separate envelopes, placing Pierre's on the still body of Alexis, the other carefully and prominently propped up against the mirror. She then took out a small revolver from the drawer of the night table, lay down on the bed alongside Alexis, placed the muzzle of the gun against her temple and pulled the trigger.

* * *

Colonel Reichart was surprised when he found her. She had seemed strangely quiet when he'd accused her, but he'd assumed that was merely resignation and fear. It hadn't occurred to him that she'd do this. . . . Actually, he'd thought she'd try to escape and be shot, and they'd be done with her. Even by her death she had deceived him. . . . He noted the envelope, then, and quickly read it, shaking his head, feeling more than ever cheated, and worried about the reaction of his superiors to this latest in his repeated failures to stop the underground. He still didn't know their headquarters . . . even though they'd confiscated numerous short-wave radios in individual homes, attics, that sort of thing. He was not altogether convinced by her accusation about Jean-Paul Dupré, who seemed too ambitious and cynical for such last-minute heroics. But never mind, Kessler thought him a likely suspect, others would too, and just now Reichart badly needed *something* to begin to redeem himself with. . . . He picked up the phone and called Gestapo headquarters. "This is Colonel Reichart. Pick up Jean-Paul Dupré immediately for questioning in connection with the escape of Jeanette Hack Dupré. . . ."

Twenty-six

With the curfew, getting out of Paris in the early morning hours was extremely difficult. Etienne took to the narrow alleys and side streets, proceeding slowly to avoid the patrols.

Finally they were on the road toward Creteil, the first village on their itinerary. Etienne stayed off the main roads, even going through pastures when possible. Henri slept until dawn, and when he awoke he became restless and hungry. Jeanette gave him a sandwich and poured a cup of milk from the thermos, which spilled out of the cup as they went over the bumpy roads.

Etienne spoke softly now as they drove on. "Henri, papa is going to ask you to do something."

"Yes, papa?"

"We have a long way to go, and I know this is very difficult for you, but will you try and be patient?"

"Where are we going?"

"On a holiday, we'll have a fine time—"

"I don't want to go. Please, papa, I want to go home . . ." and he started to cry.

Jeanette's heart pounded as she said, "Henri, please don't cry. Papa is right, we'll have a wonderful holiday."

He looked at his mother and sniffed back the tears. "But where are we going?"

"To a place called Switzerland."

"Where is it?"

"It's a beautiful place. You'll see, you'll love it. Papa and I have always wanted to take you there with us. It's a favorite place of papa's. There's snow and high mountains and you'll play and we'll make a snow man—"

"Will it look like papa?"

"Yes, we'll make him look just like papa."

"When will we go home?"

"After our holiday."

"Can't grandma and Lucien and Nicole and Desirée come?"

"Yes . . . later."

He seemed more content as Jeanette took him up on her lap and held him close to her. God, the terrible things she'd brought into their lives. All of this was because of her. . . .

She looked at her husband's bearded face, and the eyes straining ahead. She didn't deserve him. . . . She saw herself lying with Jean-Paul, and involuntarily shuddered . . . in a way it was fitting that he was the one finally to "expose" her . . . but how unfair that her son and husband should be brought down with her. . . . If only she had died before Etienne had given life back to her, *that* would have been a blessing . . . her husband and son would not be on their way with her now to . . . She pushed the thought from her mind and prayed that *they* would somehow live through this. . . .

Etienne's eyes were bloodshot, his body ached with fatigue, and it was clear that he was barely able to keep from falling asleep at the wheel. When they reached Vitry-le-François, half-way between Paris and Basel, Jeanette pleaded with Etienne to stop for a moment. It was a tiny village, picturesque, far off the main highway.

"Please, Etienne, we must stop. You can't go on without at least a few minutes rest—"

"No, the only thing we have on our side is time."

"But a few minutes . . . or at least let me drive for a while."

He reluctantly agreed to the latter, and stopped the car so they could change places. On their way again, Etienne's eyes would involuntarily close in sleep for a few moments, then he would rouse himself and strain to stay awake.

When they reached the village of Neuf Château, which was one hundred and fifty miles from the border, Etienne once again took over the wheel.

Up to now they had been able to stay off the main

roads, but that was impossible now as they neared the border. Mulhouse was the last place before reaching the checkpoint between France and Basel. This was the moment he most feared, but surprisingly there were only a few truckloads of soldiers going in the opposite direction.

Only once were they stopped. Etienne, motioned to halt, veered off to the side of the road, a corporal got off his motorcycle and came toward him. They held their breath. "Why are we stopping, papa?" Henri asked.

"It's nothing, Henri, the man just wants to see my driver's license. Now go back to sleep, little one," Etienne said quietly to reassure the boy, but Henri watched wide-eyed as the soldier walked around the car and then came to Etienne's side. He was dusty and dirty from the miles he must have traveled. He did not remove the goggles as he questioned Etienne in German; his voice was hard, clipped. He asked Etienne what was he doing on the road, where was he going?

Etienne answered in German that he was a Swiss citizen, that he and his family were on their way home to Geneva. He didn't wait for the soldier to ask for the passport—which one of Anjou's practiced forgers had, with near-miraculous speed, provided for Etienne, as well as Jeanette and Henri—instead immediately took it out of his breast pocket and handed it to the man, who looked it over, then at Etienne for a long moment, scrutinizing him, and then waved them on.

Etienne began to breathe easier, and Jeanette relaxed her hold on Henri. With luck, they would arrive at the border within two hours. . . .

Just before they reached the border checkpoint, Etienne steeled himself. When they came to a stop, he looked beyond. Just a few feet away was Switzerland. He could almost reach out and touch it.

The border guard came to Etienne's side and once again Etienne had his passport ready. But the guard didn't even look at it. Instead, he ordered them to get out of the car and follow him into the station house. Etienne protested that they were Swiss citizens and he had no right to detain them, but the guard opened the door and poised his gun. It spoke for itself . . . and for him.

Etienne guessed what must have happened. His mother had called Jean-Paul after all. Why else would they be detained? He should have gone along with his logic and not told her where they were going. Of course, poor *maman* had no way of knowing that Jean-Paul was the architect of this horror. But thinking of it now, it might have been better to have told her the truth than to risk her having to bear what was about to happen now. All very well by hindsight, but there had been so little time to think, the shock was so great, and she already had suffered so much. . . .

They were taken to an anteroom where they sat on a wooden bench. The stillness was ominous. The only sound was of their own breathing, except once they heard car doors slam and the sound of footsteps outside.

Henri began to cry. He said he was cold, and hungry. Etienne picked him up and held him until the crying stopped.

It seemed hours before two armed guards finally appeared to escort them across the hall to a spare, crudely furnished office.

Behind the desk sat Herr Kessler, who had been flown to the border and had just arrived. A black trenchcoat was buttoned up to his neck against the cold. He did not look up as they entered but continued to read the documents on the desk. There was no place to sit down.

Etienne was holding Henri in his right arm, balancing himself on his cane. Jeanette stood beside him. They waited at least two full minutes before Kessler acknowledged their presence with an abrupt "What is your name?"

"Robert Bochet."

"And your wife's name?"

"Marie Bochet."

"Is that your name?" He was looking at Jeanette.

"Yes, Marie Bochet."

"And what is your name?" This question, softly put, was for Henri.

The little boy began to answer, and Etienne interrupted: "His name is André Bochet, he stutters, I'm sorry . . ."

Kessler waved it aside. "Where were you born?"

"In Geneva . . . Switzerland."

"And your wife?"

"Geneva."

"And the child?"

"Geneva."

"Where are you going?"

"Home."

"Where is that?"

"Geneva."

"Why did you choose to come by way of Basel?"

"It's the shortest route from Paris."

"What were you doing in Paris?"

"I was working there."

"Doing what?"

"I worked in a bank."

"What bank?"

"The Bank of Paris."

"On what street?"

"The Rue de la Paix."

"Why did you suddenly decide to leave?"

"My mother is very sick."

Kessler glanced down at the documents, then looked up again. "Is the name Dupré familiar?"

Etienne paused, as though to search his memory. "Yes, I would say so . . ."

"You've heard the name before?"

"Yes."

"When?"

"It's not an uncommon French name."

"Do you know anyone by that name personally?"

"No, I don't believe so."

Kessler's face tightened in exasperation. "I suggest you stop these lies. There's no point in it, you know." He held up a thick file, complete with case histories, and spread it out in front of Etienne, whose body seemed to slump. What was the use of going on with the charade? It was there, all there. Courtesy of Jean-Paul. . . . He wanted to scream out, and was about to when he felt Jeanette's hand on his, though she was looking straight ahead, straight into Kessler's eyes.

"Well," Kessler insisted, "is the name familiar to you?"

"Yes."

"How familiar?"

"I am Etienne Dupré."

"And your wife?"

"Jeanette."

"Jeanette what?"

"Jeanette Dupré."

"Her maiden name, damn you."

"Her maiden name, damn *you*," Jeanette said, no longer willing to let Etienne bear all the brunt, wanting desperately, finally, to declare herself, "is *Hack*."

"And what is the origin of that name, Madame?"

"A fine and honorable man, which is something you wouldn't understand—"

Kessler nodded. "And what was the *race* of this fine and honorable—"

"For God's sake, stop it," Etienne broke in. "*Stop it. You know*—"

"I'm waiting," Kessler said, looking at Jeanette.

"I am a Jew," Jeanette said, never taking her eyes from him.

Kessler smiled, nodded. "And no doubt proud of it—"

"Never more than at this moment," she said.

Kessler got up, put the documents into his briefcase, then motioned to the guards. They were taken out of the room, then down three wooden steps. Etienne held Jeanette's hand tightly. When they left the building the guards pulled them apart, and transferred Henri from his father's to his mother's arms. Jeanette, breaking down finally at being separated, screamed as she and Henri were being led to one waiting car and Etienne to another. Suddenly Etienne tore loose from the guards holding his arms and began to flail at them with his cane. . . . "You can't, goddamn you, you can't separate us, you can't—"

But he didn't get the last words out as the butt of a rifle swung by one of the guards grazed his head, momentarily dazing him. Shaking his head, he had put up his hands to ward off the next blow that was being aimed at him when a confusion of yelling and shooting broke out all around them, and from behind the hedges surrounding the station house appeared nearly a dozen ragtag men with guns, men who minutes before might have been mistaken for ordinary local citizens, but who were actually partisans, alerted by the network that had begun with Magda's word to Pierre, passed on to Anjou, and from him eventually to these skilled men who knew their job and proceeded to do it with fine and deadly skill. Within moments Kessler, riddled by a spray of bullets, was on the ground, his briefcase landing beside him, and six guards, taken completely by surprise, quickly fell around him. Immediately one of the partisans instructed Etienne and Jeanette to get into their car and crash the barrier gate, which was all that was left between them and Switzerland, and then he and his small group dispersed, leaving seven still bodies behind them.

Jeanette, with Henri in her arms, ran to the car, and Etienne, still slightly dazed from the head blow, hobbled after them. Once they were all in the car, Jeanette put Henri between them, got behind the wheel, started the engine, and drove off. A few yards ahead was Switzerland. She pressed her foot down hard on the accelerator. As the car crashed through the gates, one guard, fatally wounded but still able to watch their progress, managed to lift his body just enough to prop his rifle up and fire after them.

The bullet went through the back window, splintering it, and from the corner of her eye Jeanette saw Etienne slump forward, heard a curious, hissing sound, and his almost gentle intake of breath. She didn't dare stop driving until she was across the border and then somehow she slammed on the brakes, bringing the car to a screeching halt as the Swiss border guards came running up.

By the time she got out of the car Jeanette was hysterical, telling the guards that her husband had been shot, that she was afraid he was dead, please for God's sake somebody help . . . and they tried to calm her as one of them quickly took Etienne's pulse and assured her he was alive, and the other called for an ambulance that arrived within minutes. Etienne, unconscious, was lifted onto the stretcher and placed inside, an intravenous needle was inserted, and blood given while he also received an injection to help stop the bleeding. Finally, a dazed, weeping Jeanette and a thoroughly bewildered and terrified Henri were helped into the front of the ambulance, and it sped away.

Etienne was taken to the operating room immediately. Jeanette stood outside, praying. There was nothing else left. Henri clung to her hand, and she tried to reassure him that papa would be fine, the doctors would make him well, just as they had mama when she'd been sick . . . when she'd been so sick she would have died if Etienne hadn't given her his kidney, his life. God . . . he mustn't die . . . he, more than all the rest of them, had earned the right to live, not just because of what he had done for her, but for what he was . . . the kind of man he was. . . .

When a doctor finally came out of the operating room, his mask pulled down from his face but still tied around his neck, she quickly went up to him and asked . . .

"It's too soon to know, I'm afraid, madame," and the doctor quickly walked away. Soon after a nurse came and took her and Henri for a snack in a place downstairs. Henri ate, but Jeanette sat like a statue, unable to eat or speak.

Two hours later Etienne was being wheeled down the hall to his room. From the glimpse she was able to manage, it seemed to Jeanette that he was barely alive, his face a ghastly gray, contrasting with the sterile hospital white of the sheet tucked all around him. Jeanette followed down the hall until they reached his room. She was asked to remain outside. She refused a seat, choosing to stand, leaning against the wall.

"I'm Dr. Engelmann."

The voice startled her. She had allowed her eyes to close, in spite of herself. Now she looked at him uneasily. "My husband . . . how is he?"

"He's sustained considerable chest damage, the repairs were extensive . . ."

"Will he . . . live?"

"There's no way to make a good prediction now . . . in forty-eight hours . . ."

For two days Etienne lay in a coma. . . . Jeanette could do nothing but sit by and wait.

Meanwhile, the nurses had fallen in love with Henri. They allowed him to play in the children's ward, where some of the young patients, recovering from ski injuries, were done up fearsomely in elaborate assortments of splints and casts, which fascinated Henri. He particularly liked one little girl. She had, in fact, become his best friend, the first one he'd ever had. "When my papa gets better," he told her, "we're going on a holiday, and I'm going to make a snow man that looks just like him. Would you like to come and visit us?"

"If my mother says I can."

"We could have fun. I have three cousins."

"I have six."

He was even more impressed with her now.

At dawn on the third morning Jeanette awakened after an almost sleepless night and lay looking out her window toward the snowcapped mountains. Today they would know, and she told herself that if anything happened to Etienne, if he did not recover . . . well, she would live for Henri, but it would be winter for all the seasons of the rest of her life without Etienne. . . . And then there was a gentle knock on the door, and she was too frightened to move, even to speak out. She was trying to prepare herself for the worst. . . .

Now the door was opening, and the doctor's voice was saying, "Madame, you are very lazy this morning. Your husband is waiting for you—"

She was out of bed, running without her robe or any other thought to Etienne's room, which was next door. His eyes were open, a weak smile was on his face. He slowly held out his hand to her, and in a voice barely above a whisper, said, "Good morning, darling. It seems we've managed to survive, after all."

In answer, she bent down and kissed him, over and over, smiling and laughing and letting her tears of gratitude fall freely onto that precious face.

Survive, indeed. Could the daughter of Magda Charascu have done otherwise?

ABOUT THE AUTHOR

CYNTHIA FREEMAN was born in New York City and
moved with her family to California. She has lived
most of her life in San Francisco with her husband,
a prominent physician. They have a son, a daughter
and three grandchildren. A believer in self-education,
Cynthia Freeman has been determined since childhood to pursue knowledge for its own sake and not
for the credentials. Her interest in formal education
ceased in the sixth grade, but, at fifteen, feeling
scholastically ready, she attended classes at the University of California as an auditor only, not receiving
credit. Her literary career began at the age of fifty-
five, after twenty-five years as a successful interior
designer. Cynthia Freeman is also the author of *A
World Full of Strangers* and *Fairytales*.

The World of
Cynthia Freeman

Amazingly, she began writing at the age of 55. Mrs. Freeman, housewife, mother and grandmother had been an interior decorator, but an illness forced her to end this occupation. Then she turned to writing. Four years later, her first novel *A WORLD FULL OF STRANGERS* was completed. But only after a number of rejections was it published. Readers soon found in this unknown author a writer who could create spellbinding characters and stories. Her first book went on to sell over 1,500,000 copies in paperback. Mrs. Freeman followed this with *FAIRYTALES* and *THE DAYS OF WINTER*, and her audience continued to grow. At the age of 65 her national bestseller *PORTRAITS*, followed by *COME POUR THE WINE*, has made her a national figure.

COME POUR THE WINE

In her latest bestseller, Cynthia Freeman delineates the insightful and moving story of Janet Stevens. As a naive teenager from Kansas she comes to New York in search of fame and fortune. The pursuit of her dream leads her into marriage, motherhood, a heart-rending separation and then divorce. At the age of forty-five, she meets a man who not only gives her a renewed sense of her Jewish heritage, but also offers her the chance for total fulfillment as a woman.

A WORLD OF STRANGERS

A sweeping saga spanning three generations in America. The novel traces the lives of Katie and David Rezinetsky as they struggle from the New York ghettos to the world of success among the glittering hills of San Francisco. David destroys his past to live a life of power and glory. Katie cannot forget her past. And their son must make a courageous decision about his heritage.

FAIRYTALES

The turbulent story of Catherine and Dominic Rossi—set against the enchanting backdrop of San Francisco. Strong-willed and passionate people, the Rossis' battle for life and each other is climaxed when Catherine disappears in the middle of her husband's campaign for the U.S. Sentate. "A sweeping story . . . Take this entertaining book to bed and prepare to enjoy a big slice of life, Italian-American style," said the *San Francisco Chronicle.*

THE DAYS OF WINTER

The setting is Europe in the tense period between the two world wars. It is the bittersweet story of the wealthy Hack family whose pride and sins were redeemed by their passionate humanity. Rubin Hack jilts his intended and marries a beautiful mysterious woman whom his family detests. But it is their daughter who is doomed to relive her mother's sins as the wife of one man and a mistress to his brother.

PORTRAITS

The captivating chronicle of four generations of the Sandonitsky family—immigrants from a Polish ghetto. This is the powerful drama of their struggle to achieve the American dream without losing their spiritual heritage as success drives them westward to Oakland, California. A compelling novel about human needs, passions and conflicts which reach tempestuous heights.

All Mrs. Freeman's books are available from Bantam Books, wherever paperbacks are sold.